MURDER OF IDENTITY

A completely unputdownable cozy mystery

VERONICA HELEY

The Ellie Quicke Mysteries Book 8

JOFFE
Ostara
CLASSICS

Revised edition 2023
Joffe Books, London
www.joffebooks.com

First published by Severn House in Great Britain in 2007

This paperback edition was first published
in Great Britain in 2023

Cover art by Dee Dee Book Covers

ISBN: 978-1-83526-155-2

CHAPTER ONE

Ellie Quicke, a fiftyish widow with a comfortable figure, did not consider herself to be a brave woman. She'd never learned to drive, her efforts to fend off a bullying daughter had met with only partial success, and she got the shakes if she had to speak out in a public meeting. On the other hand, she had managed to bring various wrongdoers to justice without having to spend time in hospital. Until, that is, she undertook an errand for Mrs Dawes . . .

* * *

They were both drunk, but Lee was on his feet while the other man had crashed out on his bed.

To Lee's mind, his landlord was a waste of space. He lived like a slob, his only amusements being his dirty magazines and the occasional pint. Yet he'd plenty of money and his own house.

It wasn't fair. Lee slaved at the supermarket for a pittance, barely managing to pay maintenance for his wife and the kids he never saw and who he wasn't sure were his, anyway. And what did he have to look forward to? A miserable old-age pension.

Lee pulled the pillow out from under his landlord's head and placed it over his face. The man on the bed woke up and began to fight for his life.

The victor then had to dispose of the body.

* * *

Ellie Quicke had begun to think and act for herself after years of being under the thumb of her husband and daughter, yet there were still times when she could be reduced to slavery, and her old friend Mrs Dawes knew exactly how to do it.

Mrs Dawes, head of the flower arranging team, had demanded Ellie's help that Friday morning to prepare for a wedding at church the following day. It seemed that Mrs Dawes' usual assistants were not available . . . or had found a good excuse not to be there.

Ellie was not to be trusted to insert flowers into the displays. No, she was there to act as plumber's mate, to hand over secateurs and wire and tape on demand. She was required to stand aside, holding her breath, while Mrs Dawes — majestic in a capacious artist's smock — placed lilies one by one into an arrangement on a pedestal beside the altar.

'Not quite right yet,' said Mrs Dawes. She was rarely satisfied with her own — or other people's — work. 'But we must get on, I suppose. Ellie, you may fix the containers to alternate pew ends. I've filled them with damp oasis already. Use plenty of tape so they don't fall off in the middle of the service.'

Ellie sat on an impulse to say, Yes, miss! She was not best pleased that Mrs Dawes had commandeered her time that morning as she'd been planning to work in her garden, getting it ready for winter. On the other hand, they'd been friends and neighbours for years, Mrs Dawes really *was* queen of the flower arrangers, she *had* been let down by some of her usual helpers, and they *were* both anxious to see that the church looked good for the wedding.

Mrs Dawes had a magnificent bust — she was also an alto in the choir — and simply raised her voice a couple of notches to converse with Ellie as the latter made her way along the pews.

'You know Englefield Road, don't you, Ellie? Up the hill and over a bit from where I live? A woman there is selling her house and going into sheltered accommodation. We got talking about plants a couple of days ago, and she told me she was getting a man in to clear the garden for her. It's a dump, that garden, except for one or two good shrubs. I admired her Portuguese laurel and she said I could take as much as I liked. I couldn't carry much at the time, and I could really do with some more. You know the shrub I mean? Evergreen, with glossy leaves. A wonderful basis for flower arrangements.'

Ellie also sang in the choir, but her voice was not as powerful as Mrs Dawes'.

She called out, 'What's her name? Do I know her?'

'I really couldn't say.' Mrs Dawes' jet-black earrings swung as she lifted sprays of white chrysanthemums from a bucket to add to her arrangement. 'She said I could take some of her variegated Canary Island ivy, too, which is useful because apart from what I need for today, I want to give cuttings to the members of my flower arranging class next week.'

Ellie could see where this conversation was going. She was going to be asked to collect the greenery for Mrs Dawes. Since Ellie didn't drive, it would mean asking one of her friends to help her collect the stuff, or pay for a cab.

Ellie felt this was one demand too many, so tried to head it off. 'You know my daughter Diana is setting up as an independent estate agent? She's looking for clients. Is your friend going to her?'

Mrs Dawes' back registered disapproval. 'I really don't know her well enough to say.'

Ellie kept her head down and taped another container on.

Mrs Dawes was not to be deflected. 'When you go up there, all you have to do is remind her she said I could take what I wanted. Don't forget your secateurs, and take one of those big folding bags from the vestry to put the stuff in. If you go now, you can bring it back straightaway and I can use it for the pedestal in the porch.'

Ellie straightened up. 'No, I can't possibly. I'm sorry, Mrs Dawes, but Diana's got an open day today to launch her estate agency and I promised to take in some nibbles for that. Then this afternoon I have to go over to Felicity and Roy's, to make sure everything's all right and put some flowers in the sitting room, because they're due back this evening from their honeymoon . . . not that they've been able to take much time off, with all the work he's got on.'

Mrs Dawes' tone softened. 'It's good to see them both so happy, although I really can't approve of their waiting so long before they took a proper break.'

'I know. But at least he did take her to Paris,' said Ellie, smiling. 'I'll see what I can do about the greenery for you after the weekend, right?'

'Or,' said Mrs Dawes, persistent as a migraine, 'you could go now. I usually keep some extra greenery in a bucket outside, but someone's tipped it over and the stuff's useless. Normally it wouldn't matter, but I've only got enough to do this one pedestal, and I need more to do another in the porch.'

Ellie put the last container on the end pew with care, realizing that she'd been dumped in it. Mrs Dawes had known all along she didn't have enough greenery to finish the job. One last try: 'If I go, how would you manage? There's still so much to do.'

'Two of my ladies will be arriving to help me in fifteen minutes. They don't drive either, but I can trust them to do the pew ends. I'll be perfectly all right, dear, if you just toddle up and get me what I need. You can always take a cab back, can't you?'

Ellie considered stabbing Mrs Dawes in the back with the scissors she'd been using to cut tape. Could she penetrate those mounds of solid flesh accurately enough to reach Mrs Dawes' heart? It would be like stabbing a haystack with a needle.

She heard herself say, 'All right, but I'll have to go straightaway.'

Mrs Dawes gestured widely. 'Leave me, dear, leave me. I can probably manage better all by myself. Don't forget to take your secateurs and the bag to put the foliage in.'

Ellie almost ran out of the church. She considered banging the heavy door behind her, but didn't — just. A few leaves were still drifting down from the trees on The Green around the church, and beyond that was the alley which gave access to her own back garden. For two pins she'd march across The Green, go through the garden gate and up the sloping garden to the back door of her own dear little house. She could do with a cup of coffee, too. The wind was chill.

She pulled up the zip of her blue jacket, hoping she'd left some gloves in the pockets. Yes, she had. Well, the sooner she did it, the better. She had low-heeled shoes on, and there was about an hour and a half before she was due at Diana's with her nibbles.

Diana and an acquaintance called Denis had set up the 2Ds estate agency in the Avenue, in competition with an old-established firm. Maybe it would work out. Most of the housing projects that Diana touched hadn't, but Denis seemed to have his head screwed on the right way.

Ellie plodded up the hill, the road twisting and turning. It wasn't far as the crow flew, but it took a while by road. Nice little houses, all looked after pretty well in the main and most of them with loft conversions. The primary school on the other side of The Green had an excellent reputation, and they were near a good shopping centre, too.

She reached the turn-off to Englefield Road. It was a long road; Ellie began to get cross. How much farther was it going to be? Why hadn't Mrs Dawes given her the number of the house? That would have been helpful.

She came across a house for sale, but the garden was neat and tidy, no ivy or laurel to be seen. So it wasn't that one. Englefield Road went on and on, and there were no more houses for sale to be seen.

Ellie walked along, checking gardens for signs of the precious laurel. And yes, right at the end of the road there were two houses for sale, one on either side of the road. Both were being advertised by the old-established local estate agent, and not the 2Ds. One had a skip in front, with a tarpaulin tied over it.

One house looked slightly more decrepit than the other, but both had unkempt gardens; neither looked as if they'd had the attentions of a gardener recently. Was that Canary Island ivy growing up the side of one house? It looked as if it were going to bring the drainpipe down. The gate was off its hinges. Of course. Concrete slabs served as paving stones to the front door. The slabs were cracked. Naturally.

Ellie rang the doorbell. At least, she pressed the button and listened for a chime. Nothing. She knocked on the door. Still nothing. There was a hint of chilly rain in the air. Ellie wished she'd brought a scarf.

'She's out, luv.' A voice from next door's porch. An ancient man was prodding his way down the path with the aid of a walking stick. 'Gone to the day centre.'

'Oh. Do you happen to know if . . . ?'

He went on his way, ignoring her. He was probably deaf.

It probably wasn't this garden Mrs Dawes meant, anyway. Now Ellie had had a closer look at it, it was ordinary ivy climbing the side wall, not the variegated sort. And that bush was privet run amok, not Portuguese laurel.

Ellie checked her watch. Diana would kill her if she were late for the opening day at the agency. She crossed the road, and had a closer look at the overgrown garden on the other side. No one was working there at the moment; it looked as if someone had started on it and given up. She didn't blame them. What a mess!

She spotted a tangle of variegated ivy tumbling off a fence which had once divided this property from its neighbour. The fence posts had rotted, and some of the fence panels had broken away and lay on the ground. Between it and the house there was a partially cleared border dominated by an evergreen bush. Glossy leaves? Portuguese laurel? Yes.

Next door's garden was no better cared for: an abandoned baby buggy lay on its side amid a tangle of weeds, fast-food wrappers and the odd drinks can lay strewn around. This end of the road was definitely going downhill.

Ellie hesitated. Was this the right house, after all? She rang the doorbell and knocked straightaway. Why wait for a bell that wasn't going to ring? She simply couldn't afford to waste time.

Ah. Someone was coming to the door. At last.

A young-to-middle-aged man opened the door. Curly hair, but not much of it. A painter or decorator by the look of his stained overalls. 'Yes, luv?'

Ellie hated being called 'luv' but told herself he didn't mean any harm. 'Is the lady of the house around? She promised a friend of mine some greenery from the garden.'

'Gone to visit her nevvy, probbly. Not here, anyways.'

'Oh. Well . . . I'd better not take . . . no.'

'Shouldn't think the old luv would mind, seeing as she's going.'

'Yes, but do you know when she'll be back? It is rather urgent, you see.'

'Dunno. Thought she might be here today, but she wasn't.'

Ellie looked at her watch. Time was getting on: Mrs Dawes wasn't going to be able to finish without the greenery, and Diana would be tapping her foot, looking out for her refreshments. 'Well, I wonder . . . it's for the church, you see. She said we could take what we wanted.'

He took a cigarette out from the pocket of his overalls, and lit up. 'Why not? Help yourself. But don't say I said so, right?'

He shut the door, which was just as well as Ellie's nose had begun to register that he hadn't bathed recently. Or perhaps it was some peculiar new-fangled resin-bonding agent or grouting that he'd been using? An unpleasant smell.

Only, the smell didn't seem to go away now that he had shut the door.

Ellie nerved herself to step into the undergrowth to reach the laurel. 'Oh, the holly and the ivy . . .' The choir would be practising that soon in readiness for Christmas. They were supposed to be doing some rather complicated new carols by modern composers this year. All rather a strain.

It looked as if someone had taken a hatchet to the laurel bush. A couple of branches, partially severed from the main stem, had come to rest over a collapsed section of fence. Those would be the easiest to separate from the bush.

She tried to get closer. Perhaps if she tackled it from the other garden? Bits of broken fence were sticking out all over the place, so with care not to snag her tights, Ellie got into next door's garden, only to find she couldn't reach the laurel from there, either. Bother! And she was running out of time.

Holding on to a fence post that was still more or less upright, she clambered back to the other side. As she did so, her foot slipped off the fence panel and she stepped into something that squidged underfoot.

Yuk. She couldn't quite see what it was, under all that chopped greenery and bits of fence. Something wrapped in plastic, and seeping out on to the ground. The smell . . .

A dead cat, perhaps? Or . . .

She put her secateurs back into her pocket and tugged at a particularly thick stem of ivy. This dislodged a couple of broken laths of fencing, to reveal a torn black plastic bag which in turn showed . . .

She didn't scream. No. She wasn't sick, either. But she did try to breathe through her mouth. She closed her eyes, and counted to ten. And then another ten.

What was she to do? Faint? Ridiculous! What good would that do? She lifted her right foot and placed it behind her. Then her left. She made her way back to the porch and hammered on the door. She felt sick.

She was going to be late for the launch. As if that mattered now. The decorator had his tranny on inside the house. Loud. He probably couldn't hear her.

She tried not to look down at her shoe. They'd been nice shoes, had cost quite a bit, but she didn't think she'd ever wear them again.

The man was not going to come to the door again. She sat on the doorstep, with her right leg sticking out, well away from her clothing. She found her mobile phone and dialled 999.

A bored voice. 'Which service do you want?'

'Police. I've just found a dead body. I think it's been there some time, because—'

'Name, please?'

'It's rather discoloured. And she's . . . at least, I think it's a she . . . and not a he . . .'

'Can you give me your name, please?'

'Oh.' Ellie tried to pull her wits together, but it seemed they'd gone wool-gathering. 'Ellie Quicke. Mrs. Widow. But she's very, very dead. I don't think a doctor will be needed, if you see what I mean.'

'What address?'

Ellie screwed her head round. Was there a number on the door of the house?

'I can't see from here. Maybe it's on the gate.'

'Your own address, please.'

'I'm not at home.'

'Your address, please.'

Ellie took a deep breath, told herself she was not, definitely not, going to be sick. She said, 'I'm so sorry, but I think I'm going to have to move away. It's the smell, you see.'

She put the phone down on the step, and stood up. It was better, standing up.

She took a few deep breaths, telling herself firmly that she'd never been sick in public before, and she wasn't going to start now. She walked down the path to the pavement and studied the gatepost, which didn't have a number on it.

She could hear the phone quacking at her.

She went back up to the house, picked up the phone, gave her own address and directions as to how the police should find her and the body. She said no, of course she wasn't going to leave, and yes, she'd stay exactly where she was until the police came.

At least, she'd wait in the road because of the smell, if they didn't mind.

The voice on the phone said they didn't and that an officer would be there as quick as they could.

She got down to the path and sat on the low wall at the end of the garden. The wall looked as if it were going to collapse at any minute, but her legs weren't up to supporting her. She'd seen dead bodies before: her husband — but that was in hospital and he'd been nicely tidied up by then; the cleaner who'd died in Aunt Drusilla's bedroom — but that corpse had been quite fresh and honestly there'd been nothing really disturbing about it. But this . . .

She rather hoped some kind neighbour would stop by and ask if she were all right, and would she like a cup of tea. But no one did.

Come to think of it, she hadn't seen anyone walk by, all the time she'd been in the road. A couple of cars had passed, perhaps. A very quiet road.

Mrs Dawes was not going to get her foliage in time to complete her decorations. And she was going to be late getting to the 2Ds open day.

* * *

It would have been better, of course, if he'd been able to bury the body properly before the old biddy ordered him off her property. But they couldn't trace it back to him, so who cared? He had to laugh. No head, no hands . . . no identity.

Luckily, he'd not been on chatty terms with the neighbours. Only one had asked — weeks after the event — and that was Mr Nosy Parker, who'd been about to go off on holiday with his elderly sister. A coach tour round Austria, would you believe. So he wasn't going to be around for a while.

It was easy enough to account for a solitary man's disappearance.

'Him? He had a drop too much the other night. Said he'd never done any of the things he wanted to do. Like going round the world. Said if he didn't do it now, he never would. Backpacking in the Far East . . . Australia? I told him he was daft. Made him worse. Packed a rucksack and was off. Said he'd get a bus to the airport. Sent me a card from there, cheeky devil. Singapore next, I shouldn't wonder. I said I'd look after the house for him while he's gone, and so I will.'

Yes, that covered all the points. He was quite safe.

Apart from paying the bills. He hadn't realized how much it cost to keep the house going. He'd have to have a think about that.

CHAPTER TWO

Long before the police arrived Ellie was shivering with cold. She rather thought she was going to have nightmares about stepping on corpses in future. She tried to turn her thoughts away from what she'd seen, but they kept zipping back to the moment when her foot went into . . .

She shut down that thought. Presumably the corpse was that of the woman who lived in this house, or the one next door? It must be someone who'd been missing for some time. Did that apply to the owner of this house? Yes, if you judged by what the decorator had said. The police would sort it out.

She worried about letting Mrs Dawes know there wouldn't be any more foliage for her decorations. Mrs Dawes didn't own a mobile phone.

Then Ellie remembered Thomas, their vicar, who was also a very good friend of Ellie's. He might not be in his digs, in fact probably wasn't. The vicarage site was currently being redeveloped by Ellie's architect cousin Roy who, Ellie reminded herself, was due back from his honeymoon this evening.

The old vicarage had been vast and hugely inconvenient, with a large garden at one side. All this had been cleared away. A well-designed vicarage had been built on part of the site while a small block of flats was rising beside it, to defray the cost of rebuilding.

The vicarage was nearly finished, and the parish had promised itself that it would have a party to end all parties there when the keys were finally handed over . . . hopefully before Christmas.

Thomas could be anywhere in his parish, or up in town or . . . well, anywhere. Ellie was one of the few people who had his mobile phone number since they enjoyed one another's company.

She dialled. Engaged. Should she leave a message?

She didn't know what to say. She shut off the phone, to think about it.

The police would be here any second.

She rang again. Relief! Thomas answered.

'Thomas? Ellie here. In a spot of bother. Mrs Dawes sent me up the hill to get some foliage for her for the church decorations and I've found . . .' She took a deep breath and gagged.

'Ellie? Where are you? Are you all right?'

'I'm at the far end of Englefield Road. I've just found a dead body. I've rung the police and they're coming straightaway, but I . . . could you tell Mrs Dawes that I can't get the laurel for her?'

He was brisk. 'I'll do that. Give me ten minutes. Then I'll come and fetch you, right?'

She felt weak with gratitude for his quick understanding, and for his care of her. 'No, better not. I don't know how long I'll be. I think that's a police car just coming up the road now.'

'It's Friday, remember . . . ?'

Friday was supposedly his day off, though he often didn't manage to take it. He usually tried to have lunch with Ellie at a little Italian place off the Avenue on Fridays, but for some reason he hadn't been able to make it this week. 'Listen, Ellie. I'm in the middle of something right now, but I'll finish up here and go round by the church in a minute or two. Then I'll come to get you.'

The police car drew to a halt. As if by osmosis two pedestrians appeared — one from either end of the road — and stopped to gape.

One policeman, one policewoman. Ellie stood up and waved to attract their attention. She thought she'd seen both before, but couldn't remember their names. She gestured up the slope to the house. 'Under the fencing that's fallen down. Take care.'

The WPC stopped to sniff the air as she went up the path, but the man merely got out his notebook.

'Name?' he asked.

'Mrs Quicke. Address . . .' She repeated the details she'd given before on the phone. How many times did they need to take it down?

The policewoman exclaimed something, but Ellie didn't turn her head to see what she was doing — or seeing.

The PC joined his mate. Ellie could hear them trying to shift the ivy and the pieces of fence. Did they think the woman could still be alive? Wouldn't one glance tell them she'd been dead for ages? Never mind the smell.

Ellie pressed buttons on her mobile. She must get through to Diana to tell her she'd be late.

Diana had turned her mobile off. Bother.

Ellie heard someone retching behind her. She didn't turn round to see which one of the officers it was, but she heard the woman telling her partner not to contaminate the evidence. The two pedestrians had met and were avidly watching from across the road.

Ellie left a message on Diana's answerphone. 'Diana, something's come up. I may be a few minutes late. I'll get there as soon as I can.'

The policewoman hurried down the garden, gulping, white-faced. She steadied herself with an effort, breathing hard. She said, 'You found her? What's your name?'

Ellie went through it all again.

The policeman joined them, wiping his mouth, speaking on his mobile, calling up the troops.

Ellie looked at her right shoe. It didn't look too bad, if you didn't remember what it was that was sticking to it. I mean, it might have been just a snail she'd trodden on. Think snail. Hard.

Then the questions. How did she come to be trampling around someone else's garden, did she know the owner of the house, where was the owner of the house?

Ellie answered as best she could. 'As for where the owner is, I thought at first it might be her in the shrubbery, but then I thought probably not.'

'Why did you think that? Do you know her?'

'No, I don't know her, but the decorator said . . .'

The policeman thundered on the door of the house. No response. One of the two sightseers across the road had gone home, but a young mother with a buggy had stopped to chat with the remaining pedestrian.

Eventually the decorator opened the door, wearing a jacket over his overalls.

'What's up, then? What you lot doing here?'

'What's your name?' one of the officers asked, and so on. Ellie closed her eyes and lifted her face to the sky. Was that a drop of rain? It was all they needed.

The decorator was by turns bewildered and angry. He said he'd been booked by the householder's nephew to put in a new bathroom and kitchen so as to help sell the house quickly. No, he said, he hadn't seen the old woman for a couple of days, not that that bothered him, it was easier to work in a house by himself, especially when he had to turn the water off. He'd thought she'd just moved out for the duration, because it stood to reason that she couldn't stay on without any water, didn't it?

'Her name? And her nephew's?'

'Ball. Nephew's the same. Ball. I've got his number on my mobile, if you want it.'

Ellie faded out the rest of the conversation because up the road came Thomas in his rather flash car. She had hoped he might be wearing his dog collar because that might have impressed the police, but he wasn't. Sweatshirt and jeans for his day off. She stood up as he got out of his car and made his way towards them. She was very, very glad to see him, even more so than usual.

Thomas was a big man in every way, dark and bearded. A heart of oak. And, since he'd been watching his weight recently, not too much of a paunch, either.

Everything settled down after Thomas arrived. He had a calming effect on people. Ellie gave her statement to the WPC and promised to go into the station tomorrow to sign it. More cars arrived, and a van. A doctor came to pronounce the corpse deceased and some police produced a tent affair to cover the scene of the crime.

The crowd across the road kept growing.

Thomas inserted Ellie into the front seat of his car and drove off down the hill. She put her head back and breathed deeply. 'Was Mrs Dawes cross?'

'She'd fallen back on plan B before I left; she thought of another place where she can get some foliage. She says it won't be as good but it will pass muster. Don't worry about her. How are you coping?'

'I need to get back home and change my shoes. I trod in something. I'm trying not to think about it. I've never found a dead body before.'

'Was it the old lady who lived in that house? I spoke to her once, after her husband died in the hospice. He'd told me he wanted to have a church funeral, but she wouldn't hear of it. Said he'd lived and died an atheist.'

Ellie began to giggle. She told herself to stop. Then she told herself that Thomas wouldn't mind if she had a small fit of hysterics. Just a small one. That made her stop. 'Did she get her way, or did he?'

'She did, of course. She told the funeral director what she wanted, and she paid the bill. We can't win all the time.'

No, no one could win all the time. Ellie wound down the window to breathe in the fresh air, even though it looked more and more like rain.

Thomas still wanted an answer. 'Was it Mrs Ball?'

'I don't know. It was a woman wearing a pink dress, as far as I could see. The smell was awful.'

'Been dead some time, then.'

Ellie nodded. He drew up outside her house. 'Do you feel like lunch?'

'I don't think I could face it. Anyway, Diana's expecting me at their new place in the Avenue. Open day. I promised to take some nibbles and I'm late.'

'I'll wait for you and drop you over.'

'I thought you had something on today?'

'All done and dusted. Five minutes, right?'

Ellie got out of the car. She was still feeling shaky, but managed to find her key and let herself into the house. Inside the hall she sat down and took off her shoes. She tried not to focus on what was clinging to the right sole. She took them both into the kitchen, found a plastic bag, dropped the shoes in, tied the bag up, then pushed the bag into the bin.

She ran the cold tap and held her hands under it, dashed water over her face, filled a glass with more water and drank it down. Ignoring the flashing light on the answerphone, she went upstairs for another pair of shoes.

Don't let yourself think about you've just seen, Ellie had to tell herself. Concentrate on doing the next thing. Get yourself some tunnel vision. Go downstairs. Open the fridge door, take out the foil trays on which you'd already laid out the tit-bits for Diana's open day. You'd been thinking about warming them up, but there's no time for that now.

She went out to the car, and laid the trays one at a time on the back seat. Thomas was on his mobile to someone, moving an appointment back half an hour. She hoped he wasn't going to get into trouble through helping her out.

She got back into the front seat. Thomas put his arm around her and held it there while he finished his phone call. She rested her head against his shoulder, and closed her eyes.

'All done,' he said, closing up his phone. 'Can you cope, do you think?'

She nodded. She felt worn out, but she'd manage. Of course she would.

'Do you want me to come in with you?' he asked, parking neatly in front of Diana's new premises in the Avenue. He knew Diana's temper of old.

'I'll manage,' she said. 'Thanks, Thomas.'

'I'll be free again about five. Supper?'

'I've got to go over to Felicity's place to get things ready for their return. I don't know what time I'll finish. I may be too tired to go out, after all this. Shall I give you a ring?'

Thomas nodded, extricated himself from the parking space and purred away.

Ellie balanced the trays on her arms, looking up at the brand-new shop fascia.

Diana was her only child; greedy, ambitious, and a bully. She was also brave and resourceful. She'd exhausted her father's patience with demands for money long before he died. Diana had considered she deserved better than the pleasant but rather stolid man she'd married, so she'd divorced him to play the field. Their only child — another Frank — spent weekdays with his father and his father's second wife, and the weekends with Diana. But Diana always put her own convenience first, which meant that Ellie frequently had little Frank as an unexpected guest on Saturdays and Sundays.

Ellie sighed, thinking that Diana had too high an opinion of herself, and too low an opinion of her mother. Diana wanted everything, and she wanted it *now*! She'd alienated her great-aunt Drusilla, who was a successful property developer, and her own forays into that field had met with mixed fortunes. It irked Diana to realize that Miss Quicke had refused to help Diana with her projects, but had gone into partnership with her architect son Roy in the redevelopment of the vicarage site.

Ellie wondered how long it would be before Diana's new partner Denis would get fed up with her rapacity, not to mention her tendency to cut corners. Still, Denis was old enough to know what he was doing; he'd certainly been in the business long enough.

Ellie couldn't help worrying about this new venture. She'd been left very comfortably off when her husband died, so had put most of her inheritance into a trust fund. Fending off Diana's demands for financial backing for this project and that, Ellie had finally agreed to fund the launch of the 2Ds estate agency with a six-month rental of their premises, to be repaid on commercial terms. She had an interest in seeing that this time Diana would prosper, in spite of the fact that the Avenue already boasted an old-established estate agency.

Well, the new fascia looked good. The furniture and furnishings inside the huge window also looked good. So did Diana, power-dressed in black. There were a few people inside already, milling around with glasses in their hands.

Denis was by the door: large, blonde, chatty and smiling. Ellie distrusted that smile of his, but couldn't cross her fingers while holding on to the trays of canapés. He held the door open for her to enter. 'Welcome, Ellie. I hope you don't mind me calling you Ellie but I consider you a partner in this venture of ours.'

She didn't like him calling her by her Christian name, but could hardly say so in other people's hearing. She looked around for somewhere to put her trays of food. Diana swooped on her, relieving her of the trays while simultaneously hissing, 'Mother, what are you wearing? You look like a bag lady! How could you, when you know how much this means to me!'

Ellie glanced down at the old jacket and skirt she'd worn to help Mrs Dawes with her flower arrangements, and winced. She'd meant to change before she went out again, but had forgotten all about it. Thomas hadn't noticed. Thomas never did notice that kind of thing.

'And your shoes!' Diana's voice vibrated. 'What on earth . . . ?'

Ellie had thrust her feet into the first pair of shoes that had come to hand, and they happened to be a pair of tan sandals that were comfortable but shabby and definitely not right for this gathering of rather smartly dressed people.

'Oh. Well, the thing was . . .'

Diana tore off the foil that protected the trays and shrieked with horror. 'Homemade! I can't give those to our guests! Mother, how could you!'

Ellie blinked. It was too much. She'd spent all day making them the day before. There were cheese straws and homemade crisps and a dip, tiny sausages wrapped in bacon and even tinier tartlets filled with a tomato and onion mixture. They looked good, and tasted even better.

Only now did she realize her mistake. She ought to have gone to the supermarket and got ready-made canapés which looked fantastic but tasted of nothing much. And cost the earth.

Denis appeared to put his arm around Diana. 'Eats? Splendid. Well done, Ellie.'

Ellie had heard of people whose smile didn't reach their eyes, and had always wondered what it meant, but she hadn't been treated to a Denis grin before. Now she knew what the phrase meant. The lips twitched but the eyelids didn't pouch as they should do.

'We can't serve these!' hissed Diana.

'Of course we can,' said Denis, taking a tartlet and putting it in his mouth. 'Smile, Diana, smile. Many thanks, Ellie.'

He whisked one tray away, and Diana took another. Ellie found herself a chair, noting that Diana was apologizing for the homemade fare as she worked the room. People took one bite out of courtesy. Ellie wished that she were elsewhere, wished she'd never come, wished she'd had the brains to ring Diana and tell her she couldn't make it. Then she noticed that everyone was returning for another bite, and another.

At this rate, the trays would soon be empty.

Denis put his tray down and poured more drink. The level of conversation rose. A tall woman plonked herself down beside Ellie.

'Haven't seen you at the golf club for some time, Ellie. Have you fallen out with Bill, or is that a tactless question?'

Bill Weatherspoon was Ellie's solicitor and at one point had also expressed a desire to marry her, but the relationship was no longer as close as it had been.

'Lovely to see you.' said Ellie. trying to remember the woman's name. 'How are the children?'

It was a happy thought to ask after her children, for the woman then launched into a long tale about how well they were doing. And then — talk of the devil — Bill himself hove into sight and made a beeline for Ellie, leaning down from his considerable height to kiss her on both cheeks.

'My dear, how are you doing? Lovely eats. I assume you provided them, did you? Quite a good crowd here, considering. Do you think Diana will make a go of it this time?'

'It all depends,' said Denis, materializing at their side, 'on whether we can get enough footfall. We'll be having a full page spread of adverts in the local papers, of course, and doing a mail drop. I've managed to get sole rights to sell the new flats that are going up at the end of the Avenue as the developer is a friend of mine, but we'll need more than that. Ellie, you won't mind if I put up a 'Sold' notice outside your house, will you? Just to get our name registering in people's minds.'

Ellie did mind, and it showed.

Denis gave her his toothy smile again. 'Established practice, my dear. I know you want us to succeed.'

Which she did, of course.

Bill was listening, but not interfering. 'You look tired, Ellie. Been overdoing it?' Bill had always deprecated Ellie's habit of getting mixed up in her friends' problems. What would he say if he learned she'd just discovered a dead body? And yet it was bound to be in the local paper next week, even if it didn't make the nationals. So she might as well come straight out with it.

'I do feel a bit shattered. I stumbled across a dead body this morning, and that's what made me late.'

'What?'

'You don't mean . . . not really!'

'Yes, really. I was trying to cut some greenery for the church when my foot slipped and . . . Ugh! There she was. Gruesome!' She shuddered.

'Where . . . ?'

'I don't believe it!' Bill exclaimed.

'Oh, it's true,' said Ellie. 'There's a couple of houses for sale at the end of Englefield Road, and it's in the garden of one of them.'

'Who was it? Some wino?'

'Houses for sale,' said Denis, not smiling. 'The competition, I assume.'

'An elderly lady's selling up,' said Ellie. 'Her nephew's managing things for her, as far as I can make out. Putting in a new bathroom and kitchen.'

'Fancy that. Was it her, then?'

'I really don't know,' said Ellie. 'I called the police, gave a statement and left.'

'I wonder . . .' said Denis, plucking at his lower lip. 'What's her name?'

'Someone did say, but I've forgotten,' said Ellie, tired beyond endurance.

'Well, do you think you could find out for us? Maybe there's an opening for 2Ds there. We could undercut the commission our competitors are asking, and get the sale for ourselves. How about it, Ellie?'

She couldn't think what he was on about. Bill was looking down his nose, not taking part in the conversation, but also not approving of the way it was going. Bill wouldn't want her to get mixed up in anything dicey, and it was becoming clear to Ellie that Denis was probably as conscience-free as Diana when it came to business affairs. Probably that meant they'd do well together. Probably. But it also meant that Ellie didn't want any part of it.

She got to her feet, noting that both her trays had been emptied. 'Must go,' she said. 'So glad to see you're off to a good start.'

Bill took her elbow to help her outside. His kind, slightly melancholy face looked anxious. 'Are you all right, Ellie? Shall I see you home?'

He was a busy man, even though partly retired. 'I do feel washed out. I don't normally have a little nap in the afternoons, but maybe I will today.'

'Hop into the car. It's just outside the office on the other side of the road. And don't forget that I'm always at the end of the telephone.'

'You are very kind, Bill, and I'd love a lift but I don't think there'll be any repercussions from my find this morning. After all, I didn't even know the woman.'

'That hasn't stopped you in the past.'

She got into his car, hoping that this kind offer of his didn't mean he was going to renew his courtship. They hadn't happened to run across one another for a couple of months, and though in some ways she'd regretted the break in continuity because their friendship went back a long way, she was always aware that Bill, deep down, disapproved of many things about her. Whereas Thomas . . . Well, Thomas was different. Very different. She smiled to herself. It would be pleasant to go out for a meal with Thomas that evening, provided he didn't get caught up with something or somebody needing his help in the parish. Thomas never really seemed to be off duty.

She thanked Bill nicely when he deposited her outside her house.

'I might ring my friend at the police station,' he said. 'Find out what I can. All right?'

'Thanks, Bill. I just want to put it behind me. Felicity and Roy are due back from honeymoon tonight, you know, and I've promised to check up on the house for them.'

Bill nodded. 'Perhaps a bite to eat later on? I'll ring you, see how you feel, right?'

She couldn't argue any more. 'Thanks for the lift, Bill. See you.'

The house was quiet, save for the tick of the central heating as it clicked on. Midge, her marauding ginger tom, appeared from nowhere, expecting to be fed. Ellie fed him. She scrambled herself some eggs, adding mushrooms to the dish. Bread and butter with lots of butter. Milk to drink. Some squares of chocolate to finish up with. She ignored the winking light on the answerphone. Let it wait.

Midge mounted the stairs in front of her, and settled on the bed while she chucked off her outer clothes and collapsed under the duvet. Midge settled down for a good wash, shaking the bed.

She thought, Dear Lord above, how terrible . . . that moment when I saw . . . wearing pink . . . I suppose she tripped and fell in her garden and then got covered over by the broken fence and . . . I don't understand it . . . poor creature. I hope she was peaceful . . . I hope she had time to pray.

Midge altered position to pay attention to his hind quarters. Ellie was asleep before he'd finished.

* * *

Lee laid the bills out on the table. Electricity, water, telephone and council tax. It had taken him some foraging to find out where Russell's money had come from, but he'd worked it out in the end. Russell had been paid a large sum of money for letting a lorry run over him when he was out cycling. Total disability. No wonder he'd moved like an arthritic tortoise. The money was invested in an annuity, which was paid into Russell's bank account monthly. Russell had been a bit of a miser, never splashed out on holidays or a car or maintaining the house. So the money had mounted up nicely.

Lee got Russell's cheque book, debit and credit cards out, and laid them on the table, too. They all wanted you to pay by direct debit nowadays, didn't they? So, all he had to do was make out the direct debit slip, and sign it with the murdered man's name. Simple.

He drew a piece of flimsy paper towards him, laid it over the murdered man's signature and traced it through. He moved the piece of paper down a bit, and did it again. And again. Until it began to feel natural. Then he tried writing it out on another piece of paper. It didn't look too bad. Getting better all the time.

It amused him to think of having a double identity. His, for everyday.

And Russell's for money matters.

CHAPTER THREE

Ellie awoke with a start, remembered she had to go to Felicity's house, and scrambled out of bed and into the clothes she'd worn that morning. However had she managed to sleep for a whole hour? She must find some proper shoes, and not those sandals she'd worn to the estate agency.

Midge slept on while Ellie skittered down the stairs, trying to remember what she needed to take over to Felicity's house. Roy had moved in after their quiet civil ceremony and not-so-quiet blessing in church, but they'd only just managed to find time to go away. Roy was so busy nowadays, and Felicity so happy. Cynics had said it wouldn't work because of the age difference, he being sixteen years or so her senior, but they'd both had bad first marriages, and with a bit of luck . . . They did seem very happy together.

Ellie had made a list somewhere — where had she put it — of bits and pieces she needed to take. She'd bought some things yesterday . . . where were they? A couple of chops, some fresh vegetables, some fruit, a pint of milk. Ah, there was the azalea, too. It was just coming into flower. Felicity loved flowers but at this time of year there wasn't much in the garden except for the odd chrysanthemum plant, and many people associated them with death, so . . .

Ellie grimaced. She packed things into a couple of plastic bags and rang for a cab to take her over to Felicity's on the far side of the park. As she didn't drive, she had an account with a local mini-cab firm, who were always happy to oblige and often helped her carry her shopping up and down the driveway. While she waited for the cab, she thought she'd better check on her messages.

There was a message from Miss Quicke, her elderly and autocratic aunt, who was also Roy's mother. 'Ellie, when you come to lunch on Sunday, bring some of your homemade redcurrant jelly, will you? I told Rose that we could perfectly well make do with some from the shop, but she's fretting because she says it's not the same and she's run out. Oh, and tell Felicity that I expect them straight after church. I don't want Roy dilly-dallying with his friends from the golf club and making the roast dry out.'

Short and sweet. Rose must be cooking roast lamb for lunch. Goody.

Next was Diana. 'Mother, just to remind you to put the eats on a good china dish. We don't want people thinking they come from a supermarket, even if they do. Oh, and don't be late, will you?'

Those two messages must have been recorded while Ellie was helping Mrs Dawes at church. Bill Weatherspoon was next. 'Ellie, long time no see. Are you going to the bash at Diana's new venture? I thought I might pop in, as your solicitor, check on the prospects for success. Anyway, if you're going to be there, perhaps we can have a bite to eat afterwards?'

Oh. Ellie wondered if Bill had really gone to see her, rather than to suss out Diana's latest. He'd be wary of whatever she did next, since he'd been involved in several of Diana's attempts to extract money from her mother in the past.

One last message was from her nice next-door neighbour, heavily pregnant with her second child. 'Ellie? Kate here. A parcel came for you this morning. I'll hold it till you get back. Cheers.'

That would be the bedlinen Ellie had ordered for Christmas presents. She was glad it had arrived, but hoped Kate wouldn't try to lift it, in her condition.

The cab arrived. Ellie piled herself and her packages in, and gave the driver the address. The sky seemed to have gone a thicker grey since morning. It was going to get dark early.

Felicity had bought a neglected three-bedroom property overlooking the park after her first husband died. Roy had turned it into a delightful house, extending the kitchen at the back, installing en suites, building on a double garage, and updating all the facilities. Felicity had created pretty gardens back and front, but there wasn't much in the way of flowers to be seen.

Before their marriage, Roy had lived in the old coach house at the side of his mother's house. He'd furnished his place with a mix of old and new, including some valuable paintings and objets d'art. To his relief, Felicity had insisted on swapping the slightly bland furniture she'd had, for his. So now their house was a visual delight as well as being comfortable to live in, while his old quarters in the coach house had been turned over to his growing practice as an architect.

Ellie let herself into the house, stopped the burglar alarm from sounding off, collected the post and laid it with the rest of the mail on the hall table. She turned up the central heating a notch because it had got a lot colder in the last couple of days. She put the food in the fridge, and went round shutting curtains and closing blinds, because the honeymoon couple would be arriving back after dark.

She made a quick foray into the garden for a few twigs of sweet-smelling pink viburnum fragrans, some red-berried pyracantha, and a few shoots of winter jasmine, which she arranged in a small vase on the table in the kitchen/dining area. The azalea she put in a copper pot in the sitting room. Should she leave a couple of lights on, to welcome them back home? Yes, perhaps.

She left a note on the hall table reminding them that Miss Quicke and Rose expected them for lunch promptly the following day, and was about to lock up and leave when her mobile phone rang.

Thomas? Bill?

Denis. Oh. Diana must have given him her number.

'Ellie . . . or would you really prefer me to be formal and call you Mrs Quicke?'

He had the sort of gravelly, deep voice that was supposed to charm and didn't. Or rather, she supposed it might charm some people but she didn't like it much.

He laughed, gently. 'I feel we're on much too close terms to stand on formality, so I'll continue to call you Ellie, shall I?'

Ellie didn't reply, her mind whirling with uncouth words that she'd never allowed herself to use.

'Well, the thing is that I got to thinking about that house you said was for sale up on the hill. An elderly lady, you said? The nephew selling it for her? Awful tragedy, of course, but maybe it's an opportunity for the 2Ds to get in there, make ourselves useful. Englefield Road. That's it, right? I thought I might wander up there now, and if you're free you could meet me there, introduce me to the neighbours, see if we can get the nephew's phone number, right?'

'No, I . . .'

'It won't take you five minutes. Diana says you were going round to Felicity's . . . oh, I beg her pardon . . . Mrs Bartrick as she is now, to her house this afternoon, so I thought I could pick you up there. Perhaps I could have a word with Roy at the same time. Useful contact, you know. All in the same line of business, ha, ha.'

Ellie tried to stem the flow. 'I'm there now, but they won't be back till later on. I'm just leaving, as it happens.'

'Don't move! I'll be there in just a tick! We can't let our benefactress get chilled on a day like this.' He shut off the phone.

Ellie expressed herself with one or two words that had never, in all her born days, crossed her lips before. The man was worse than Diana, and that was saying something!

She zipped up her jacket, pulled on her gloves, set the alarm and locked the house up. With any luck, she'd be well on her way down the hill before Denis caught up with her. But as she hurried down the path to the road, he drew up outside. He must have been on his mobile in the car when he phoned her. Not giving her a chance to get away. She believed it was illegal to drive and be on the phone, but that didn't seem to have stopped him.

Not knowing what else to do, she got into the car and he drove smoothly off, taking the shortest route to Englefield Road. 'The far end?'

She nodded, rehearsing the words she wanted to say to him. Part of her noted that the road did indeed seem to become shabbier as they drove along. There were more people on the pavements now, hurrying to get home before dusk overtook them; mothers with small children in buggies and larger children returning from school; teenagers loitering, no overcoats, no gloves, no scarves — didn't they ever catch cold? — a council minibus delivering elderly people back to their homes from the day centre; a council worker with a broom, leaning on it, and not working; an elderly woman in a wheelchair being pushed along the pavement to her house — the one that Ellie had tried first that day.

Incident tape was still in place across the front of the garden in which Ellie had discovered the body, and it had also been spread over the front of the garden next door. A policewoman was coming down the pathway from next door's house; a middle-aged woman standing in the doorway was glaring after her as the WPC retreated. So the neighbour was not the victim, either.

A police car and a police van were still on the scene, but it looked as though they were about to pack up for the night, because several large men and women were in a huddle by the police car, notebooks out, talking on phones.

Denis slowed down and parked well beyond the house. 'Well, where do we start?'

She took a deep breath. 'I'm sorry, but I've decided I don't want any part of this. It's . . . tacky. If you want to make a nuisance of yourself, then go and ask a policeman. Thanks for the lift. I can see myself back home, no bother.'

'Oh, come on, now! Don't be so faint-hearted. For Diana's sake, if not for mine. I know you really want her to succeed at this.'

Words failed her. She shook her head, got out of the car and walked off, checking that she still had both her gloves. Had she lost one already? Where? Had she left it back at Felicity's? She was sure she'd had two when she left, but maybe she'd been in such a hurry . . .

She stopped directly under a street light that had just come on. Left-hand pocket. Right. She found it. She heard Denis get out of the car and hail a policeman, all friendly. She hoped the police would tell him to get lost. She rather thought she recognized at least one of the police in the group round the car — not that she'd tell Denis that. If he and Diana couldn't make a go of their business without descending to ambulance chasing tactics, then so be it.

The police were telling him to get lost, to move on. Good.

She didn't want to be caught hanging around by Denis, so she began walking along the road, back the way they'd come. The road was too narrow for him to make a three-point turn here, so he'd have to go on.

'That you, luv?' She was passing a large, rather dirty white van from which came the sound of pop music. The decorator she'd met that morning had been poking around in the back of the van, both doors wide open, until he saw her.

'Yes, it's me,' she said, relaxing. 'Are you all right? It was awful, wasn't it? Did they make you look?'

He leaned against the half-open door. 'Shook me up, I can tell you. One minute I was looking forward to some nosh, and the next . . . phooh! Turned my stomach, I can tell you.'

'Me, too. I stepped on it and . . .' She swallowed.

He caught her arm. 'You're not going to faint, are you? Here, come and sit in the van a little. If I had some tea left, I'd give it you, but . . .'

'I'm all right, really. It's just that . . .'

He closed the van doors at the back, opened the front and pushed her up into the passenger seat, shoving aside an empty thermos, a tabloid newspaper and some sandwich wraps. The van reeked of cigarettes. Ellie began to laugh. Which was worse? The memory of the other, or the reality of the cigarettes? And the pop music!

He swung himself up into the cabin and pulled out a packet of cigarettes, offering one to her. She shook her head. 'Do you think we could have a window open just a crack?'

He wound down a window and muted the radio. Nice man.

'Thanks. It's just . . . you know?' Ellie tried to explain.

He lit up and inhaled. Coughed. 'They said would I look, see if I recognized the body. I said, how could you tell? But it wasn't Mrs Ball, anyway. You knew her?'

'No. Not at all. A friend arranged for me to get some greenery from her and . . .'

'Ah, I remember. You said. I told them, Can't be Mrs Ball, 'cos I saw her early this week. It suited me fine, her not being around. Get on with it, no women under my feet, begging your pardon, but you know what I mean.'

Ellie nodded. 'With the water turned off . . .'

'That's it. With the water turned off. I told them she was likely staying with her nevvy, but I didn't have his work number, did I? And his mobile was switched off. The fuss!'

Ellie nodded. 'I can imagine.'

'I said, Look, no way can it be Mrs Ball, 'cos she's a biggish woman. Make two of you, missus. Besides, I seen her Monday or Tuesday. When we was taking out the old bath and putting it in the skip.'

Ellie nodded. 'Not big. Wearing pink, as far as I could see.'

'Wrapped in a pink blanket, I thought. Stained, though. You could hardly tell.'

'No, you couldn't, could you? I thought it was a dress because the bit I saw clearly was pink, but . . . yes, it might have been a blanket.'

'Not that I'm an expert, like, but a body couldn't get into that state since Monday. Or maybe Tuesday. It does the mind in, thinking about it.'

'It does.'

He stubbed out the cigarette he'd been smoking, and took out his pack and offered it to her again. She refused. One part of her mind said, You've never smoked in your life. Why not try it? But the sensible part said, You'd better not start now.

He lit up, and she didn't object. He seemed to need it.

She said, 'I'd have thought the police would have let you go before now.'

'They thought the house might have been the crime scene, would you believe? Wanted to know what work I'd been doing, and where. I told them I'd been all over, floor-boards up, hatch to the loft down. That plumbing was a disgrace, and as for the wiring! I told her — Mrs Ball — that wiring's way past its sell-by date, not been touched for thirty years. First she said to give her a quote, then the nevvy puts his oar in, and he says not to bother.

'Typical of the way they carried on. She'd say, We don't need a bidet. And I'd get the plumbing sorted without one. Next day he'd say, We need a bidet, and I'd have to start all over again. I tell you, I'd have been finished and out of there a week back, if they hadn't kept changing their minds. Then I wouldn't have been there when it happened. 'Cos the police say we must have been working there in the house when . . . whenever.'

'You . . . and a mate?'

'Mmm. Nevvy said he wanted a modern washbasin, you know, the kind you can hardly dip your fingertips in, and she said she wanted something she could wash her hair in. She won that one. So my mate had to go and get a new basin for the bathroom this morning. He got back maybe half an hour after you left. The plod was all over him, and he'd only been to B & Q. My mate's a bit short with his temper and didn't like it when they said we must have seen something, or heard something, when we didn't. I thought he'd lose it, and we'd both be taken down the station, and then . . . and then . . . she turned up, didn't she.'

'Who?'

'Mrs Ball. With the nevvy, as he'd brought her over to fetch some extra things, she having tripped over something at his place and got her leg all bandaged up and stayed over, not bothering to let me know. I might have been worried sick.'

Ellie forbore to say that he'd just told her he'd been glad Mrs Ball was out of the way. So she shook her head in sympathy. 'So it isn't Mrs Ball in the shrubbery.'

'I'd told them so, hadn't I? But they didn't listen.' He started to laugh. 'There was a right old row when she arrived, I can tell you. She can yell with the best of them, while the nevvy's one of those quiet, creepy little men that has all the right names in his address book. Probbly a Mason. He got on the phone to someone and before you could say Jack the Ripper, the police were out of the house and I was told to get on with my work, or else.'

'I don't suppose you felt much like working, after all that.'

'No, I didn't. But he's paying the bills, so we didn't argue. Got the basin plumbed in. That's the bathroom finished, bar the tiling, which my mate's just been down to get. That's what I had to hang on for. Mrs B told me to get some in pale blue, which is what we'd got for her, but he's wanting white, so we had to change them, sharpish.'

'You'll be glad to finish with this job.'

'I wish. Should have been done and dusted by now. As it is, we'll have to go back week after next. She said, Why not Monday? And I said, You must be joking! I got another client been screeching his head off for me to get a wet room put in. I've had to put him off twice already, and I'm not putting him off again. I'll come back week on Monday or nothing. So she said she'd try to find someone else, but I bet she doesn't. Nevvy wasn't best pleased, either. Said it was all her fault the house wasn't finished by now, and she said, Whose house was it anyway? I left them to it.'

Ellie sympathized with him. 'A good plumber's always in demand.'

'Right on. You feeling better now? You never got your greenery, did you? I'll run you home, if it's not too far.'

'You're very kind. Thank you. Just to the bottom of the hill, anywhere round The Green by the church would be wonderful. This sort of thing takes it out of you.'

He threw away the butt of his cigarette, and pulled on his seat belt. Looking into his driving mirror, Ellie saw that the police vehicles had gone, but . . . she peered round the side of the van . . . Denis' car was still there, and he was talking to the elderly man with the walking stick that Ellie had seen earlier.

'What's Mrs Ball's nephew's name?'

'Ball. Same as. Lives in one of those big old houses the other side of the Avenue. Solicitor, or lawyer or accountant or something. You interested in her house when it's finished?'

'No, but someone I know may be. Have you got his number?'

'Give it you when we stop.' The steering on his van seemed a trifle wayward, but he slid to a halt neatly enough when they reached The Green. True to his word, he scribbled some details on a flier. 'And that's my phone number, if ever you need something doing about the house.'

Ellie read his name out loud. 'Mr . . . Hurry?'

'I know, I know,' he said, gloomily. 'Everyone laughs when they see it, and says, "You'll do it in a hurry, won't you?" And I say, "More haste, less speed."'

Ellie tried not to grin. 'My name's Quicke. Ellie Quicke.'

He thought that was great. 'Give it a high five, luv!'

Ellie had never given anyone a 'high five' before, but she'd seen youngsters doing it, and it seemed she acquitted herself creditably. 'Thanks. You've been very kind.'

He jumped out of the van, and came round to open her door and help her down to the pavement. It seemed to be her day to be treated as if she were made of glass. He said, 'It was pink flannelette, I think. My mum had some like it. Take care now. You look like you could do with a good lay down.'

'Thank you, Mr Hurry. I'm trying not to think about it too much.'

He lifted his hand in a sketchy salute, and drove off. His exhaust was pumping out blue smoke. She hoped the police wouldn't get him for it.

* * *

Ellie couldn't think what day of the week it was, never mind what time of day. She let herself into her house and made a pot of tea. Emergency treatment — hot tea with milk and sugar and a chocolate biscuit or two. What had she got for supper?

She couldn't remember.

Midge arrived, pretending he hadn't been fed for a week, and she fed him. She went into the conservatory which she'd had built across the back of the house, and fed the goldfish swimming in their lead tank. She pulled out a chair and sat down to sip her tea and watch them. Soothing. The geraniums had all been cut back for the winter and she wasn't feeding or watering them now. Likewise the bougainvillea. She'd bought some orchids, which were flourishing; they looked like white butterflies, clustering around their stems.

She had a mental flashback to . . . And stopped it, right there. Stopped it dead. Dead. Oh, dear.

It was getting dark. She switched on the dimmer lights, and tried to make herself get up and draw the curtains; couldn't.

Somebody quite small. Wrapped in a pink flannelette sheet.

Ellie remembered those sheets. Her mother had had some like it, swore by them for wintertime. But, of course, in those days they hadn't had central heating, or duvets. Who used flannelette sheets nowadays? Old people, presumably?

Mrs Ball? Someone could have taken one of Mrs Ball's stock of flannelette sheets and used it to . . .

Gruesome.

Anyway, Mrs Ball wasn't missing, and neither was her nevvy. Nephew. Mr Hurry was a kind man. Ellie hoped he got lots of work.

Which reminded her, going back across the events of the day, that she'd left her two baking trays at Diana's launch party. Oh. Would Diana return them? Possibly. Possibly not. Bother. Ellie was going to have to ask for them, then.

She heard a tapping sound in the distance, and wondered what it might be. She helped herself to another biscuit. The sugar rush gave her enough energy to get her to her feet in order to draw the curtains. A lorry was just drawing away from the road in front of her house and in silhouette she saw, with mingled fury and resignation, a For Sale sign from the 2Ds agency, attached to her low front wall. There was a Sold notice tacked across it.

That did it!

She snatched up the phone and tried Diana's mobile. Engaged. That wasn't going to stop Ellie. She opened the front door to take note of the 2Ds office phone number which was on their notice board, and rang that. Denis picked it up on the third ring.

'Denis, this is Mrs Quicke here.' She was not going to allow him to use her first name again if she could help it. 'I'm sorry to tell you that someone's made a mistake and put a Sold notice up outside my house. I'm having it taken down straightaway, of course. If I can't get anyone else to do it, I shall do it myself. Understood?'

'Now, now, my dear Ellie—'

'Don't you "dear Ellie" me!' said Ellie, keeping her voice down with an effort.

'Do you read me? I don't care if your van is or is not going to be out here in the near future. Either you or Diana will remove that sign tonight. And you may leave my two baking trays in the porch at the same time.'

'But . . .'

'I am not open to negotiation. Understood?'

'Diana said you'd understand exactly how important it is for us to—'

'To gain your clients' trust, right? Well, you've yet to earn mine. By the way, did you succeed in getting an address or telephone number of the people who are selling the house in Englefield Road?'

'Well, as a matter of fact, I didn't.'

'I did. I have it right here.'

Silence. 'Does that mean that you'll give it to me when I get the sign removed?'

'It might. It depends on how quickly it's removed, and how charitable I feel towards you and Diana tomorrow morning. Oh, and a note of appreciation for the food I provided for you today wouldn't come amiss.'

'Wait a minute, I'm sure we can work this out. Look, how about I take you out for supper tonight—'

Ellie dropped the phone on to its rest. Supper with him? It would choke her.

Which reminded her. Bill. And Thomas, dear Thomas. They'd both asked her out to supper. Bill would take her to somewhere smart where the prices reflected the décor and not the food. Thomas, on the other hand — and here she smiled — was a great trencherman and the sort of person to whom you could say whatever came into your mind, without worrying what interpretation he was going to put on it.

Her answerphone light was flashing again. Had she deleted the messages she'd had that morning? She couldn't remember. No, she hadn't. She listened to them all over again. Redcurrant jelly for Aunt Drusilla, that was the important one.

Then, at last, a call from Bill, saying he'd pick her up at eight for a bite to eat. Eight was too late. She was ravenously hungry and it was only half past five now. She rang Bill

— luckily or otherwise, he was out — and left a message to say that she was so sorry, but she couldn't make it that night. All the best, Ellie.

Then she rang Thomas. He sounded distracted. Exactly what had he been up to today, his one day in the week off duty?

'Ellie here. Are you able to get away for supper?'

'Can't wait. Can we eat early? What do you fancy? Thai, Greek, French, fish and chips? Or shall we hop in the car and go further afield?'

'How about the Carvery? Then you can have double helpings.'

'Good choice. Pick you up at . . . what time? Six?'

'Best scruff, or do we dress up?'

'Come as you are.'

'I'm wearing the scruff I was in this morning. Which reminds me, did Mrs Dawes get her extra greenery?'

'Would her scouts dare to disobey her? The church looks marvellous. Be with you at six.'

Satisfactory.

* * *

He must have practised the signature fifty times. It felt right. He'd become Russell. He could pay all the bills without worrying about them. For the first time in his adult life, he had no financial worries.

He'd chucked in his job at the supermarket. No need for that piddling pay cheque any more. No need to pay the maintenance for his wife any more, either. If he was Russell, then he wasn't Lee. Lee was dead, and his wife could go hang herself. Anyway, she'd probably moved someone else into her bed already. She'd not be skimping. Long live Russell.

He'd better see to cleaning out that bath again. You could never be too careful, when you got blood on the grouting.

CHAPTER FOUR

Ellie glanced at her watch and decided that even if she were a few minutes late, she wanted — no, needed — a shower and change of clothes. In fact, she rather thought she'd not wear that skirt and jacket again, at least until after they'd been dry-cleaned.

A chilly November night needed warm clothing; a blue jumper with lacy inserts over a swishy midnight blue skirt, and court shoes rather than sandals because they did keep her feet warmer. A scarf, a change of handbag, and she was hustling into her best winter coat as Thomas rang the doorbell.

He'd changed, too. A thick, cable-knit blue sweater over a decent pair of trousers for a change. And a chunky car coat. Most people, when they looked at Thomas, saw only his calm, bearded face which reminded them of Players Cigarette adverts if they were old enough, or Captain Birds Eye adverts if they were not. Though Thomas' hair and beard were still dark.

Ellie saw deeper lines around his eyes.

'A bad day?' she asked.

He nodded. 'You, too, I gather. I suggest we don't talk about it until we've eaten and had a chance to relax.'

Sensible man.

He pointed to the 2Ds sign. 'That's new.' Meaning: what's going on?

'Put up without my consent. I told them to come and take it down. Would you like to knock it over for me?'

'A pleasure.' He was a big, heavily muscled man. A couple of heaves, a well-placed kick, and the board lay on the ground.

'Well done,' said Ellie.

The Carvery was divided into booths and the lighting was soft. Ensconced in a quiet corner, Ellie felt herself unwinding. She hadn't realized quite how tense she'd been. She had a flashback of torn plastic sheeting, stained pink flannelette and . . .

She took a deep breath, banishing it, and picked up the menu. 'You'll have soup to start with, I suppose? I'm not sure I could cope, although come to think of it I don't think I've eaten properly today.'

'Mushrooms? Garlic bread?'

'If you will, too.'

'A glass of wine. I know you don't normally, but you're as white as a sheet.'

A sheet. Oh. She tried to smile. 'I just need something hot inside me. You'll have a beer though, won't you?'

They talked about the wedding tomorrow, which was for the daughter of a nice lady called Maggie who sang in the choir and helped on the coffee roster. The girl was getting married to her boss and everyone liked him, so it was going to be a happy wedding. Some weren't . . . sigh.

They talked about what time Roy and Felicity might be back, and . . . oh, trivia. They ate and drank. Thomas had roast beef with Yorkshire pudding, twice. Ellie had a smallish helping of roast pork because she didn't normally cook that, being on her own. He had cheese and biscuits. She had a chocolate ice cream.

'Coffee?' said Thomas, looking over her shoulder. 'We could have it in the bar, because it looks like they're wanting our table.'

His gaze sharpened, and she turned her head to see what had attracted his attention. A tall, handsome man with silver hair was urging a beautiful blonde to a table on the other side of the room. He had his right hand on her shoulder in proprietorial fashion, and she was laughing up at him. Roy and Felicity. They must have got back and decided to come out for a meal rather than cooking for themselves.

They disappeared from sight as they sat down.

Thomas switched his eyes to Ellie. 'We don't want to disturb them, do we?'

Ellie shook her head. When Roy first started paying serious attentions to Felicity, Ellie had been a little put out because he'd been paying court to her before. But now . . . no, she was really pleased for them.

The way Felicity had come on since she and Roy had got together was remarkable. To think what a downtrodden little slavey she'd been in her first marriage to an extremely unpleasant man! Now, she looked radiant.

She looked . . . Mmm. Could it be?

Thomas said, 'I know that look. You're counting on your fingers.'

'No, no.' But she had been, of course. 'It's not really likely.' The doctors had said Felicity probably wouldn't conceive again, after a miscarriage some years ago.

'I've noticed that happiness improves your physical health.'

They made their way to the bar end of the Carvery for coffee.

'Now,' said Thomas. 'Tell me all about it.'

So she did, thinking how wise he'd been to insist that they eat and drink before talking about their day. New impressions overlaid the old. A comfortably full tummy helped to allay her nervous qualms. But still. 'It was pretty awful. It keeps coming back at me and to that nice man, Mr Hurry, as well. Also, I'm going off Denis, big time. I suppose he and Diana deserve one another, but if he thinks I'm going to be sucked into helping them find work for their agency, they've got another think coming. Except that I suppose I am doing precisely that, bargaining that they remove the board in exchange for Mr Ball's telephone number. Do you think I should?'

He grunted. 'If you've promised, you'd better do it. About the corpse . . . someone small, you say? I haven't heard of anyone going missing, have you?'

She shook her head, wrinkling her nose. 'I suppose the rest of her was under the fence. Wrapped in something pink, and then in plastic. I couldn't really see.'

'I suppose the police will want to know why Mrs Dawes sent you up there to collect greenery for her. They'll think she knew the body was there, and wanted you to find it for her.'

Ellie giggled. 'I'd like to see them try that on. Except she might have a stroke. I don't suppose they come across people like Mrs Dawes often. Normal people have a mental map of houses and shops and how to get there. Her mental map marks where to find flowers and foliage which might be useful for flower arrangements. I bet she can pinpoint exactly where she can scrounge the first hazel catkins in spring, and the best branches of holly in winter. If ever someone is gardening and cuts down or throws out a plant which might be useful to her, she's right there, suggesting she relieves them of it.'

Thomas ladled sugar into his coffee. 'Come to think of it, when the old vicarage garden was being torn up, she got someone to cart away a cartload of lavender and some pampas grass that I thought was only fit for the bonfire.'

Ellie knew she ought to have her coffee black, but put in cream and sugar. She felt she needed it. 'Now, Thomas. Your turn. I know it was something bad.'

'Yes, apart from the fact that an old friend is dying . . . well, enough of that. It's Felicity's mother, "Lady" Anne as they call her at the retirement home, though she's no right to the title. Well, it's likely she's going to be asked to leave.'

'What's she done now?' asked Ellie, seeing at once how very difficult this was going to be for Felicity, whose life had been overshadowed by her mother's criticisms. It was Anne who had pushed her daughter into marrying a rich tycoon, thinking it would ensure her the lifestyle Anne craved for herself . . . and never mind if he did abuse her daughter. Unfortunately for Anne, her disappointment in all the men she'd married or flirted with — and there'd been a considerable number of them — had led her to drink, which in turn had caused the accident which had left her in a wheelchair in a retirement home. Anne had been furious when Felicity had married Roy, because she'd persuaded herself that he'd fallen victim to *her* charms, and not to those of her daughter. She'd declined to attend the ceremony, while upping her demands for attention.

Thomas said, 'You know Anne threatened everything under the sun if they went off to Paris and left her alone?'

'If she's all alone, it's because she's a horrible snob and nobody likes her,' said Ellie, viciously for her. 'She sucks the life out of everyone who comes near her.'

'Mmm. It can be a cry for help, of course. Cutting your wrists, or taking an overdose.'

Ellie clattered her cup into her saucer. 'She's actually gone and done it?'

'The people at the home are very good. They wouldn't let her have enough pills to do any damage, so she cut her wrists two days ago. Not badly, of course. With her nail scissors. They called me in because Anne was screaming that the people at the home were conspiring to keep her daughter from her side.'

'What? But . . .'

'The battery on her mobile phone had run down, so she demanded that the home rang Felicity and get her to return from Paris straightaway. Unfortunately,' said Thomas, with a bland expression, 'no one could find the charger for her mobile and Felicity's own mobile number was stored on it.'

'She wanted to ruin their honeymoon. Oh, how could she!'

'Easily, given her fixed impression that she's the most beautiful, most unfortunate and abused creature on earth.'

'She is a pampered, devious . . . ! I'm sorry to say this, Thomas, but she is not a nice woman. Did she need stitches?'

'The cuts were superficial, but the nurse on duty showed me a letter they'd found by Anne's bed. It said she was going to commit suicide because life wasn't worth living since her only daughter had rejected her. The nurse asked what she should do about it. I said to put it in Anne's file. They don't want to keep her now, of course.

'I can imagine,' said Ellie, sympathizing.

'I've been in to see her a couple of times. At first she wouldn't listen to reason, but today she was calmer . . . I went back to see her after I'd collected you from Englefield Road. She'd refused to listen to anyone at the home, but for some reason she thinks I'm "on her side", so I managed to get through to her today.

'The home is going to bring in a psychiatrist to evaluate her condition in view of her suicide attempt. It will probably mean she'll be transferred to the local hospital for a while, and then if the home won't have her back — and they're saying now that they want her to look for alternative accommodation — she might have to go into a council home somewhere. I said the ones in the neighbourhood were all full at the moment and she might have to go out to Kent or, well, anywhere they could find a bed for her. Probably sharing a room.'

Ellie suppressed a smile. 'She'd loathe that.'

'She said Felicity wouldn't allow it. She said Felicity would never let her go into council accommodation. I said that Felicity was married now, and would have to take her husband's wishes into account, so it would be advisable for Anne to think about making the best of things. She tried tears. She said I didn't realize how hard life was for her, that Felicity was the only thing that made life worth living, etc. She cries beautifully.'

'You weren't fooled?'

'She wanted me to ring Felicity there and then and tell her what a terrible state she was in. I said that when I next had a chance to talk to Felicity, I would. Luckily, I haven't had a chance to speak to her yet.' He sat back in his chair, folding his arms, smiling.

Ellie laughed. 'Sneaky. But wise.'

He jerked his head at the restaurant. 'How far along do you think she is?'

'How should I know? It was only a guess. I'm probably wrong.'

'I like your guesswork. I don't understand how you do it, but you sum people up quicker than I can down a pint. Don't try to think, just answer off the top of your head.'

'Well, then. Not far along. Three months, maybe four.'

Thomas stroked his beard. 'They've been married four. Hmm. It might be better not to tell Anne that she's expecting a grandchild just yet. Felicity shouldn't have to face tantrums for a while.'

'But as soon as she visits her mother . . .'

'I'm going to suggest you ask Roy to handle it. Let him do the visiting for a week or so. I expect Felicity's got a slight sniffle. Most people do, after flying. Anne won't want Felicity anywhere near her, if she's infectious.'

'You want me to arrange it? We're all having lunch at Aunt Drusilla's on Sunday. I could mention it then. But knowing Felicity, she'll have been worrying about her mother and will be round to see her first thing tomorrow.'

'No, she won't,' said Thomas. 'Both she and Roy are invited to the wedding, remember, and the reception after. I'm hopeful we can keep them apart for a bit.'

'You wind us all round your little finger, don't you?'

'You look worn out. Come on, let's get you home before you fall asleep on me.'

* * *

Lee trundled the broom and wheelbarrow into the shed at the bottom of the garden. He'd found the fluorescent council-issue jacket — slightly torn — in a skip, and mended it with tape. Wearing it made him invisible. You could stand in the street pretending to sweep the gutter, and no one paid you any mind.

He could kill that interfering old witch.

If she hadn't stopped him from burying the body in the first place, it would all have been done and dusted by now.

It had been such a good plan, too. Off with the head and hands — he'd done that in the bath, no problem. Without the head and hands, it was much harder to identify the body. Bury the rest of him in the garden.

But she'd popped her head over the fence and said, 'You're never going to dig up those good rose bushes, are you?'

And he'd had to say, No, he was just digging around them, going to put some manure on them, improve them no end. Which meant he couldn't dispose of the body in his garden, because the rest of it was laid to grass and anyone could see he'd disturbed the ground if he dug up the lawn.

His second plan was good. He'd burn the body, like the Hindus did. He'd built a bonfire and was just about to light it and put the body on, when her head popped over the fence again. 'Don't you know you can't have a bonfire here? It's against the law.'

So he'd had to improvise. By this time the body was stinking, even wrapped in an old blanket and black plastic bags. He'd looked around for another garden that needed clearing, and when he'd found one he'd got the old lady to agree a fee for doing the work, taken the body round there in his wheelbarrow with his tools on top and started to dig the grave. He'd dumped the body right next to where he'd started digging . . . phooh! What a stink. But it would soon have been over for good.

Then she'd only gone and changed her mind, hadn't she! Said her nephew didn't want things torn up after all, and she'd marched him off the premises. Luckily he'd been able to pull the fence down over the body first, but . . . it hadn't been properly hidden. And now, it had been discovered.

He told himself not to panic. No one could connect him with the body. The plod had been round, asking if he knew of anyone missing. He'd given his name as Russell and played dumb, said no, he didn't know of anyone missing. The only one who could give him away was, he supposed, the old biddy.

She'd had a good look at him. He bit his fingernails, thinking what he'd like to do to her.

It was only five o' clock and already dark outside. It wouldn't take long. No one would see him if he went over the fence. There was going to be another hard frost tonight by the look of it, and he wouldn't leave any traces. A good strong spade would prise open any back door and then . . .

Curtains for biddies.

* * *

Ellie slept better than she'd expected to. It rained in the night, and Midge stayed curled up at her back, keeping her warm. A little too warm, if truth were known. Had she left the central heating on all night? She hadn't intended to do so, but it had been cold of late so she might have left it turned up high.

She was late — for her — having breakfast. But what did that matter? All she had to do was get ready for the eleven o'clock wedding. One of the beauties of living opposite the church was that it didn't take long to get there.

The phone rang. For some reason Ellie jumped. Her heart rate went up. She told herself not to be silly, but she took her time answering it.

Diana. 'Mother? Is that you? I've got an emergency. How soon can you get over here?'

'What sort of emergency?' She could hear Frank wailing in the background. Something to do with him, no doubt. Was he ill? Had an accident?

'I have to be at the agency by half past eight, and it's a quarter past now. I'm supposed to drop Frank off at Denis' place first — his wife's got four boys and she's prepared to let him muck in with them — but he's crawled under his bed and refuses to come out and I simply don't have the time to make him!'

Ellie had met Denis' rumbustious boys, all of whom were far older and bigger than little Frank, and observed that the youngster feared them. Granted, Frank was no angel, but it did seem hard that he had to be left at the mercy of those big lads whenever it proved inconvenient for Diana to have him with her.

'Can't his father . . . ?'

'No, they're away for the weekend. I've told Frank, promised him a trip to Alton Towers if he's good, but he's just screaming at me the whole time and I daren't be late on our first day; Denis will kill me!'

Ellie registered that Diana appeared to be afraid of Denis. Was that a good thing, or a bad one? 'Diana, I can't help you. I've got a wedding on today and—'

'Mother, you can't be serious! You can at least come and get him out from under the bed, and find someone else to look after him for me.'

'Who?' Frank could be a little devil at times. Who could she think of, who could take charge of him? Kate next door was just about to have her second child, Frank's one-time babysitter didn't take anyone at weekends.

'I don't know, do I? Look, I've got to go and I can't just lock him in the flat and leave him there all day, can I?' exclaimed Diana.

'No, I see that. All right, I'll come and coax him out and maybe I can find someone at church to look after him, but—'

'Bless you, bless you. Oh, and that reminds me, Denis says you've got the address of the man who's selling that house in Englefield Road?'

'You may have his phone number when you've taken away the Sold notice from outside my house. It's on the ground just inside the wall.'

'But . . . oh, I must go. I'll lock him in, so remember to bring your key. Speak to you later.'

Ellie heard the phone click off. She looked down at herself. She'd dressed in a good warm suit in a heathery colour over a jumper which was — an inexcusable extravagance — cashmere. Well, she was going to a wedding, after all. She hadn't put any lipstick on yet, or good shoes. Poor little Frank. Locked in? It didn't bear thinking about.

She phoned for a cab. It would take too long to walk over there. Poor lad, distressed and locked in! She ought to report Diana to Social Services. She hurried to get some shoes and put essentials into a handbag which matched. Keys, mobile, purse, lipstick and comb. Hankie. She locked the back door, banged the front door till it clicked shut and noticed that the postman had left an elastic band on the pathway again. The post hadn't arrived yet.

The cab drew up outside and made good time to the large house which Diana had bought a couple of years back and converted into flats, one of which she'd retained for her own use.

Silence as Ellie let herself into Diana's flat. She called out, 'Yoohoo! It's me!'

A pyjama-clad figure hurtled itself into her, and clutched her knees. She stroked his dark head, thinking how odd it was that it took a threat from outsiders to make Frank realize how much his granny meant to him.

'There, now,' she said, abandoning all hope of attending the wedding and the reception afterwards. She could ring Mrs Dawes and explain. 'It seems we've got an unexpected treat today, you and I. Have you had any breakfast? What would you like? Boiled egg and soldiers? Suppose you go and get dressed, while I see to it for you, right?'

'A bacon sandwich. I can stay with you all day?'

'I expect so. I'll have to ring one or two people, arrange for them to cover for me, and then we'll see what we can do.'

'I don't have to go to Denis'?'

'No.'

'I don't have to sit in the shop and be quiet all day?'

'No. Now you let go of my leg, and I'll ring Mrs Dawes to say I won't make the wedding this morning.'

He let go of her leg. Even tear-stained and tousled, he was a handsome boy. 'Can I come to the wedding? Will there be sausages on sticks?'

Dare she take him to the wedding and on to the reception? Mmm. If he decided to behave himself, it might be possible. On the other hand, it might not. As he left for the bathroom, Ellie tried Mrs Dawes' phone number. But that dear lady wasn't answering. She might well have gone to the church early, to make sure that nothing had gone wrong with her precious flowers overnight. A twitch here and the removal of a fading flower there made all the difference.

Then Ellie remembered Felicity, and how essential it was to head her off from visiting her mother for a while. Would Felicity agree to help look after Frank in an emergency? It might help deflect her from any desire to visit her mother.

Ellie got through and Roy answered. 'Ellie, is that the time? I'm afraid we got up rather late . . .' Ellie heard Felicity laughing in the background. Roy also laughed. Well, good for them. 'So, what can we do you for today?' Roy asked pleasantly.

'I gather you had a good time?'

'You can say that again,' said Roy, still laughing. 'Felicity's just trying on her hat — at least, she calls it a confection, not a hat — that she bought specially for the wedding. So we'll see you at the church, then?'

'Diana's failed to make suitable arrangements for little Frank, so I'm looking after him today. I've tried ringing Mrs Dawes to say I may not be able to make the service, so if you get there first, will you tell her?'

'Bring him along,' said Roy, generous in his happiness. 'We'll look after him during the service, and I don't suppose Maggie will mind one small boy extra at the reception. It's a buffet, I gather, not sit down.'

'I didn't dare suggest it,' said Ellie, 'but yes, that would be wonderful. We'll be there as quickly as we can.'

'Will there be Coca-Cola to drink?' asked Frank, appearing in respectable enough clothing. His fingernails were not particularly clean, but they'd have to do.

With one eye on the clock, Ellie fed Frank, had a quick cup of coffee herself — that was one good thing about Diana, she always kept a supply of ground coffee — and called a cab to take them to the church. Felicity and Roy were walking down the path to the main door as they arrived. Felicity looked stunning. Her 'confection' was a dance of tiny feathers on trembling stalks, and she was wearing a silvery-grey silken coat with matching dress beneath. Roy was so proud of her that Ellie thought he'd grown another inch, and he was tall enough as it was.

'Good timing,' said Roy, who'd always been tolerant of little Frank, even though he cordially detested Diana. 'Frank, you'll sit with us, will you? Then we can all go on to the beanfeast together.'

Frank stroked Felicity's coat and she, smiling, put her arm around him and urged him into the porch, while Ellie fled round to the vestry entrance, hoping against hope that Mrs Dawes had managed to sort out any extra pieces of music they might both need for the service. Their organist had been known to spring a new descant on them at the last minute and though Ellie could follow a tune once she'd heard it, her grasp of notes which went up and down on the page was tenuous, to say the least.

Ellie hoped that the bride would be a little late, as was traditional. It would give Ellie time to get her music sorted.

'Only five minutes late,' said someone. 'Remarkable.'

Everyone was hustling into place, choir robes on, bundles of music clutched in hand. Ellie threw on her gown and grabbed her pile of music. Someone hissed at her that she was late and she nodded, whispering back that there'd been a bit of a domestic crisis.

'We were worried, what with Maggie being out front today . . . and Mrs Dawes hasn't turned up.'

No Mrs Dawes?

The choir was getting into processional order. Ellie looked sharply around. Mrs Dawes wasn't there. Oh. Thomas appeared at the door, the crucifix was readied. The organist gave the signal, and the service began.

Ellie couldn't concentrate. All during the processional hymn, she kept wondering why Mrs Dawes wasn't there. It was so unlike her. She hadn't missed singing in a wedding for . . . well, Ellie couldn't remember her ever having missed a wedding before. It was one of the highlights of Mrs Dawes' life, to decorate the church for a big occasion, and then sit back and enjoy it. She didn't care whether or not people complimented her on her flower arrangements — although of course she liked it when they did — but it was her way of exercising her talent.

Maggie's daughter looked lovely. A little on the plump side, but that didn't matter when you saw how much she loved her husband-to-be, and how much he adored her. From the choir stalls you could see everything. Including Felicity's 'confection', and Roy hoisting little Frank up on to the pew, so that he could see what was going on.

Ellie couldn't settle. If Mrs Dawes hadn't come to check on her flowers earlier, then why hadn't she answered her phone? Perhaps she'd slipped and fallen. She was a heavily built woman, and her right knee did play up from time to time. Suppose she had had an accident . . . but those little houses were not all that soundproof, and she ought to have been able to make a neighbour hear her. Or get to a phone.

Suppose she couldn't get to a phone?

Ellie was hemmed in by sopranos on either side of her. If she tried to make her way out, it would create quite a disturbance. She didn't know what to do. With every minute that passed, she became more convinced that something dreadful had happened to Mrs Dawes. The second hymn was announced. The sopranos were decidedly wobbly today. If Ellie left, they'd be worse. Oh dear. And nice Maggie, sitting solidly in the front pew, deserved the best.

Ellie whispered to her neighbour that she had to get out. The neighbour was not amused but allowed Ellie to wriggle past her. Thomas caught the movement and lifted his eyebrows. She sent him a smile which she hoped was not too anxious, and managed to get back to the vestry without treading on anyone's feet. In the vestry she got out her mobile and rang Mrs Dawes' number. And let it ring.

The service was continuing in the church. She mustn't disturb that. She went outside, striding up and down, trying the number again. Nothing.

She rang for a cab. The lines were engaged.

Roy came round the corner of the church with Felicity in tow and Frank running along beside them. 'What's up, Ellie? Are you ill?'

'No, but I'm worried about Mrs Dawes.'

As Ellie explained, Roy was getting his keys out. 'I've got the car nearby. Hop in and I'll take you up there. We can't have Mrs Dawes lying there in agony while we enjoy ourselves.'

Frank raced them to the car. 'Do you think she'll be all bluggy?'

'I hope she won't be bloody, no,' said Ellie, following him into the car. She realized she was still wearing her choir gown, but it was too late to bother about that.

'Belt up, everyone,' Felicity said as they moved off.

Up the road, twisting and turning. They parked outside Mrs Dawes' house, with its immaculate garden. The house looked as neat and well-maintained as usual, except . . .

'The curtains are closed in the front room, and I think there's a light on inside,' said Roy, getting out of the car. 'In the hall, too. You lot stay there.' He rang the doorbell, and peered through the letter box, calling out for Mrs Dawes.

There was no reply.

'A neighbour might have a key,' said Ellie, getting out of the car.

Felicity followed, with Frank scrambling out behind them.

Roy stepped over a low fence and tried the front door of the neighbouring house. A middle-aged woman in a sari came to the door.

'Mrs Dawes? No, I do not have a key for her. Is something wrong?'

Roy said, 'Look, do you mind if I go through your house and check on Mrs Dawes' house at the back, see if I can spot anything?'

He disappeared inside the house, and they waited. It began to drizzle, and Felicity put her hands over her 'confection' to protect it, and then ran up the path to shelter in Mrs Dawes' porch.

Frank jumped up and down. 'I bet she's lying there, all bluggy.'

'She might have had a stroke,' said Ellie to Felicity. Felicity nodded. Mrs Dawes was overweight and ate well but not always wisely.

There came the sound of bolts being drawn back at the front door, and Roy appeared. 'It looks as if someone jemmied the back door open. Frank, you stay here.'

Frank, of course, had already got himself inside the house. The neighbour joined them. 'Is she all right?' she asked with concern.

Ellie tried to grab hold of Frank. 'Frank, no! Stay here!'

Frank slid out of her grasp and into the front room. 'I've found her, I've found her. And she is all bluggy!'

* * *

He wrapped the few parts that remained of Russell in newspaper and put it out on the drive in the container the council provided for recycling food waste. Smashed to small pieces, the head and hands were unidentifiable. Lee approved of recycling. In a way, he'd recycled his own life — as well as Russell's.

CHAPTER FIVE

Mrs Dawes was in the sitting room, stretched out on her back with her head almost under the table. There was a large bruise on her jaw, and a black stain under her head on the carpet. Since the stain was black and not bright red, Ellie imagined that Mrs Dawes must have stopped bleeding some time ago. Her eyes were closed. The gas fire was on and made the room feel close.

Ellie told herself she was not going to panic. Mrs Dawes wasn't dead. She couldn't be!

It was difficult to see in that light. The curtains were still drawn, and a ceiling light had been left on. A drinking glass in a holder lay on the floor way beyond one of Mrs Dawes' outstretched hands, and the contents — milk? — had splashed across the carpet and up over the wallpaper. A paperback with a lurid cover had landed up behind her chair. Mrs Dawes was dressed in a padded housecoat over a long brushed cotton nightdress, her black hair in a plait. One slipper was standing by itself at the foot of her big armchair, but she was still wearing the other. Her arms and legs were all over the place and her nightie had ridden up.

Roy knelt down and tried to find a pulse in Mrs Dawes' neck.

'Let me see!' The neighbour pushed into the room. She saw Mrs Dawes and gave a frightened scream, which didn't help matters at all.

Ellie felt like fainting, but told herself she couldn't afford to give way. This was dreadful! Dear Lord, let her not be dead!

It was too late to stop Frank seeing Mrs Dawes, but Ellie stirred herself to shield Felicity from the sight. 'Go into the back room and sit down, Felicity.' She heard her voice quaver. Felicity nodded but didn't move. Her nod of agreement meant that she either knew or suspected that she was pregnant, but she seemed incapable of movement. She'd gone very pale. Possibly as pale as Ellie felt?

Four months, thought Ellie.

The neighbour collapsed into Mrs Dawes' big chair by the fire, and began to wail.

'Is she really deaded?' enquired Frank in a tiny voice.

'Not sure,' said Roy, changing his position and trying again.

Ellie found she was trembling. Dear Lord, no! She's my oldest friend! She's a cantankerous, difficult old so and so, but she can't die!

Ellie ordered herself not to shake. For little Frank's sake, for everyone's sake, she mustn't go to pieces. She took Frank by the hand and turned him towards the door. 'Frank, this is important. I want you to be very grown up and look after Felicity for me. She needs a lot of care at the moment. Take her into the back room and make sure she sits down. If she wants a glass of water or anything, will you come and tell me, so that I can get it for her?'

Frank gave her a straight look. Sometimes he could act older than his years. He nodded. He went to Felicity, took her hand and led her towards the back room. 'Come along, Flicky. I'll look after you.'

Felicity sent a distorted smile in Ellie's direction, and went with the boy.

The neighbour was being no help at all. What was her name? Had Ellie ever heard it? Possibly, but if so she'd forgotten it.

Roy was standing up when Ellie got back. He'd pulled Mrs Dawes' nightdress down and covered her legs with his jacket. 'I think she's still alive, but I can only just feel a pulse. It's a miracle she's lasted this long, with the nights so cold.'

He took out his mobile phone and tried to punch in some numbers. Failed. Cursed. Tried again.

Ellie noted that there was a smear of blood on the edge of the table. It looked as if Mrs Dawes had been whacked into the middle of next week and hit her head as she went down. Head injuries bleed a lot. It didn't look as if she'd broken anything, because, although her legs and arms were all over the place, they were all at acceptable angles.

Roy still couldn't get through to the emergency services. His hands must be shaking as much as Ellie's. She said, 'Let me try,' and got her own phone out.

He said, 'I don't think we should move her till the ambulance gets here, but I'll see if I can find a blanket to cover her with.'

Blanket, thought Ellie. Pink winceyette. She shook her head at herself. No, there couldn't be any connection. She keyed in the emergency number.

'Which service do you want?'

'Ambulance, please.' This was getting to be a habit. 'Oh yes, and the police, too.'

The neighbour continued to wail. Ellie felt an impulse to hit her, but restrained herself. Roy came back with a blanket, cream wool honeycomb, and not pink winceyette, thank goodness.

Ellie looked around the room. Mrs Dawes' capacious handbag was on the table, the contents strewn all over the place. Mrs Dawes used it to contain the tools of her trade, including secateurs and wire, as well as the usual things to be found in a handbag: a large diary, lying open with the pages bent back, tissues, a makeup pouch, spectacles for reading, a tube of cough lozenges. Her keys had dropped to the floor, together with a flutter of letters and bills. A wallet and a change purse gaped, empty.

Roy said, 'Looks like robbery.'

'Our mothers used to keep money in a pocket in their drawers,' said Ellie, light-headedly.

'What?' said Roy, who'd never heard of women doing that.

'Oh, never mind,' said Ellie. Into the phone, she said, 'Ambulance to Oaktree Road. And will you inform the police, too? My name is Ellie Quicke, Mrs. We've found an elderly lady on the floor, unconscious. Her name's Mrs Dawes. It looks like a robbery gone wrong.'

Roy was looking lost. 'I feel we ought to do something for her, but I don't know what, do you?'

'You could take Mrs . . . whatever her name is . . . into the kitchen and give her a glass of water. Or return her home? She's doing no good here.'

'No, no!' gasped the woman. 'Me, Mrs Kumar. I stay — please! Oh, dear Mrs Dawes! Whoever is doing such a wicked thing?'

Roy asked the woman if she'd like a drink of water, while Ellie looked around, trying to work out what had happened. Mrs Dawes must have been sitting in a chair beside the gas fire, dressed for bed, but not yet ready to go up. She'd been reading, sipping hot milk; it had to be hot milk because the glass she was drinking from was in a holder. She hadn't finished the milk when she was interrupted.

Perhaps she'd heard someone at the back door? As she got to her feet — rather slowly because of her bulk — he or she had burst in and clouted Mrs Dawes, sending her flying and causing her to hit her head on the table as she fell. Probably a man, and a big man at that, because it would have taken some force to knock Mrs Dawes for six. He'd upended her handbag, taken the money and made his escape. It had probably all been over in sixty seconds.

Roy fetched the neighbour a glass of water, and stood over her while she sipped at it. He said, 'It looks like a drug addict wanting a quick fix to me.'

The phone quacked at Ellie, and she gave the operator Mrs Dawes' details. She shut off the phone. 'They'll be here as quickly as they can.'

Roy bent down to look at the gas fire. 'It was a cold night. It's lucky she had this on. It's probably kept her alive. Otherwise she might well have died of hypothermia.'

Frank came to the doorway, and hovered. Ellie stirred herself to go to him.

'Flicky wants to know if the lady's all right? Is she really deaded?' His first excitement over finding a body had worn off, and now it was his turn to look pale.

Ellie took his hand. 'Let's go back and tell Felicity that it's all right. Mrs Dawes has had a nasty fall, but the ambulance is on its way.' This time Frank wasn't unwilling to leave the scene.

Felicity was sitting on an upright chair in the rarely used dining room at the back of the house. She still looked white, but tried to smile when Ellie came in. 'I'm all right, really I am. It's just . . . I mean, I haven't told Roy that . . . I might well be . . .'

'I know,' said Ellie. 'You'll be just fine. Deep, slow breathing. Think of something pleasant. Clouds passing across a sunny landscape, birds on the feeder in your garden, the roses you're planting this winter. Tell Frank a fairy story.'

'Fairy story.' Frank went to Felicity's side. She put her arm around him, and kissed the top of his head. For a wonder, he let her do it. He even nestled into the soft grey of her coat.

It was cold in the back room. Ellie put the gas fire on, and its cheerful glow made them feel better straightaway.

Roy called out, 'I think that's the ambulance now.'

Ellie shut Felicity and Frank into the back room and joined Roy in the hall, but the neighbour was recovering fast and fluttered to the front door ahead of them.

'Is Mrs Dawes!' she cried to the ambulance men as they came up the path. 'Oh, so terrible! We must phone her daughter and her son, and oh, the grandchildren, too!'

'All right, missus. Stand aside and let's have a look at her, shall we?'

Like a brightly coloured bird, Mrs Kumar led the way. 'Such a fright she give me! I am worrying because her milk is still on the doorstep you see, and she is always up and about, so busy all the time. But today, not! Then her friends knock on my door and I say, Will you come through my house and look over the garden fence? And this is how we found her.'

'Could you draw the curtains back, missus? Let the dog see the bone, right?'

Someone shouted at the door, 'Anyone there?'

Mrs Kumar squealed, 'Oh, oh! The police. Everyone, all at once!'

She rushed to the front door again, excited as a child at Christmas. 'This way, this way! The ambulance men are just here, but perhaps she is dead already. I am saying, when I see her, I nearly fainted . . .'

Ellie and Roy exchanged glances and by mutual consent joined Felicity and Frank in the back room. Felicity looked up at them and smiled. She'd taken off her pretty hat and transferred to a big old armchair in the window with Frank on her knee. She'd undone the buttons on her pretty coat, and Frank was nestling close to her inside it.

'And the brave little boy married the princess and lived happily ever after.'

'More!' demanded Frank.

'Later, perhaps,' said Felicity. Her eyes asked the question, but she didn't put her anxiety into words.

'All right so far,' said Roy. 'The ambulance men have arrived, and so have the police. The neighbour's acting as hostess.'

Felicity nodded and they all stretched their ears to listen except for Frank, who was playing with a string of crystal beads around Felicity's neck.

Ellie noticed with a start that she was still wearing her choir gown over her ordinary clothes. She took the gown off and laid it over the back of an upright chair. She was thinking that if Mrs Dawes had died, the ambulance men would leave her where she was for the police to deal with. If she was still alive, Ellie would hear them taking her out of the house.

Oh dear, oh dear . . . please Ford, don't let her die. She's such a part of my life, always been there since I got married over thirty years ago. I know she orders people about and criticizes them but she only gets cross with people if they don't do as well as they might. She sets high standards for herself and everyone else and yet she can be so kind . . .

Was that footsteps retreating? The door banging? Were the ambulance men leaving, which meant . . . ? A long pause.

Felicity lowered her head, so that her cheek rested on the top of Frank's head. The footsteps returned. Mrs Kumar was still twittering next door. Why didn't someone shut her up?

There was a bumping sound. 'There we go!'

'Watch it!'

A short wail from Mrs Kumar. Then retreating footsteps, slow and heavy. They were taking Mrs Dawes to hospital. So she was still alive. Felicity and Roy had come to the same conclusion. Their strained expressions relaxed into a smile.

Ellie said, 'Perhaps I ought to go with her?'

'I'll take you to the hospital later, but the police will want a word first.' Roy was right, of course.

Ellie wrung her hands, thinking of all that had to be done. Someone would have to tell Mrs Dawes' children. Her son lived . . . where? Think Ellie, think! Ah yes, she had it now. Her son lived in Birmingham, her daughter in Leeds. The grandchildren were all over the place. One of the girls was in Australia, but the lad Neil — the one who set up in business as a handyman locally with the help of a grant from Ellie's trust fund — didn't live far away. Hayes? Yeading? She had his phone number at home somewhere.

'I'll ask how they're getting on,' said Roy, leaving the room.

Felicity crooned a lullaby to Frank and, retreating to babyhood, he smiled and twisted his fingers in her string of beads.

Ellie plumped herself down on an upright chair and began to pray hard. Please Lord, please. Mrs Dawes is such a good person, does so much good, she really does. I know she can be sharp, but that's understandable . . . her bad knee . . . such high standards, so caring about other people. Lord, in your mercy, hear my prayer.

Her mobile phone rang, and after a moment she realized what it was and fished it out. Thomas, worrying about her.

'I'm all right, Thomas, really. Mrs Dawes was attacked last night at her home. Someone knocked her for six and left her to die, but she didn't die, though she's still unconscious. It's too soon to tell if . . . we won't know for a while whether . . .' Her voice faded out on her. 'Sorry, Thomas. Sorry. The ambulance men have just left to take her to hospital, but the police are still here so we can't leave. Sorry to have messed up the wedding ceremony, too. Will you tell Maggie, make my apologies?'

'Of course, of course. Shall I come and fetch you?'

'No, you mustn't leave. It would spoil everyone's enjoyment of the reception. Roy's dealing with the police and he'll drop me back home later. I'm quite all right, really. Just shocked, you know.' She tried to laugh. 'I bet my name's mud, leaving in the middle of a church service.'

'*Eccentric* is the word they use to describe you. Give me a ring when you get back home, right?'

She rang off as Roy came back with a couple of policemen. They flashed their cards and mumbled their names, which Ellie didn't grasp. She thought they were a couple of plods. Neither was of any great calibre. One of the policemen had large ears. Very large ears. Red. Ellie told herself not to look at his ears, which must cause him embarrassment, but there, no sooner do you tell yourself not to look at someone's embarrassing feature, than you find your eyes going straight to them again.

'You all arrived together, I understand,' said Ears, taking in the presence of a small boy and their party gear. 'Mrs Kumar has told us how she found the body when you arrived, so really all I need is your names and addresses and then you can go, though we may need a statement from you later.'

Mrs Kumar had found the body? This was a slight variation on the truth of what had happened, but they were all feeling too subdued to object.

Except for Frank, and he wasn't having anyone steal his thunder. 'I found her first,' he said.

Ears frowned. This was messing up his notes.

Ellie said, 'We all came in together. I was right behind my grandson when he discovered the body. My cousin and his wife were just behind us, and Mrs Kumar followed them in. You won't want to report that a small boy discovered the body. You can put my name down, instead.'

Ears thought a man would be better, and addressed Roy. 'So, what's your name?'

'Roy Bartrick, and this is my wife, Felicity. We were at the church, at a wedding, when we realized—'

'Just a minute,' said Ears. 'How do you spell your name?'

He got it right at the third attempt. He looked at Ellie. 'Now, your name and address, please?' She spelled her name out for him, and noticed he'd written it down wrong. Kwik as in Kwik Save. She couldn't be bothered to correct him.

Felicity asked, 'Which hospital are they taking her to?'

The policeman shrugged. 'Ealing, I suppose. You're none of you any relation to the old lady, are you? Just friends, right? Well, Forensics have just arrived. They'll want to know if you touched anything.'

'Only her, I think,' said Roy, suppressing a shudder.

'In here,' said Ellie. 'I put the fire on. That's about it for this visit, although I've often been here in the past, of course.'

'I sat in that chair over there,' said Felicity, 'and then moved here. That's all.'

Ears said, 'They'll want your fingerprints though I doubt there's going to be anything worth having.' He closed his notebook, looked at his watch. 'It looks a straightforward case. Druggie wants a quick fix, strikes old lady, lucky he didn't finish her off. We'll ask around, but . . .' He shrugged. 'We might be lucky, and he might not have been wearing gloves. If so, he might have left us a print that we can identify.' What he meant was, don't hold your breath.

His colleague looked slightly more intelligent but was obviously number two in the partnership, not number one.

Ellie said, 'What about the back door? He got in that way, didn't he?'

Number Two said, 'Forensics will have a look.'

Ellie wondered if she should voice a deep unease about what had happened. She told herself it was only asking for trouble to do so, and that these men wouldn't listen to her, anyway. But she tried. 'You know, it's something of a coincidence. Mrs Dawes sent me along a road not far from here yesterday to get some greenery for her, and I stumbled across a body then. But that one was very dead.' She shuddered.

'Oh?' said the number two.

'Really?' said Ears, looking at his watch. 'Not our shout.'

'You don't think there's anything in it?' asked Ellie. 'I mean, I can't see how there could be, but . . .'

'It wasn't this Mrs Dawes that found the other body, was it?'

'Well, no. But . . .'

'You don't think she knew anything about it, do you?'

'No, certainly not.'

He put his notebook away. 'Don't you worry, then. Mrs Kumar is going to make us all a nice cup of tea, and when Forensics have taken your prints, you can go.'

Ellie tried again. 'We ought to phone her family.'

'Don't worry. We'll be doing that.'

Ellie reflected that Mrs Dawes' phone book would give them all the information they needed, and probably Forensics had it now and would release it in due course. But when would they release it? Surely, if Mrs Dawes was still alive, her family would want to be at her side?

Ellie wished she'd brought her big address book with her. But there, you don't cart such things around to a wedding, do you?

The two policemen went out, talking loudly about where they intended to stop for a bite to eat after they'd finished their shift. There were bumps and other noises from the front room, and a youngish woman put her head through the door, and said, 'You lot waiting for me?'

'We found the body,' said Roy. 'You'll want our prints, no doubt, even though I don't think any of us touched anything in there.'

Frank looked up. 'I've never had my fingerprints taken before. Does it hurt?'

It didn't take long, once the woman got down to it. Then they were free to go.

Roy looked at his watch. 'Too late to go to the wedding reception. Anyone hungry?'

Frank said, 'I am.'

Felicity buttoned up her coat. 'I've a freezer full of food. Let's get back and eat at home.'

'And have a good rest this afternoon,' said Ellie, giving Felicity a meaningful look.

Felicity ignored the look, giving her hand to little Frank. 'Come along, little man. The sooner we get going, the sooner we can eat.'

'Can I tell them at school that I found her all bluggy and lying down? And that I've had my fingerprints taken?'

The adults shivered, but Roy managed to say, 'I expect so.' Ellie was conscious of something missing, something overlooked. Roy put his arm around Felicity and grabbed hold of Frank, fearful that he stray again. 'Come along, then.'

'Will you all be having a nice cup of tea?' Mrs Kumar appeared in the doorway, holding a tray with mugs on it.

'I'm afraid we're just off,' said Roy. 'I'm sure the police will be delighted.' He led his charges out of the room.

Ellie picked up her handbag, and looked around the dining room, wondering if Mrs Dawes would ever see her much-loved little house again. There was an ancient pair of binoculars beside the chair in the window, the one Felicity had sat in. Ellie could imagine Mrs Dawes sitting there, watching the birds as they came to feed in her pretty garden.

Ellie spotted Felicity's little hat, which she'd taken off earlier and left on the table. Ellie retrieved it and also her choir robe. She wasn't thinking straight, was she?

'Will you be staying, then? Will you like some tea?' Mrs Kumar was still hopeful, poised in the doorway with her tray.

Ellie manoeuvred herself around the tray into the hall. 'Thank you, I expect the police would love it, but we're only in the way here and have been told to go. Are you all right? Do you have someone to be with you at home?'

'My husband is at home, asleep. He works nights at the airport, you see. I ring my son. He is also working at the airport. He will be here in an hour, maybe.'

There was a bump from the front room, and both women shivered.

Roy called out, 'Ellie, are you coming?'

The front door was open, and she could see Roy helping Felicity into the car. He'd already got Frank into the back. He'd have to argue with Frank to get him to belt up, but Roy could probably manage it.

'Poor Mrs Dawes,' said Mrs Kumar. 'Her nice room will need redecorating altogether, I think.'

'Yes,' said Ellie, wincing at the thought of the spoiled carpet and splashes on the wallpaper. 'I'd offer to stay with you, but I have to look after my grandson.'

'I know, I know. I will go back home next door when you go.'

'Do you have any of the family's telephone numbers? I've got Neil's — her grandson's — at home, but no others.'

'The police said they will do it. I say the grandson — he lives near and often comes to see her, and they say when was he here last, and I say it was yesterday afternoon, I think. Yes, I am sure of it, because I see his van outside, and they are shouting at one another as they always do. Always, always shouting. And the police said, Ah-ha! as if they think he did it.'

'Oh, he wouldn't,' said Ellie, knowing the boy well. 'Mrs Kumar, will you give me your telephone number just in case, and I'll give you mine?'

Roy called out, 'Ellie, are you coming?'

With a warm 'Goodbye, and take care of yourself' to Mrs Kumar, Ellie went to join the others in the car.

After such an attack, would Mrs Dawes ever regain consciousness? And if she did, would she still have the use of her arms and legs, not to mention her tongue? And even if she did regain her faculties, might she not be too broken to resume her old life? Such attacks often heralded a descent into frailty and a retirement home.

Which reminded Ellie that Mrs Dawes' indoor plants would need watering, or there would be Words Said when that lady returned home. If she ever did. Perhaps Neil would see to it? Ellie decided that she wasn't going to wait for the police to contact him, but would try to get through to him herself.

'The sun's come out,' said Roy. No one else said anything on the drive down the hill, while Ellie worked out what she needed to do.

'Roy, if you don't mind, I think I'd like to go straight home with Frank. The police said they'd contact Mrs Dawes' next of kin, but I know Neil will be half out of his mind when he hears his gran is in hospital, and I've got his number somewhere in my desk.'

Roy nodded. They were all — including Frank — unusually subdued.

Roy dropped them off and sped away.

Ellie was greeted in the hallway by Midge, and got some food out for him and for Frank. She couldn't be bothered to eat herself, but went into the study to see if she could find Neil's number. Eureka! His business flier was exactly where it ought to be, for a wonder.

NEIL CAN FIX IT!
Property & Garden Maintenance.
Lawn-cutting and garden care.
Interior decoration.

He'd given both his home and mobile numbers, and she caught up with him on his mobile.

'Neil, Mrs Quicke here. I've got some bad news, I'm afraid. Your gran has—'

He sighed, noisily. 'Oh, no! She hasn't been on to you as well, has she? I told her only yesterday I'd keep my eyes peeled for any more of that something laurel, but I haven't spotted any more around and I'm not going back to ask that woman again, and that's flat!'

Ellie wondered if he were talking about the same laurel that had been concealing a dead body but didn't stop to ask. 'No, listen. Neil, your gran was getting ready for bed last night and someone broke in and knocked her out. The police think it was someone after money for drugs.'

'What? Why, the . . . ! Is she all right?'

'Well, no. She isn't. She was unconscious when we found her this morning, and she's been taken off to hospital. It doesn't look too good.'

'I'll get down there straightaway.' Pause for thought. 'I'm in the middle of doing this woman's ceiling, but she'll understand. I'll give the hospital a ring now, find out what ward she's in.'

'I rather think it'll be Accident and Emergency. Maybe Intensive Care.'

Heavy breathing from Neil's end. 'You mean, it's that serious? That I'd better ring the family?'

'You'll want to get down there straightaway, and they won't let you use your mobile in A & E. Give me the numbers to contact your family and I'll tell them. Then when you've found out what's happening at the hospital you can either go outside or use a payphone to give them an update. I'll see if I can get down there later myself.'

He kept his head, though obviously shocked. He reeled off a couple of numbers, which she jotted down on the back of a kitchen equipment catalogue. Then he clattered off, and she started to spread the bad news.

Neil's father had long since divorced his wife and set up with a younger woman, but when reached he, too, was horrified to hear what had happened. He said he'd drive down as soon as he could, probably reaching the hospital about ten that evening. Ellie asked where he'd stay. He said he couldn't think as far as that. In his mother's house, he supposed. Ellie said he'd better check the police would let him in. Perhaps he'd like to stay with her, instead?

'No, no. Oh, well . . . maybe. I'll ring you.' He would have rung off without taking Ellie's phone number, but she managed to get him to take it down, hoping he'd remember to take it with him.

Ellie then rang the number Neil had given her for Mrs Dawes' daughter. The only person at the end of the phone was one of the granddaughters, who was playing such loud music that Ellie could hardly make herself heard, but who did finally understand that something serious had happened, and gave Ellie another number to ring her mother, who was at work.

When reached, Mrs Dawes' daughter had to talk through her shock, but then said she'd see if she could get her husband to drive her up to London tomorrow, after she'd made arrangements for the rest of the family to be looked after in her absence.

Ellie rang the hospital only to be told that as she wasn't a relative, they couldn't release any information. Bother. She couldn't go round there and make a nuisance of herself, either, because she had to look after little Frank. However, she knew a man who could get information out of a stone, never mind a frosty hospital receptionist. She rang Thomas.

'Update, Thomas. It doesn't look too good. I've managed to contact Neil and he's going round to the hospital straightaway. I've got hold of Mrs Dawes' son and daughter and they're coming down, but the hospital won't tell me anything . . .'

'Leave it to me,' he said. As she'd known he would.

She relaxed, slightly. Frank had by this time finished his late lunch and gone into the sitting room to turn on the telly. Of course.

'Want to watch a DVD?' she asked.

'Mmm.' He selected something from the pile she kept handy for him. She did hope it wouldn't be anything too gory, or she'd have to keep leaving the room. But it wasn't too bad. *The Lion King*. Perhaps the events of the afternoon had made him realize that human beings didn't bounce back as cartoon characters did.

She sat down beside him on the settee and muted the sound from thunderous to a murmur. He knew the dialogue by heart, anyway. He curled up beside her. She'd taken off her jacket, and he nestled into her cashmere sweater.

'You're all soft,' he said. 'So's Flicky. So's Maria.' Maria was his stepmother, who loved him no matter how bad he'd been, but didn't let him get away with anything.

Ellie realized he hadn't said his mother was all soft. Well, Diana wasn't. Sigh.

For the umpteenth time, Ellie thought it might be better for Frank if he didn't have to spend weekends with his mother, because she alternately spoiled him and screamed at him.

Was Diana now going to have to work at weekends to make the agency a success? Diana seemed to think it was a perfect solution for Frank to be dumped in with Denis' children at weekends, but Frank was scared of Denis' brood and Ellie didn't blame him for that.

How much — if anything — should Ellie interfere?

Probably not at all. She stroked his head, noting with a touch of despair that he'd got a baked beans stain on her brand-new, very expensive jumper. Oh dear. Would dry cleaning get it out? She went on stroking his head and his eyelids fell, lifted, and fell again. It would probably do him good to have a little nap. Such a shock for a little chap to have seen the body.

Her own head sank back to rest against the back of the settee. The DVD murmured on. Frank slept and she tried to nap.

* * *

The plod interrupted him while he was vacuuming the hall. A different set of plods from the first lot.

'Yes?' he said, switching the vacuum cleaner off, heart beating no more rapidly than usual.

'You're the householder? Your name?'

'Russell. What's the matter?' He was pleased with the way that had come out. Slightly concerned, but not worried.

'You've heard there was an incident in the neighbourhood . . . ?'

'Yeah, someone came round, yesterday. They found the body of a drug addict or something.'

'We're here on another matter. An incident last night. Were you in?'

He nodded. 'Watching telly. What happened?'

'Did you see or hear anything unusual? Someone taking a short cut down the alley between this house and the next?'

He pretended to think about that. Then shook his head. 'The telly was on. Someone been burgled?'

'Have you seen a strange vehicle around?'

'Wasn't looking'. He rubbed his chin. His beard was growing in nicely. 'You don't mean the white van, do you?' It wouldn't do any harm to point them in another direction. 'There's been a white van coming up and down this road a fair amount recently. Doesn't live here. A builder, I reckon. You don't mean that, do you?'

'Do you know the licence number? Was anything written on the side?'

He shook his head. 'Never noticed. It weren't none too clean, I know that.'

'Was it here yesterday afternoon or evening?'

'How should I know? What you on about, anyway?'

'Well, thanks . . . Mr . . . er?'

'Russell.'

The plod had nodded at the vacuum cleaner. 'Don't you get your missus to do that?'

'Never felt the need to bring a woman in,' he said, and it sounded — it felt — so right. He switched the vacuum cleaner on again, even before he closed the front door.

CHAPTER SIX

Ellie woke with a start when the front-door bell rang. One prolonged, insistent ring. Diana. It must be.

Ellie eased Frank out of her arms — he was still fast asleep — and covered him over with her jacket before going to the front door. Yes, it was Diana. And Denis. Denis was smiling. Ellie wondered, uncharitably, whether he smiled even in his sleep.

Denis handed over Ellie's two trays while Diana stalked through into the conservatory, shedding her jacket and handbag as she went. She didn't observe her son, curled up on the settee in the sitting room, but she did comment on the mark on Ellie's jumper.

'Honestly, Mother. Food stains! Whatever next!'

Denis bent down, still smiling, and took Ellie by surprise by kissing her cheek.

'Dear Ellie!'

Flustered, Ellie dumped the trays in the kitchen, and offered coffee or tea.

'Something stronger?' said Denis, rubbing his hands. 'To celebrate.'

Ellie tried to slot back into their world. 'Would you like a sherry? I think I've got some in the other room, but I don't drink much nowadays. You had a good first day?' She dived into the sitting room to rescue the bottle, and a couple of glasses, taking care not to wake Frank.

'What, no champagne?' said Denis.

Ellie's eyes widened at the thought of keeping champagne in the house. Whatever next! She poured him a small sherry, which he was graciously pleased to accept.

Diana said, 'It will be better when we can contact your friend up the road, Mother. And before you ask, yes, we've removed the Sold sign.'

Ellie handed Diana another sherry, and scrabbled in her handbag for the telephone number of Mr Ball which Mr Hurry, the decorator, had given her. 'Here it is. The house is owned by a Mrs Ball. Her nephew — same name — doesn't live there, but is involved with the plans to modernize and sell it. They're often at cross-purposes, it seems. The garden is a wreck . . .' Ellie swallowed. 'But there's a new bathroom and kitchen being fitted. That's his mobile phone number, not hers.'

'You are quite brilliant, Ellie,' said Denis, smiling. He took Ellie's hand in both of his. 'We'd never have got this house without you.'

Ellie thought, but managed not to say, You haven't got it yet.

'And I want to assure you that you will receive a cheque for a percentage of our profit when the sale goes through.'

'Oh, but I wouldn't dream of it.' said Ellie.

'Nonsense, my dear.' He pumped her hand up and down between both of his. 'We regard you as a partner in our little agency, don't we, Diana? You have a stake in our success, right? As such, I'd like to propose a little contract between us. You are in an ideal position in church to learn about who might be wanting to downsize or, indeed, to go into better accommodation around here. You will get a percentage each time you bring us a lead which goes through to a sale.'

Ellie removed her hand. 'A kind thought, but it's not really my style.'

Diana threw herself on to a chair. 'Oh, come on, Mother. It'll be easy money for you, and help us to get established. As Denis says, it's in your interest for us to succeed.'

'I wish you well,' said Ellie, diplomatically, 'but I'm no saleswoman. I'm sure that dealing honestly with people will be your quickest road to success.'

'Yes, of course,' said Denis, losing his smile and narrowing his eyes.

Diana yawned. Shrugged. 'Well, we offered.'

The doorbell rang again, twice. Thomas.

Ellie hastened to let him into the hall. He looked serious, was wearing his dog collar with a good navy-blue suit.

Ellie asked, 'Mrs Dawes?'

'Still unconscious. They thought at first she might have a broken jaw, but apparently that's all right. It's the head injury that's worrying them now. They're going to do a scan, see if there's a depressed fracture and if so, they'll need to operate. But, it's Saturday and they may have trouble trying to find a safe pair of hands. There's talk of moving her to another hospital, but they think that's too dangerous. It all depends on the results of the scan. Neil's at her side.'

'Prognosis?'

He shook his head. 'They say it was right to call the next of kin. Neil's beside himself. He only saw her yesterday, when she tore him off a strip as usual. I've got another visit to pay first but I said I'd go back and sit with him later on. Have you eaten? Could you manage something?'

Ellie tipped her head to the conservatory. 'I'll come with you when I've got rid of them. Diana and Denis are here. They seem pleased with the open day at the agency. Little Frank's here, too. Asleep. Yes, I do need to eat, I suppose.'

She led the way into the conservatory. 'What's he doing here?' asked Diana on seeing Thomas.

How rude! Ellie felt herself flush with embarrassment. 'Thomas has just come from the hospital. Our old friend Mrs Dawes has been attacked and is in a critical condition. We're all terribly upset.'

'Oh?' said Denis. 'You mean . . . it's serious? I don't think I know the lady, do I?'

'An interfering old buzzard,' said Diana. 'But maybe it's an ill wind, if it means her house comes on to the market.'

Ellie gasped, 'Diana!'

'I'm only being realistic,' said Diana, with a shrug. 'Anyway, where do we all fancy eating this evening?'

Denis tried to grasp Ellie's hand again but she moved away to avoid him. He said, 'Ellie, we want you to come out with us to celebrate. You're such an important member of the partnership. We want to show our appreciation.' He bestowed one of his toothy smiles on Thomas, who was standing by, stroking his beard. 'You understand, old man, don't you? Family comes first, doesn't it?'

Thomas said, 'I'd never try to come between Ellie and food.' Which didn't help.

Ellie tried to defuse the situation. 'Denis, that's very sweet of you, but I've promised to go back to the hospital with Thomas, and we'll pick up a snack on the way. Diana, you'd better wake little Frank up and take him home or he'll not sleep properly tonight. He's only had baked beans for lunch and that was a bit later than usual for him.'

'I thought we'd let him sleep here for a while, and then he can muck in with Denis' kids while we three go out to eat,' said Diana, beginning to frown.

'I dare say.' Ellie wasn't having it. 'But I have to go out now, and I can't leave you all behind in the house.'

'Don't you trust us?' Denis held on to his smile.

Ellie fought with the desire to say 'no', which would be the truth. Perhaps silence would be best.

Thomas lifted his mobile phone out of his pocket. 'Excuse me while I make a couple of phone calls, people who need to know about Mrs Dawes, and an old friend in trouble.' He went back to the hall to get some privacy.

Diana marched into the sitting room to gaze down at her son. 'What shall we do with him?'

Denis followed, shrugging his shoulders. 'Let his father look after him.'

'He's away this weekend. I was relying on Mother to help out, but if she insists on being so selfish . . .'

'Oh well, he can always doss down with my brood.'

'Of course.' Diana shook Frank's shoulder, not unkindly. 'Time to go.'

Frank was muzzy, confused. He mumbled, 'I saw her, I did . . .' His voice trailed away, then he started into full consciousness. Recognizing his mother, he dived into her arms with a wail, only to be held away from her as she spotted the baked beans stain around his mouth. 'Not on my best suit!'

Ellie mumbled something about checking that the back door was locked and fled into the kitchen via the conservatory. Thomas, still talking on his mobile, realized something was wrong and followed Ellie, putting his arm about her as she reached for a tissue. He finished the call, but kept his arm about her.

She said, fiercely, 'I know it's considered best for a child to have contact with both parents.'

He patted her shoulder.

'What's all this?' asked Diana, leading Frank into the kitchen to wash his face.

'A spot of comfort in a cold world,' said Ellie, expecting Thomas to remove his arm — which he didn't.

'I thought the clergy weren't supposed to cuddle their parishioners,' said Diana, wiping Frank's mouth with a J-cloth. 'It lays them open to all sorts of gossip.'

'A cuddle in time saves many a breakdown,' said Thomas. 'Your mother is eminently cuddlable, in my humble opinion.'

'Now, now,' said Ellie, trying to regain her composure. 'Stop it. Both of you. Frank, didn't you have a jacket, earlier? Thomas, I'll just pop upstairs and change. Give me fifteen minutes?'

'Take twenty, if you wish,' said Thomas, once more busy on his mobile phone.

Diana followed Ellie into the hall. 'Mother, is that man trying to flirt with you?'

'To comfort me, yes.'

'If he carries on like that, people will talk.'

'The parish is getting used to it, and so will you.'

'It's obscene.'

Ellie was tired, hungry, and getting cross. 'Listen to yourself, Diana. Thomas is a grown man and I'm a grown woman. If we choose to spend time in one another's company, then it's none of your business.'

'It is my business! Heaven's above! An impecunious vicar and a wealthy widow! He'll strip you of everything you've got!'

'How dare you!'

Their raised voices had brought Denis to the doorway from the sitting room, and Thomas from the kitchen.

Ellie reddened. 'I'm sorry, Thomas. Diana, that was not called for. I think you'd better go.'

Diana exploded. '*I* should go? It's *he* who should go, not me!' She turned on Thomas. 'Please go. I need a private conversation with my mother.'

'Diana!' said Denis, a warning note in his voice.

Thomas stroked his beard, looking sideways at Ellie. 'If your mother asks me to leave . . .'

'I don't!' said Ellie, glaring at each one in turn. 'Diana, Denis, see yourselves out, will you?'

'But . . . what! Do you mean you're throwing me out? That's just not—'

'Yes,' said Ellie, opening the front door. 'And please remember that a certain small boy has had a bad time today and doesn't need grown-ups rowing over his head.'

Diana's face changed. 'Oh. Well, I was just going to say, about tomorrow . . .'

'I can't look after Frank tomorrow. I have church in the morning followed by a family lunch, and I suspect any spare time will be spent at the hospital and looking after Mrs Dawes' family.'

'Will Thomas be at this "family" lunch?'

Embarrassed, not knowing how to deal with the situation, Ellie held the door wider. 'Will you please go?'

Denis took Diana by the elbow, and manoeuvred her towards the front door. Rubbing his eyes sleepily, little Frank followed them. As she closed the door on them and the nasty cold night Ellie hoped they'd remember they'd got the boy in tow.

Thomas was still standing four square in the door to the kitchen. She couldn't read his expression so she said, 'Sorry about that,' to a point somewhere above his head, and almost ran upstairs to change.

What would Thomas think! How could Diana!

Pray heaven they don't forget poor little Frank . . . and please Lord, remember to look after Mrs Dawes. I don't know what to pray for her, but you know what's in your mind for her, so I'll pray for that . . . and for poor Neil, at his wits' end . . . and his father, driving down from the Midlands . . . drive carefully, won't you . . .

Suddenly, she remembered Roy and Felicity, and that difficult woman Anne. Ellie shot out on to the landing, pulling a long woollen skirt around her.

'Thomas!' He appeared in the doorway to the sitting room, holding the prayer book that he always carried with him. 'Thomas, I'd quite forgotten. Weren't we going to ask Roy to deal with Anne, to stop Felicity getting upset?'

Thomas said something more or less under his breath. Ellie grinned. Sometimes Thomas seemed just too good to be true. It was nice to have it confirmed that he was human, after all.

'Use my telephone,' said Ellie. 'Roy's number is in the memory.'

He put his prayer book away and got down to dealing with the next problem.

* * *

Thomas put capable hands at ten to two on the steering wheel. He'd only a couple of parking tickets and a speeding fine in thirty years of driving, and Ellie felt safe in the car with him. She wondered if he'd mention Diana's outburst, and decided — a little hysterically — that she'd ignore it. It was all too embarrassing.

Thomas and Ellie had drifted into spending time with one another some months back. He'd given her his mobile phone number and he had hers. They were taking it gently, enjoying one another's company, without feeling any need to set boundaries. He knew that she wasn't thinking of getting married again soon. Perhaps she never would. Diana's intervention had upset Ellie's comfortable view of their relationship. Were other people going to think the same way as Diana? What would this do to Thomas' reputation?

What a mess!

Thomas said, 'I suggest I drop you off at the hospital. You find Neil and make him eat something. There's quite a good café in the basement of the hospital. Do you know it?'

Ellie nodded.

'I've spoken to Roy. Felicity said she had a bit of a headache when they got back and she's been lying down all afternoon, so she hasn't yet done anything about contacting her mother.'

Ellie nodded again. Good.

'I told Roy what Anne had done. He agrees with me that Felicity may well be coming down with something infectious . . .' Ellie smiled. 'And that they'd both better keep away from the retirement home for the next few days. I said I'd call in tonight to see how Anne was getting on . . .' Ellie now frowned. 'Because, whether we think she brings her troubles on herself or not, she is a woman in pain.'

Ellie sighed. 'You're right, of course. I'll stay with Neil till his father gets here, and try to persuade him to eat. I've given Neil's father my mobile number, so he can contact me so long as I'm not actually in A & E.'

He drew up outside the entrance to the Accident and Emergency department.

Ellie pulled her coat around her and got out of the car. She remembered her handbag but found she was missing one glove. Again. 'You're a special case, Thomas.'

He said, 'I'll come back when I've finished there.' He drove off, leaving her to reflect that his day threatened to be a long one, starting with an SOS from the home for Anne, then the big wedding. After that he'd dealt with the problems for the church of the attack on Mrs Dawes, then made another visit to the home, and finally he was going to end up in A & E.

She found Neil in the waiting area, staring blankly at the floor while rubbing his hand over his shaven head, bobble cap on the seat beside him, one big hand clutching a magazine that he was clearly not reading. A half-empty packet of crisps lay beside him, with an opened can of Coca-Cola.

The place was thronged, trolleys passing to and fro, nurses bustling, doctors hastening, blank-eyed relatives staring; there was a pool of yellowish liquid on the floor which someone was mopping up.

Saturday night in A & E: drunks, fight victims, overdose victims. Plus the usual chest pains and unexplained stomach upsets. A child wept in his mother's arms and was swept away to a cubicle. Policemen and women wandered in, conferred at the desk and wandered over to cubicles or left the department.

Ellie touched Neil on the shoulder, and sat beside him. 'It's me, Neil.'

He looked up at her. There were tears in his eyes. 'She's not back from the scan yet. Still unconscious. Been down there for—' he consulted an outsize watch on a bony wrist — 'nearly an hour.'

'She's very strong. A fighter.'

He nodded. Looked down at the magazine in his hands again. 'I'll kill them,' he said, meaning it. 'Why did they need to pick on her, when she's hardly two pence to rub together? I've been thinking and thinking. Why her? I mean, it's not exactly on their doorstep.'

'On whose doorstep, Neil?'

'Those scumbags that hang around the take-aways in the Avenue at night, selling dope. It must have been one of them. I told her, don't you say nothing to them. I don't care if you do think what they're doing is wrong. It's best not to interfere.'

'Did she say something to them?'

'Boasted of it. Said she'd given them a right mouthful when she caught them selling to some schoolkids. I mean, it's not as if she's often that way late at night, but she'd been to an event at the library with a friend who'd gone home a different way afterwards. Trust Gran to step in. She sees something wrong, and she has to have her say. I told her, sometimes it's best not to see something, if you know what I mean. They're a mean lot, specially that very thin one. I reckon he carries a knife — not that I've seen it, but that's what they say.'

'It wasn't a knife that laid her low, Neil.'

'Whatever. They must have followed her, or seen her going into her house, maybe one of them lives up that way, I dunno. And then they decided to pay her a visit, teach her a lesson. She never *listens* when I talk to her! She always thinks she knows better.'

'You saw her yesterday?'

'Wish I hadn't! She was still going on about that greenery she wanted, and I'd told her before that I'd look out for some more for her, but I hadn't seen any elsewhere.'

'You'd tried Mrs Ball?'

'Big woman, way up the hill? The house that's being done up inside but the garden's a right mess? Yes, Gran had me go round there some time last week, asking if I could get some greenery for her. While I was there, I asked the old woman if she'd like me to do the garden for her, but she said I was too expensive. Honest, Mrs Quicke, it was a proper price.'

She patted his hand. The chaos in A & E continued as two drunks were brought in, still trying to fight one another. 'Neil, how about we go and get a bite to eat?'

'Couldn't.'

She used guile. 'Well, I must confess, I'm about dropping. Finding the body took it out of me. I haven't been able to fancy anything to eat, but I'm afraid I might faint if I don't.'

'You poor old thing.' He put his arm about her, helped her to her feet. 'I'll tell them at the desk where we're going, and then we'll see what we can find for you. I think there's a café somewhere . . .'

She steered him in the right direction. If she dithered enough, perhaps he'd take a firm, manly stand and bully her into eating something. It was child-play, manipulating someone like Neil.

* * *

Normally on Saturday nights he'd be down at the pub, which is where he'd met Russell in the first place. Two men drinking alone, both liking Young's Best Bitter.

The pub had been crowded and some youngster had jogged Russell's arm so that he'd spilled beer over Lee's jacket. The youngster had bought them both a fresh pint, and somehow Lee and Russell — the ex-bank clerk and the wiry supermarket shelf-filler — had started talking.

Lee was skint, as usual. Russell was flush and bought them both another pint, and then another. Lee was looking for new digs where he could leave his car in the street without it being graffitied overnight. Russell's parents had left him a house which he hated but hadn't the courage to leave.

Marginally the soberer of the two, Lee offered Russell a lift home in his ancient Volvo at chucking-out time, and stayed overnight on Russell's settee. And moved in there the following day.

Now he had the house to himself, Lee swore he'd not give it up for anybody.

It was what he'd always dreamed of: a place of his own with no one to shout at him, and money coming in. He was riding high. He could do anything he wanted.

There'd been a spot of bother, yes. But poof! It had disappeared, just like that.

He'd never realized before how easy it was to remove people who got in your way.

CHAPTER SEVEN

Ellie got some food into Neil and ate some herself. She was not a fan of junk food, but there was no denying that on occasions like this it hit the right spot. Neil topped off his meal with some black coffee but Ellie settled on a fruit juice. If ever she did get back home that night, she wanted to be able to sleep.

Meanwhile Neil talked . . . and talked . . . and talked.

Ellie heard about his latest girlfriend and how that affair had been going, what her parents were like, what he'd said about them to her, and what she'd said to him about them. And all about their last row . . .

Well, there was no need to listen to every word, was there? Ellie got the impression that he didn't consider this particular girlfriend a long-term project. When Ellie reminded Neil that it would be kind to let his girlfriend know that he was waiting for news of his gran at the hospital, he turned sulky, said she didn't care what he did, so why should he bother?

He did have one bit of good news for her, though. Neil had got started his garden maintenance and decorating business with a grant from Ellie's charitable trust. His business was doing well, even in the depths of winter. There was no grass cutting to be done for the moment, of course, but he could mend and replace fences, attack overgrown plots, clear out ponds and tackle most smallish outdoor jobs. And there were always people who wanted decorating done in time for Christmas.

He'd not impressed the members of the trust with his book-keeping skills, but after trying out various girlfriends in that direction, he'd now found someone capable to help him: a young single mother who was a friend of a friend. She worked part-time at a school so she could look after her little one. She was glad to have some extra work she could do at home, and he could trust her to keep the books straight.

Ellie realized that he was talking to keep depression at bay. Fair enough. She did that herself, sometimes. At last, though, he pushed back his empty cup and said he thought they ought to be getting back. At the beginning of the meal he'd been making positive remarks about how his gran would come through this, no problem. With all the carbohydrates he'd been stuffing into himself, he ought to have been more positive, but the opposite seemed to be true.

'If only I hadn't shouted at her that last time.'

'Maybe your father will be arriving soon,' said Ellie with one eye on the clock.

'Much good he'll be. I only hope he doesn't bring *her* down with him, his totty bird. Gran never liked her. "Mutton dressed as lamb," Gran said. It took me a while to work out what she meant, but she's right.' He grinned. 'Likely she'll not come, what with the surprise packet and all. A surprise to him, too. He hadn't reckoned on another mouth to feed at his age.'

They made their way back to A & E to hear that Mrs Dawes had come back from the scan and was now in Intensive Care, no visitors allowed yet. There was some good news: the scan showed only a hairline fracture of the skull, so an operation would not be needed. On the other hand, with head injuries they couldn't tell how long it might take for the patient to wake up.

Neil's father arrived; another big-boned man, dark-haired and dark-clothed. He and Neil greeted one another with lowered eyes and an avoidance of physical contact. Not close, then. The department was as busy as ever, but Ellie found them a corner in which to wait. Had Mr Dawes eaten? It appeared he'd stopped on the way down for a burger.

Mr Dawes asked if the police had been informed. Ellie filled him in as best she could. She asked if he'd like to come back to stay the night with her. He shook his head.

They waited.

Soon after midnight, Thomas appeared, apologizing for his delay in getting there. He'd had yet another call to make on his way over. He looked much as he always did, save for a slight darkening of the shadows under his eyes. A strong man, capable of bearing many people's burdens. Ellie was concerned for him. Even strong men need to eat, drink and take a rest sometime.

He checked in at the desk, waiting patiently while the victim of a mugging was admitted. He suggested that he take Ellie home, but Neil looked so alarmed — possibly at the thought of being left alone with his father? — that Ellie said that she'd prefer to stay. Thomas sat down to wait with them. He talked for a while with Mr Dawes, but after a while they all fell silent. Waiting. Time limped on.

At half past one, a doctor came to see them. Mrs Dawes was to be kept in Intensive Care for a while, but one member of the family could go in to see her for a short time if they wished.

Mr Dawes vanished with the doctor. He returned after a short while, looking shocked. Neil hit his eyelids with the back of his hands. He said he'd wait to see her in the morning.

A nurse suggested that if they'd like to go home, the hospital would be in touch if . . . Please leave details of where you will be . . . it might be some time before . . .

They nodded. Thomas said Mr Dawes could doss down at his place, if he liked. It wasn't much, but Mr Dawes could have the bed and he'd take the chair that turned into a bed, if Mr Dawes knew what he meant. It appeared that he did.

'Thanks. Yes. My gran had one of those when I was a kid. It's been a long day. We never sleep through the night at home, with the young one. I told Sylvia I'd ring and let her know what's happening, but not till morning or she'll not be best pleased.'

Ellie smothered a yawn. 'Neil, would you like to come back with me for the rest of the night or do you want to get back to your place?'

Neil, too, shied away from the thought of waking his girlfriend up. 'She'll think I've gone to one of my mates. She won't be worried about me, not her. I'll give her a ring in the morning, mebbe. I can kip down anywhere. In the van, probbly.'

'Certainly not,' said Ellie. 'I always keep a bed made up in the spare room, and you want to be fresh for your gran in the morning.'

'Give you a lift, then.'

Neil took her back in his van, which reminded her, as she climbed up into it, and then climbed down on to the driveway when they reached her house, that vans were not really suitable methods of transport for someone in their fifties with less than perfect statistics. She ached all over with tiredness, but forced herself to make sure Neil had everything he needed. Then, of course, she had to feed Midge, who'd plopped through the cat flap to greet her as she let herself in. Finally, she could fall into bed herself.

Her last thought was that it wasn't long before she had to be at church, fed, clothed and in her right mind, to sing in the choir. It was Sunday morning already, but perhaps, just for once, she'd not set the alarm, and manage to sleep through . . .

* * *

Midge woke Ellie at her usual time of seven o'clock. Midge usually managed to adjust fairly quickly to the hour going back in autumn, but his internal clock insisted that food be provided for him at regular intervals, and no nonsense about his provider sleeping in.

Bleary-eyed, Ellie fed him and managed to take a shower without waking Neil. She hoped he'd sleep on for a while. She dressed and went downstairs, trying not to let the third stair squeak. Black coffee never had appealed to her, but she made herself a brew, telling herself sternly that it would do her good, only to reach for the milk and sugar before she had taken more than a sip. She then had some cereal and half a slice of toast for breakfast.

Eight o'clock, and still Neil slept. She knew it was no use ringing the hospital for news of Mrs Dawes because they'd refuse information to any but next of kin. It was better to let Neil sleep on. It was a good sign, surely, that they hadn't rung Neil here in the night?

Should she go back to bed herself? It was a temptation, but she knew she'd never sleep soundly if she did. She drew back the curtains, watered her indoor plants, kept the wireless on low so as not to disturb Neil. An unmarked car drew up outside, and two policemen got out and came down the slope to her front door. Ears and his partner. Ellie felt herself grow rigid. Had the unthinkable happened and Mrs Dawes died?

She ran to the front door and held it open. 'Mrs Dawes . . . ?'

'We understand you brought her grandson home with you. Can we have a word with him, please?'

For a moment Ellie couldn't think what they meant, and then she realized they thought that Neil had had something to do with the attack on Mrs Dawes. Ridiculous! A second later she understood that from their point of view it wasn't at all ridiculous. Mrs Kumar had told the police that Neil and Mrs Dawes had been shouting at one another. Neil had been open about it, too. In the eyes of the police, that probably meant they'd quarrelled.

'He's still in bed, asleep,' she said. 'Come in. I'll wake him. Would you like some coffee?'

Her brain was going into overdrive. She desperately needed to think, but her brain wasn't functioning as well as usual. It was a Sunday morning. Should she see if she could get her solicitor, Bill Weatherspoon, out of bed to look after Neil? Would Bill want to be involved? The answer to that was, no, he wouldn't. What's more, he wouldn't want her to get involved, either. He'd tried to get her to promise never to get involved with the police again, which was one of the reasons she'd stopped seeing so much of him. If a friend got into trouble, she wanted to be able to do something about it.

'No coffee, thanks,' said Ears, stepping inside. 'If you'll just get him downstairs for us, we'd like a quiet word.'

'He didn't do it,' said Ellie, and as she spoke she saw their faces relax into a 'poor old girl, thinks butter wouldn't melt in his mouth' smile.

'Didn't do what, missus?' said Ears. 'He's not accused of anything — yet. We just want a word, quietly. Right?'

Ellie showed them into the sitting room and went up to shake Neil's shoulder. He was still deeply asleep. 'Neil, wake up! There's no news of your gran, but the police are here, wanting a word.'

She steered him into the bathroom, then went to make some more coffee. He stumbled downstairs eventually. She had to admit that he looked pretty villainous what with his shaved head and unshaved chin. And earrings.

He saw the police and did a double take. For a moment Ellie thought he was going to make a run for it. Perhaps the thought did cross his mind. He gave Ellie a look of horror, probably thinking she'd betrayed him to the plod.

She said, 'They just want a quiet word, Neil. You'd like some coffee, wouldn't you?'

She ushered him into the sitting room and went out through the French windows into the conservatory, not quite closing the door behind her. She wanted to hear what went on. Their voices rumbled. She pushed the plunger down on the cafetière, found some biscuits that Thomas had overlooked and took the tray in for Neil.

Neil was looking belligerent, saying, 'I told you, she often shouts at people. If she shouts at me, I shout back. It's just the way she is.'

Ellie said to the policemen, 'Are you sure you wouldn't like a cuppa?'

'No thanks, missus.'

She left the room but continued to lurk in the conservatory, out of sight of the policemen.

Neil was just about keeping his temper under control. 'Yes, I saw her Friday afternoon. Yes, we had words, but it wasn't serious. What was it about? She'd been on at me about some greenery she wanted for the church. She'd asked me to go up and collect it for her, and that's what I'd tried to do, only it didn't work out.'

A murmur from the police.

'Why didn't it work out? Well, the woman said it was OK to take the greenery because she wanted to get someone to clear the garden for her, and I offered to do it, but she said I was too pricey, which I wasn't. But then a man come out of the house and said no, the garden looked bad enough as it was without me taking anything, and he wasn't prepared to pay for some poncey gardener to charge the earth for tearing it up, and they started arguing about that. So I had to leave it.

'Gran was in a fidget about it, said I must have been rude or something. Only that morning she'd sent someone else to get it, and that had gone wrong, too. She said that if I'd only done as she asked in the first place, she'd have had her greenery and not been put to a lot of extra trouble. She said it was all my fault.'

Murmur, murmur.

'Listen, that's the way she is, my gran. She doesn't like it when people don't do what she wants. It happens all the time . . . What about? Well, almost anything. About my earrings and shaving my head, and not keeping my van spotless. I ask you, in this weather, keeping a white van clean!'

Murmur, murmur.

'What did I do after I left her? I went home, of course. I was in a foul temper. I thought me and my girlfriend could go out down the pub, but she was in a right mood, too. So we had words about that . . . Why? She's always wanting me to go round her parents' house at the weekend and me, I like to sleep in of a weekend, so it ended up with me slamming out . . .'

Murmur, murmur. Ellie couldn't quite hear what the police were saying.

'No,' said Neil. 'I didn't go back there, not after what she'd said. It weren't called for and I told her so. No, I don't know exactly where I went when I banged out of the flat. I drove around for a bit. Then I thought of going to see my mate over at Isleworth, but he weren't in. So I went in the pub there, but it was crowded and smoky, and I hate cigarette smoke, so I ended up walking down by the river . . .'

Murmur, murmur.

'No, I don't suppose I did see anyone I know. Well, I wouldn't, would I?'

Murmur, murmur.

Neil's voice raised in protest. 'What? But I haven't done anything wrong!'

A police voice raised. 'Then you've nothing to worry about. All we want is to ask you a few more questions down the station.'

Ellie shot into the sitting room, aware that Neil was on a short fuse and that it wouldn't do him any good to resist, or worse, to throw a punch.

'What a fuss about nothing,' she said, laying a calming hand on Neil's arm, very much aware that his blood pressure was mounting to danger point. 'Neil, shall I ring your father, get him to go with you?'

He looked as if he'd made a false step in the dark. 'What? My father?' But his colour began to subside.

Ellie spoke to the policemen. 'You're making a mistake, you know. What Neil says is true. He and his gran are always shouting at one another, but that's because she shouts at everyone.'

Ears smiled forgivingly. 'We just want a word down at the station.'

'Of course.' Ellie tried to think what was best to do. She could ring Thomas — no, she couldn't. Thomas was on duty today, Sunday. He'd have taken the eight o'clock communion by now, but he still had two services to take, two sermons to give, lots of people to speak to. She couldn't ring Thomas.

She said, 'I'll just fetch my coat and come down with you, Neil. Give me a minute.'

'No need for that, missus,' said the other policeman.

'I think there is,' said Ellie, slamming the lid on the biscuit tin, and scooping up Neil's mug to take out to the kitchen. She'd have liked to have had time to ring Kate next door and tell her what was happening and to leave a message for Thomas, too, but no, she'd better not. Now, where had she put her mobile phone? In her handbag, she hoped.

Someone rang the doorbell. Everyone looked at everyone else.

'You expecting someone, missus?' asked Ears.

Ellie shook her head. She didn't like the sound of that doorbell. Sometimes it rang with a perky, joyful note. And sometimes it seemed to toll. This was a definite toll.

Closely followed by the two policeman, one of whom was grasping Neil by the elbow, she opened the front door to find a snotty-nosed, weeping, dishevelled five-year-old boy on the doorstep, clutching an Action Man toy, broken, and a DVD.

'Frank?'

Diana's car was just driving off.

Frank was huddled into his jacket, looking up at her as if he expected her to turn him away from her door. Poor little mite! Ellie thought of everything that the little boy had been through the previous day, and wanted simultaneously to kill Diana and to hug the little boy.

'Come on in,' she said, realizing that Frank was her priority now, and that Neil must take his chance. 'Neil, I'm so sorry, but you see . . . ?'

Neil nodded. 'If you can get hold of Dad?'

Ellie said she'd try and then the phone rang. What a busy morning this was turning out to be. As Ellie ushered little Frank into the house, Ears and his colleague led Neil up the slope to their car in the road. Ellie slammed the front door, scooped up the phone, and drew the little boy close. He was still crying, still clutching his broken toy and the DVD.

'Yes?' Ellie was uncharacteristically terse.

'Ellie, are you all right?' It was Kate, her next-door neighbour and very good friend. 'We saw the police car and wondered . . .'

'It's all right. Or almost all right. All right in bits,' said Ellie. 'Mrs Dawes—'

'Yes, I had to ring Felicity . . .' Kate had been something in the City until she had her first child, and now she looked after Felicity's business affairs. 'She said you'd found Mrs Dawes unconscious. What a shock! How is Mrs Dawes getting on? Are you all right and what's going on with the police? Why were they carting young Neil — it was Neil, wasn't it? Isn't that his van outside? — off in their car?'

'He and Mrs Dawes had a shouting match on Friday afternoon, and they think . . . oh, it's ridiculous of course. It's far more likely to be one of the drug pushers from the Avenue.' She tried, gently, to disengage Frank from his jacket, but he resisted her.

'Why would drug pushers target Mrs Dawes?' Kate always thought clearly. In this particular case, Ellie wished Kate didn't. It would be so convenient to put it on the drug pushers.

Ellie sighed. 'They got across Mrs Dawes and she had a go at them. I know, I know. It's not a good enough reason for them to attack her in her own home, but I'm sure it wasn't Neil. I sat with him at the hospital last night and brought him back here when Mrs Dawes was moved to Intensive Care. The hospital has this number for Neil and they haven't rung, so she hasn't taken a turn for the worse. That must be good, mustn't it?'

Frank was pressing himself into her good skirt; oh, what a sticky face he had, her poor skirt. He was still clinging tightly to his toy and DVD. 'Look, Kate. I've got to go. Diana's brought Frank round.'

Kate sounded amused. 'Are you going to take him to church with you?'

'I don't think I can. He's had a rough time. I'll ring them and say I can't make it.'

'I'd look after him myself, but he teased Catriona last time he came round, and if he takes it into his head to run off I'm not in any condition to run after him. Is there anything else I can do for you?'

'Thank you, Kate. No. Just look after yourself.'

Kate sighed, the heavy sigh of late pregnancy, and cut off the phone.

Ellie concentrated on little Frank. 'Now, what's all this about, little man?'

He still wouldn't let go of his toy, but he now held it out to her. 'Broke.'

Ah. Denis' boys were all much older than Frank, and rough. Frank had probably become their latest play thing, in a not nice way. He never liked going there.

Ellie took the DVD off him, noting that it was adult rated and a highly unsuitable choice for a boy who'd found Mrs Dawes in a pool of blood the day before. She said, 'Well, we can always buy you another Action Man. So, what about breakfast?'

How many breakfasts did that make this morning? And — a glance at the clock — what was she going to do about church? If she cried off singing in the choir, they'd be not just one alto down, but an alto plus a soprano. If she didn't turn up to help with the coffee afterwards, Jean, who organized the coffee rota, would be incensed. Jean was the sort of bully every church needed to keep people up to the mark, and Ellie always seemed to be making excuses when she was on the coffee roster. Jean would not be pleased.

But Frank had to be her first concern. She managed to lift him on to her lap — he was getting almost too big for this, and oh, was that a twinge in her back? — and made another attempt to peel off his jacket. This time he let her. His shoe laces were undone. There was a tear in his jumper. And was that a bruise coming up on his cheek?

'There, there,' she said, promising herself a word with Diana about leaving Frank with Denis' boys. 'There, there.

How about you go upstairs and have a good wash and then you can put on some clothes that you can be comfortable in.' Luckily she always kept a change of clothes for Frank in 'his' little bedroom at her house.

He threw his arms around her neck, and buried his face in her sweater. He'd stopped crying, almost. She rocked to and fro, patting his back, holding him close. She didn't fool herself that he loved her in any great depth: he'd had a nasty fright, his father and stepmother were away, and his mother didn't want him around. Granny was next best. And Granny did love him.

'There, there,' said Ellie, thinking of all the phone calls she needed to make, and wondering how on earth she was going to cope.

She couldn't phone Bill to arrange a solicitor for Neil, because Bill didn't want to get involved in that sort of thing any more. Anyway, Bill was pretty well retired now. And yes, it was Sunday morning and who would want to turn out for someone like Neil, whom they'd think probably deserved a session in the cells for something or other, if not for this? Ellie could see their point of view. If Neil would go around looking like a bovver boy, he'd only himself to blame for being treated like one. Also, there was no denying he had a short fuse.

Ellie couldn't think how to solve that one. She really ought to ring Thomas if she could get Frank unstuck from round her neck, and it was no use telling herself that the little boy was overreacting, because he wasn't. Only, he might be, of course. He might be putting it on because he'd not been able to get his own way in everything and because his favourite toy had got broken. She might be maligning Denis' boys because Frank could be a mite destructive with his toys, and they'd probably looked after him very well.

She really ought to ring Jean, and the choir master, and tell them she couldn't make it. And oh! How could she have forgotten that she was due at Aunt Drusilla's for lunch? Could she take Frank with her? He wouldn't be a terribly welcome guest, that was for sure. His table manners were just about all right on a good day, but appalling on a bad one. This was obviously a bad one.

She shifted him into a more comfortable position on her lap, and her back twinged again. Surely she wasn't going to start having a bad back, was she? On top of everything else? She told herself that she was falling into the self-pity trap. It got you nowhere, just paralysed you. She would try a spot of prayer, see if that unstuck her.

Dear Lord, help. I can't sort out my priorities. I know I need to get moving, speak to Neil's father, get a solicitor, ring Jean and Thomas and everyone. Please help this little boy, who's so unhappy and show me how to talk to Diana, to persuade her to make a different arrangement for her son.

Dear Lord, that's no sort of prayer, is it? Just a shopping list. Sorry about that. Look, I know you're listening. I know you're trying to get through to me, to tell me what to do. So. Right. I've stopped shouting at You. Now I'll listen.

She kept on rocking little Frank, but made her mind go quiet . . . and receptive.

The grandmother clock nearby chimed the half hour. In half an hour she ought to be in the vestry with her choir robe on, holding her music, ready to go into church. In half an hour, the police might have reduced Neil to tears. Or a fit of rage, in which case he might well lash out, which would do him no good at all. Oh dear.

All her married life Ellie had put her husband and daughter first, fitting in her own needs around theirs. After he died, she'd found other needs to fill her life with: working for the church was only one of them, though an important one. She'd made new friends such as Kate and Armand next door, and Felicity. She'd spent a lot more time with her aged Aunt Drusilla and Roy. She'd enjoyed it. She'd also enjoyed the feeling that she could be of use to other people. It made her feel, well, important. And valued.

Everyone needed to feel valued, didn't they?

Diana had continued to demand special treatment, since her father died, for herself and for little Frank. Mostly Ellie had been able to fend Diana off, and although it had sometimes been inconvenient, Ellie had been happy enough to look after little Frank as required. She couldn't honestly say it had always been a pleasure, even though she loved him dearly. The fact was that he wasn't a particularly loving child. Or even a really nice child.

She stopped that thought from going any farther. He was what he was, a product of a selfish mother, and a loving but perhaps slightly weak father. His stepmother had drummed some manners into him, and her loving care was slowly improving his manners.

Ellie could cope, more or less, with the pull of family loyalties versus that of friends. But when they clashed, as they did now . . . oh boy!

She really couldn't decide what to do. Of course, she ought to concentrate on the little boy, but at the expense of everyone else? There were some very hurt people out there, relying on her to do this and that. Maybe some of the things they wanted her to do — like serving coffee after the service — were not that important. But others — such as keeping Neil on an even keel — were very important.

More important than soothing Frank?

She wasn't sure.

Equally important? Yes. Definitely.

So how to do both?

Little Frank unstuck himself from round her neck, and clambered off her lap. 'I'm hungry. What's for breakfast?'

At the same time the front-door bell rang, sharply, twice. It was Kate, carrying her bulge before her, as well-groomed as if she'd spent the morning in a beauty parlour instead of dealing with her toddler. With a big smile on her face.

'I've sent Armand off with Catriona to have a second breakfast at the coffee shop. She can play with their toys, and he can read the paper in peace. So I'm all yours for an hour. What would you like me to do first?'

* * *

He stood at the window, gently tipping himself backwards and forwards in Russell's shoes. Comfortable shoes, they hardly pinched at all, nothing to bother about. He'd been surprised at how comfortable good shoes could be. He'd worn nothing but trainers for ever, usually until they were cracked across the sole and letting the water in. A good shoe made you stand tall. Made you feel different. Russell's clothes fitted him well enough, too, once he'd put them through the washing machine. A trifle on the tight side, but that was fashionable now, wasn't it?

He was keeping the Baxi fire going all the time in this cold weather. It was a bit old-fashioned, but it heated the front room and gave him plenty of hot water as well. It was useful in other ways, too. He'd burned all traces of Lee's identity on it, and his old clothes, too. Bye bye, supermarket. Bye bye, little wifey with her incessant whine for money.

It was pleasant, being Russell.

CHAPTER EIGHT

Ellie couldn't help thinking that Kate's arrival was the answer to her prayer. It made her feel like crying, that her neighbour would put herself out for her when anyone else would have taken the chance to put their feet up for a while.

'Can you wash Frank, change him, and then get him some food? I have to make some phone calls, try to get hold of Neil's father.'

'Of course,' said Kate, holding out her hand to Frank who took it without whinging. Frank trusted Kate, as most people did. She wasn't the obviously maternal type, she never talked down to her own little one, never mind other people's babies, but she expected — and got — good behaviour from them. Perhaps that was her secret.

Ellie attacked the phone, thinking hard. Who to phone first?

Thomas. He might still be at home, or he might be on his way to church or he might be ferrying Mr Dawes to the hospital before going to church.

His landline phone rang and rang. No reply. She tried his mobile, worrying that he wouldn't be best pleased to be interrupted on his way to wherever on the busiest day of the week.

‘Yes?’

‘Thomas? Ellie. Sorry to ring you so . . . the thing is, do you have Mr Dawes with you still?’

‘Ellie? Are you at church? I’ve just left him at the hospital and dashed home to get the notes for my sermon. What’s up?’

‘Is there any news of Mrs Dawes?’

‘Still unconscious. I’ll be with you in . . . oh, five minutes.’

‘I don’t think I’ll make church this morning. Have you Mr Dawes’ mobile number? Can I ring him?’

His tone sharpened. ‘Ellie . . . !’

Ellie suppressed the urge to pour the whole story out to him, while knowing very well that he hadn’t time to listen at the moment. His priority must be getting to church where a hundred people would be waiting for him to take the service.

Kate was slowly making her way down the stairs, followed by Frank, who was now wearing his Arsenal strip and trainers.

With an effort to keep her voice level, Ellie said, ‘It’s all right, Thomas. I’ll tell you all about it later, after the service. I just need to contact Mr Dawes, now.’

‘You know he can’t use his mobile in the Intensive Care Unit.’

Ellie ground her teeth. No, of course he couldn’t. ‘I’m being stupid, aren’t I?’

‘Ellie . . .’ A pause. ‘Ellie, you are the most capable person I know. Ring me when you can, right?’

Ellie found she was smiling. A moment before she’d been jelly, but his words had transformed her from amoeba to something almost human. She heard Kate clashing dishes in the kitchen and little Frank beginning to chirrup away. Good for Kate.

She looked at her watch. She was not going to make the morning service, no way. She tried to phone Jean who ran the coffee rota, but the phone rang unanswered. Probably Jean was already at church. She must ring someone in the choir, then. The choir master would be there already, but Mrs Dawes might still be making her way down the hill to . . . Oh. Mrs Dawes wouldn't be there, would she? How could Ellie have forgotten? Well, not forgotten, but . . . her mind was misplacing things.

The quickest way to sort that was to run down her garden and up over The Green to the church and tell someone, if only Kate would hold the fort for a few minutes.

'Kate, Frank, I've got to pop over to the church for a moment.'

Frank slid off his chair and made a run for her, burying his head in her skirt. 'Don't leave me!' Ellie couldn't blame him for being so clingy, but it was very awkward.

She stroked his head, thinking furiously. 'No, I won't leave you.' Perhaps Thomas would tell someone at church that she wouldn't make it. They'd be annoyed at being one down on two fronts, but that couldn't be helped. That was low priority.

What about Neil, being grilled by the police? She threw a glance at the kitchen clock. What was she to do about him? It would be easiest to do nothing, because it was none of her business what happened to him, right? He was no relation of hers. But she was in a position to help, wasn't she? Or was she? She sat on a chair and drew Frank into her arms. He kept his head down, and huffed a bit. Stifling tears?

'Listen, Frank. This is a bad time for all of us, isn't it? You ran into the house yesterday when we told you not to and saw something really nasty, something that made you feel bad.'

He didn't speak, but nodded his head vigorously.

'It upset you, didn't it?'

He nodded again, and mumbled something about waking up all wet. Oh. He'd wet the bed, had he? At Denis'? Oh dear, oh dear. Those boys of Denis' would make the most of that, wouldn't they.

'I didn't like seeing poor Mrs Dawes like that, either,' said Ellie, conscious of Kate's frown across the table. 'It got me all upset, too. Mrs Dawes' grandson was awfully upset when he heard about it, too. And so was her son. I want to help them, but helping them means that I may have to call a cab and go to the hospital and—'

His grip tightened on her. 'Don't leave me!'

'No, I won't leave you.' That far ahead she could see. 'But I do have to make some phone calls and I may have to go to the hospital—'

'No! Stay here!'

'I'd like to, but if someone asks us for help, we ought to try to help them, don't you think?' How best to get through to this angry, confused, hurt little boy?

What was the best thing about him? Probably it was his love for his little half-sister, Yaz, whom he adored.

Ellie said, 'I know you're very good at looking after your sister. I saw how good you were yesterday, looking after Felicity. I think you're very good at looking after everyone who is hurt and needing help. I want you to be very brave and sit quietly here while I make some phone calls, and then come with me to the hospital. That way we'll be helping Mrs Dawes and all her family who are feeling so bad about her being hurt.'

His grip relaxed a trifle. 'You're not going to send me back to Denis'?'

'Definitely not. I think this is something that you and I have to do together, because we saw how badly Mrs Dawes was hurt, and now we can do something to help her.'

He lifted a snotty-nosed, tear-stained face. 'Like Batman and Robin.'

'And all those who are kind to others. Like Shrek.'

'I like Shrek.'

He nodded.

Kate eased herself to her feet. 'I'll come with you.'

'No need,' said Ellie.

'Yes, there is,' said Kate, extracting her mobile from a back pocket with some difficulty. 'I can't get under the wheel of my car at the moment, but you run a tab with the local mini-cab firm, don't you? I'll leave a message for Armand, while you order one of those cabs which is easy to climb into and has upright seats. Preferably one which has a DVD machine in it . . .'

'Yes!' Frank punched the air.

'And then Frank and I can sit in the cab and he can look after me and we can watch a film while you make your phone calls and extract Mr Dawes from Intensive Care, right?'

Frank appraised Kate. 'Do you need looking after, too?'

'I'm afraid I do, at the moment,' said Kate. 'I can't move very fast, you see.'

'Like Maria,' said Frank. 'I have to fetch things for her, too, sometimes. And then she gives me a hug and tells me I'm a good boy and she loves me.'

'Hug coming up,' said Kate, bending at the knees to get down to his level, and gave him a hug.

Clever Kate. Ellie pulled a tissue from the box and blew her nose. Sometimes God provided the most unexpected answers to prayer. Now where had she put her short coat and handbag? She hadn't time to look for another pair of gloves. Such a nuisance, losing one, but she didn't suppose it would turn up now.

* * *

The cab was large and roomy with upright seats and a DVD which was currently showing a rap singer surrounded by his friends, but that was soon remedied as Ellie had had the forethought to bring a cartoon DVD with her. The cab driver found a space in the crowded car park at the hospital and said he'd wait, while Ellie fed the meter.

Kate asked Frank to help her out of the cab so that she could walk around for a bit. He did so, proud of his new status as carer. Instead of being bottom of the heap, as he was at Denis', he was promoted to being a Great Help, and a Good Boy. He blossomed under this treatment.

Ellie found her way to Intensive Care, and asked a passing nurse if she might speak to a Mr Dawes who was sitting with his mother, on urgent family business. Glancing at her watch, she started worrying all over again about Neil being at the police station. She didn't have a high opinion of the two young policemen who had taken him in. She could see how easy it would be for them to decide that Neil was responsible for everything from drug pushing to murdering his gran in a fit of rage. Easy. But wrong.

She could also see them pushing Neil beyond the fragile limits of his temper, and then . . . she didn't like the thought of that scenario at all. He might well lash out, and then they could have him on a charge of assault and . . . no, something had to be done.

She hoped they wouldn't be too long fetching Mr Dawes, because she couldn't trust little Frank to behave himself for long, could she?

At last Mr Dawes appeared, looking anxious. 'Something's happened? My wife . . . ?'

'No, no. It's Neil that's in trouble. Is there anywhere we can talk?'

They were shown to the relatives' room. Quiet enough. Pleasant enough.

'Neil? What's he done now?' Mr Dawes was not in haste to find out. He kept looking back at the door. 'I should be with my mother.'

'Of course,' said Ellie, sitting on an impulse to scream and trying to understand his point of view. 'What do the doctors say?'

He swung his head back to her, and then returned to watching the door. 'Oh, you know. Holding her own. I keep telling them, she's a strong woman, she'll pull through. I need to be with her. So what's Neil done now that you have to fetch me away?'

Ellie was grim. 'The police have taken him in for questioning, and—'

'What? Why would they do that? They don't think . . . ? That's ridiculous!'

'I agree. A couple of rookie policemen acting on their own initiative, I should think. They know Neil had words with his gran on Friday afternoon, you see.'

Mr Dawes buried his head in his hands and groaned, 'Oh, don't tell me, I can't believe it, he wouldn't, would he? Not our Neil. I mean, I know he's got a temper and he can be really hasty. I suppose if she shouted at him he might well have lashed out and—'

'No, he wouldn't!' said Ellie, in a sharp tone. Was the man so stupid that he couldn't see the danger to his son? 'Neil wouldn't hurt his gran, and you know it.'

'Sylvia always says that . . . Sylvia's my wife, my second wife. They've never got on, him and her, and he's an adult now and ought to know better than to call her names.'

'I daresay,' said Ellie. 'But calling your stepmother names isn't on a par with trying to murder your grandmother.'

He reddened, but didn't reply. He then hauled himself to his feet — he was carrying far too much weight for his age and height — and made for the door.

Ellie stopped him. 'I realize you're worried about your mother, Mr Dawes, but she's in good hands at the moment, whereas your son is in the sort of trouble that you could put a stop to. He needs you.'

'He made his bed and he can lie on it.'

Ellie wanted to shake the man, despite the fact that he would have made two of her. Stupid, stupid, short-sighted man. No, that was not the way to deal with this. She calmed her breathing. 'Mr Dawes, I do understand that you are torn two ways. I know you want to be with your mother, but Neil really needs you, now. If you could only come with me to the police station, and—'

'I'm not leaving my mother's side for any snivelling little—'

Ellie played what she thought must be a master card. 'Surely, because he's your son . . . ? He's all alone and afraid . . .'

'He should have thought of that before he attacked her.'

Ellie lost her temper. 'You stupid, stupid man! I don't care what problems there may have been between Neil and his stepmother. I don't care what you think of his present way of life. Neil is a good-hearted, hard-working lad who's earned my respect and affection, and if you can't see that, then—'

The door opened, and a nurse popped her head in. 'Could you keep it down, do you think? Oh, and there's someone else come to see Mrs Dawes.'

A heavy-set woman in shapeless casual gear pushed into the room. She greeted her brother without so much as a smile. 'So you're here already, are you?' And to Ellie: 'Who are you?'

'A something busybody, that's what!' Mr Dawes' blood pressure was going through the roof. 'Came here, trying to tell me what my duty is . . .'

Ellie told herself to calm down. 'Mrs . . . you're Mrs Dawes' daughter, aren't you? I'm an old friend of hers, the neighbour who spoke to you yesterday. The police have jumped to the conclusion that Neil attacked her, and have taken him in for questioning. He needs his father to—'

'Angie,' said the newcomer, shedding an enormous parka with ratty fur trim. 'I'm Angie. Couldn't get down yesterday. My husband's parking the car. Why have the police taken Neil?'

'Because he had a shouting match with your mother . . .' Ellie started to explain.

'Because he's a no-good son of a—'

The nurse put her head around the door again. 'Please!'

'Yes. Sorry,' said Mr Dawes.

Angie eyed her brother up and down. 'You're an idiot, always were, and always will be.' Her unforgiving tone was that of a bossy elder sister. She turned to the nurse. 'How is my mother? May I sit with her?'

'One at a time, family only. And please, keep your voices down.'

'I'm going back to her.' Mr Dawes blundered to the doorway.

'No, you don't, Jack,' said Angie. 'You sit right down there and calm down while we talk things over quietly. Right?'

Somewhat to Ellie's surprise, Jack Dawes sat, putting his large hands on his knees. He even began to look sheepish. Definitely elder sister time.

'Now, Mrs . . . ?' Angie looked to Ellie for information. 'Fill me in.'

Ellie did so, succinctly as she could. She glanced again at her watch. 'Of course, Neil didn't attack his gran, but he does need someone to extract him from the police station before he makes an ass of himself. It's been nearly two hours. If they shout at him enough, he might start shouting back.'

'And this idiot,' Angie said, indicating her brother, who sank his head and rounded his shoulders under the weight of her scorn, 'has done nothing to help, I suppose.'

Ellie held her tongue. She wasn't sure what she'd have done in Mr Dawes' case, either. Especially if his new wife had a waspish tongue.

Angie addressed her brother. 'I'm here now to sit with Mother, so you can take an hour off to rescue your son, can't you?'

He hunched his shoulders even more and muttered something which both women decided not to hear. 'Flaming no,' he said, conveying the impression that he'd rather be burned at the stake than do as Angie asked. 'Besides,' he said, 'I was here first, so I ought to be sitting with her.'

'I'm the eldest, and she'll want to see me when she wakes up.'

'Ha, ha!' said Mr Dawes. 'Why should she want to see you? You couldn't even be bothered to get down here last night while—'

Angie reddened. 'I didn't have the car, and anyway—'

'Lost your licence again? Ha, ha!'

Angie's blood pressure was rising. 'I have not! It's just that it's only sensible to run just the one car at the moment, and—'

'Hubby out of work again, is he?'

Ellie tried to intervene. 'Look, I've got to go. If you could decide who is going to sit with—'

'I am!'

'No, I am!'

Ellie made one last attempt. 'Toss a coin for it. Who's going to look after Neil?'

'That's *his* job!'

'I was here first!'

'When my husband gets back from parking the car—'

'*If* he gets back from parking the car. He's probably in the nearest pub, drowning his sorrows. I can't blame him, being married to you!'

Ellie had suffered for years trying to produce a brother or sister for Diana. Each successive miscarriage had caused her more and more misery. She wondered for the first time whether she hadn't wasted valuable time and energy mourning for what was not to be. What if she had produced a sibling for Diana who argued with her as these two did? It had been hard enough trying to bring up Diana. What if there'd been two of them like that?

It didn't bear thinking about.

'Well, so long as one of you goes to Neil's rescue. Sort it out between you. I've had enough.' Ellie got herself out of the room somehow, and blew her nose.

A passing nurse said, 'Trouble?'

Ellie tried to get a grip on herself. 'Mrs Dawes is one of my oldest friends, and it was I who found her yesterday. Do you think there's any chance I could see her for a second? I can't stay because I've a neighbour looking after my grandson in the car park, but I'd feel so much better if I could just be sure she was holding her own.'

The nurse glanced at the door to the relatives' room, where World War Three was still progressing. 'I don't see why not, if you promise to be quiet. Just one minute, mind.'

Ellie nodded. There was a man sitting beside the bed already. A plod? Yes. Waiting to see what Mrs Dawes would say about the attack on her when — if — she woke up. The immobile figure on the bed didn't look like Mrs Dawes. Her eyes were closed, her face bruised, her head swathed in a bandage. Machines reported on her life signs. The only good thing was that she appeared to be breathing on her own.

Ellie tried to pray, and couldn't think of the right words. Somewhere she'd read — or Thomas had said — that words weren't necessary when you were at the end of your tether. Perhaps this was one of those times. You said 'Please' to let Him know that you were trying to connect, and He knew what you meant.

She whispered, 'Thank you,' to the nurse, and left the ward.

The outside world seemed to have been carrying on all right without her. There was a spit of rain in the air, and it was chilly. Where had she left the cab? For a moment she couldn't even think what day of the week it was. Every day was the same, more or less, in hospital. She looked at her watch and realized with a start that it was nearly lunchtime and Aunt Drusilla would be expecting her. Should she cancel that?

Little Frank spotted her from some way off, and ran towards her. 'I took Kate to the loo, and we had some crisps but she wouldn't let me have any fizzy drink. She said it's bad for me, but it's not, is it?'

'Well, yes. It can be,' said Ellie, giving him a hug, and trying to force a proper smile to her face. 'Good for you, Frank.'

'He's looked after me beautifully,' said Kate, as Ellie climbed up into the cab. 'Though I must admit I was getting a bit anxious about lunch. Armand phoned five minutes ago. He's back home and trying to cook something.'

Normality. Ellie filled Kate in on what had happened, saying she only hoped someone from his own family would deal with Neil, but it didn't seem likely.

Kate was soothing. 'It's not really your problem, Ellie. You've done your best to see that someone looks after him, and I'm sure he'll be perfectly all right. He's probably back at your house now, wondering where you are. Except,' Kate frowned, 'Armand would have mentioned it if Neil had turned up at your place and couldn't get in. But don't fret, Ellie, Neil's a grown man, and able to look after himself.'

Ellie was gloomy. 'Some men never grow up enough to keep their tempers when provoked. I hope he arrives home before I do but I don't count on it, and I don't trust either his father or his aunt to think of anything but themselves. I'll have to think of something else. But first, let's get you home.'

Her priorities kept changing, and she didn't know whether that was a bad thing or a good. Now her priority was to get Kate home and feed little Frank. And then, perhaps she'd be able to think clearly about Neil's predicament. Of course Kate was right and Neil wasn't in any real danger or anything. She was fussing unnecessarily.

Probably.

As the mini-cab driver took them home, Ellie phoned Aunt Drusilla and asked if she might bring little Frank for lunch. Aunt Drusilla was surprised and not too pleased, but said he might come if he behaved himself. Ellie asked Frank when his mother was going to collect him, but he didn't know. He was absorbed in watching another cartoon, and hardly bothered to wave goodbye when Kate was decanted at her own house.

'Thank you, Kate. A thousand times.'

Kate waved goodbye. Armand already had their front door open to welcome her home. It was then — and not a moment too soon — Ellie remembered Aunt Drusilla had asked her to bring some redcurrant jelly when she arrived for lunch. Leaving Frank in the cab, she darted inside, only to find Midge wanting to be fed and the phone ringing; how long would little Frank stay put in the cab?

Priorities! Every minute they changed. She fed Midge, ignored the phone, collected the redcurrant jelly and made it back to the cab just as the DVD finished and Frank became fractious.

The cab took them on to Aunt Drusilla's early Victorian mansion, the house in which she'd been born and in which she fully intended to die. The house had actually belonged to Ellie's husband and now belonged to Ellie herself, but she would never turn her aunt out, and Miss Quicke knew it.

Roy had modernized the place, contriving separate quarters in it for Rose, his mother's treasured housekeeper. Rose was an old friend of Ellie's from the days in which they'd both worked in the charity shop in the Avenue. Ellie slept more easily knowing that her elderly aunt was being well looked after.

Rose loved plants, so the previously formal appearance of the garden had been softened with the introduction of annuals, perennials, bulbs and shrubs galore. Miss Quicke pretended indifference to her own comfort and to what was grown in the garden, but had erected a heated conservatory in which Rose could indulge her hobby during the winter months, and she had made sure that a gardener and cleaning lady took on the heavy jobs.

As Ellie and Frank went up the steps to the front door, it was opened by Aunt Drusilla herself, propped up on her stick. She was frowning. 'You're late. Roy and Felicity are late, too. What's going on? What's all this about Mrs Dawes, and how is she?'

Before Ellie could explain, Frank said, 'I saw her first and she was all bluggy, and I saw them carry her off to hospital, and then the police took my fingerprints and Mummy took me to stay with Denis . . .' He hesitated, remembering the misery of a night spent at Denis', then resumed, 'This morning I looked after Kate and we went to the hospital to see the lady but I wasn't allowed in, and there was a cartoon playing in the cab . . . and who's going to play with me now?'

* * *

He'd expected the two biddies to have had more money on them. He hadn't had time enough to turn their houses over to see where they kept their bankrolls. In fact, it hadn't occurred to him till he got home with what cash they'd had in their handbags, that they might have had enough money stashed away in their houses to keep him going for a while.

He riffled through the few notes he'd collected and slipped the coins back into his pocket. This wouldn't keep him going for long. It was a bit of a worry, working out how to get hold of some cash without going back to work. He had Russell's bank cards, of course, but not the pin numbers. He'd found a chart on the back of a calendar in the kitchen which had lots of numbers on it. Presumably these were Russell's pin numbers. The only problem was, which set of numbers was for which card?

Well, now he had time to work that out. And if the money ran out before he had cracked the codes, he'd proved how easy it was to get some more, hadn't he? Those two women had lived alone, no man about the place. Easy pickings. And there were plenty more like them around. But he could do with finding someone with a bit more money than they'd had. No point in taking unnecessary risks.

Perhaps he'd indulge in a six pack tonight, to get the old brain cells going?

CHAPTER NINE

Ellie started to explain what had been happening over the last day or so, but before she could finish, Roy drove up with Felicity. Frank, seeing someone who'd been kind to him the previous day, flung himself at Felicity, repeating his demand for someone to play with.

Felicity was wearing the same outfit that she'd worn to the wedding. She fended the little boy off but held his hand as they mounted the steps to the house together. She kissed Aunt Drusilla, apologized for being late and, taking off her beautiful coat, dropped it over Frank's shoulders. He loved that. He strutted around, letting the coat trail on the ground behind him, and making little jumps to see if he could catch his reflection in the hall mirror.

Ellie noticed that though Felicity was smiling, she looked tired. Was this the result of her pregnancy or had she been to see her mother in spite of everything that had been done to prevent it?

'Ellie, are you all right?' Felicity gave her a quick hug.

'I'm fine,' lied Ellie, trying to put all her worries behind her. 'How about you?'

'What's happened?' demanded Miss Quicke. 'What are you two hiding from me? Mrs Dawes . . . ?'

'Thomas rang the hospital after the service and they say she's still unconscious but stable,' said Roy, shedding his own coat. 'Sorry we're a bit late. We had to make a call on Felicity's mother on the way over, and it delayed us a bit.'

Felicity took off her delicate headgear and fluffed up her hair. 'My fault entirely. Roy didn't want me to go till tomorrow, but I insisted.' She faced them with an apology for a smile. 'My mother is . . . has never been a happy woman. But don't let's talk about her now.'

Roy put one arm around his mother and the other round Ellie, urging them into the sitting room. 'I want you both to say how charming Felicity looks in that outfit. It's the only way I can reconcile myself to paying so much for it.' He smiled, indulgent, pleased with his wife.

'I thought if I didn't wear it again today, I'd never want to see it again,' said Felicity, also holding on to a smile. Answering Miss Quicke's enquiring look, she said, 'I wore it yesterday, you see, when we made that dreadful discovery. I do love it, but now I'm beginning to think it's jinxed.'

'It's a beautiful outfit,' said Ellie, 'and you delight the eye in it.'

'Yes, but . . .' Aunt Drusilla never liked to be left out of things, and she'd caught the undercurrents in the reference to 'Lady' Anne.

At that point Rose appeared to say that they'd better take their seats in the dining room, because she really couldn't answer for the lamb if it wasn't eaten straightaway. Rose loved cooking and her roast dinners were famous, so they collected Frank from the hall and made their way into the dining room. This cavernous room usually served Miss Quicke as an office, but today had reverted to its original status.

Frank was given an adult chair, with a cushion on it. The only problem was, he refused to take off Felicity's beautiful coat.

'It doesn't matter,' said Felicity, bending over the little boy and rolling up the sleeves for him. 'It will need cleaning after today, anyway.'

Roy rolled his eyes. 'More expense! Little did I know, when I promised to love, honour and obey, that it meant dry cleaning bills as well.'

Felicity smiled up at him as he pulled out a chair for her. Neither of them realized how closely they were being watched by the other women, including Rose at that moment bringing in a succulent roast leg of lamb.

Ah, how sweet! thought Ellie, noting that Miss Quicke was also looking at the couple with an indulgent smile. Long may it last, she thought, remembering that Love's First Dream usually fades quite soon. She sighed. It hadn't lasted that long for Ellie and her husband. They'd become, well, accustomed to one another within a couple of years. Well, there had been love, of course. But not romantic. More . . . comfortable? More enduring? Perhaps romance would last longer with Roy and Felicity, since both knew how lucky they'd been to find one another. Both had been through bad first marriages, and they'd had time to become good friends before their second foray into matrimony.

Rose added roast and boiled potatoes, roast parsnips, leeks and carrots to the table. She'd already carved the meat, knowing she did it better than anyone else. Aunt Drusilla usually asked Rose to eat with them, because she was her friend as well as her housekeeper, but Rose said she wanted to check on the pudding and vanished.

'A sight for sore eyes.' Roy shook out his napkin, and looked around to see if his mother was serving wine as she usually did. This time there didn't appear to be any. Maybe Rose had forgotten it.

Ellie exchanged a flick of an eye with Felicity. Rose never forgot anything. So Rose guessed that Felicity was pregnant? Ellie poured water for herself and Frank first, and then for Felicity, while Roy passed the dishes around.

'If someone doesn't tell me what's been going on soon,' said Miss Quicke, 'I shan't be able to eat my lunch.'

Ellie looked at Felicity. Roy looked down at his plate.

Frank said, 'I don't have to eat carrots, do I?'

'Just one to please me?' said Felicity, helping him to just one, and a liberal helping of everything else.

'All right, Flicky, just one,' said Frank. 'Just to please you.'

Miss Quicke said, 'Ellie, let's start with you. Why were you late? You went to the hospital and . . . ?'

Ellie sighed. It would be best to put an amusing slant on what had happened, if she could. 'Why do I always have to poke my nose into other people's business? Mrs Dawes' grandson is a nice lad—'

'He's done the odd job for me,' nodded Miss Quicke.

'And was very upset at what happened to his gran. We were at the hospital till late, he'd had a row with his girlfriend, so I took him home with me last night. Meanwhile Mr Dawes, Neil's father, arrived. They don't seem to get on, so when I took Neil home with me, Thomas took Mr Dawes home with him. This morning the police carted Neil off for questioning.'

'Do they think he did it?' Interested, Roy almost suspended operations on his plate.

'They were two rookies — I think that's what they call them. Young policemen, wet behind the ears. They knew Mrs Dawes and her grandson had had words, and I suppose it seemed an open-and-shut case to them. I didn't know what to do. I had Frank to look after and . . . well, I went back to the hospital to see if I could extract Mr Dawes, get him to ride to his son's rescue . . .'

Frank said, 'Has he got a horse?'

'Well, no. Probably not. I meant . . . well, it doesn't matter what I meant. But Mr Dawes wouldn't budge because his elder sister arrived and they reverted to childhood — "You broke my doll!", "You killed my hamster!" — that sort of thing. I think — I hope — that one of them will bail Neil out. I told them to sort it out between them, but goodness knows what they will have done about it, if anything.'

'Unsatisfactory,' pronounced Miss Quicke.

Ellie inclined her head. 'I know.' She dug into her food, remembering that Diana had wanted to know if Thomas had been invited to the meal. A pity he hadn't been; he'd have enjoyed it. Thomas loved his food. He wasn't greedy exactly, but he did appreciate good cooking.

What was that? Everyone was looking at her. Had she missed something?

Roy was patient. 'Ellie, could you pass the redcurrant jelly?'

Ellie made haste to do so. Roy was enjoying his plateful, as was Frank. Felicity had taken small portions of everything, but was managing pretty well. Miss Quicke had given herself minute portions of meat, boiled potatoes and leeks, no gravy. It was probably all she needed for the day because she took no exercise at all. Except with her brain, and that was in Olympic condition. Ellie knew her aunt was circling her prey. So, the next person to be questioned would be Roy.

'What about you, Roy? How was Paris?'

'Splendid,' said Roy. 'We must do it more often, eh, Flick?'

Felicity smiled at him. A full-blown, lover's smile. Roy smiled back.

Aaah, thought Ellie. And then she thought, Urrrk. Oh, well. Lovers! She glanced at Aunt Drusilla, who looked as if she'd had the same reaction. Was there a touch of vinegar in her aunt's smile?

Miss Quicke homed in for the kill. 'And how is your mother, Felicity? I really must get round to calling on her now we are related by marriage.'

Ellie thought, And pigs might fly. Miss Quicke had no patience with Anne.

Felicity dropped her fork on her plate and blushed, but kept her voice steady. 'I'm afraid I'm going to have to find another place for my mother to stay.'

'What a pity,' said Miss Quicke. 'Isn't she in the very best of the local retirement homes?'

Roy was frowning. 'No use trying to cover up, Flick. My mother is discreet.'

Felicity took a sip of water. 'My poor mother's had a sad life. She was born and brought up in a beautiful manor house in the country, but couldn't afford to keep it up. She still hankers for it, all these years on. She's tried all sorts of ways to earn her living but never succeeded, and it's little wonder that she has a little, well, failing . . .'

'Drink,' said Roy, helping himself to seconds. 'And don't forget she's been through three husbands so far.'

'I'm not forgetting anything,' said Felicity, indignantly. 'I know she's very fragile, but she's my mother and it's up to me to look after her as best I can. I didn't realize how much it would hurt her if I got married and had less time to spend with her.'

'If you married and were happy,' amended Roy.

Felicity blushed, and cast down her eyes. 'Yes, I didn't realize that it would hurt her to see me so happy.'

Roy looked at his mother. 'When she found out that her daughter had been left a rich woman, she wanted Felicity to take her out of the retirement home and look after her, twenty-four seven. She was "dreadfully disappointed" when Felicity was selfish enough to get married again. To cap it all, she threatened to harm herself if Felicity were so unfeeling as to go away on honeymoon and leave her behind.'

Felicity murmured, 'We did go.'

Miss Quicke was fascinated. 'Did she fulfil her threat? What a clever woman she is, to be sure.'

'We went,' said Roy. 'We enjoyed ourselves. She complained, and the day before we returned, she cut her wrists. Not very effectively, of course.'

'Of course not,' said Aunt Drusilla. 'She knows how to press all the right buttons, doesn't she? How are you coping, Felicity?'

Felicity managed a smile, though her eyes were starry with tears. 'I know in my head that it was selfish of her and manipulative. I know all that, but I can't help worrying about her. She's completely dependent on me.'

'Only because you let her be,' said Aunt Drusilla. 'Cut the umbilical cord, my dear, and see how quickly she finds someone else to cling on to. So, the home refuses to keep her?'

'She doesn't want to stay. She said . . . she said she would have to come to live with me and Roy, and we could put in a stairlift and look after her and then she'd be happy. Only—' she gave Roy a glowing look — 'Roy put his foot down.'

'With a firm hand,' said Roy, polishing off the last of his food. 'I said we were not trained to look after invalids, and she'd best apply to the council for sheltered accommodation.'

'Roy was wonderful!' said Felicity, smiling at him.

At which point Ellie felt like making a retching sound. Yuurk! Though on the whole, she had to admit that Roy had turned up trumps on this one.

Rose appeared to remove the dirty plates.

'Can I help?' asked Ellie.

'No, no,' said Rose, preoccupied with getting the next course on the table.

'Excellent,' pronounced Miss Quicke, as Rose bore a steaming hot apple pie and custard into the room.

'Please can I get down?' asked Frank, over whose head — hopefully — much of the preceding conversation had passed. He got down without being given permission and, drawn as it were by osmosis, approached the bank of computer equipment which Miss Quicke used on a daily basis, and which had been temporarily placed on the sideboard.

'If you touch any of that, Frank,' said Miss Quicke, in a conversational tone, 'you'll be struck by lightning. Leave Felicity's coat here and go and run round the garden five times. See how many different kinds of birds you can spot.'

Frank departed, still wearing Felicity's coat, and leaving the door open behind him.

'Never mind,' said Felicity. 'He needs a comfort blanket after what he saw yesterday. If my coat helps him, then I'm not bothered.'

Rose shook her head, but kept quiet. Rose kept looking sideways at Felicity. Was she counting on her fingers, too?

Roy helped himself to apple pie and custard. 'Poor little tike. What time is Diana collecting him, Ellie?'

Ellie shrugged. 'I wish I knew. I suppose she's working at the new agency today and will contact me when they close this evening.' She thought, How on earth am I going to see that Neil gets out of this in one piece?

'I have never approved of shops opening on a Sunday,' said Miss Quicke, who worked as hard at weekends as on weekdays. 'But I suppose if it keeps Diana out of our hair, it's something to be thankful for.' She took some custard, but no apple pie.

Ellie said, 'Do you know of a solicitor who will turn out for a client on a Sunday?'

'For your young protégé, Neil? Yes, of course. My own solicitor has a couple of youngsters in his practice, and they are not without merit. Try Mark Hadley. I'll give you the number when we've finished. I've never believed in discussing business at the table.'

To their credit, nobody smiled at this statement. What, wondered Ellie, would Aunt Drusilla define as 'business' in this context? The price of oil shares? The dip in the housing market? Perhaps she divided conversational possibilities into her investment portfolio on the one hand, and on the other into people and their problems?

Ellie glanced at her watch. How long had little Frank been out of their sight, and what was he up to? How was Neil faring? And poor Mrs Dawes. Dear Lord, look after her . . . and Thomas. The busiest day of the week for him, and yet he'd had to play host to Mr Dawes last night, he'd probably gone haring off to the hospital before and after the morning service, missed his lunch, and still had to be back in good time for Evensong. A day like any other. Or worse than.

'Ellie? You've gone all distant on us.' Roy was smiling at her.

'Sorry. Counting my worries instead of my blessings.'

Roy and Felicity took coffee in the drawing room with Miss Quicke, while Ellie checked that Frank wasn't up to anything too dreadful and helped Rose clear the table and stack plates and cutlery in the dishwasher. Both paused every now and then to look out on to the garden, where Frank — still clad in Felicity's coat — was stalking a neighbour's cat.

'He'll get scratched for sure,' said Rose.

'I'm tempted to say that it would serve him right,' said Ellie. 'I know it's awful of me, and of course I love him . . .'

'And worry about him.'

'Now more than ever. I used to think that when he was old enough to go to school he'd be easier to cope with, but he seems to have a knack of finding things to do which you'd never have thought of telling him not to, because you'd never have thought he'd get into such trouble — if you can unscramble that! Sorry, Rose. I'm in a bit of a tizzy today. Not thinking straight.'

Rose halted by the window, staring out. Felicity had gone into the garden to fetch Frank in. She was clutching her arms around herself in her pretty dress. Frank still had her coat on. It must be filthy around the hem by now. Felicity stood there, laughing and talking to the little boy while he looked up at her with an answering grin. She began to lead him back to the house.

'Do you think . . . ?' asked Rose. 'May next year?'

'Let's hope. I doubt if she'll say anything till she's well past four months, because of having had a miss before.'

Rose nodded, and resumed putting cling film over the few remaining vegetables. 'They'll do for a soup in the week. Do you think Miss Quicke knows?' Rose's only daughter had had a miscarriage once and didn't seem anxious to start another pregnancy. Rose was suffering from granny fever.

'Hard to say. Best not mention it, in case.'

Nothing could dampen Rose's happiness at the possibility of Felicity bearing a child. 'It would be good to have children living in this house once more.'

Ellie forbore to remind Rose that this house actually belonged to her, Ellie, and not to Miss Quicke. Also Roy probably wouldn't want to move into it when his mother eventually passed on. Roy was happier than he'd ever been before in Felicity's pretty little house overlooking the park, where children could be set free to play in the enclosed playground. Besides, Felicity might still miscarry. Please, Lord, not. At least, if that's the way you want it. But you can't blame us for hoping.

She glanced at the clock. It was more than time to go. It would be getting dark soon, and presumably Diana would be wanting to retrieve her son. Or would she want Ellie to take him back to his father's house? Presumably Stewart and Maria would be back soon from their weekend away? Best to check.

She went in to thank Miss Quicke for the lovely lunch. No one stayed long after lunch at Miss Quicke's because she always had a nap in the afternoon and insisted that Rose took a rest at that time, too.

Miss Quicke handed Ellie a piece of paper. 'Mark Hadley's telephone number. Let me know how you get on with him. Make it clear that *you* are paying for his services in this instance.'

'Of course,' said Ellie, thinking that her aunt never missed a trick. 'Come along, Frank. Let's see if Mummy's finished work yet. I'll call us a cab, and we'll be home in no time.' And then, Ellie thought, we'll have to see whether Neil has surfaced or not.

'Give you a lift?' said Roy, helping Felicity into her once beautiful, but now rather dirty coat.

Did Roy guess that Felicity was pregnant? Possibly. No, probably not. Would it be the sort of thing that he'd notice? And, because he was a good ten years older than Felicity, would he really want to become a father at his age? Ellie couldn't decide and didn't want to raise the subject until Felicity herself did so.

'Can I sit up front?' asked Frank.

'No!' said three adults together.

'Ooooh!' whined Frank.

Ellie sighed. 'He's getting tired. Frank, you can sit on my knee and have a cuddle if the seat belt will go round both of us. How about that?'

Roy got them into his car, sorted out seat belts, and they drove away waving goodbye to Miss Quicke and Rose. The wind was getting up, threatening rain or, possibly, sleet. The adults were silent, wrapped in the warmth of the car, thinking — or trying not to think — about the unpleasant tasks that the future would bring. Frank curled up beside Ellie and fell asleep. He whimpered in his sleep and Ellie cuddled him, trying to keep her own eyes open. A nap seemed like a good idea to her, too.

Roy took one hand off the wheel when they came to the lights at the end of the Avenue, and placed it over Felicity's knee. She turned her head to smile at him. Ellie closed her eyes. It was all very well telling herself she was very content with her widowhood, but sometimes, just sometimes, the thought of having a man to love her like that . . . well, she had to put such thoughts aside and deal with reality. Her dear dead husband had been accustomed to patting her on the shoulder when she needed comforting. Ah well. Strange how much she was thinking about him lately.

She remembered that Thomas had put his arm about her to comfort her. Was that only yesterday? She smiled. That had been a good moment. If anything did come of it in the dim and distant future, then it wouldn't matter that Thomas had no money, because Ellie had enough for two. Thankfully.

When they arrived, she woke Frank up and managed to get him to walk down at her side, clinging to her coat. Half awake. She avoided Neil's van, still parked outside. There was no Diana waiting for her. And no Neil. Ellie went into full worrying mode. There was an answerphone full of messages. The central heating needed bumping up. Frank wouldn't let go of her.

Patience! She instructed herself. One thing at a time. Prioritize. Feed Frank. Again. Check on Diana. Check whether Frank's father was back or not. Then, and only then, could she move on to doing something about Neil. Only, she worried about Neil. It was all very well saying she had to look after little Frank first, but she'd started trying to get help for Neil a number of times and failed to follow through. Suppose Neil had got into real trouble while she'd been letting herself get sidetracked? Yet, if she'd let Frank fend for himself . . . no, that was unthinkable. Neil was old enough to take care of himself, wasn't he?

* * *

The problem was, what to do about his old car. It wasn't new or even very reliable, but he'd always run a car, from the day he left school. He'd left it in Russell's garage for now, but that could only be a temporary solution. Russell had never owned a car, had gone everywhere by bike till he'd had his accident. After that he'd gone on Shanks' Pony. Limped, rather. He'd walked to the shops for convenience food, sent out for pizzas, that sort of thing. Hadn't cooked for himself.

Once the kitchen had been cleaned up, it wasn't a bad place in which to fiddle around, throwing together this and that. He'd always enjoyed a good curry, for instance.

He knew he ought to get rid of the car. He didn't dare drive it any more in case he was stopped for a faulty brake light or a blown exhaust. If he was stopped, he'd be asked for his papers and he'd burned those, hadn't he? That was another of the problems that being Russell had thrown up. He couldn't afford to get into his car and go for a run. Or even do a week's shopping in one go.

If he'd kept Lee's papers, he could have sold the car. Maybe. Even if it was an old banger, there'd be some cash in it for him. But he couldn't sell it without papers, and he couldn't afford to have anyone find it. It was a puzzle. He'd have to give it some thought. It wasn't roses all the way, taking on another identity.

CHAPTER TEN

Ellie listened to her phone messages while Frank proceeded to get outside a plateful of sausages and baked beans. How could he eat again so soon after that big lunch? The food this time was from a tin, but he didn't object and she didn't have time to cook properly.

The first message was from Diana, saying she was sorry to have had to drop little Frank off with Ellie for the day, but would phone to say when she could pick him up again. She didn't sound sorry.

Then there was Thomas, who sounded weary. He wanted to know how things were going. He himself was just off to visit someone in the hospice — not Mrs Dawes — but would be back for Evensong.

Then Kate from next door, wondering if there was any news, and saying they were all going out to tea but would be back sixish.

Nothing from Neil, or any other member of the Dawes family.

Ellie nerved herself to ring Diana on her mobile. She didn't like interfering but the present arrangements for Frank were not working. Somebody was going to have to say something, sometime, and it looked as if it would have to be her.

Ellie edged the door of the kitchen shut with her foot. She didn't want Frank to hear this.

Diana answered. Very curt. 'Well, Mother? Don't tell me you're having a problem looking after little Frank for a few hours. I should have thought you'd realize I've got to work to—'

'Enough, Diana. I've got him here with me, and assume you will collect him to take back to his father's later on. But I'd like a chat about your weekends. The present arrangement isn't feasible if you have to work Saturdays and Sundays, is it? Do you think that perhaps—'

'Don't interfere, Mother. I know what's best for my child. And now, I really must get on.'

She rang off.

Ellie took a deep breath to recover, and decided that — interference or not — she would have to say something to Frank's father. She didn't like going behind Diana's back, but maybe it wouldn't be out of order to tell Stewart how concerned she was about what was happening. She rang Stewart, hoping he'd have got back from his weekend away, and was lucky enough to catch his wife, Maria instead. Nice as Stewart was, it was Maria who made the decisions in that household.

'Ellie here. Can you talk for a moment?'

'Is it about bringing Frank back? I'm confused, not knowing quite who's got him at weekends, you or Diana.'

'I don't like to interfere,' said Ellie, and she really didn't. 'I've tried to talk to Diana about this, but she's so busy she's not able to cope with it. Maybe you or Stewart would have better luck? I'm really worried about what's happening with Frank at weekends now that Diana's working at the agency. Putting Frank in with Denis' boys hasn't worked out. He's terrified of them. Yesterday he was with me, and unfortunately he was the first to find a neighbour lying on the floor with her head bashed in. It's affected him, as you can imagine.'

Maria gave a long whistle. 'Who . . . I mean, how . . . ? Oh dear. How dreadful. Poor little mite. Was it anyone we know?'

'Someone from church. Mrs Dawes. He knows her, at least by sight. He behaved pretty well after that, all things considered, but I suspect he's more deeply affected than he pretends. He's been a bit clingy, may have wet the bed at Denis' place.'

Silence.

'Maria, are you there? Has he been wetting . . . ?'

'Not for ages, no. Has he behaved himself, otherwise?'

It was a relief to talk freely to someone who also loved the little boy. 'He doesn't always take notice of what I say, but he responds to cuddles and praise. You're doing a good job there, Maria.'

'He's a great lad, and a wonderful help with Yaz. You know I'm expecting again?'

'I'm so pleased for you. When . . . ?' Some baby talk ensued. Then Ellie said, 'I'm so pleased that Frank loves little Yaz, too. I'm sure it will be the making of him, helping to look after somebody smaller than himself, while constantly being reassured that you love him. And that you don't stand any nonsense. You're a clever woman, Maria.'

'I think we're on the right lines with Frank, but do you have any tips for handling Diana? Stewart and I foresaw there might be a problem at weekends when she started at the agency and I did try to talk to her about it, but she cut me off, saying she's got the right to have him with her when she wishes. We did ask Frank if he'd like to come away with us this weekend, but he said he hadn't seen his mother all week, so of course we let him go to her.'

'Saturdays are important days for an estate agent. Maybe Sundays as well. Perhaps you could suggest she have him a couple of nights in the week?'

'Would she get him to school on time, though? And remember to collect him at the end of the day?'

Ellie was silent. Maria had a point, there.

Maria sighed. 'I'll talk to Stewart, see what he says. Shall we pick him up from you in about an hour, say?'

'I'll give you a ring if that's necessary. Diana's said she'll let me know when she'll collect him, but it's—' she looked at the clock in the hall — 'it's nearly half past four now and pretty dark. Surely they must have closed for the night? Give my love to Stewart.'

She put the phone down as Frank came out of the kitchen, demanding to see the film he'd brought with him: the unsuitable, full-of-violence film. Ellie persuaded him to see one of his old favourites, and he settled down happily enough with *Five Children and It*.

Diana might ring any minute and if Ellie were on the landline, Diana wouldn't be able to get through. But Diana also had Ellie's mobile phone number, so Ellie decided to go ahead with making her own calls.

First she must see what had happened to Neil. The obvious thing to do was to ring his girlfriend, see if he'd gone back to their place. The girlfriend was called Trace — short for Tracy? — and sounded sullen on the phone. No, she hadn't seen Neil for days, and she wasn't sure she wanted to see him ever again, anyway, and if he wanted to come and fetch his things, he was welcome, and that was all she wanted to say about him.

Ouch. So Neil hadn't gone back there. Could he be at the hospital?

How to find out?

She rang the hospital and asked for the Intensive Care Unit. When a pleasant voice replied, Ellie said she realized they couldn't give her any information about Mrs Dawes' progress since she was not a relative, but only an old friend.

'Making good progress.'

'Oh. Great! Would I be allowed to see her if I came in tomorrow?'

'She may be moving out of Intensive Care. Ask when you get here.'

Ellie realized this was excellent news. 'There is one other thing. If I could speak to one of the members of her family, could you get a message to them to phone me?'

The nurse covered the phone over with her hand, but Ellie could hear her call out a question to someone, and get an answer. Then the nurse came back on the phone. 'There's no one sitting with her now. I think her relatives had to go home. They came from a distance, didn't they?'

Oh. So both the son and daughter had returned home? And Neil wasn't there?

If he wasn't anywhere else, he must still be at the police station. Not good news. She dialled the number that Aunt Drusilla had given her for a young solicitor, and got through to a pleasant bass voice, interrupted by yawns. On hearing that Miss Quicke had given her his number, he apologized and said he'd been at a cracking good party last night and only just woken up. Could he ring her back in ten minutes, when he'd got some black coffee inside him?

'You'll need my telephone number. My name is Ellie Quicke, by the way.'

He mumbled something about caller ID, and rang off. Ellie wasn't sure whether to laugh or scream. But if Miss Quicke had recommended him, he must be good.

She rang Thomas on his mobile phone, only to find it was switched off. Ah, he'd be preparing for Evensong, no doubt. She didn't leave a message.

She tried Mr Dawes' home number. No reply. His new wife must be out and he must be on his way back up to the Midlands. She hoped one or other of the siblings had done something about Neil, but had no great confidence that they had. She tried his sister's home number. No reply. She left messages on both phones. What else could she do to help? She couldn't think.

She was relieved when Mark Hadley phoned back, sounding very much more awake. 'Mrs Quicke? Sorry about that. I've heard about you from Miss Quicke. What can I do for you?'

'Will you bill me for this, please? Not my aunt.' She explained about young Neil and the attack on Mrs Dawes, and why the two policemen might have leaped to the wrong conclusion. 'He's got a short fuse, you see. He's not back here, he's not with his girlfriend and he's not at the hospital.

Could you find out if he's still at the police station and if so, what's happening? Say you'll represent him if they're thinking of charging him for anything.'

Mark Hadley gave another giant yawn, but said he'd see what he could do when he'd found his car keys, which he'd left somewhere around the flat. And rang off.

Priorities.

Frank was all right, sitting watching the DVD with a rather dazed look on his face, but quiet. Ellie felt the need for a cuppa and was on her way to the kitchen when the doorbell rang. It was Diana, smelling of wine and looking a trifle less well-groomed than usual. Her colour was unusually high. 'Have you still got him? I hope he's not been too much of a nuisance today.'

Ellie started to say that considering everything Frank had been through, he was managing pretty well but Diana wasn't listening, so Ellie continued on her way to the kitchen. Should she have a cup of instant, or some strong tea? She heard Diana bustle into the sitting room, and say something in a low, intense voice to Frank. And then there came the unmistakeable sound of a slap, followed by a yelp from Frank which made Ellie abandon her idea of making a cuppa and hurry back to the sitting room.

Frank was holding his hand to his bare leg, and was on the verge of tears.

Diana was trembling with rage. 'How could you let me down like that?'

Ellie held her own temper down with an effort. 'Diana, a word with you in the kitchen.'

'Say what you have to say here. He knows he blotted his copybook.'

'You shouldn't hit him. It wasn't really his fault.'

Diana mimicked Ellie. 'It wasn't *really* his fault. All the bedding will have to be dry-cleaned, and I shall have to buy a new mattress. So whose fault is that, pray?'

'Those rough boys at Denis' are rather too much for him, on top of everything else.'

'You *would* make excuses for him.'

For once Ellie took the initiative. She grasped Diana's arm and bundled her, squawking, through to the conservatory, closing the French windows between the two rooms.

'Diana, sit down. That is one very confused and unhappy little boy. He wants to spend time with you, but you have no time to spend with him. He knows he's welcome here, but I do have other things to do with my life.'

'Such as sleeping with the clergy?'

Ellie felt herself grow hot, and then ice cold. 'I think we'd better pretend you didn't say that. It's not true, and anyway . . . no, we'll not discuss Thomas now. The point is that I love Frank and of course I want to help look after him, but I do have other commitments and sometimes it's a struggle to fit everything in. I can't always cancel things just because you decide at the last minute that you don't want him around.'

'For crying out loud, I'm a working woman!'

'If you have to work at weekends then you should perhaps come to an arrangement with Maria to have Frank for a couple of nights in the week.'

'I can't do that. I have to pull my weight at the agency, if it's to survive.'

Ellie made a mental note that Diana was now talking as if the agency might not survive, though they'd only just opened their doors. Yet she and Denis had projected a glowing future for it when they'd applied to Ellie's trust fund for a start-up grant to cover the first year of rental for their premises. Well, this was not the time to go into that.

Ellie tried to sound conciliatory. 'Perhaps you'd better arrange to have him for just the odd weekend when you can concentrate on him properly?'

'I can't do that, either. How would that look to everyone?'

'Better than if it were known that you'd been smacking him for wetting the bed in a strange house.'

'Denis' wife is a very capable woman.'

'But not, I think, a loving one. Frank is too young to be boarded out whenever you want to get rid of him for a night. And what about this evening? What time did you close? Four? Five? Why didn't you fetch him then?'

'It was a business do. I couldn't get out of it.'

Did Diana believe what she was saying? Perhaps she did. Ellie held back a sigh. 'I realize that this is a difficult time for you and I will gladly help to look after him when I can, provided you give me enough notice and I'm able to rearrange things. Perhaps you'd like to have a word with Maria and Stewart, see if they'd agree to keep him at weekends until you can sort something better out for him.'

Diana sneered. 'Oh, they won't want him at weekends. Only too glad to see the back of him.'

The door opened behind them, and there stood Frank. He'd heard, of course. Ellie swooped on him, picked him up and carried him back into the sitting room. He was heavy, of course, but she could manage in an emergency. She kept saying, over and over, 'She didn't mean it. She didn't. Maria loves you dearly, you know that.'

'And I don't?' Diana had gone white, and there were tears in her eyes. 'Frank, darling. Come to Mummy. I didn't mean that Maria doesn't love you. Of course not. I'm sure she does, in her own way. But not as much as I love you.'

Frank clung to Ellie, who thought for one wild moment that it would be best to hang on to him . . . and perhaps bring on a permanent break between mother and son. Wouldn't Frank be better off if he didn't have to suffer Diana's damaging intermissions into his life? But no. Diana did love him, in her own way. And he certainly loved her.

Ellie gradually loosened the little boy's arms from around her neck, and pushed him gently towards his mother. Frank burrowed into Diana's shoulder, weeping. She hugged and kissed him, over and over again.

Ellie went to make her longed-for pot of tea. Frank's leg was still red where Diana had hit him.

* * *

Peace and quiet. Diana had gone, taking Frank with her and promising him new toys and DVDs and games of all descriptions. Promising him the earth.

Ellie felt as if she'd been through five rounds with Jack Dempsey or whoever that boxing champion had been in her youth. Cassius Clay? She shook her head at herself. She'd never really been interested in sport. That had been Frank's domain.

Sleet hit the windows. She drew the curtains, dug out some homemade soup from the freezer, made herself a cheese sandwich. She heard Kate and Armand return next door. Catriona wailed a bit. Tired, no doubt. Ellie ate some supper, paid some bills. Answered a letter from an old friend.

The phone rang, and she fell on it. 'Yes?'

It was Kate, worrying about Ellie.

'No news of Neil yet,' said Ellie, 'but it sounds as if the hospital is thinking of letting Mrs Dawes out of Intensive Care. She's still not woken up yet, but is improving.'

'She's a strong woman.'

Yes, thought Ellie. But not young. Perhaps she will pull through, but even if she's not left disabled, won't her confidence have been shaken? Will she still be able to live by herself, take care of herself? Tell everyone else how to manage?

Kate understood all this as well as Ellie did, but they both made bright noises about how good this news was, and they'd see one another tomorrow.

Ellie found a news bulletin on the telly. More doom and gloom. She switched it off. Couldn't settle to anything. Opened a box of chocolates that she'd been keeping for a special occasion. Well, there was nothing like comfort food when you were worrying about something.

Finally, Mark Hadley rang. 'Sorry, no good news, Mrs Quicke. Neil has been charged with assault on a police officer and they're keeping him in custody, pending further enquiries.'

She'd more than half expected it, but it was still a blow. 'I suppose they pushed him till he snapped. Did you manage to see him?'

'Yes. He wasn't very cooperative, I'm afraid. He knows he's in trouble for hitting the policeman, and he's beginning to realize that worse is in store. He's angry and frightened. He hardly gave me the time of day.'

'Worse? What's worse?' She didn't want to hear. 'So, what happens next?'

'He'll be up in court tomorrow. I'll ask for bail, but I doubt if it will be granted. They want to resume questioning on the other matter, of course.'

'He didn't attack Mrs Dawes.'

'He attacked a police officer, which will harden their belief that they've got the right person.'

Ellie made herself face an even worse fear. 'The news on Mrs Dawes is better. She may be out of Intensive Care tomorrow. That reduces the charge against him, doesn't it?'

'It's still a serious offence.'

'I'm even more afraid that they'll try to pin the other murder on him.'

'What other murder?' exclaimed Mark.

'They found — well, actually, I stumbled on it myself — a body quite near Mrs Dawes'. In a garden not far away. Badly decomposed.'

He sucked in his breath. 'This just gets better all the time. Tell me who, why, what and where?'

'I really don't know much about it. I sort of trod on it, trying to collect some greenery for Mrs Dawes. I can't think the two incidents are connected.'

'The police will try to connect them if they occurred in the same locality. They've already got Neil for assault, they'll certainly push to make him responsible for the attack on his grandmother, so why not clear the books with the body in the bushes? The lad's his own worst enemy, isn't he?'

Ellie grimaced. 'I stand by my original statement: Neil didn't put his gran in hospital.'

'Can you rustle up another suspect? Is this Mrs Dawes popular with her neighbours? Has she had words with anyone else? A long-standing feud would be good. Or perhaps an argument with another member of her family?'

'She's a hard-working member of the church, on several committees, has a circle of old friends. I don't think she's in close touch with the other members of her family, from what I can gather. I mean, they came down overnight to see her in hospital, but it sounds as if they've both gone back to their own homes already.'

Ellie sought for a handkerchief, 'Look, no one that I know of would want to kill her. Except, if you don't think it's too far-fetched, Neil thought that the lads who sell drugs in the Avenue might have got it in for her, because she had words with them one evening.'

'Better.' He sounded doubtful. 'I'll follow that up. But I don't want any more nasty surprises when I get there tomorrow. Tell me everything you know about the body in the bushes.'

'Sounds like Moses in the bulrushes,' said Ellie, subduing a tendency to hysteria. She wondered if Mr Hadley would think her a giggly airhead, but he actually laughed and said he knew just what she meant. If she could concentrate, please?

She concentrated. She told him everything she remembered, including the subsequent encounter with Mr Hurry, the builder, who had given her a lift home in his white van. 'Now, don't start thinking that Mr Hurry could have done it, because he was as shattered as I was when we found the body.'

'His presence would be a useful diversion to throw in the path of the police, if they try to pin that murder on Neil.'

Ellie thought about that. 'I follow your reasoning, but I don't want you to push another innocent man into the arms of the police, just to save Neil.'

He seemed to be treating this far too lightly. 'Well, can you turn up any other suspects?'

Ellie decided that she didn't really like his jocular tone. 'I am *not* a private detective. I do *not* go round looking for crime.'

'I know, I know. You're just an innocent bystander with a knack for discovering the truth.'

'I'm an innocent bystander, no more, no less. You'll let me know what happens tomorrow?'

'You'd better have my mobile number, and I'll take yours.'

They exchanged numbers. Ellie felt limp. It had been a long day. Midge arrived from nowhere and jumped on to her lap. He always sensed when she was disturbed about something, though he rarely showed affection. She stroked him for a while, until he decided he needed to be fed.

What she really wanted to do was to ring Thomas and tell him all about it. He had a knack of putting things into perspective which would have been very helpful at this moment. She tried his mobile number, carrying it into her darkened conservatory to look down over the slope of her garden, and up to the pretty Victorian church on The Green. There were no lights on in the church, so Evensong was long past. But Thomas still hadn't got his mobile switched on.

She tried the landline to his digs, and left a message there. While the inconvenient old vicarage had been pulled down and a new one built on the site — designed by Roy — Thomas had been renting a small furnished flat nearby, but was hardly ever there. The parish was planning a big party to mark the occasion when he moved into the new place. Ellie went upstairs and peered out of the window in the spare bedroom. With the leaves almost all gone from the tree, she could catch a glimpse of the new vicarage, but no, there were no lights on in there, either.

It wasn't all that late but the television programming didn't attract, so she had a long soak in the bath and went to bed. Once in the night she got up and went to stand in the back bedroom, looking out over the church. Moonlight turned a scene she saw every day into something out of a Christmas card. There was something very soothing about looking at a church spire, wasn't there?

* * *

The cab decanted him at the front of the house. He'd been too drunk to risk the walk, but it took most of his remaining cash to pay the driver. He cursed the gatepost when it caught his thigh in passing, and cursed the keys he dropped while trying to get back into the house. He fell over the first step of the stairs and slid down to the tiled floor of the hall.

He wept a few tears.

Why was life so difficult?

Didn't he mean well? Hadn't he always meant well?

It was them that took advantage of him, kicking him around when he was down. And now, just when things were looking up, he was short of cash. It wasn't fair.

It was all Russell's fault, hiding his pin numbers like that. No honest man would need to hide them away from his friends. Hours he'd spent, trying to crack the codes.

Well, he'd just have to get some cash another way. There were plenty of old biddies living alone around here. Or old men.

He'd think of something, when he'd had a little nap.

CHAPTER ELEVEN

The central heating ticked away, providing a bubble of warmth in what looked, from the window, to be an unfriendly world. Dull. Cold.

Ellie held back a shiver as she drew back her curtains. It probably wasn't going to snow because it rarely did in London, but it looked as if it would like to. Wind was blustering around the garden. It looked as if the Argyranthemum by the sundial had died. They did last through the winter sometimes, but it was a bit of a gamble.

She found a woolly jerkin to put on over her jumper. That was better. Where was Midge? He'd need feeding, for sure. Her phone rang. The landline. Who would ring at this hour? It was only half past seven, and still not really light outside.

'Ellie?' A rough voice. Deep. He cleared his throat. 'You wouldn't by any chance . . . could I cadge breakfast?'

'Thomas, is that you?' He didn't sound like himself.

'Sorry. Forget it. I shouldn't have bothered you.' He rang off.

Puzzled, Ellie put the phone down and went into the kitchen to feed Midge, who wasn't there. Instead, he was sitting on the window sill among her precious flowers in the conservatory, where he knew very well he wasn't supposed to be. Midge was gazing raptly out on to the back garden at a man who was just leaving her garden by the gate into the alley. Thomas.

Ellie hastened to unlock the door. 'Thomas?'

He halted, turned and plodded up the garden path. He still had his mobile in his hand. He looked even more sailor-like than usual, with a heavyweight short navy coat over his jeans. There were brown shadows under his eyes and the line between his eyebrows was very marked. Had he slept at all? It didn't look like it.

Ellie held open the door, and he came in. His hand, brushing past hers, was icy. 'Sorry,' he said, not making eye contact. 'Stupid of me to think . . . a hard day's night.' He attempted a smile.

Ellie could recognize exhaustion when she saw it. 'When did you eat last?'

'Eat?' He didn't seem to understand the word. It must have been a very hard day's night.

She gave him a little push in the direction of the table and he sat, still buttoned into his coat.

'Orange juice? Tea or coffee?'

He just looked at her.

A really truly grim night.

She had some orange juice in the fridge because Frank sometimes liked it. Would tea be better, or coffee? A big plate of cereal to start with; a pity she had no oats for porridge, which would probably do him more good, but there it was, she hadn't got any and he'd have to make do with what she'd got.

She put the orange juice on the table, and he just looked at it. She picked up his right hand, inserted the glass in it and hoped he wouldn't drop it. He seemed to get the idea, so she left him to pour some cereal into a dish and add milk. Better not give him a choice; he probably couldn't cope with that. He'd drunk the juice by the time she had the cereal ready. She removed the glass from his fist, and started throwing things into the frying pan.

She'd give him scrambled, not fried eggs: better for his digestion. Bacon, a couple of sausages which she'd been saving for her lunch today, mushrooms . . . bother, there were no tomatoes. She could have some of the scrambled eggs herself.

Double quantity of sliced bread into the toaster. Butter, spreadable. Marmalade, homemade. Or would he prefer jam or honey? He could have marmalade and lump it. Tea or coffee, that was the question. Usually he drank strong dark tea with milk and sugar, but coffee might be better in view of the state that he was in. But she couldn't find any good ground coffee, though she was sure she'd bought some a couple of days back. Tea would have to do.

He'd demolished the cereal by the time the toast was done. As she took in the rest of the meal, he stirred himself long enough to unbutton and throw back his jacket. Was that sort of jacket called a reefer? It was piped round the edges with leather. A durable coat for a durable man. A man who seemed to have lost the plot temporarily.

She wondered if any of his parishioners would have believed their eyes if they could have seen him at that moment. In Ellie Quicke's house! At breakfast time!

Scandalous!

Midge arrived on the table top, looking for food. Ellie shooed him off, and then remembered he hadn't been fed that morning and would have got up to give him something, if Thomas hadn't taken a scrap of bacon from his plate, and held it out to the cat.

'Thomas, you shouldn't feed him at the table.'

He produced a faint copy of his usual grin. 'Sorry.' He'd probably do it again in a minute.

She poured tea into the largest mug she had, added milk and sugar and handed it to him. He closed his eyes, savouring it, as he drank. Then he tackled his plateful, which vanished before Ellie had finished her much smaller helping.

'More?' she asked, wondering if she had any more eggs. Or bacon.

He shook his head, reaching for the toast. She refilled his mug with tea, and this time he was able to add milk and sugar himself.

She fed Midge, and put more toast on. Then she found the bag of ground coffee exactly where she'd left it on the top shelf of the fridge.

'Would you like some good coffee for afters?'

'Thanks, no. I can never sleep on good coffee. This is hitting the spot nicely.'

Ellie reflected that some people seem born to provide for others. Since her husband had died she'd tried to lose that image, but first little Frank and now this great galumphing monster had pushed her back in time. Ah well. There were worse fates in life.

'Sorry,' said Thomas, when he'd eaten the last of the toast and drained the big teapot dry. 'Awful thing to do to you. But I just couldn't face going back to the flat. I knew I hadn't any food in, and . . . no excuses. I shouldn't have come.'

'Mmm?' said Ellie, pressing the right button. 'Want to tell me about it?'

He sighed deeply. 'An old friend went screaming into the night. Died, I mean. Cancer. He was in terrible pain, which they couldn't seem to alleviate until the very end. Cursing and . . . blaspheming . . . and I couldn't do anything to help. Nothing.'

'Except to be there. And pray.'

He nodded. 'For what it's worth. I comfort myself by saying that he didn't want me to leave. But . . . I can still hear . . . see.'

'How did you get back here? Where's your car?'

He washed his face with his hands. 'I think . . . yes, I think I must have left it in the pub car park near the hospital. I couldn't find a parking space at the hospital. You know what it's like. It'll probably get clamped or towed away. How ridiculous of me. After he died this morning, all I could think of was getting back home, so I called a cab and must have fallen asleep. Without thinking, I'd told him to take me to the vicarage. I got out and paid him, and that was when I realized that, of course, the old vicarage wasn't there anymore and the new one isn't habitable yet. Then I saw you draw the curtains and thought . . . sorry, Ellie. Sorry. I shouldn't have dumped myself on you.'

'It's what I'm here for,' said Ellie, not unhappy about it.

'What?' He wasn't connecting very well, even now. He tried to stand up, and didn't make it. Tried to laugh. 'I'm bushed. Fit for nothing. I used to be able to keep going for forty-eight hours without sleep. Would you call me a cab? The sooner I'm back at the flat and can get some kip, the better.'

'Can you get up the stairs here? I always keep a bed made up in the spare room.'

He shook his head. 'What would the parish say? No, no, Ellie. I couldn't do that to you.'

'Everyone else does it.'

'Men of the cloth are not supposed to, even if others do.'

'Then take a nap in the big chair in the sitting room. When you wake up, I'll get you some good coffee and you can toddle off under your own steam.'

He began to protest, but she steered him through the doors and into the biggest of the armchairs; the one which her husband used to regard as his own. She pushed a stool in his direction and he lifted his feet to rest them on it, as if he'd done it a thousand times before, which he hadn't. By the time she fetched a light blanket to cover him, Midge had taken up his position on Thomas' broad chest. Thomas hadn't acquired the nickname of Tum-Tum without reason. Midge was purring. Correction; it wasn't Midge who was purring. Thomas was snoring, gently, lightly. But snoring.

Mercy me, said Ellie to herself. What a turn-up for the books. Who'd believe we weren't having serious nooky, if they saw him now?

Well, I don't care. I *like* the fact that he came to me for help.

She went into the hall to mute the telephone bell. Let Thomas sleep it off. He deserved a bit of peace and quiet after all he'd been through.

The phone rang as she left it. She pushed the door of the sitting room closed, and answered it. It was Angie, Mrs Dawes' daughter, ringing in response to Ellie's call the previous evening. Full of excuses, lots of worry, had had to return home, one of her daughters had been in a car accident, nothing serious as it turned out, but Angie was glad she'd gone back, especially since she had to work today. And she had to work today because her husband was temporarily out of a job . . .

She'd have gone on and on, excusing herself, but Ellie cut her short. 'It's all right. I understand. I'll go into the hospital to see your mother today, if I can.'

'The hospital said . . . oh, this is all such a worry, but my brother should be there still. He'd gone for a snack when I left, but he was due back.'

'It seems he's returned home, too.'

'Oh.' There wasn't much to be said to that. Angie and her brother would no doubt continue their feud into old age. 'So, what about young Neil?'

'He assaulted a police officer, and he'll be up in court today.'

'What did he do that for?'

'He was provoked, I expect.'

'My brother promised me he'd sort Neil out.'

Silence. They both knew her brother hadn't lifted a finger to help his son. Guilt was rolling backwards and forwards over the telephone.

Ellie said, 'I've got hold of a solicitor who's going to try to help Neil.'

'Oh.' Much relieved. 'Well, that's probably best, under the circumstances. You'll get the bill sent to my brother?' Not to her, she meant.

I'll probably have to pay it myself, thought Ellie. She said, 'Of course. And I'll keep you informed.'

'Oh, good.' Angie's name was being called by someone in the room with her. 'Must go. I'm ringing from work. The news from the hospital seems good, doesn't it? I'll try to get back down next weekend.'

Ellie put the phone down, only for it to ring again. This time it was Mr Dawes. The conversation went much as it had with his sister, except that he blamed her for not staying with his mother and not seeing to Neil. He was not happy, though, about Ellie having contacted a solicitor to help Neil, because he couldn't afford to fork out for that sort of thing himself, could he?

Ellie suppressed unkind thoughts about the Dawes family and said she'd pay the bill herself. Which she'd fully intended to do from the start. That is, until they'd made it clear they wouldn't be paying. Oh, bother! Drat them both.

The door from the conservatory to the garden opened, and a bulky Kate negotiated the final step and let herself in. Ellie made sure the doors from the sitting room into the conservatory were closed, but couldn't prevent Kate from seeing who was stretched out asleep in her big armchair.

Kate lowered herself on to one of the conservatory chairs. 'Armand spotted Thomas arriving this morning. He said you hadn't sent him away. I was supposed to be tackling some correspondence over at Felicity's this morning but she rang to put me off, saying she has to make alternative arrangements for her mother or something. Armand and I decided he should take Catriona to the childminder's as arranged, and I'll sit with you till Thomas goes. And if anyone asks, I was here before he arrived. Right?'

Ellie got a tray and started clearing the table of breakfast dishes. 'You've no need.'

'Yes, I have. You'd think people wouldn't think anything of it in this day and age, but it's different for a man in his position. That sort of thing still makes headlines in the yuckier tabloids. The parish think you're fairly eccentric as it is . . .'

'Thank you.'

'Granted. You'd survive the scandal because you've always had men hanging around you, and they don't expect anything else. Your goings-on give the gossips considerable pleasure, something to talk about: 'have you heard the latest about Ellie Quicke?' sort of thing. But Thomas doesn't need mud thrown at him.'

'Let me tell you how he came to be here . . .' Ellie filled Kate in. 'I went into my Earth Mother mode, I suppose. I thought I'd grown out of it, but it seems I haven't.'

Kate shifted in the chair. 'My back's giving me gyp, and the baby's not due for another ten days. I'd help with the breakfast things, but . . . no, I won't even offer.'

'A restless night?' Ellie took her tray through into the kitchen, and returned to clean down the table.

There was a scratching noise at the French windows leading into the sitting room, and both women froze. Thomas hadn't stirred, but Midge had decided he didn't like being shut in when the action was elsewhere. Ellie let him out into the conservatory, where he made a leap for the table top and sat there to give himself a good wash.

'Divert me,' said Kate, twisting in her chair. 'What's the latest?'

'On Mrs Dawes?' Ellie started to stack the dishwasher. 'Some improvement. I'll try to get up there later. Both her children have returned home. If you ask me, they care more about scoring points off one another than about looking out for their mother. No wonder Mrs Dawes doesn't talk about them much.

'As for the latest on Neil. He assaulted a police officer while he was being questioned so they're holding him at the station . . . don't ask! I reckon they yelled at him till he reacted. He was so upset about his gran that the very thought of anyone laying the assault at his door would be enough to make him see red.

'I've got a solicitor involved — a real oddity, and I'm not sure I take to him — but he should be good because Aunt Drusilla recommended him. The problem, as I see it, is that if the police can prove Neil has a short fuse — and now they can — they can make out he must have been the one who assaulted his gran. And they'll probably also try to make out he's responsible for the body that I stumbled across as well.'

'So what do we do next?'

'Make a shopping list,' said Ellie, scrabbling in her handbag for some scrap paper and a biro. 'The last resort of those who've got too much to do and don't know which job to tackle first. Routine is a wonderful thing. Routine means you don't have to think what to do next, you just do it. Monday morning I hoover and dust downstairs, and then go shopping for food.'

With a surge of annoyance, she realized she couldn't follow her routine today and that she almost regretted her impulse to let Thomas in. 'Bother, I can't get into the sitting room and I can't leave him here asleep while I go shopping. I wish I'd never let him in.'

Kate was amused. 'But you are fond of him?'

Ellie squiggled the pen to make the ink flow. 'I like him very much indeed. This morning I felt all maternal and loving towards him. It even crossed my mind to drop a kiss on his fevered brow as he lay asleep. You know? And now I could willingly kick him out because he's upset my routine. Isn't that just like a woman?'

'Hormones, dear,' said Kate, shifting again.

Ellie snarled, 'Hormones? At my age? I'm long past all that nonsense. This is Ellie being a frustrated housewife.'

'But you do like him better than any of the other men who've been sniffing around you?'

'I don't see him through rose-coloured spectacles, if that's what you mean. Shall I get you a cushion?'

Kate stood up, massaging her back. 'Have you any of that herbal tea?'

Ellie put the kettle on, popping the bag of ground coffee back into the fridge. Kate hadn't been able to face coffee for months.

The doorbell rang. Both women froze, but there was no movement from the sitting room. Ellie went to the door to find another parcel of Christmas goodies she'd been expecting. Also the postman was coming down the drive. She dumped the parcel in the hall and took the handful of bills and letters into the kitchen. She extracted two envelopes and groaned. 'The first of the Christmas cards. Why will people send them in November?'

Kate limped around the kitchen, easing her back. 'When I was a child, we never sent them out before the twelfth of December. I had two Christmas catalogues at the end of August this year.'

Ellie poured boiling water on Kate's herbal tea bag. 'What's Felicity going to do about her mother?'

Kate shrugged. 'She's dithering between various alternatives. Put her in respite care? Bribe the home to keep her? What's more to the point is, what are you going to do about Neil?'

'Now don't you start. Mark Hadley wants me to find another suspect, but what can I do about it? I don't even know who the missing man — or woman — was. It wasn't in the local paper, was it?'

'They print on Thursday, come out on Friday, so it was discovered too late for that. You could ask around, see if anyone's gone missing.'

'Don't be daft. The police will have done that. My only hope is that when Mrs Dawes wakes up, she'll tell them it wasn't Neil.'

Kate was silent. They both knew the effects of a head injury couldn't be foretold. Mrs Dawes might never wake up. Or wake up and be in a vegetative state. Or not remember anything of the attack.

'You could get Thomas to make some enquiries,' said Kate. 'Everyone talks to him.'

'Yuk,' said Ellie. 'If you don't shut up, I'll make myself some good coffee and waft it in front of you and then you'll be sorry.'

'I take it all back. My lips are zipped.'

'I need to replace eggs, bacon, sausages, mushrooms,' Ellie murmured to herself as she made out her shopping list. 'Butter, a half of mince, cheese, tomatoes. Veg. Teabags. Biscuits. Some bleach for the loo. Oh, and a pair of gloves. Except I might have to go to Ealing Broadway for those. I lost one the other day and the weather's not going to improve, is it?'

They looked out at the wintry garden. The wind had dropped, and flakes of snow were drifting past the window.

'Snow?' said Kate. 'Catriona hasn't seen snow. She'll be delighted.'

Adults wouldn't be delighted. Ellie thought of treacherous patches on the pavements, and car wheels spinning on icy roads. 'I suppose I'd better take the bus to the Broadway and get everything there. I need some cash, anyway. Oh, why does everything go wrong all at once?' She slammed the biro down, and her list wafted across the table towards Kate. Kate flicked it back. It skidded across the table and fell to the floor. Both women looked at it. Ellie sighed. There was no way Kate could pick it up with her bulge, so Ellie did, throwing it back on to the table. It landed upside down.

'Who's Mr Hurry? What a name!' Kate exclaimed.

'What? Oh, that's the flier he gave me the other day when he gave me a lift back in his van. He's a builder, working on the house where we found the body in the garden. Nice man. I wonder . . . Neil said he was halfway through painting a ceiling for a customer when he got called to the hospital. They must be furious that he's left them in the lurch. I wonder if we can find out who it was.'

'Would this Mr Hurry provide a distraction for the police? Did you tell the solicitor about him? Mr Hurry might have seen something, heard something. Try him!' Kate liked to use her brain and unlike Ellie, fancied herself as a bit of a detective.

The doorbell rang, one long, loud peal. Kate spilled some of her tea. Ellie peered into the lounge through the French windows, but Thomas hadn't moved.

'It would take the last trump to wake him,' said Ellie, getting crosser by the minute.

Kate was already on her feet. 'I'll go. I need the exercise.'

'To the door and back?'

Kate laughed, and swayed along to the door. She opened it and said in a loud voice, 'Why, Jean! What a pleasant surprise!'

Ellie went rigid with shock. Jean the bully? Jean who ran the church coffee roster with terrifying efficiency? What was she doing, calling on Ellie at this time on a Monday morning? Did she know that Thomas was here? Uh-oh . . . !

Ellie mentally reviewed her recent sins: she'd disrupted the wedding on Saturday, leaving the choir short of sopranos; she'd failed to attend church and sing in the choir on Sunday morning, and been absent from the coffee roster afterwards. All deadly sins in Jean's book, probably equated with 'sloth'. And now Jean was about to find Thomas asleep in Ellie's sitting room, which she'd certainly regard as 'lust'.

Kate was cheerily welcoming Jean in. 'No, you haven't come to the wrong house. I'm keeping Ellie company this morning. Do go through the kitchen into the conservatory at the back. Nasty old day, isn't it? We were just wondering what to do about a rather knotty problem when you rang, and I really do think it was an answer to prayer, because if anyone can do something about it, it's you.'

Jean was wafted into the conservatory, willy-nilly, on the wings of Kate's chatter. She looked puzzled, but alert. She looked rather like a Yorkshire terrier with her fringe of gingerish hair, but a Yorkshire terrier quite prepared to take a bite out of someone's ankles if they crossed her. She might be under five foot in height, but could make grown men quail when she fixed them with her eye.

'Ellie,' she said, as Ellie got to her feet, not knowing quite what Kate was up to. Then Jean spotted Thomas through the windows, and took a half-step back. 'Oh!'

'Exactly,' said Kate, in a grim, meaningful tone. She drew out a chair. 'Join the think tank. What exactly are we going to do about Thomas? I always thought he was perfectly capable of looking after himself, but I suppose even the strongest of men needs a spot of tender loving care occasionally.'

'What . . . ?' Jean looked to Ellie for enlightenment, but Ellie couldn't think what to say, so merely shook her head sadly.

Kate was in full flow. 'What I think is that the parish ought to find him a housekeeper. Someone to see he has food in the fridge if he has to stay up all night with a dying parishioner. He arrived back at the church more by good luck than judgement. The walking dead. Can you think of anyone, Jean? You'd know the right person, better than anyone else. I mean, this time Ellie and I were here to see that he ate something and had a nap when he arrived on our doorstep, but suppose we hadn't been in? He might have collapsed in the Avenue.'

Ellie could see where this was leading. 'I didn't mind cooking for him, but it's my day for turning out the sitting room and he is in the way, rather. Besides, I want to get to the hospital to see how Mrs Dawes is doing.'

Jean turned her head from one to the other, with the bemused stare of someone watching the conjurer. She suspected the worst of Ellie; she wouldn't have been surprised if she'd found Ellie canoodling with Thomas — although naturally she'd have expressed horror and indignation at the sight of the vicar wrapped around one of his parishioners. On the other hand, she didn't really want to think the worst of Thomas, and she respected Kate as everyone did. It was a dilemma. 'How is Mrs Dawes? That was a terrible thing.'

'Dreadful,' said Ellie. 'Would you like a coffee, Jean?' Kate turned a peculiar shade of greyish-white and Ellie hastened to add, 'Only instant, I'm afraid.'

'Thank you, no. I came round to see if you were all right, since you missed church yesterday.'

'I know. I was at the hospital all morning. I'm a bit of a bent reed, aren't I? Letting you down like that.'

'Well . . . yes, but now you've explained. What time did he . . . ?'

'Breakfast time,' said Ellie. 'He told the cab driver to take him to the vicarage, being completely disoriented and forgetting that it was being rebuilt. Then he didn't know what to do with himself, and couldn't face trudging off to his cold flat which hasn't any food in. He spotted me drawing the curtains . . .'

'My husband saw him coming up the path from the church, looking dazed,' said Kate. 'So I came round to help.'

'Not *drunk*?' asked Jean, eyes gleaming with imagined horrors.

'No, no,' said Ellie. 'Just worn out. How do you think the parish should handle this, Jean? Advertise for a housekeeper?'

'Mmm, no. We don't want everyone thinking . . . well, what they might think if they had that sort of mind. I might ask Maggie if she'd take him on, if her husband agrees. A couple of hours two days a week might do it. He'll need someone to look after him when he moves into the new vicarage, anyway. Yes, I'll do that. We don't want a repetition of this, do we?'

Kate and Ellie both shook their heads.

Jean hesitated, then said, 'I can rely on you two to keep your mouths shut?'

Kate and Ellie both nodded.

'Good.' Jean took one last look through the French windows at the recumbent Thomas, and sighed. 'There's men for you. Well, I must be off. Sorry you've been lumbered, Ellie. It's lucky Kate was here to help.'

'Glad to,' said Kate, ushering Jean to the front door. Jean disappeared.

Ellie sank back into her chair. 'Ooof! Thank you, Kate. I owe you one.'

'A pleasure,' said Kate. 'Now I have you in my power for evermore. What shall I ask for?'

* * *

He was furious. Livid. Some time in the early hours he'd got himself up the stairs and put himself to bed after drinking several glasses of water. When he woke about eleven, he didn't feel too bad. Almost hungry. Yes, for once he really felt hungry.

He'd counted out his small change — all he had left — before he left the house. There'd been enough for a small fish and chips and a can of Diet Pepsi. He'd dived down the sides of chairs, and gone through the pockets of every piece of Russell's clothing to find enough money. He really fancied some fish and chips.

By the time he'd got to the Avenue, he'd remembered it was a Monday and the chippy didn't open on a Monday. So he'd gone along to the kebab shop, and decided he'd make do with some of that and dived into his pocket for the money, only to find a good half had gone! That was when he'd found that hole in his pocket. In Russell's pocket. He could shoot his little finger through the hole, and that's how the change had gone.

He bought a couple of bread rolls from the baker and a lump of cheese from the supermarket, and that was all he had money for.

He was still hungry after he'd finished the last crumb. That did it. He was going to have to try out those pin numbers again, or starve. He'd go down to the Broadway this evening after dark, and see if he could beat the system. It would be a gamble. He knew that. There were five rows of numbers on the back of the calendar.

One was for a cash card. One for a deposit card. One for the building society machine. He didn't know what the others were for. If he put in the wrong number, after a couple of tries the machine would eat up his card and he'd have lost his chance of ever getting money out that way. If he guessed right, he'd be in clover for life!

He'd have to wait till it was dark, and maybe wear a hat of some kind, in case there was a security camera pointed at the cash machine.

CHAPTER TWELVE

Ellie got off the bus at the Broadway and realized she'd lost her shopping list. Surely she'd put it in her handbag before she set out? Or had she left it on the kitchen table?

Well, she'd have to try to remember what she needed. She must get some money from the bank first. Then buy some gloves. Then do the food shopping.

If she hadn't left Kate standing guard over Thomas, Ellie would have indulged herself in a coffee and a piece of cake at one of the cafes in the Broadway. As it was, she took a taxi back home with all her bags. One of these days she'd master shopping by internet, but at the moment she could only do it if Kate stood over her. Besides, for one person, it was hardly worth it.

There was another flurry of snow as she paid off the driver back at the house, but it wasn't settling on the ground. Just as well.

The house was warm and welcoming, but quiet. Too quiet? Thomas was still asleep in the sitting room, but there was no sign of Kate. Instead, that nice woman Maggie, from the choir, was in Ellie's kitchen, knitting something pink and reading a magazine.

'All's well,' said Maggie, helping Ellie in with her shopping. 'Jean phoned and asked if I could help out for a bit.'

'Kate's all right, not been rushed off to hospital? Wait a minute. Don't you have masses to do, clearing up after the wedding? Which was lovely, by the way. Thomas did give you my apologies, didn't he? You know what happened?'

Maggie had the sweetest of smiles. She lifted her fingers from her knitting to tick off the points Ellie had raised. 'Kate's fine. She left a note for you. She'd remembered a dental appointment so she phoned Jean, who asked if I could spare an hour to look after Thomas. I'm fine. There's hardly any clearing up to be done, and what there is can wait. Yes, of course I heard what happened to you. Poor Mrs Dawes. That was a dreadful thing. And poor Thomas. These men will overdo it, if we don't look after them, won't they.'

'True. Coffee? You should have helped yourself. No? We ought to call ourselves The Friends of Thomas.'

'I don't think he ought to sleep on much longer, or he won't sleep tonight.'

'I'll wake him when I've got my breath back.' Ellie could see Mr Hurry's flier propped up against the toaster. So she had left her list here. Kate had scrawled P.T.O. on it. Ellie turned it over: Your solicitor phoned. You can get him on this number before twelve. Followed by a mobile phone number.

Ellie excused herself to Maggie, and went into the hall to phone Mark Hadley.

He seemed slightly more awake than before, but the news wasn't good.

'Neil's been up in court, charged with assaulting a police officer. I managed to see him in the cells beforehand and he says it was more of a jostle than an assault, but the police say otherwise. He's been remanded in custody, pending further enquiries, which means they want to continue questioning him on other matters. I told him to insist that I had to be present before any further questioning, and to shut his mouth and say "No Comment" to everything. He agreed to do that, though I don't know that he'll keep to it. He's very worried about a decorating job he's started and not finished, and wants you to tell the woman what's happened. Alice

Horton, Greys Road. She paid him something on account. He keeps saying he's never let a client down before.'

'How's he bearing up?'

'Frightened, but hiding it under bluster.'

'Any chance of you getting him out on bail?'

'None, I should say. Two policemen swear Neil attacked them.'

Ellie said, 'Tell him I'll contact Mrs Horton. Tell him I believe in him.'

'Humph!' said Mr Hadley, and rang off.

Oh dear, thought Ellie. I suppose solicitors do get cynical, dealing with so many dodgy characters, but I would have preferred him to believe Neil to be innocent.

'Bad news?' asked Maggie, rolling up her knitting.

'Could be better.'

Maggie stowed her belongings into a strong-looking basket with a waterproof cover on it. You didn't see many baskets like that around nowadays. Perhaps it was like Maggie herself: not particularly in fashion, but durable. 'My husband will be wanting his lunch, so . . .'

'Many thanks for helping out. Are you knitting for another grandchild?'

'No, no. My grandchildren are past wanting something knitted by me. But there's always someone having a baby and I like to keep my hand in. Do you know if Kate is having a boy or a girl?'

Ellie shook her head. Kate had said she didn't want to know, though Armand had vociferously expressed a desire for a boy.

Off Maggie went. Ellie stood, listening, in the hallway. If Kate were back from the dentist's, she might like to come round for a sandwich lunch. But there was no sound from the other side of the wall.

Ellie traced a Horton in the phone book, and gave her a ring. Mrs Horton was, it transpired, furious that Neil had let her down. She'd got the sitting room furniture pushed into the middle of the room — except for the table, which was in the hall in pieces — and covered with dust sheets, and the carpet rolled up, and the ceiling only half painted with the first coat. As for the television, Neil had put it on the kitchen table for her, and it was far too heavy for her to move back again, and she couldn't get at the fridge-freezer because it was right in the way, and what was he going to do about it?

Mrs Horton vowed she'd never use Neil again, no matter how well he'd come recommended. He'd no business, she said, being taken up by the police, and if she'd known that he was the sort to be charged with grievous bodily harm, she'd never have taken him on, which her daughter had said from the beginning that she shouldn't, and that proved it, didn't it? And she'd paid that villain up front for the paint, and who was going to reimburse her now, and in any case, who could she get to do the job for her at this time of year when everyone was decorating to get their home ready before Christmas?

Ellie tried to get a word in edgeways, but didn't succeed. Finally she was reduced to shouting at the woman, 'I'm trying to get someone to finish up for you, right? And if necessary, I'll pay.'

She put the phone down on Mrs Horton, guiltily aware that in that lady's place, she'd probably be hopping mad, too. She rang Mr Hurry, but could only get his answerphone. She left a message, saying a friend had started painting a ceiling for a client but couldn't finish it, due to circumstances beyond his control. Could Mr Hurry fit the job in? The client had already paid some money up front, so it was going to be awkward to sort out the bill, but Ellie said she'd make up the difference if necessary. Oh, and had he found a glove of hers? She might have dropped it in his van the other day.

The front door bell rang. It could be Jean again, could it? No, this was a tentative sort of ring, the sort that Felicity gave when she called. And yes, it was Felicity, looking worried.

'So sorry to trouble you, Ellie, but might I bend your ear for a moment?'

'Come on in. Don't mind Thomas. He's been up all night and has just dropped off.'

'Oh, really?' Felicity was too worried about whatever it was to care. She followed Ellie out into the conservatory and sank into a chair, refusing coffee or tea.

'You're all right?' said Ellie, seeing Felicity was having difficulty in making a start.

'Oh, yes. I'm fine. Taking care, of course. Roy doesn't know yet, and I don't want him to. Not yet. Just in case. Another week or ten days, perhaps.'

Ellie nodded, subduing an impulse to look at the clock. How many times this morning had she had to sit and listen to other people wanting her to do something for them. But surely Felicity wouldn't want her to . . . ? Ah. Perhaps she would.

'You've just been to see your mother again?'

Felicity nodded. 'Roy didn't want me to, but I felt I had to. I know she can be a little selfish at times, but she is all alone and miserable and she'd set her heart on getting out of the home and living a more normal life . . .'

At your expense, thought Ellie.

'It's only natural that she'd look to me to make it happen. But, now I'm married, she can't understand why I keep refusing her, so eventually I told her I'm having a baby and she . . .' Felicity covered her eyes with trembling fingers. 'Oh, dear. I'm so sorry. I didn't mean to give way like that.'

Ellie reached for the box of tissues and pushed it towards Felicity. 'I suppose she said you were being very selfish to have a baby, when you could be looking after her twenty-four hours a day, seven days a week.'

Felicity gave a muffled laugh, wiping her eyes. 'Something like that. I'm trying to think logically about this, Ellie. She *is* a lonely old woman. If only she had a friend, someone she could talk to, someone who'd visit her several times a week, perhaps even take her on outings. In addition to me, I mean.' Felicity concentrated on blowing her nose, her head lowered.

Ellie got the message. And despaired. It was a sensible suggestion, of course. Ellie could see how 'Lady' Anne would flourish under such treatment. Felicity had called round to see if Ellie would agree to be the unselfish, undemanding, patient saint who'd fit the bill. For a couple of seconds, Ellie wondered if she ought to agree. It would be miserably hard work, of course. But if it would ease the burdens all round, wouldn't that be a good thing?

Think how Thomas had eased his friend's passage out of this life, with his generosity of spirit, his unselfish Christianity. Ah, but remember how it had worn Thomas down. And he a professional to boot.

'I think,' said Ellie, 'that you have the germ of an excellent idea here. Someone that Anne could trust, someone who'd listen to her and make her feel special, wanted again. You need a professional, a therapist, a shrink . . . right?'

Felicity frowned, and then eased the frown away. She was no fool; she realized Ellie had considered her proposition and turned it down. 'A therapist? You're probably right. It would cost the earth, but it would be worth it. If it worked, I think I could persuade the home to keep her on. Do you know any?'

'No, but I bet your father does.' Although long divorced, Felicity's father had kept in touch with her over the years and was currently paying his ex-wife's bills at the retirement home.

Felicity looked startled, and then thoughtful. 'Yes, he could find one for us, couldn't he?' She examined her fingernails. 'I'll have to make it clear that I'll pay the bills. He's done enough for me — and for her.'

Ellie had met the man: she liked and respected him. 'You must work that out between you.'

Felicity glanced at the clock. 'Roy said he'd try to get home at lunchtime so's we could discuss it. Mind you, he'll probably forget. Once he's back at work . . .' She shrugged, smiling.

'Tunnel vision,' said Ellie. 'He's a good architect and a lovely man.'

'So he is,' said Felicity. She kissed Ellie and wafted herself away.

Ellie looked at the clock and went to wake Thomas. Not an easy matter, but she did finally get him to open his eyes. He still seemed shell-shocked, looking around him in bewilderment. Ellie made him a cafetière of good coffee, and put it at his elbow. She then had to pour it out for him. He still didn't seem capable of coherent speech, though. Ellie wondered if he were always like that when he woke up and if so, how early did he have to get up to be in his right mind for the eight o'clock service.

She talked to him in a soft voice, telling him what had been happening, checking every now and again that he understood what she was saying. She said Kate had come in to save his reputation, and then Jean and after her, Maggie.

Did he shudder slightly? He wasn't giving much away this morning.

'We put it to Jean that you needed someone to look after you, and she's arranging for Maggie to keep your flat stocked with food in future. So you needn't worry about that any more. And in any case, you'll soon be moving into the new vicarage. Perhaps Maggie could continue to keep an eye on your home comforts there as well.'

He nodded, his eyes fixed on her as if she might disappear if he looked elsewhere. However kindly she put it, she was telling him she did not want him to rely on her for food and refuge again, and he was getting the message. She felt as if she were telling an old and trusty dog that he was going to be put down.

It was absurd to feel so guilty about it, wasn't it?

Perhaps he had wanted her to claim him as her 'significant other', to use a phrase which Ellie had always found risible. Perhaps he had. Perhaps, in coming to her for help, it had crossed his mind that she might acknowledge their relationship had reached a certain stage, and make it official?

It was she who had insisted on taking him in, and on making him have a nap afterwards. She felt guilty, and annoyed with him, and with herself. Yes, she liked him enormously, and yes, they had been making the first moves in the courting game. But no, she hadn't yet reached the point of agreeing to marry him. If ever.

'You do understand, don't you, Thomas? If Jean had found you here alone with me, there would have been all sorts of gossip. It was my fault entirely for not throwing you out after you'd eaten. Anyway, no harm done. There were four of us taking turns to look after you while you slept, and no one's going to suggest you're setting up a harem.'

A poor jest, but he twitched a smile.

'So, it's all turned out for the best,' she said. And to herself she added — with a feeling of having had a lucky escape — that no, she really didn't want to take him on as a permanency. Not with everything else that was happening.

His priority now was to rescue his car, so she phoned for a cab to take him in search of it. He went off as meek as a lamb.

* * *

It was noon, and she hadn't done any cleaning yet. She didn't feel like it, either. She did a quick tidy up, threw out some chrysanthemums which were past their best, put some sprigs of winter jasmine into a tiny vase, and pushed the duster around. She had a sandwich lunch, debated whether or not to take the two buses which were needed to reach the hospital and decided to spoil herself with a cab.

She eased herself into her winter boots, found a soft hat to keep her head warm, and pulled on her new gloves. She quite liked her new gloves, though she didn't think they'd last as long as her old ones.

Now to see how Mrs Dawes was getting on.

* * *

Snow swirled around the windows of the side room to which Mrs Dawes had been moved, high up in the tower block at the hospital. She lay prone, still hooked up to various instruments but making a restless movement now and then. She was, the nurse said, coming out of it nicely, though of course they wouldn't know for some time how much damage had been done. The nurse said it would be all right if Ellie talked softly to Mrs Dawes, who might not be fully conscious yet, but could probably hear her.

There was a policeman on guard duty, sitting on a chair by the door. Now and again he shifted his feet, and crossed his arms over his body. He avoided Ellie's eye, and she avoided his. It was the same man as yesterday.

Ellie turned her back on him, took a seat and stroked Mrs Dawes' hand. In a soft voice she commented on the weather, the flowers in her garden, what flowers they might have in church next weekend, and what she'd planned to have for supper that night. She didn't mention Neil, or Thomas, or Mrs Dawes' children.

The hair showing under the bandage around Mrs Dawes' head revealed a rim of white. Ellie had long suspected that Mrs Dawes dyed her hair black. It saddened her to have her suspicions confirmed. The bruises on Mrs Dawes' face seemed worse than before. The nurse said bruises always did look worse a couple of days on, but that they'd soon disappear. The nurse had been cheery. She'd made Ellie feel even more depressed.

The shop on the ground floor sold flowers, plants, confectionery, newspapers. Ellie had bought an orchid in a pot to stand on the bedside cabinet. Maybe Mrs Dawes would be pleased with it, if she woke up and were in her right mind. More likely — if she were in her right mind — she'd complain that the orchid had been put in the wrong light, or been overwatered. Or was too dry.

When it got dark, Ellie went home. Neil's van was still there. Midge needed to be fed. Ellie supposed she ought to eat something herself. There would be choir practice that evening, and they'd expect Ellie to be there; they would no doubt talk about Mrs Dawes, and wish her well. Probably someone would produce a Get Well card and they'd all sign it.

She could hear happy family noises next door: Catriona crowing, Armand laughing, the phone ringing, Kate calling out to Armand that it was for him. Ellie couldn't hear them distinctly, but it was good to know that normality continued next door. If not everywhere.

Ellie hoped Thomas had managed to retrieve his car. She wondered, idly, if he would have a lot of work to do, clearing up his friend's place. Perhaps he was an executor. People like Thomas were often asked to be executors. Tidying away the estate as well as setting the immortal spirit off on its last journey.

The doorbell rang, and Ellie let Mr Hurry into her hall. Presumably he'd come from work because he was still wearing overalls. He wasn't holding her glove but she presumed that's why he'd come.

'This is kind of you, Mr Hurry. I wasn't sure where I'd dropped my glove. In your van, I presume?'

He stared at her. Shell-shocked? Like Thomas. But presumably not for the same reason?

She thought, Oh, he hasn't discovered another body, has he? For a moment she considered turning him away, but instead she said, 'It's a nasty cold night. Could you do with a cuppa?'

He shook his head, and then said, 'Yes, if you've got the kettle on. I didn't fancy it, down at the nick. I came about the job up at Mrs Horton's.'

Ellie blinked. He'd been down at the police station? Did this mean the police were considering him an alternative to Neil? No, how absurd. But as she looked more closely, she saw lines of strain on his face. Of shock. His hair was all over the place, as if he'd run his hands through it. And he hadn't brought her glove with him.

She led the way to the kitchen and put the kettle on. How many times today had she fed and watered other people? Her late husband would not have been amused. He hadn't wanted her wasting her time and energy on other people, when she ought to have been concentrating on her husband and child.

To tell the truth, she was getting a bit bored with playing Mother Earth.

Mr Hurry put four sugars into a mug of strong tea. She opened a couple of packs of biscuits and put them in the tin. Pushed it towards him.

The central heating ticked. Midge plopped through the cat flap, to enquire who this stranger might be in his territory. After a good sniff at his trouser legs, Midge decided Mr Hurry was an acceptable guest, and leaped on to a spare chair for a nap.

Ellie let the silence lap them around. Mr Hurry was having to hold the mug in both hands to stop the tea from slopping all over the place. He was definitely in shock. He emptied the mug, and she filled it again. He ate three chocolate biscuits, and sighed, sitting back in his chair. Unwinding a notch.

He looked at the clock. 'The missus'll be wondering where I am. I said I'd be home early today. Some do on at the school for the kids.'

Ellie nodded. 'You came about the job at Mrs Horton's?'

'I got your message, saying you'd pay something towards it, so I thought I'd come round, check it out with you. I've got a bit of a cash-flow problem, see, because of the arguments up at Mrs Ball's and him not wanting to pay me till the job was finished. I left my mate up at the new place where we started this morning, and popped round to see Mrs Horton. Told her I couldn't fit it in till the end of the week, and then it would be tricky, but I thought I could manage it. Shifted her telly, and the table. You did say you'd pay something towards it?'

Ellie nodded again.

'When I got back to the job, my mate said he couldn't find his spanners. Said he'd left them in the van — my van — so we had everything out and that's when I found your glove.' He passed his hand through his hair. 'I've only gone and left it on the dashboard, haven't I? I'll get it in a minute. We couldn't find the spanners in the van. Then he remembered he'd left them at Mrs Ball's. I said I'd go round there at lunchtime. I'd still got the key, because we were going back to finish off later, weren't we?'

Prickles ran down Ellie's back. Did he mean . . . ?

He rubbed his eyes. 'She was lying at the bottom of the stairs. I thought at first she'd tripped over her nightie. A heavy woman like that. Could have done. I think I laughed. Laughed out loud. Shock, you know? Then I said, "Up you get, missus." She didn't move, so I bent down and picked up her hand to help her up, you see. It flopped away from me.'

He stood up and made for the sink. Retched, but wasn't sick.

Ellie held the kitchen door open for him. 'The bathroom's upstairs.'

He nodded, went past her with his hand over his mouth.

She called out, 'Second door on the left.' She busied herself with putting away the biscuits, rinsing out the teapot. The dishwasher was almost full. She set it going.

He came down looking pale and tired but in command of himself. 'Sorry about that. I spent the rest of the day at the nick but I didn't fancy using their facilities.'

He resumed his chair. She said, 'We're an unlucky pair, aren't we? Finding bodies. I presume you called the police straightaway?'

'My mate was furious. All this . . . it's put us right behind and there's bound to be a right row about who pays for the work we did at Mrs Ball's. That's the worst of working for yourself, if you don't get paid, you don't eat.'

'Never mind about that now,' said Ellie. 'If you need a loan, I'm sure I can find some money — I have access to a trust fund — which will tide you over.'

He wasn't listening. 'I tell you for nothing, I don't want to go back there no more. First that . . . that thing in the garden. And now this.'

'You think it was an accident?'

He looked uneasy. 'At first I did. Tripped and came down the stairs at a run and straight into the wall. But one of her bedroom slippers was still on her foot, and the other was lying right beside her as if she'd just stepped out of it. Loose slippers, not tight-fitting like some of them are. I phoned the police, and then I phoned my mate, and then I just stood there, staring. Those slippers bothered me. I kept looking at them, and thinking that if she'd lost one halfway down the stairs, it would have looked . . . right. Natural. I thought, I don't want no more trouble. I thought if I took one of her slippers off and tossed it up the stairs, it would look better.'

'But you didn't.'

'Wish I had. Then they wouldn't have gone on at me so much. Her neck was broke, you see. You could read it easily enough if you knew. One of my aunties — rest her soul — she died that way. Tripped over the sash of her dressing gown and tumbled down the stairs, arse over tip, night-clothes all over the place, ran her head into the wall at the bottom. Broke her neck.'

'And Mrs Ball?'

He shook his head. 'Her clothes were all in place. She'd been in bed, or about to get into bed. Forgot something? Heard something? Came down the stairs calm as you please and when she reached the hall, someone hit her for six, knocking her into the wall behind her. You could see the dent in the wall, but no blood. And she just slid down and died. Feet to the hall. Head to the wall.'

'No blood at all?'

'There might have been at the back of her head, but I didn't shift her to look. She was cold. The central heating wasn't on. We'd set it to come on in the day-time, but she'd gone and altered the thermostat, hadn't she? To save money, I suppose. It was freezing in there. I knew I shouldn't touch anything, but I went into the kitchen to get a drink of water. Her handbag was on the table, everything pulled out. No wallet, no purse to be seen. And the back door was open a bit. Been jemmied, probbly.'

'Just like Mrs Dawes.'

'Who's she?'

‘A neighbour who was attacked on Friday evening. Left for dead, but may survive. Her handbag was ransacked, too.’

‘Filthy druggies!’

‘You think? The police are trying to pin it on Mrs Dawes’ grandson because they’d had words that afternoon.’

A frown. ‘Could he have done Mrs Ball as well?’

Ellie shuddered. ‘You have an alibi?’

‘Dunno when it was. But probbly. They asked me where I was over the weekend and I told them. Just the usual. Family stuff, you know? They didn’t seem that bothered.’

No, they wouldn’t be, thought Ellie. They were going to throw the book at Neil. And what could she do about it? Nothing.

He got to his feet, making a move with reluctance. ‘Must ring the missus. She’ll be worried. Can’t face the school do.’

Ellie accompanied him to the front door. ‘It might help, take your mind off things.’

‘What my mind’s on is money. When will I get paid for the work we did at Mrs Ball’s? And we’ve lost a whole day today, too.’

‘Bring me the bill when you finish off Mrs Horton’s ceiling, and I’ll give you a cheque for it.’

‘Thanks. Maybe I could get started on it tonight . . . no, I keep forgetting the do at the school. I’ll get you your glove.’

Ellie didn’t tell him not to bother. He’d come out of his way to bring it to her and give her the news. And to make sure she’d pay something towards Mrs Horton’s ceiling. It didn’t look as if Neil were going to be able to finish it. Mr Hurry didn’t need to know that she’d already thrown the other glove away. Correction, it might still be in the bin, in which case she’d rescue it. She’d liked those gloves.

He got into his van, flicked on the lights, saluted her through the window, and drove away. Forgetting her glove again! She didn’t know whether to laugh or cry about that. Poor man. He’d been badly shaken by finding not one but two bodies. She didn’t feel too strong herself.

As she went back into the hall, she noticed that the answerphone light was blinking. Oh, she'd forgotten to turn the sound back up after Thomas left. How many messages were there going to be on the phone for her? As it turned out, only one, and the person hadn't left a message.

But as Ellie was moving away, the phone rang again. This time it was the police, a woman's voice, reminding her that she hadn't been in to sign her statement about finding Mrs Dawes on Saturday. Oh dear. She'd forgotten completely about that. She promised to do it first thing on the morrow.

'While we're on the phone, could you tell me what's happening about Neil Dawes?'

But they'd rung off already.

Ellie rang both the numbers that Mark Hadley had given her. They rang and rang. He was not available. She left messages.

She wondered if Thomas had managed to retrieve his car. She felt guilty, really sad, about the way she'd handled matters that morning. He'd looked so hurt, so little boyish, when she'd informed him of the arrangements that had been made for his well-being. Oh well, it was done now. And she really did not want to have to take on another burden. Not that Thomas was a burden, precisely.

She put her front-door key in her pocket and went round to ring Kate's doorbell. She didn't want to be alone to think. She was really worried about Neil. He'd hate being locked up, shouted at. She could see why the police thought they'd got the right man, but they hadn't. Waiting for news was awful. She wondered how people managed if they had to wait weeks, maybe months, for a trial.

Armand opened the door, wearing an apron and flourishing a spatula. 'Come in, Kate's been worrying about you. I'm cooking, she's bathing the infant.'

'Come on up,' cried Kate, so up Ellie went to enjoy the sight of Catriona splashing about in the bath. Kate was also wearing an apron.

'Up you come!' said Kate, pulling out the plug and wrapping a protesting toddler in a bath towel. Catriona started to yell. She hated being put into the water, and she hated being taken out of it again.

Armand called up that supper would be fifteen minutes and was Ellie staying.

'Yes, of course,' Kate called back.

'Don't you lift her,' said Ellie. 'Let me.' Ellie plucked the child from the bath, towel and all, and sat on the stool to dry her. Catriona was so surprised at being lifted by someone other than her mother that she forgot to yell. Ellie hummed a nursery song as she dried the little girl. The bathroom window clouded over with steam as Kate produced a clean set of pyjamas from the airing cupboard for her little one, and the world turned right side up.

It was Ellie who carried Catriona into her bedroom, and tucked her up in her cot, while Kate tidied the bathroom. Catriona tried to keep her eyes open, but clearly she was ready for sleep. Kate murmured a prayer over the child, and the adults tiptoed out, leaving a glow-worm light on in the room.

'Glass of wine?' asked Armand when they went downstairs.

'Daren't. Choir practice in just over an hour.' Ellie winced at the thought. How could they practice carols with Mrs Dawes so ill? And Neil on remand?

'Eat, then. There's plenty.'

There was, indeed, plenty. Armand was a good cook though perhaps a trifle heavy-handed with the garlic. But the spaghetti bolognaise was undeniably tasty. Ellie discovered she had an appetite after all.

Kate said, 'What's been happening? What's that white van doing parked outside your house, and was that another one I saw just now? Which one is Neil's?'

Ellie brought Kate up to date with everything she knew. 'And I can't get in touch with this solicitor, and Mr Hurry's in such a state he doesn't know whether he's on his head or his heels, and I forgot to go to the police station to sign my statement. The good news is that Mrs Dawes is showing signs of coming out of it. We can only hope . . . well, we have to hope for the best, don't we? So what's your news? Did you see Felicity this afternoon, and what's happening about her mother?'

Kate pulled a face. 'She's been trying to get hold of her father all afternoon. She's bearing up very well, all things considered. Roy's not much help, though. There was some tangle with delivery dates on the vicarage site, something that someone was supposed to fix but didn't. So he's out of it. He told Felicity he'd be home at lunchtime, but of course he wasn't.'

'Danger: men at work,' said Ellie.

'Watch it!' said Armand, with his mouth full.

Kate pushed away her empty plate, and caressed her bulge. 'So what's the latest on Thomas?'

Ellie told herself she was not going to blush. 'He went off in search of his car when he woke up. Come to think of it, he probably needs a therapist himself after watching his old friend die.'

'Aren't you his sympathetic ear?' asked Armand.

'Shut up,' said Kate, 'or I'll kick you under the table.'

Armand was wounded. 'What did I say?'

Ellie did her best to laugh. 'He's a lovely man, isn't he? Or, no. I don't mean lovely. You know what I mean. But he's not *my* lovely man. Now I must go or I'll be late for choir practice.'

* * *

He couldn't remember when he'd last been so angry.

Well, perhaps when he'd done away with that fool, Russell . . . though of course he'd been drunk then.

He'd always thought of himself as an even-tempered man. All that stuff his wife had said about his temper — a load of old cobblers.

He'd tried two of the cards and lost them. Swallowed by the machines. And he still hadn't got any cash. He'd been so careful, too.

He'd copied out the numbers he'd found on the back of the calendar, and tried them out, one by one. The machines had still swallowed the cards! He couldn't believe it!

The machines must have broken.

AND HE COULDN'T COMPLAIN!

He had one card left. He'd almost tried it, but hadn't quite dared. He needed the card in case he had to sign a cheque somewhere.

He was hungry. He dipped into the nearest waste bin on his way home, and found some chips left over from a takeaway. They were cold, but he ate them, anyway.

How to get some cash?

There was one way. He'd noticed that the police had left a man on guard outside one of the biddies' houses, but not at the other. He laughed to think how long they'd taken to discover that first body. He could go back to the house which wasn't being watched and see what he could lift: a television, a stereo, a mobile phone. It couldn't be anything large, or he wouldn't be able to carry it. Unless, of course, he took the car and loaded it up and drove it over to a certain pub in Hanwell where he knew he could flog the stuff.

But it was too much of a risk to take the car out, wasn't it?

And neither of the biddies had had a telly worth looking at.

Maybe they had something else he could sell, though. The odd piece of jewellery. A ring or two? It was worth a try.

HE WAS HUNGRY!

A thought: there'd be food in their fridges, wouldn't there? And maybe a deep freeze with more in it? If he took a black plastic sack, he could fill up. It would last him for days. Till he'd worked out what to do about that one last card.

CHAPTER THIRTEEN

Ellie woke with the dragging feeling that something unpleasant was hanging over her.

She opened one eye to look at the bedside clock, groaned, and turned over, only to be awakened by the alarm ten minutes later. It was a new clock alarm. She hated it. It squawked. It had the raucous, angry buzz of a road drill.

Midge was still at the bottom of the bed, which must mean that the weather had been too dire for him to venture out. Ellie inspected the sky outside, and agreed with Midge that driving rain and sleet did not encourage one to leave the house. But, she must do so.

She had promised to go to the police station that morning, and do it she would. What's more, she wasn't going to be fobbed off with a desk sergeant, or whatever member of the lower echelons might be around. She was going to ask to see — no, demand to see — Detective Inspector Willis, whom she'd encountered on a couple of occasions in the past.

True, DI Willis' judgement was not infallible, as instanced by her choice of an unbecoming mahogany dye for her hair. Equally true, her manner was brusque to the point of rudeness, but the woman was not without brains and if only Ellie could get across to her that Neil was innocent . . .

A tall order. Ellie knew that, and dressed accordingly. Something businesslike was required. Ellie didn't *do* businesslike in her wardrobe. She did feminine or practical-for-gardening-and-housework. She did clothes for visiting relatives. She even had a couple of reasonably smart outfits for accompanying friends to events at the golf club or for going out to supper. When she had the trustees round for a meeting, she wore something clean but didn't bother to dress up; after all, they'd both known her for ages, and she didn't need to impress them. She had less than perfect statistics, black did not suit her, and when she went to buy clothes, she looked for comfort and something with a pocket to put her keys and hanky in. Practical rather than classic.

Today she chose an off-white woolly jumper over a grey skirt. She added a red scarf because the outfit looked too bland. Then took the scarf off because it made her skin look too pale. Then put on a gold chain which had been her mother's, and decided that would have to do.

What she needed was just one piece of evidence to prove that Neil couldn't have done it. Her belief in his innocence was not enough. She knew that.

She'd prayed about it a bit last night. Please God, show me how to prove Neil innocent. She'd also prayed a bit for Thomas. Truth to tell, she was rather worried about Thomas. Was he going to be all right? She'd heard that ages ago — long before he'd arrived in this parish — he'd had some kind of breakdown after his wife died. He'd been teaching at some theological college or other. Had he been the principal? Something like that. He'd had to take a break, and then he'd joined them in the parish. He'd written some books, hadn't he? They were probably far above her head and no doubt very clever. Men could be clever but idiotic at the same time: brilliant minds in bodies that forgot to eat and sleep and therefore landed them up in hospital.

She really did hope that Thomas was all right.

She wasn't going to ring him, or anything like that. No.

He hadn't turned up at choir practice last night, but he often didn't. He didn't sing regularly with the choir, but on occasion he was given a solo to sing and then he'd muck in with them all, jollying everyone along, making everyone feel better just because he was there.

The phone rang as she was on her way downstairs, and she nearly fell over Midge in her haste to answer it, but it wasn't Thomas.

'Mark here.'

Who was Mark? Oh. The solicitor.

'Sorry I didn't get back to you yesterday. We had a bit of a problem with another case.'

Yes, and a lad like Neil would be at the bottom of his priority list.

'I wanted to tell you that I saw Neil again. He's calmed down a bit now . . .'

From when he hit the policeman?

'And he understands the position he's in. I asked him if he could keep his mouth shut and not lose his temper again, and he said he thought he could. He's adamant he didn't hit his gran, and that the only time he went near Mrs Ball's place was when his gran asked him to get some of the ivy or whatever it was . . .'

'Portuguese laurel. It has rather distinctive leaves. You don't see it about very often.'

'Whatever. He says the nephew was there when he went to Mrs Ball's, and it was him who told him to get lost. He can't be sure exactly when it was, but it was about a fortnight ago, probably on a Wednesday. He says they were both very much alive when he left. He also says that the garden, though overgrown, hadn't been touched for ages. When you went up there, it had been disturbed, right?'

'Hacked down, torn up, and ready to be carted off in a skip. Did he say whether the fence was standing or not? When I saw it, it had been partially pulled down, over . . . over the corpse. Do they know who it was yet?'

'They didn't say. I must warn you I think they're going to charge Neil with manslaughter for Mrs Ball, and probably keep the charge for the John Doe on file. If Neil hadn't hit the policeman, we could say the case was all circumstantial and a first-rate barrister could probably get him off, though it would cost an arm and a leg. As it is, if they can't get a conviction on his assaulting Mrs Dawes, they'll get him on assaulting the police officer. They've got him coming and going. Do you want me to continue representing him?'

How depressing. 'Continue for the moment, please. And keep me informed.'

'Will do.' He rang off.

Oh dear. However much was it going to cost? Would the other members of the trust agree to her underwriting Neil's defence? It wasn't exactly what the trust had been set up for, and they'd have every right to object. She was comfortably fixed for money, but probably couldn't afford to finance a good barrister while a second-rate one probably wouldn't be clever enough to get Neil off.

Justice for the rich, and not for the poor? No, no. She mustn't let herself become cynical. She would consult Kate about it. Kate was one of the trustees, and always thought clearly.

She made herself some tea and toast, and the phone rang again.

This time it took her a good while to understand who was phoning. An agitated female voice kept repeating, 'Is it one of them that is there? Is it?'

'Who is it speaking? Please, slow down. Say that again.'

'Is Mrs Kumar.'

Who was Mrs Kumar? Oh, Mrs Dawes' neighbour. 'Of course, Mrs Kumar. What's the matter?'

'It is last night, very late, my husband is working late shift at the airport, and my son and his wife are with me all evening but after they have gone, I hear this noise next door, so I say again, is it one of them?'

'One of who?'

'Her family, of course. I think the house is empty, but there is someone there, I am not mistaken, I assure you. I phone to my son to come back, but he is almost home, and his wife doesn't want him to go out again. She thinks I am silly old woman making it up that there are noises in the night when it is only a dog prowling around, but I say no, it isn't a dog, it is more like a man. Only then she say it is one of Mrs Dawes' family that is staying there, and of course I see it must be that. I go to bed but I listen and listen, and soon the noises stop and I think yes, they are gone to bed, too . . .'

The voice ran on and on, while Ellie gripped the hall table. Neither of the Dawes children had stayed down in London and Neil was still in prison on remand. So who could it have been, moving around in Mrs Dawes' place?

'And then this morning, when my husband is come back home, I say to him that I hear someone in the house next door and they are sleeping still, and he go outside to have a look and he say that her back door is broken open again.'

'Did he go into the house? Is anything missing? Has she been burgled?'

'He not go into the house, no. He is tired after working all night. He say to me, someone will tell the police but not him because he is tired and wishes to go to sleep. He say I not to tell, either, because he doesn't like to go to bed and then someone come to wake him up as soon as he is asleep. He say, it must be one of the family, come back after seeing her in hospital, right? Am I not right? It is one of them? He's got me so up and down that I don't know which is up and which is down.'

'It can't have been Neil,' said Ellie, trying to think. 'He's still with the police. If you like, I'll try to ring Mrs Dawes' son and daughter, see if they sent one of their children down here by any chance.'

'If it is, why they not have key, eh? I say this to my husband, and he say I am silly woman, and not to poke my nose. But Mrs Dawes is always nice to me, and I say if it is her ghost then she wouldn't hurt me, and if it is not her ghost and not her children, then I want to know who it is.'

'Quite right, too. Mrs Dawes is still in hospital. I visited her yesterday, and she's coming out of her coma but is still unconscious. I'll check with her children, shall I? Give me fifteen minutes and I'll ring you back and let you know what's happening.'

'My husband, he gone to bed now. He cannot have phone ringing while he is sleeping.'

'Turn down the volume for the bell on the side of the telephone. Can you see there's a sort of notch thing that you can slide up and down? Turn that right down, and he won't hear it ring.'

Heavy breathing. 'Like that?'

'Probably,' said Ellie, hoping for the best. 'I'll ring you back as soon as I can.'

Well, well. She went to fetch the Dawes' family telephone numbers. It might just be possible to catch them before they went off to work. Or it might not.

She got Angie's out-of-work husband first. He said that no, none of them had been able to get away to visit Mrs Dawes yet, though they were hoping to do so that weekend. He said he'd rung the hospital a couple of times, and it seemed Mrs Dawes was getting on as well as could be expected.

He gave her a number for Mr Dawes at his workplace. Mr Dawes wasn't best pleased at being phoned there but confirmed that no, he hadn't been down to see his mother again. He said it was probably that layabout son of his, out on bail. Ellie found herself disliking him more every time they spoke. She told him Neil was still in custody, and what was he prepared to do about it?

Nothing, of course.

Ellie rang off in a temper. One more try: Trace, Neil's girlfriend. Trace was on the point of leaving for work, and said she couldn't care less what happened to Neil, and she'd packed up all his stuff and he could collect it when he liked, and if he was kept in jail then she supposed someone would come and take it off her hands, but no, she wouldn't dream of going round to his gran's, why should she, she'd never liked the old cow anyway.

So that was that.

Ellie rang Mrs Kumar back, and gave her the bad — or good — news. Mrs Kumar had regained control of herself by now, and was anxious to obey her husband and not be drawn further into the case. 'You tell the police, no? Tell them a man is in there last night, and what are they doing about it? If they come round, tell them they must be quiet. My husband needs to sleep now.'

'I'll do my best.'

Armand had gone off to work. Through the party wall Ellie could faintly hear Catriona chirruping away to her mother. Kate had the wireless or the television on. Kate was a good neighbour, she never had the wireless or the television turned up high, but you could hear it murmur if you listened hard. Ellie debated whether to consult with Kate before she went to the police, but decided that informing the police was her priority. Besides, if Mrs Dawes' back door had been broken open again, then the rain might be sweeping into the kitchen and doing even more damage than the burglar had done.

If it was a burglar.

How would a burglar know that the house was empty? Did burglars go round looking for houses where there were no lights on? Possibly, yes. But she wouldn't bet on it in this case.

Ellie nerved herself to ring the local police station. She gave her name and asked to speak to Detective Inspector Willis. A longish wait. Ellie fidgeted. Finally a voice — not that of DI Willis — said that DI Willis was just about to go away on leave, but would see Mrs Quicke for a few minutes if she liked to come down to the station that morning. Which meant, probably, that Ellie would be in for a long wait and fobbed off with some underling. What could Ellie say to get the DI's attention?

The weather was even nastier now than it had been early on. Sleet was turning to hail. Ellie looked out a library book and put it into a strong plastic bag, together with the daily paper and a bag of toffees. Winter coat, squashy hat, new gloves, mobile phone in handbag. She looked around. What else? Ah, she still had her bedroom slippers on. She sat down to put on her winter boots and the phone rang.

If she hadn't been sitting right next to it in the hall she'd have let it ring, but as it was, she picked it up. It was Felicity, wanting to talk, wanting to say that her father was looking out a good therapist for Anne, and did Ellie think it really was a good idea? Wasn't it the case that Felicity was just pushing her mother's problems on to someone else's shoulders? And what if her mother refused to see the therapist? The home still wanted her to leave.

'I'm sure you've done the right thing.' Ellie tried to be soothing, while easing her boots on with her free hand. 'You've no cause to feel guilty.'

'Oh, I don't. Well, perhaps a little bit.'

'It's always difficult to deal with emotional blackmail.'

'It isn't . . . oh, I suppose you could say . . . but she doesn't mean it that way, I'm sure. She's just so lost and lonely.'

Ellie suppressed a desire to tell Felicity that her mother was a selfish old cow, who had ruined her own life through self-indulgence, and was now trying to ruin her daughter's. 'I think you've hit on the very thing that would help her. It was very clever of you, Felicity.'

'It was your idea, really.'

'No, no. You realized exactly what she needed. Someone to talk to. Someone who will understand her problems, but won't allow her to sink into self-pity.'

'I don't know that it's self-pity, exactly. She's a lot to put up with.'

'You've done the right thing in getting her professional help. You have to think of, well, other people now.'

A long sigh. 'Yes. Thank you, Ellie.'

She rang off. Ellie reflected that it was easier to advise other people on family problems, than it was for Ellie to deal with her own. Ellie — like Felicity — could see what ought to be done, but had difficulty facing up to it.

Ellie sighed, pulled on her other boot and gathered up her things. She could walk to the police station. Give her some exercise. She opened the front door and wilted as a blast of sleet struck her. She went back inside and phoned for a cab.

While waiting for it, she wondered about phoning Thomas. It would be good to know that he was all right, not gone into a depression or anything. But she didn't phone him.

* * *

The police station had been in the same building for years, but had had a facelift with what looked like armoured glass on the doors to the vestibule. As the doors could only be opened from inside the building, Ellie spoke her name into a tin box and waited.

She was allowed into the vestibule by remote control. She was informed that DI Willis was busy, so was asked to wait. She sat down and got out the day's paper and made herself comfortable.

Two toffees and the fashion section later, DI Willis herself appeared and said they could go into an interview room. Ellie gathered up her belongings, and was ushered down a corridor into a bare room which contained just four chairs around a table. It was clean enough, but the air was fusty. Perhaps someone had been smoking in there?

DI Willis looked reasonably pleased with life. Perhaps she was planning to go to some Mediterranean or Caribbean island for her leave? There was a slight tan on her usually pale skin. Perhaps she'd been having a couple of sessions on a sunbed to prepare herself for exposure to the sun? Her hair had that dry, brittle look caused by poor conditioning. It was still that unconvincing mahogany colour, though perhaps in a darker shade than before. Was it an improvement? Ellie couldn't decide.

'I assume you've come in to sign your statement about finding the body,' said the DI, hovering in the doorway.

'Well, you don't need me for that. I'll find someone to look after you.'

'Which of the bodies would that be?'

DI Willis snapped to attention, looking wary.

'The first body, wrapped in a pink blanket?' asked Ellie. 'Or that of Mrs Dawes? Or were you referring to the third body, that of Mrs Ball? I didn't find that one. As for the break-in last night—'

DI Willis ground her teeth. 'What break-in? If you've had a break-in, why didn't you report it at the desk when you came in? You don't need to speak to me about a simple break-in.'

Ellie decided that the new hair colour was an improvement. Marginally. 'Look, I know that I'm only a housewife—'

'Who thinks she's got a nose for crime that would shame a sniffer dog.' The woman was being sarcastic. They'd never really got on, had they?

Ellie went pink. 'The thing is that people do talk to me, and sometimes I hear things that the police might not. Or things that they might not consider important, but which are, if you see what I mean. And in this case—'

Now it was DI Willis' turn to turn red, but not with embarrassment. 'Are you trying to accuse the police of—'

'No, no. Or . . . well, not precisely, no. I'm making a hash of this, aren't I? I wasn't going to poke my nose in, honest, until Mrs Kumar—'

'Who the whatsit is Mrs Kumar?' DI Willis was on the verge of losing her temper.

Ellie blinked. 'I really am sorry. I thought you'd have been properly briefed. Who should I ask to speak to? Not Ears, I imagine.'

'Ears?'

Ellie blinked again. 'I'm sorry. I shouldn't have said that. I don't know his name, but he's got bright red ears that stick out.'

DI Willis did some deep breathing exercises, and walked around the room, calming herself down. 'He's on my team. Do you have a complaint to lodge against him?'

Ellie was cautious. 'Would incompetence be grounds for complaint?'

DI Willis closed her eyes momentarily, then sat down opposite Ellie, taking deep breaths to calm herself. 'If you wish to make an official complaint, we'd better get on with it. Shall we get this down on tape?'

Ellie thought about that. She didn't want to make a formal complaint, did she?

No, because she couldn't substantiate an accusation of incompetence. Ears had jumped to the wrong conclusion, he'd proved himself a poor speller, but could that be classed as incompetence? And wouldn't it sidetrack the investigation? Which was more important: making sure that Ears went for spelling lessons, or that she put forward the case for Neil?

'I'm not laying a complaint against anyone. I just want to tell you what I've observed and what I've surmised. But you might like to send someone — preferably someone with more brains than Ears, and I'm sorry to have to call him that but he mumbled his name so that I didn't get it — to Mrs Dawes' house, which was broken into again last night. I don't know how much was stolen, but—'

'You discovered that, too, I suppose.'

'A neighbour, Mrs Kumar, rang to tell me about it this morning.'

'Why didn't *she* ring the police?'

'Her husband is on night shift at the airport and wanted to get to bed. He told her not to interfere in case they woke him up just when he'd dropped off to sleep. She rang me.'

'Why didn't *you* ring the police?'

'I came here to report it, knowing I had an appointment with you anyway.'

DI Willis smothered a few words which Ellie chose not to hear. DI Willis left the room and, before the door shut behind her, could be heard shouting for someone outside. Ellie took out her paper, and immersed herself in the Agony Aunt column. Not that it was called an Agony Aunt column nowadays. Now, it was called something posh. But that's what it was, all the same. Fancy that! she said to herself glancing at one reader's story. What people will do when they think their husbands have been cheating on them! She wondered what she'd have done, what she'd have felt like, if Frank had cheated on her. She shook her head. She was pretty sure that Frank hadn't cheated on her. If he had, would she have known, or at least suspected? She knew wives who'd suspected and pretended not to know anything and, in nearly every case, the man had stayed with his wife. Especially if she were a good cook.

Ellie went on to look up what would be on the telly that evening. She could do with a quiet night in at home, watching something that would leave her feeling better and not worse after having seen it.

DI Willis came back with the plumpish policewoman Ellie had met the day she discovered the body in the pink blanket. It was this WPC who'd had the nerve to inspect the body, leaving her colleague on the path.

Ellie had formed a good opinion of her, so got to her feet and held out her hand. 'Oh, it's you. Nice to see you again under happier circumstances. It was pretty awful, wasn't it?'

The policewoman avoided her hand, but smiled and ducked her head, taking a seat and laying a typed form and a notebook on the table before her.

'You've met?' asked the DI.

'When we discovered the first body,' said Ellie, smiling at the newcomer. 'I'm afraid I didn't catch your name because I was so upset at the time, but I can tell you—' she switched her eyes to the DI — 'that she's a lot braver than her partner.'

DI Willis said, 'I suppose we should be grateful for small mercies. This is WPC Mills.'

Ellie said, 'WPC Mills took my statement and got my name right.'

Mills pushed the form towards Ellie. 'Ready for you to sign.'

'Thank you,' said Ellie. 'Now, may I start at the beginning?'

* * *

Food, glorious food. He'd eaten himself silly last night, and not fancied anything for breakfast. He spread the rest of the food out on the kitchen table. The stuff from the fridge would be all right for a couple of days, but he hadn't dared spend long in the house, not long enough to search it thoroughly. He'd contemplated taking several bits and pieces while going through the house: a brooch here, a necklace there, a silver-framed photograph. But he'd realized he'd have to use the car to flog them, and he daren't use the car. So he'd left them. Which meant he still hadn't solved his cash-flow problem.

CHAPTER FOURTEEN

'You wish to make a formal complaint against WPC Mills?' asked the DI.

Was the woman being wilfully obtuse? 'No, I don't,' said Ellie, getting cross. 'I want to tell you what I've been thinking, and that won't be in the statement you've got there.'

DI Willis stood up, preparing to leave. 'You don't need me for that.'

Ellie played her trump card. 'What about the gardener? Have you located him and what does he have to say for himself?'

DI Willis looked annoyed, hovering over her chair. 'What gardener? No one's mentioned a gardener that I know of.'

Ellie said, 'Surely you knew there was a gardener working at Mrs Ball's? About a fortnight ago Mrs Dawes spotted some Portuguese laurel and a variegated ivy in Mrs Ball's garden. She's always on the lookout for unusual foliage for the church and for the flower arranging classes that she gives, so she fell into conversation with Mrs Ball and learned that she was going into sheltered accommodation.

'Mrs Ball gave Mrs Dawes permission to take what greenery she wanted. Mrs Dawes did take some, but couldn't carry away as much as she wanted that day. So she sent her grandson, Neil, to collect some more for her later on.'

'Ah-ha,' said the DI. 'So that places *him* on site.'

'There's no "ah-ha" about it,' said Ellie. 'Neil went up there at his gran's request, to ask Mrs Ball if he could have some more of the laurel. At the time of his visit the garden was still a jungle untouched by human hand. Mrs Ball said she was getting a professional in to clear the site and was going to let Neil take what he wanted, when her nephew interfered and told Neil to take himself off.'

'Ah-ha,' said the DI, again. 'So there was an argument about it, was there? Better and better.'

Ellie told herself it would do no good to lose her temper. 'Cut to last week when I arrived, sent by Mrs Dawes on the same errand. It was clear that Mrs Ball had indeed had someone in to work on the garden. Someone had hacked greenery down and started digging a trench. So I say again, who was it, and what do they know about the body?'

The DI shrugged. 'Neil Dawes, of course. He does odd gardening jobs.'

'Well, no,' said Ellie. 'Neil does do garden maintenance jobs when the weather's good but it's the wrong time of the year for outside work, so he's switched to painting and decorating for the winter months.' She was not going to mention that Neil had tendered for the job and been turned down. That was irrelevant, surely.

'All local jobs,' said the DI. 'He could have popped back there any time to dump the body.'

Ellie felt slightly sick. Had she unwittingly led Neil further into trouble? With an effort, she resumed. 'You can't be sure of that, can you, until you've found the gardener?'

'This is all supposition and hearsay,' said the DI, looking at her watch. 'It's not evidence.'

Ellie tried to keep going. 'What does the nephew say? He was heard to quarrel with his aunt.'

'Alibis from here to eternity. Besides which, he's got friends in high places. We have Neil Dawes right on the spot.

He's got a short fuse and admits arguing with Mrs Ball about taking some of the greenery. He hasn't yet told us whose body it was that he tried to bury there, but he will. We've conducted a house-to-house search, asking if they know of anyone who's gone missing recently. Nothing so far, but some member of the public is bound to come forward to report a missing person soon. In the meantime, Neil Dawes has been charged with assaulting a police officer and with the assault on his grandmother. Further charges are in course of preparation.' She stood, preparing to leave.

'Are you going to try to pin the murder of Mrs Ball on Neil as well? Why should he have attacked her, for heavens' sake? I tell you, Neil didn't do it.'

The DI was amused. 'You have proof?'

'No, but . . . have you really exhausted all the other possibilities? Neil thought some of the gang that hang around in the Avenue might have done it, because Mrs Dawes told them off one night.'

'They wouldn't bother with someone living so far from the shops.'

Faint but persevering, Ellie said, 'Neil couldn't have done the break-in at his gran's house last night, could he?'

'What? Well, no. It's clear the two events are unrelated.'

'You have someone working on it now?'

'Are you trying to teach me my business?'

Ellie made calming motions with her hands. 'I didn't mean to upset you. Of course you didn't know about it until just now.'

'The alleged burglary will be investigated by . . .' She clenched her hands into fists. 'One of my team.'

'Not by Ears?' asked Ellie in a tiny voice.

The DI ground her teeth. 'Unless you are prepared to make a formal complaint?'

'Only that he can't spell,' said Ellie. And then realized that she shouldn't have said that.

The WPC kept her eyes on her notebook.

DI Willis moved into heavy sarcastic mode. 'I agreed to see you this morning because I thought — mistakenly as it happens — that you might have some information for us. I even hoped you might have some local knowledge about the John Doe. To tell the truth, I'm a little surprised you haven't come up with a name, complete history including childhood illnesses, and the maiden name of the corpse's grandmother.' She looked at her watch. 'You'll forgive me, but I'm due to start for the airport in half an hour. So, unless you can come up with anything to help rather than obstruct our investigations, I suggest you return home and mind your own business.'

Ellie made one last try. 'Who will be in charge of the investigation while you are away? I thought all leave was cancelled if you had an unsolved murder on your hands.'

'Fortunately, that is not the case.'

Which meant they *did* intend to pin the lot on Neil; not only the assault on his gran, but Mrs Ball's death, and that of the body found in her garden. If only Neil hadn't lashed out when he was being interrogated!

The DI banged the door to behind her as she left.

The WPC pushed a form across the table. In a soft voice she said, 'Would you like to sign your statement now?'

Ellie searched her handbag for a hankie. She found a tissue and blew her nose. She felt wretched. How stupid of her to think she could help Neil by talking to DI Willis. She'd fancied herself as a white knight riding to his rescue, and had merely added weight to the evidence against him. She was sure that this new solicitor, Mark Something, would have advised her against taking her half-baked theories to the police. He'd probably disown her, when he found out what she'd done.

She blew her nose again, and tried to appear normal. She picked up the form and started to read the statement. It was all right, she supposed, as far as it went.

The WPC said, 'Would you like a cup of tea?'

Ellie sniffed, shook her head and tried to smile. 'I haven't heard of anyone going missing around here. Was it a woman? It seemed too small for a man, somehow.'

'It's a man, so far unidentified. A male body without an ID is called a John Doe. A woman is called a Jane.'

Ellie was bemused. 'I suppose the rest of him was under the wreckage of the hedge and fence, but somehow the body seemed too small for a man.'

The WPC nodded. 'You're right, but it was a man.'

Ellie said, 'They can't close the case till they find out who the body was and why he was killed, can they?'

The WPC shook her head. 'We did a house-to-house in the neighbourhood and put out the usual plea for information. Nobody's missing, and there's no match from Missing Persons.'

'How long ago did he die, do you know? How long does it take a body to decompose like that? Perhaps it was a natural death?'

'It might have been. We can't tell yet.'

'A week? A month?'

'Tests are being carried out. I can't tell you any more.'

'I might have another word with Mr Hurry. Or would that be interfering in your investigations?'

The WPC addressed her notebook. 'I'm not going on leave for at least a month. Maybe longer. But you can reach me at any time through the station.'

Was that a promise to listen to anything else Ellie had to say? Ellie's measure of self-worth had sunk to nil. Why couldn't she learn to mind her own business?

The WPC was showing her out. 'I believe you've lived in the neighbourhood for a long time. You haven't heard of anyone going missing?'

'No, I haven't. Could it have been a homeless person, who wandered this way?'

'Definitely not. We can tell from what we have of him that he's not been living rough, though he did seem to be fond of a drink.' A professional smile. 'If you did come across anything, you know my name and I'll be around for at least a month.'

Ellie buttoned up her coat. 'Thank you.' She pulled on her hat, and made sure she'd got everything with her. It was still windy outside, but the rain had died away.

It was only when she got outside that she wondered if the WPC had been trying to tell her that the body at Mrs Ball's house must have been dead for at least a month. And what was that about 'from what we have of him'? What on earth did that mean? That they'd only got half a corpse? Ellie shook her head at herself. She'd be imagining all sorts of things, if she weren't careful.

She set out to walk back home but instead found herself approaching Aunt Drusilla's. She wasn't quite sure why her feet had taken that route, except that sometimes — if Miss Quicke were not too busy at her money-making activities — she could be a good listener. Only, this was a week day and she was probably busy.

Well, even if her aunt were busy, Ellie could probably cadge a cup of coffee off Rose. She could do with something to cheer her up.

Rose was out shopping, but Miss Quicke was in, toying with a bowl of homemade soup. 'I was thinking of ringing you, Ellie. Help yourself to some soup. Rose has left a big pan of it in the kitchen in case I should fancy another helping, which I don't. At my age a little is enough.'

Ellie appreciated the soup and tried to put her troubles out of her mind. She did her best to listen to her aunt's problems which, it transpired, were concerned with Christmas celebrations. Ellie could hardly believe her ears. Miss Quicke hadn't concerned herself with Christmas celebrations in living memory.

'But, dear Aunt, won't it put you to a lot of trouble?'

'It's different now,' said Miss Quicke, gazing out of the window at the scatter of snowflakes falling gently upon her garden. 'Rose is upset, and I want to do something about it.'

'Ah. Her daughter doesn't want her for Christmas?' Ellie had no great opinion of Rose's selfish daughter Joyce, who was rapidly climbing the ladder at the bank in which she worked. Joyce had made a sensible marriage, but seemed to have no maternal instincts. Or much concern for her mother, either.

'Joyce went to her husband's family last Christmas, so it should have been her turn to come to Rose. I suspect Joyce is ashamed of her mother being my housekeeper.'

'And friend. How dare she!'

'Agreed. Joyce's in-laws are to spend Christmas in the South of France, and Joyce wants to go, too. Rose is devastated and I'm not having that. Advise me, Ellie. We could celebrate Christmas here, couldn't we? Have a big Christmas tree in the hall, and decorate the place. Rose would love to cook a really big lunch for a change, and the dining-room table seats ten or even twelve.'

Ellie blinked. Was this the reclusive, miserly, anti-social Miss Quicke speaking? In all the years Ellie had known her, Miss Quicke had never once offered to host a Christmas meal in her own home, being content to sit at Ellie's table and criticize. As for giving presents, for thirty years she had unfailingly given Ellie a gift token from the chemist's. A small one.

'You mean, have an old-fashioned Christmas here in this house?'

Miss Quicke's expression was, almost, one of pleading. 'We could do it, couldn't we? Invite everyone? Have games and a big pile of presents? You'd have to help me, though.'

Ellie ordered herself not to gape. 'Er, who were you thinking of inviting?'

'Well, my son Roy and his wife Felicity for a start. Rose tells me Felicity wouldn't really want to cook a Christmas lunch this year. Is that right?' The old woman's hand closed convulsively round the silver handle of her stick, and Ellie realized how much it would mean to Miss Quicke if Roy and Felicity were indeed to produce a child.

'You must ask Felicity, of course. But I expect she'd be thrilled. Only—' Ellie had a nasty thought — 'you'd probably have to invite her mother for the meal as well, and she's a pain.'

'I'm well aware of it. If she comes, then I shall seat her next to someone who won't mind her complaining. Perhaps,' said Miss Quicke, with a touch of mischief, 'someone who's slightly deaf?'

Ellie wanted to laugh out loud, but managed to control herself. Whatever next? 'Who else?'

'You, of course. Diana and little Frank. Stewart and Maria and their infant, whose name I cannot for the moment recall, but whom I understand is reasonably well behaved. I thought we could feed the children at a low table at the side of the room.'

Ellie delved into her handbag for a notepad, and started to jot down names. An explosive mixture so far.

Diana had always considered — wrongly — that she would inherit her great-aunt's millions, and had been furious when Roy had come looking for his birth mother, even though he hadn't a fortune-hunting bone in his body. Diana had never understood why Miss Quicke had chosen to acknowledge her illegitimate son, even though he loved his mother dearly. It hadn't helped that Roy had gone on to marry Felicity, a wealthy woman in her own right.

Diana would hate seeing Roy and Felicity so happy together, and her blood pressure would probably go through the roof when she realized that Felicity was pregnant and any child of hers would be in line to inherit the family fortune. Diana wouldn't like seeing her ex-husband and his new wife there either, particularly since Stewart's second attempt at matrimony had worked out so well.

Of course Miss Quicke was fully aware of all of this. The resulting tensions would no doubt give her exquisite pleasure.

'An interesting mixture so far,' said Ellie, trying not to grin too widely while totting up names. 'That makes nine adults and two children. Any more?'

'My old friend and solicitor, whose family is scattered around the world. He enjoys a family occasion, provided the wine is tolerable and he can have a little nap after lunch. I rather thought we might invite Thomas, too, if he has no other plans that day.'

Ellie kept her eyes on her pad. 'A kind thought,' was all she said, wondering if this would be too strong a signal to send to Thomas. Wouldn't it be telling him that Ellie's family accepted him as a suitor? No, no. What a stupid, old-fashioned way of looking at things. Of course he wouldn't think that.

'I'm not having Rose kill herself over it, either,' said Miss Quicke. 'She can cook for us if she wishes, and I'm sure she will wish because there's nothing she likes as much as providing for other people, but I shall insist that she eats with us. She's gone out now to buy all the dried fruits for the pudding and cake, but on Christmas Day I'm having the cleaning agency send in a woman to set the table, serve the food, clear away and put things in the dishwasher to save Rose's legs.'

'That will cost a bit.'

Miss Quicke produced her nutcracker version of a smile. 'You're always telling me I can't take it with me and, after all,' she turned pathetic, 'this may well be my last Christmas with you.'

'Nonsense,' said Ellie, 'you have every intention of living long enough to get your one hundredth birthday card from the Queen.'

'One lives in hope. Now, Ellie, about presents. You'll have to come with me to buy them. Some people are easier than others. You, Ellie, are difficult. I've wanted to give you something good for a long time but I can't think what you'd like. Some jewellery? A cruise?'

Ellie blinked again. 'Not really my style. I'm not a very wanting sort of person, I'm afraid. What I'd really like is to prove Neil Dawes' innocence.'

Miss Quicke was irritated. 'I want to give *you* something, Ellie. Not your lame ducks.'

Ellie felt like crying.

'Oh, dear,' said Miss Quicke. 'I didn't mean to upset you. I thought you'd got Mark Hadley on the case.'

'Well, yes and no. He's not exactly encouraging. How good is he?'

'I'm not sure. My own solicitor doesn't touch criminal work, but he told me some time back that he thought young Mark might shine in that direction, if he weren't such a lazybones. Too much money in that family for him to have to work hard. I rather thought you might spur him on to distinguish himself.'

Which probably explained Mark's attitude. 'You might have warned me. I hadn't the slightest idea how to handle him.'

'Tell me all about it. From the beginning.'

Ellie tried to present the facts clearly. 'Some time ago — maybe four or five weeks — a man got himself killed. I don't know who he was, or how he was killed, or even where. I assume he lived alone and was local, but I might be wrong about that.'

'I don't follow your reasoning.'

'He hasn't been reported missing, which probably means he lived alone and kept himself to himself. The police have done a local house-to-house search but I don't suppose they've covered more than a couple of streets in either direction from where the body was found, if that.

'I don't think he can have come from far away. Oh, I agree the body could have been brought in from somewhere else by van or car and dumped in the garden, but why would a murderer pick such an out of the way place as a dilapidated house on Englefield Road unless he knew it, and had worked out that the garden was ripe for a makeover? Surely the murderer must be a man who knew that Mrs Ball was doing the house up to sell, and seized the chance to get rid of the body?'

'A relative or friend of hers, perhaps?'

'I don't think she's got anyone apart from her nephew, which is why she's going into a home. The nephew isn't the murderer, by the way. At least, I assume he isn't because . . . oh dear, I suppose he could have been. I suppose that if he'd buried the body in his aunt's garden, and a gardener had begun work there and was about to turn up the body, the nephew would have had every reason to stop him working there. But that still doesn't answer the question of who the gardener was and why he hasn't come forward, because he must have become aware that there was a body there . . . Am I making sense?'

'Where is this road? I can't place it. My A to Z is in the dining room. Show me on that.'

Ellie went into the dining room, which had reverted to being Miss Quicke's office. It was true that the table could easily seat twelve. Ellie retrieved the A to Z from a stack of books beside Miss Quicke's computer, and found the appropriate page for her.

'It's up the hill from the church and then way off to the right. Quite a long road, as you can see. Mrs Ball's house is almost at the end of it.'

'It looks like the end of nowhere.'

'It is, rather. No shops, no buses, even. It's a between-the-wars estate. The houses down where Mrs Dawes lived — that's down here, way over to the left — seem better looked after, though they're all much alike. Three-bedroom semis, some with recent loft conversions, small front gardens, larger back ones. Yes, it is very quiet up there. The more I think about it, the more I think the man who disposed of the body must be local, although it doesn't mean he committed the murder himself.'

'You really don't fancy the nephew for it?'

'You'll laugh if I say that he's not the type, but he really isn't. No, my money's on the gardener.'

'So why have the police targeted Neil Dawes?'

Ellie sighed. 'It's all the fault of the Portuguese laurel. About a fortnight ago, Mrs Dawes spotted some in Mrs Ball's garden, and got permission to take what she wanted. We had this big wedding at church coming up, which meant lots of flowers and greenery would be needed. At that time the garden was an overgrown jungle. Mrs Dawes sent Neil — who has a van, of course — up to collect some greenery for her.

'He found the garden as Mrs Dawes had last seen it: a mess, untouched by human hands for years. Mrs Ball said for Neil to go ahead and take what he wanted, as she was going to get someone in to clear the place. Neil tendered for the job and was turned down. Her nephew arrived and told Neil to get lost. Neil left without the greenery, which is why Mrs Dawes asked me to get some for her.

'But by the time I arrived on Friday, the garden had been attacked by someone who had axed shrubs and plants and dug a trench and pulled down the fence. That's when I stumbled over the corpse. There's no way either Mrs Ball or her nephew would or could have made such a mess. It was wholesale destruction, done by a powerful man with the right tools. I conclude that Mrs Ball did get a gardener in, but didn't allow him to finish the job, which knowing the way she and her nephew used to carry on, is par for the course. Only the police don't want to admit there ever was a gardener, and are happy to pin the murder on Neil, along with everything else that's happened.'

'Such as?'

'I failed to get the greenery on Friday morning. Friday afternoon Neil and his gran had an argument because he hadn't got it for her, either. That night she was attacked and left for dead just as she was about to go up to bed. Neil has no alibi. The police like him for it. The police also like him for an attack on Mrs Ball, which probably happened the same night. Only in her case, no one found her till yesterday morning and she was very dead by that time. And before you ask, yes, the nephew has an alibi.'

'But the gardener hasn't?'

'The police don't want to admit to the presence of a gardener. Neil didn't attack his gran, you know. He was really upset by what had happened to Mrs Dawes. I know, because he was with me at the hospital that evening and I kept him with me overnight. But when the police came to question him, well . . . I think they pushed and pushed him until he hit one of them. So they've charged him with assault and remanded him in custody while they think what other cases they can clear up at the same time.'

'Cynic,' observed Miss Quicke.

'Realist,' said Ellie. 'My only hope was in young Mark, and I'm not all that happy with what he's done for Neil so far, although, to be fair, I'm not sure what else he could have done. Then I heard this morning that someone had broken into Mrs Dawes' house last night, and I thought that might help to clear Neil, but of course the police are saying the two events are not related.'

'They might not be.'

Ellie knew that. She looked out of the window. The snow had ceased to fall, and a pale sun was visible in a sky clearing of clouds. The wind was getting up again.

Miss Quicke said, 'Rose should be back soon. Will you wait to see her?'

Ellie shook her head. 'I must do something, I don't know what, but something. The policewoman said . . . it's probably nothing.'

'Even loners leave traces in the community. A pub they frequent? A corner shop? A milk bill unpaid? If I were to die suddenly and neither you nor Rose nor Roy were around, there'd still be bills flooding in, people ringing up asking for money and wanting decisions taken. There'd be solicitors and writs all over the place.'

'Point taken.' Ellie bent to kiss the old lady's cheek, while thinking that if the victim had been such a loner, he might have confined his shopping to the supermarkets and not bothered with milk being delivered. 'Now, I must go to the hospital to see how Mrs Dawes is doing.'

'And I,' said Miss Quicke, leaning on her stick to help her to her feet, 'will ring young Mark and give him a piece of my mind.'

Ellie felt a little sorry for Mark. But not very much. He hadn't been as much help as she'd expected. She rang for a cab, and was whisked off to the hospital.

The nurse who ushered Ellie into Mrs Dawes' room said that they were pleased with her progress. A different policeman was sitting at Mrs Dawes' bedside. He gave Ellie a cursory glance and resumed scrutiny of the sports pages of a tabloid newspaper.

Ellie sat by Mrs Dawes, noting that her old friend was lying in a more relaxed position on the bed. Her eyelids fluttered now and again, and she shifted her right hand to and fro. Ellie was more aware of the policeman this time than before. He seemed to be watching her over the top of his paper. It was unnerving, as if he was waiting to see her make a wrong move of some sort. Did he expect her to interfere with the drip on Mrs Dawes' hand, or smother her with a pillow or something?

Ridiculous. Ellie couldn't think of a single thing to say to Mrs Dawes. All her doubts and worries about Neil came rushing back into her mind, though she'd intended to be very calm and relaxed.

The policeman spoke at last. 'You a relative?'

'An old friend. A very old friend.' Ellie reminded herself that she was there to help Mrs Dawes, and not to gossip with the police. She took Mrs Dawes' hand in hers, and stroked it. What could she possibly talk about? 'Dear Mrs Dawes, I brought you an orchid yesterday. Have you been able to look at it yet? I wasn't sure which colour you'd like, but I got purple — no doubt you know the botanical name for it. I suppose I could look at the label but I'd probably pronounce the name wrongly . . .'

Mrs Dawes eyelids flew open and she stared up at the ceiling. Ellie half rose from her seat and, seeing her move, the policeman sprang up and bent over Mrs Dawes on the other side of the bed.

'Can you hear me?' he asked. 'Who hit you?'

Mrs Dawes' eyes switched to him, and then closed again.

'Who was it?' repeated the policeman, in an urgent tone. 'Was it Neil, your grandson?'

Mrs Dawes' head moved slightly.

'She said yes,' said the policeman, looking pleased.

'No, she didn't,' said Ellie. 'She shook her head.'

A nurse appeared at the side of the bed, taking Mrs Dawes' pulse, checking the monitors. 'She came to, right? Please keep your voices down.'

'She opened her eyes,' said Ellie, 'but I don't think she was fully conscious.'

The policeman was on his feet, ready to leave. 'She confirmed it was her grandson who hit her.'

'No, she didn't,' said Ellie.

The nurse hushed them. 'It's quite likely she didn't know where she was, or see anything clearly.'

'I'm ringing it in,' said the policeman, leaving.

Ellie sat down again. 'Oh dear, oh dear. Now what?'

'We wait,' said the nurse. 'It's early days yet. There's someone else outside waiting to see her. Her daughter, I think. I said she could come in when you left.'

Ellie wanted to say that Angie didn't seem to give a toss about her mother, but meekly left the room. It was indeed Mrs Dawes' daughter Angie waiting outside. And Angie was in a right state.

'What's going on? I came down as soon as I could, but there'll be all hell to pay at work when I get back. It's our busiest time of the year.'

Ellie couldn't help herself. 'I thought you were too busy to come down.'

'I was, but when you phoned about the burglary, I took the first train and then a taxi. The neighbour said the police came round for a while and then left, leaving the place wide open again! What are they thinking of? My poor mother's only left the house for a couple of days, and everything's been turned over, drawers out, her bits and pieces of jewellery tied up in a scarf and left in the hall, and the fridge and freezer totally cleaned out. Anyone could walk in and make themselves at home. We could have squatters, travellers, anybody! Wiping thousands off the value of the house!'

'Most distressing,' said Ellie, realizing that her worst fears about Angie were justified: the woman cared far more about the value of her mother's house than about her mother. 'But there's some good news. Your mother's beginning to come out of her coma. I do hope you won't tell her that anything's amiss just yet.'

'What?' Angie was sharp enough to realize she was making a bad impression.

'Oh, of course not. Not till she's better. I can sleep at the house tonight, anyway, and the neighbour said her husband would do something about the back door when he wakes up. But I don't like it. It's just not good enough.'

'I agree,' said Ellie, disliking the woman almost as much as she'd disliked her brother. 'Do go in and sit with your mother for a while.'

'After that, I'm going straight to the police, see what they're doing about the break-in.'

* * *

It was killing him, this business of not being able to get at the money. He'd got some food now. Enough to last him a couple of days. Tins and stuff. There hadn't been much in the old biddy's cupboards. What he really wanted was a good cup of strong tea with plenty of sugar in it, but he hadn't liked to bring away the half bottle of milk she'd had in the fridge, in case it spilled in transit. He needed milk for his tea.

There was one thing he could do. He could take the bus to West Ealing, using Russell's travel card. Russell banked at Ealing Broadway, but Lee couldn't risk going in there to cash a cheque. West Ealing was just far enough away that no one would know Russell by sight, so it might be possible to cash a cheque there. He could do the signature all right.

Yes, that's what he'd do. Then he'd go into the nearest supermarket and buy a heap of stuff. Maybe they'd take a cheque there, too.

He just needed to be bold about it.

CHAPTER FIFTEEN

Ellie took a cab from the hospital to the Avenue. She was thinking hard. Whether intentionally or not — and Ellie was inclined to think the woman had known exactly what she was doing — WPC Mills had given Ellie a lot of information.

First, the body of the man in Mrs Ball's garden had not been that of a homeless drifter; he had not been living rough. Presumably they could tell that by the condition of the skin. No calluses on the feet, for instance. And probably well nurtured.

So far so good. But what had the woman meant by saying 'from what we have of him'? That had set up all sorts of nightmare thoughts in Ellie's head. She hadn't liked to dwell on what she'd seen when she trod on the corpse, but . . . she gritted her teeth; it had to be done. A woman, she'd thought at first. Now it seemed it was a man they hadn't yet been able to identify.

Ellie knew that unidentified bodies were often traced through dentistry. She shuddered. Did that mean the corpse had no teeth, or — worse — no head? A line from an old song came into her mind. The ghost walked 'with her head tucked underneath her arm'. Nasty.

If he had no head, that would account for his appearing to be a short man.

As for fingerprints . . . don't go there, Ellie. Either the hands had decomposed too much, or . . . no, really don't go there, Ellie.

Which meant the police were going to have to rely on someone, somewhere, reporting that a neighbour or husband or son or whatever had gone missing.

The WPC had said they'd done a house-to-house search of the streets immediately around Englefield Road. Humph! It was a densely populated estate of houses, with a number of roads criss-crossing one another. Perhaps they'd only searched a small area because they thought it would have been too difficult for the murderer to carry a decomposing body far. Perhaps they'd realized it could have been transported to Mrs Ball's garden in the boot of a car, and so considered a wider search unnecessary. Perhaps they'd been constrained to search only a small area for reasons of finance. Or perhaps they'd given up as soon as they realized they had a local boy all ready to be fitted up for the crime.

Whichever. What it meant was that they hadn't looked very far.

In a way, Ellie could understand that. Doing a house-to-house search over a wider area would have been a tremendous expenditure of men and money. Not practical.

So how could Ellie help?

It had stopped snowing some time back, and there was no sign of it now on the street. The street lights were beginning to glow cherry red. The Avenue looked prosperous and inviting, with the shops beginning to put out their Christmas displays.

Local knowledge of Englefield Road implied local knowledge on the part of the murderer though not necessarily of his victim, who could have come from, well, anywhere. Did it make sense to look for the murderer, rather than for his victim? It might do. What did Ellie know about the murderer? He had transport of some kind, he had local knowledge and he could pass himself off as a gardener of sorts. That is, if the gardener really existed. No, he did exist. She had to believe in him.

But it wasn't much to go on, was it?

Could she assume that the murderer had gone on to attack Mrs Dawes and Mrs Ball? Yes. Though why should he attack two such inoffensive people? Well, Mrs Dawes wasn't exactly 'inoffensive'. But harmless, surely. The only connection between the two women was the Portuguese laurel, and that did not make sense.

Ellie sighed, and tackled the problem from another angle, that of the unidentified victim. Suppose for the sake of argument that he were local. In that case, he'd shop in the Avenue.

She was standing in the Avenue now. What would the Avenue say to a man living alone in this area? Was he a loner, or a joiner? No, not a joiner; somebody who belonged to clubs and attended classes would have been missed by now.

A loner, then. Would the Avenue be his home from home? Would he like coming here to pick up some meat from the butcher's, some fish here, a bag of potatoes there? Maybe not, because if he were a loner, he would shrink away from the human contact necessary with each transaction.

Would he patronize the little supermarket at the far end? They seemed to change staff every five minutes. In fact, Ellie had gone off the supermarket, suspecting she'd been given the wrong change for a twenty-pound note recently.

If he were a loner, he might well prefer to shop in the supermarket, where he could fill up a basket and pay for the food without exchanging a word with another soul.

Did he cook for himself, or heat up frozen meals? Would he buy bread at the bakery? Visit the post office to cash a giro — that is, if they still had giros for unemployed people? Of course he might have a job . . . No, no job. Or enquiries would have been made for him when he disappeared.

There were blocks of flats at either end of the Avenue. Had he come from one of them?

It was beginning to drizzle and Ellie was opposite one of her favourite places, the Sunflower Café. She was known there by face, if not by name. She went in and found a place at a table at the back. Some years ago one of Mrs Dawes' grandchildren had worked here. A nice girl. Doing well out in Australia, now.

Ellie decided that she needed carbohydrates, and ordered a baked potato with tuna filling, plus coleslaw on the side, suppressing qualms about adding to her weight. The good thing about the Sunflower Café was that they always gave you a decent sized pot of tea.

She ordered and looked around. Were there any single men in here? No. It really was more a place for women to come. Women with husbands and shopping bags, small children and buggies. Many older women like her. One with a Zimmer frame; good for her! There wasn't anyone here that Ellie knew to talk to, although she recognized a couple in the window. They spotted her, smiled and nodded. It was that sort of place.

One of the waitresses was trying to pin a gold-foil Christmas decoration above the till. It fell down, and the girl fell off the chair she'd been standing on. She wasn't hurt, but she expressed her annoyance in a loud voice, which made everyone look around and smile or frown according to their temperament. Conversation resumed.

Ellie remembered Miss Quicke saying that people left trails behind them. Bills. Paper trails. But this was not the place to start looking for a lone man.

When her food came, Ellie asked the waitress if any single men came in on a regular basis. Improvising, she said she was trying to find an old school friend for a cousin who'd gone abroad. A man living by himself. Did the waitress remember anyone like that? Perhaps he hadn't been around for a while? Her cousin was worried that she hadn't heard from him for some time.

The waitress was young and podgy. She shouldn't have been wearing a cropped top which displayed far too much bulging flesh, but she was obliging enough. No, she didn't think she knew anyone like that, but she'd only been there a month. She'd ask around.

Ellie ate her potato with relish and drank her tea. The daylight faded, and the streetlights turned yellow. The manageress, a cheerful soul, came out from the kitchen to tell Ellie what she already knew: single men didn't come in very often, but there were a couple who came up from the retirement home. Ellie didn't mean one of them, did she?

No, Ellie didn't. If someone had gone missing from the retirement home, the police would have been informed immediately. She thanked the manageress and paid the bill.

There was always the coffee shop opposite, of course. That was very popular, staffed by intelligent, hard-working students from Poland and Latvia and what used to be Yugoslavia and was now called something different. It was, Ellie decided, too friendly a place for a lone man. If he sat down at a table by himself, he might be bumped into by a buggy, or a toddler might try to hand him a book to read to her. Or young mothers would encircle him, talking ten to the dozen. No, he wouldn't have gone there.

Of course, Ellie knew perfectly well where he'd have gone if he spent time in the Avenue. WPC Mills had said the victim had been fond of a drink, and she hadn't meant café latte. There were two pubs in the Avenue, one at either end. Ellie had never been inside either, and quailed at the thought of doing so now.

What would her husband have said, if he'd been around? She couldn't remember his going into a pub, either, unless it was when they were on holiday and wanted a pub lunch. But that was different, wasn't it? If he'd wanted to meet someone for a drink, it would have been at the local community centre, or the tennis club or even at the Conservative club. Frank had been a convinced Conservative. But dropping into a pub for a quick half had not been his style.

Ellie tried to think of someone in her circle whom she could ask to go into the pubs for her. The only person whom she could think of, who wouldn't be totally aghast at such a request, was out of the question. Thomas would undoubtedly have been able to do it. But . . . no, she couldn't ask Thomas.

She was uneasy about Thomas.

She switched her mind back to the task in hand. The pubs were open now, and she was in the Avenue. She told herself not to dither, but do it. Bayleys wine bar was nearest. She pushed open the heavy door and went in. Scrubbed tables with ironwork underpinnings, heavy-duty banquettes, etched mirrors and a long bar counter. Everything looked clean, including the man and girl behind the bar. Flashy games consoles, low lighting, background muzak.

There were a scattering of people sitting around, some of whom were single men. Bingo. Now that she'd found the sort of place she was looking for, she didn't know how to proceed. When she'd been in such places with her husband for lunch, she'd always gone to sit in a quiet corner while he ordered. She had no idea, even, how much drinks cost. Or what sort of drink she'd like. Did they charge astronomical prices? How much cash did she have on her? She really ought to have drawn some more out when she passed the cash machine.

'What would you like, luv?' asked the girl behind the bar, who must have been only just out of her teens, if that.

Ellie glanced at the bewildering array behind the bar. Should she ask for a short? Or a sherry? Or . . . welcome relief, they had a coffee machine.

'Might I have a coffee, white, please?' She perched on a stool at the bar, feeling extremely out of place, but determined not to show it. They didn't seem very busy.

'Waiting for someone?' asked the barmaid, twitching a cup into place under the coffee machine and pressing buttons.

'Well, no. Not really. I was wondering . . . you see, it's like this.' Ellie plunged into the story about her cousin trying to find a school friend, who might have been taken ill or something. It didn't sound any better this time round, but the girl nodded, and asked the man behind the bar if he knew of anyone.

'What was it you wanted, luv?' he asked Ellie. Was he South African, or Australian? Ellie knew it was shameful that she couldn't tell them apart.

She repeated her story, thinking it sounded more and more unlikely each time she produced it. She really must think of something better.

He shook his head. 'We do get our regulars, locals, mostly. No one's fallen off the twig lately, so far as I know. He went to school locally, did he?' Before Ellie could stop him, he called across to a craggy, ancient man with a hearing aid. 'Cecil, any of your old mates popped off lately?'

Cecil said, 'Eh? What?'

The barman repeated his question.

Cecil cackled. 'All hanging on for their Christmas bonus.'

The barman said, 'He means the winter fuel payment. Keeps them going, like.'

Ellie's coffee came. She added a creamer and some sugar, as it was stronger than she liked. 'Thanks for asking. How much do I owe you?' She paid, reflecting that it cost less than at the coffee shop.

The barman was polishing glasses. Thirty-ish. Looked reliable. Might be the under-manager? He said, 'Your friend lost contact . . . how long ago?'

'Five or six weeks. They were supposed to meet up when she was over here but he didn't turn up, and she's lost his address.' Ellie shrugged. 'You know how it is. Now she's mad at herself and can't get in touch. She wrote to me, said would I ask around. The thing is, people who don't know London, never realize how big it is. They think that if you live in Ealing, you know everyone who lives in Ealing. But of course you don't. All I've got to go on, is that he used to drink here.'

The barmaid giggled. 'Maybe he wasn't so keen on meeting up with her as she thought. Maybe he went off round the world to get away from her.'

The barman smiled, shaking his head at her. 'Now, then, that's only one of Jack's stories.' And to Ellie, 'What's this man's name?'

'Ronald, or Donald.' Ellie became vague, pawing in her handbag. 'I've got his name somewhere. What was Jack's story, then?'

'Oh, Jack's well known for embroidering a story. I don't know how much truth there is in it. He said he'd heard of a chap who'd lived here all his life and hardly ever left the house, who upped and departed for foreign parts overnight. Sends postcards back from Singapore or Bombay, all sorts. Just shows you can never tell.'

'Vanished overnight, eh? That makes a good story. Is Jack here tonight?' said Ellie, wondering if this were a lead or not.

'He's only in Friday and Sunday nights.' A couple of middle-aged men had come in, and the barman went off to serve them. Ellie sipped coffee. The girl vanished behind the scenes, returning only to add 'Cod & chips' to the menu on the blackboard at one end of the bar.

Ellie didn't fancy eating again, so finished her coffee and left.

She hadn't seen anyone she knew in the café or in the pub, but as luck would have it, someone from church now bore down on her as she reached the pavement. She hoped she hadn't been spotted leaving the pub or it would be all round the parish in no time. Then she stiffened her back. What if she had been seen? So what!

Nice Maggie was burdened with plastic bags as well as her usual shopping basket. 'Ellie, well met. How's Thomas getting on? We hoped he'd drop into the Bright Hour this afternoon. He likes our biscuits, doesn't he, but he didn't come. I was just saying to Jean that we ought to contact him, get a key to his place so's we can get the fridge stocked up and that sort of thing.'

'Jean?' said Ellie, looking around for her.

'We met in the fishmongers, terrible queue, orders for Christmas, you know.'

Ellie wondered if Miss Quicke had already placed her order for a giant turkey, or was waiting to know how many of her family would respond to her invitation. And whether Thomas would accept or not. Ellie replied truthfully, 'I'm worried about him, Maggie. He watched one of his oldest friends die the other night and it really upset him. What does Jean think we ought to do about him?'

Maggie gave Ellie an old-fashioned look. 'She thinks — we all think — that he'll take more notice of you than anyone else.'

Oh. So they all thought that, did they? Time to put the record straight. 'Of course I'll do what I can, he's a lovely man, we couldn't have anyone better for the church, but I don't want to start people gossiping about him.'

'How can you stop them?' asked Maggie, shifting packages around. 'My back's killing me today. It's all the hanging around in queues. Why don't you pop round to his digs, see if he's eating, that sort of thing?'

Ellie hesitated. She knew Maggie didn't drive, and what with the wedding the previous week, her husband being retired and demanding grandchildren, she would have no money to spare for taxis. 'All right, I'll see what I can do. If you can hang on a minute, Maggie, I'll phone for a cab and drop you off on the way. Do you know exactly where his digs are?'

'Don't be daft! It's just at the end of the shops, here. His car's outside. I saw it and wondered about going up and knocking on the door, but then I thought I'd better not. Jean said I was being silly and ought to have gone in to see how he was doing, but . . . you know.'

Yes, Ellie did know. She also knew that Maggie never complained about a chronic back problem unless it was getting fierce. 'Maggie, I run a tab at the cab firm. I'm going to ring for one to take you home, now.' She took a deep breath. 'What number did you say Thomas is at?'

'Number . . . no, I can't remember. But you can't miss it. Most of the front garden's been paved over. There's no flowers or shrubs, just an apology for a rockery in one corner.' She dumped her shopping on the floor. 'I accept your offer of a lift with thanks. I've got the grandchildren coming round for supper and I've just missed a bus. I know there'll be another one along soon, but . . . well, thanks.'

So that was that. Ellie was being pushed to do something about Thomas, whether she wanted to or not. She rang for a cab, waited till one came and helped Maggie inside with all her parcels, then walked along to the end of the Avenue. There was a run of small, three-bedroomed detached houses beyond the bus stop. She didn't normally come this far down the Avenue.

Ellie had known in general terms where Thomas was lodging, but hadn't visited him there. She didn't know who had. She'd heard that while the vicarage was being rebuilt, someone's aunt or cousin had let him have their upstairs flat, fully furnished, at a low rent. Thomas had put his own furniture into store and moved in for the duration. Presumably the churchwardens had vetted the place?

Maggie's description of the place was apt. There were no gnomes in the front garden, but it gave the impression that they'd only just left. Most of the space had been paved over in ancient crazy paving, rather uneven. For the rest there was a rockery, a sundial and a miniature well-head, all very bleak without a scrap of greenery to soften their angularity. Thomas' car looked as if it could do with a visit to the car wash; all the rain recently had smirched it.

Ellie marched round his car to the porch, a semi-circular shape edged with red brick. A window bay bellied out to the left. Upstairs and downstairs, the windows were shrouded in net curtains. There was no light on in the hall downstairs, but a faint glow was visible in the bay window upstairs.

The place looked bleak, as if it liked repelling visitors. She rang the bell. And waited.

* * *

The cheek of it! The nerve!

That something bank had only let him have a measly fifty pounds on the card he'd proffered. He'd wanted to argue, but hadn't dared.

They'd looked at him as if he were trying to cheat them. He should have realized that there was a limit of fifty pounds on that card! He could see them beginning to ask themselves why he hadn't known.

He'd told them he was just recovering from flu and didn't know which end he was up. They'd accepted that, told him to go to the side and make out another cheque, not for three hundred, but just for fifty.

He'd almost run out of the door there and then. But he hadn't. He'd gone to the side, and carefully, slowly, made out another cheque, this time for fifty pounds.

Fifty pounds only! He could spend that in a couple of days. It was beer money, that's all.

Of course he could go back in a few days' time and cash another cheque for fifty pounds. Perhaps he'd choose another bank, though. Only, if he couldn't use the car he'd have to get the bus, and in this weather, it was no joke waiting around for a crowded bus.

He wished now that he hadn't left the old biddy's bits and pieces in the hall. He could have sold them somewhere, down the pub; not the local, of course. But somewhere.

He wasn't going back to his old job, that was for sure.

He'd just have to think of something else. There were plenty of well-heeled elderly ladies living around here. Widows, mostly. He'd panicked before, leaving too quickly after he'd done the biddies in. He could have taken his time, gone through their drawers, tried under their mattresses. True, he hadn't found anything much when he'd gone back to his neighbour's, but next time . . .

He'd pick someone with some cash next time. All he had to do was hang around by the cash machine in the Avenue till someone withdrew a tidy sum, and follow her home. By four o'clock it was dark. If it were raining, all the better. They'd be out shopping for Christmas presents. A nice present for him, if he timed it right.

CHAPTER SIXTEEN

Ellie rang the bell again. Nothing happened. She rang again. She stepped back to look upstairs. There was definitely a light in the window bay behind the nets. No blind or curtains had been drawn across. So he must be in.

She rattled the letter box. 'Thomas!' Nothing happened. But the house had a listening air. Was he ill? In bed? There were no lights on in the downstairs flat, and it had an empty look.

She tried calling Thomas' name again, and ringing the bell. Finally she called through the letter box, 'I know you're in there. If you don't come down and open the door, I'm ringing the police.'

Uncertain footsteps descended uncarpeted stairs. A dim light went on in the hall.

'Who dere?' A muffled voice.

'Thomas? It's me, Ellie. Let me in.'

After a pause, a bolt was drawn back, a chain taken off, and the door opened.

She swept in out of the night to face a depressing sight.

Thomas was clutching a large handkerchief to his face. His eyes were watering. He was dressed in what looked like Marks & Spencer's black lounging pyjamas under his heavy car coat. The house was freezing cold.

'Got a code,' he said, snuffling. 'Dote cub in.'

Ellie sighed. Was she going to have to play the part of Good Samaritan yet again? 'Back to bed with you, then. I just popped in to see if you were all right, had enough food and so on.'

'Beed id bed. Bedder dow.' He blew his nose and wiped his eyes. He was feeling better now? He didn't look it.

Ellie shooed him upstairs. 'Hasn't your landlady been looking after you?'

'Gone away. Od a cruise.' He led the way into the front room upstairs, kitted out in what looked like second-hand furniture, very much the worse for wear. There was a small television on the table, and the only heat came from a tiny gas fire. There were central heating radiators around, but they were stone cold. Pushed to one side was a stout wooden chair with an adjustable back; no doubt this was the one in which Thomas had spent the night when he'd given Mr Dawes his bed. Uncomfortable, very.

Drawn close to the fire was a cracked leatherette armchair with a blanket on it. Was that where Thomas had been sitting? There was a thermos and mug beside the chair. The reason he hadn't drawn the curtains was because there weren't any. Only nets.

This was appalling! The churchwardens surely couldn't have condemned him to this cold uncomfortable place if they'd seen it.

'It's dot too bad in subber,' he said, reading her expression. Not too bad in summer? Humph!

'When did you eat a proper meal last?' She didn't wait for his reply, but explored the rest of the flat. The tiny kitchen was bare and cold. The fridge held a few bits and pieces but nothing to tempt the appetite. Everything was scrupulously clean. She peeped into the bathroom. Ditto. No shower, but an antiquated water heater over the bath.

The bedroom was spartan and cold, cold, cold. The bed had a couple of blankets on it, and he'd put an overcoat over the blankets. No duvet. No creature comforts. There wasn't even a gas fire in there. No wonder he'd flinched at the idea of coming back to this place after sitting overnight with his dying friend. No wonder Mr Dawes hadn't stayed long!

'Thomas, this is ridiculous. Why didn't you turn on the central heating, and call someone for help?'

'Can't turn it od. All locked up dowdstairs.'

'They locked up downstairs and left you in the cold, while they went off on holiday? And I bet you took them to Heathrow or wherever.'

'I couldn't. Deanery meeting. It doesn't matter.'

'Yes, it does. You can't stay here. I won't take you back with me because it'll make talk, but I'll book you into a hotel somewhere. If the parish won't pay for it, then I will.'

'Gedding bedder all the time,' he said, wiping his eyes. 'All I need dow is a tot of whisky and a square meal.'

She surveyed the pathetic kitchen equipment. An ancient microwave that looked as if it might incinerate anyone who touched it, an even more ancient fridge. No oven, and no washing machine. A toaster and an electric kettle out of the Ark.

'Not even I could cook here,' she said. 'Throw some clothes on, and we'll see about getting you fed. Come to think of it, I did hope you could pay a visit to the pub at the other end of the Avenue for me. They do food, don't they?'

'Gib me a quarter of ad hour, and I'll be right with you.' He vanished into the bathroom, shutting an ill-fitting door at the second attempt.

She hadn't meant to suggest she go out to eat with him, but come to think of it, he really oughtn't to be let out alone at the moment. Men never did look after themselves properly when they had a cold. Mind you, a man with a cold was a very different thing from a woman with a cold. Women snuffled and got through a box of tissues and dosed themselves up and got on with life. Men gave themselves up to it, staying in bed far longer than a woman would think necessary, demanding tender loving care and hot drinks every hour and pampering with special food. Men!

She took the thermos and mug through to the kitchen to wash them up. There was no hot water. There was a water heater on the wall, but it had been disconnected and a 'Do not use' notice blue-tacked to it. It was the last straw.

He must have boiled kettles to wash up in. She put a kettle on to boil, and watched it switch itself off without boiling. Even the kettle didn't work properly. She sought for her mobile phone. She was past caring what people thought if she interfered. She rang both the churchwardens. The first one was out and Ellie left a terse message. The other was in, and Ellie told her exactly what she'd found.

'No central heating, only one miserable gas fire, no hot water or oven in the kitchen, inadequate bedding, and he's gone down with a cold. We'll have him in hospital with pneumonia if this goes on!'

The churchwarden was suitably horrified and promised to get something better sorted out. Ellie promised herself that if the churchwardens didn't do something, she would!

She heard Thomas move to the bedroom, and wondered if he'd been able to get the bathroom water heater to work. She phoned Jean, and then Maggie, telling each of them what she'd discovered, and asking what they thought she should do about it. Jean was sure she could find someone to take Thomas in, and would ring back about it later that evening. Maggie said simply that Ellie had better bring him round to her place, and she'd get her husband to shift his computer from the small bedroom. Thomas could muck in with them till something better turned up.

Thomas appeared in the doorway, dressed in a thick navy-blue sweater and dark trousers. He looked sleepy-eyed, but better. 'Are you moving mountains for me, Ellie?'

'Maggie's making her spare room available for you. You can move in tonight.'

'Maggie's got enough on her plate.'

'If you want something done, always ask a busy person.'

'Like you?' He was speaking more clearly now, but stuffing a couple of large hankies in his pockets. He found keys, assumed his car coat, and turned off the gas fire. 'They'd kill me if I went out and left it on. Did you mention something about food at the pub?'

'I don't know what it's like in there. Is it all right? Only I have a special reason for . . . I'll tell you all about it when you've got something hot inside you.'

The pub was large and user-friendly. Wooden floors, panelling, mismatched but comfortable thirties style tables and chairs. A more than adequate menu and friendly Australian bar staff.

Thomas was known there. Of course. He seemed to expect her to come to the bar with him to order, and so she overcame her timidity to do so. Looking around, she saw several parties of women only, and even one or two solo women. And of course some single men.

The food was appetising. Thomas got down to a steak and kidney pudding with enthusiasm. Ellie had ordered roast pork with all the trimmings, as it was something she rarely cooked for herself. Incredibly, Thomas still had room for a banana split after his massive first course.

He said, 'Bananas give you strength, and I feel I'm going to need it when you've told me what you want me to do.'

Ellie went pink. 'Well, there was something, but of course you don't have to do anything, if you don't want to.'

'After you've saved my life twice? Coffee? Perhaps I'll have a tot of whisky with mine, to help me face the future.'

'I'm sure Maggie will look after you beautifully.'

'I'm sure she will. Now, come clean. What's driven you out of your maiden reserve to seek me out?'

Maiden reserve, indeed! But perhaps the jibe had some truth in it. He was looking better. A lot better. But still heavy-lidded. His speech had cleared, too.

'Well,' said Ellie. 'If you think you can stand it, I'll fill you in on what's been happening, including the latest news of Mrs Dawes and what the police are or are not doing.' After detailing events so far, she ended up with, 'So you see, there might well have been someone going missing from this area, if Jack's story had some truth in it.'

'Apart from my landlady and her husband, you mean? No, joke. I didn't mean it.'

'I would rather like it to be them,' said Ellie, in a vicious tone. 'What they've left you with . . . it's unpardonable. Taking your money and using it for a cruise, did you say?'

'They're both in their seventies. He's got cancer, and she's got Alzheimer's. I don't blame them for taking the money and running with it. I know I should have done something about the heating, but at first it didn't matter much, because I'm usually out all day and evening. When the cold snap came, I thought about getting a locksmith to break into their quarters and turn the radiators on, but it was all too much trouble. I should be into the new place by Christmas.'

'You'll be down with pneumonia before then. You're not spending another night there, and that's flat.'

He yawned hugely. 'What a terrible woman you are, Ellie Quicke. Now, tell me what it is you want me to do before I fall asleep.'

'Ask the bar staff, or anyone else you happen to know in here, about Jack's story.'

'Is that all?' He wandered over to the bar to order a coffee with a tot of whisky in it, and stayed there, chatting for a while. Ellie noticed how the bar staff brightened up as Thomas talked to them. Once or twice they all laughed. Another man joined him at the bar, and then another. They all seemed to know him.

Turning away from the bar eventually, he waved to someone across the room, and went over to talk to them. A middle-aged couple, man and woman. They were pleased to see him, too. A single man, youngish, passing by their table, clapped Thomas on his shoulder, and joined in the conversation.

Thomas was on his way back to Ellie when a table full of women hailed him. He spent a few minutes with them, shaking hands with some, smiling at others. He drifted over to the door which led to the toilets and disappeared for a good ten minutes.

Ellie finished her own coffee, taking her time about it. She wondered why she'd been so afraid to enter pubs all these years. This was a friendly, family sort of place. There was a large children's playground outside, which would be pleasant in the summer. She supposed that some pubs were more family-orientated than others.

How would a lone man feel, coming in here? There were several men sitting by themselves, or clustering around the bar. Yes, they'd probably feel all right here. Not pressurized to chat, because the place was too big for intimacy. If the victim had spent time anywhere locally, it would have been here.

Thomas wandered back eventually. 'Hope I haven't kept you too long. It seems several people have heard the story about a chap who suddenly and uncharacteristically decided to take off round the world at short notice. They all seem to have got it from this chap called Jack, who's not here tonight. I think I've met Jack on the odd occasion. He's the original "have you heard this one?" man. Usually there's some basis to his tall tales, but you might need a magnifying glass to find it.'

'So you don't think anyone has disappeared?'

'I didn't say that. In fact, a couple of the bar staff said that they hadn't thought about it till I asked, but there is a regular they haven't seen around for a while. It might not be the same man, of course, and they've never seen him talking to Jack, but if you're looking for a missing person, he might be it. They say he's the sort of man nobody takes any notice of: smallish, spectacles, neatly dressed in an old-fashioned way. Quiet. Didn't usually talk to anyone. Never joined in any bar chatter.

'He used to sit in that corner under the clock all by himself and drink Best Bitter till closing time. He used to be in a couple of nights a week but not lately. They can't put a finger on how many weeks it is since they last saw him, but they think it was before this cold weather set in. The bad news is that no one knows his name or where he lived, though they said he couldn't have come far, because he always came with an overcoat and an umbrella when it rained so they don't think he had a car.'

Ellie sat back in her chair. 'It's a something and a nothing. Do you think I should tell the police?'

'He might have moved away, decided to patronize a different pub, or he really has gone travelling round the world. Will you have something to drink?'

She shook her head. 'I'm not used to going into pubs, as you've probably guessed. How can we find this Jack? What's his second name and where does he live?'

'The bar staff don't know his full name. "Jack" might be a nickname and not his Christian name, even. What they do say is that he's a local man, supports Brentford Football Club; he's a widower, they think. He's been away for a couple of weeks on holiday, only got back a couple of days ago. He meets up with his sister somewhere in the Midlands, in Birmingham, they think, and they take a coach tour together some place warm. They go away at this time every year.'

'He couldn't be the missing man?'

'No, he's very much alive. He was in last night, they say. He's in one or other of the pubs in the Avenue most evenings of the week, though not if the weather's too cold or it's raining. I expect that's what's put him off tonight.'

'The barman at Bayleys said he was usually in there Fridays and Sundays.'

'You've been trying out all the bars this side of Ealing Broadway?'

'No, of course not.'

'But you want me to find him for you?'

'You've done enough. I'll think of something. Maybe I can get the police interested in finding him.'

He blew his nose again. She wondered how bad his cold really had been. He seemed to be throwing it off nicely, now. Except that she could see he was tired.

She wondered if he'd been so thrown by the death of his old friend that he'd got depressed and not been able to fight off the cold virus when it hit.

They were not really at ease with one another now. It was all her fault. She'd reversed their roles, becoming the bullying mother to his awkward small boy. She didn't know how to put that right, especially since he wasn't making any move to assert himself.

'Come along,' she said. 'We've got to pack you up and move you over to Maggie's before they go to bed tonight.'

'She'll fuss over me.' He was almost sulky. Definitely into small-boy mode.

She suppressed a smile. 'It may only be for the one night. By tomorrow the churchwardens ought to have something sorted out.'

'I'm not staying with either of them. One believes in exercising to videos and the other has the builders in.'

Dear me, thought Ellie. It is most unlike Thomas to be looking on the dark side. He really must be unwell. But the thought of their snappy churchwarden forcing Thomas to join in exercising to a video had its funny side. It would do him good, of course. But . . . no. Not his style.

She'd just thought of somewhere he could stay where he would be warm and comfortable and not fussed over. But would Miss Quicke care to invite him? She said, 'My aunt wants to have a big family Christmas. She intends to invite you to lunch. Would you like that?'

He almost snarled. 'Don't treat me like a child!'

'Time you were in bed,' she said, keeping her tone light, and inserting herself into her coat. 'How soon will you be able to move into the new vicarage?'

He struggled into his own coat. 'They're halfway through the decorating now. Roy's hurrying them up. There's no carpets or curtains or blinds, and the kitchen's not operational yet.'

She ignored his peevish tone. 'Roy's done a good job, I think. I hope he let you choose the wallpaper.'

He grunted something which she chose to ignore. She said, 'When did you last have a holiday?'

'Don't be stupid. This is my busiest time of the year.'

She gave up. She'd had enough. They walked back to his place in silence. She rang for a cab while he pushed a few things into a rucksack, and after she'd deposited him at Maggie's, she took the cab on to her own place.

It was quiet in there. The clock in the hall ticked. So did the central heating.

Kate must have been in to draw the curtains, which was kind of her. Ellie sat down at the kitchen table, still in her winter coat. She was overtired.

Images of the day passed through her mind in rapid succession: the phone call from Mrs Kumar reporting the burglary; DI Willis' rejection of her attempt to help Neil; Miss Quicke's plans for a family Christmas which were probably doomed to failure; Mrs Dawes' struggle towards consciousness and the policeman's misinterpretation of her involuntary movement; Angie's selfishness . . . and then the visit to the pub where they must have thought her a right fool; and her interfering manner to Thomas which had obviously alienated him for ever. Each memory left her feeling more and more depressed.

She gasped aloud. And then the tears came.

One part of her mind told her she wouldn't feel any better if she allowed herself to cry, but the other part said she'd earned a respite from being brave and reliable and doing good to other people. And that part won.

She sobbed and wept until a furry mask pushed itself into her face. Midge was distressed, wanting to know what was wrong with his prime carer. Ellie hugged him till he squawked to be released. Even that tiny contact with the warmth of an animal who needed her, helped Ellie to reach for the tissues and mop herself up, only to wonder whether, when she'd crashed in on Thomas he might, just might, have been crying, too. And not dealing with the aftermath of a cold. A cold which seemed to have cleared up remarkably quickly.

In which case, she'd interrupted his grieving for an old friend.

She'd pushed in, laying down the law, removing him from his flat where he'd probably, being Thomas, not cared that it was cold or uncomfortable. And then forced him to ask questions at the pub about a man who probably didn't even exist.

She felt herself grow hot all over with shame. Humiliated. How could she have been so unthinking!

She fed Midge and climbed the stairs to bed. I'm so sorry, Lord. I've been such a fool. I feel dreadful. She pulled the duvet over her head, and felt Midge leap on to her feet and begin to wash himself all over. Oh dear, oh dear. I ought to have asked him if he'd like to move.

Common sense intervened. No, I oughtn't. I'm being silly. It was doing him no good at all to stay in that cold place. Please, Lord, help me not to be so impulsive in future. Tell me what to do and how to do it. There's so much trouble all around, and I'm really just blundering about, acting on instinct.

You know what I'm like, Lord. Not heroine material. I mean, I can feed people and listen to them grumble, and help a bit with my money now and then, like giving Maggie a ride home in a cab. But when it comes to the bigger things, like Neil being arrested, and Mrs Dawes . . . I've made such a mess of things, though I meant well.

Poor Mrs Dawes. Do look after her, won't you? And Thomas. You'll have a special care of him? He's spent himself looking after others, and now . . . I was insensitive, wasn't I? Bossing him around. Oh, dear. But You forgive me, don't You?

I don't know what to pray for, exactly. So I'll just have to say Over To You.

She hadn't expected to sleep well, but she did.

* * *

His luck was right out! If he hadn't known better, he'd have thought he'd been cursed by the dead man. He'd sat in the Broadway for an hour, watching how people tackled the business of getting money out of the cash machine. He'd found the right seat from which to watch them. He'd followed one woman who'd withdrawn what looked like a reasonable wad, but she'd led him a merry dance, going into almost every shop in the precinct. And then she'd gone up to the car park above the shops, got into a mangy old 2CV, and roared off in a blue haze. He couldn't follow her without a car, and he didn't dare take his car out.

He'd had a roll and a pint in the pub nearby and picked up a paper someone had left behind. He hadn't read a newspaper for some days. The racing section had been marked up by someone who obviously knew what he was doing. Big Time had been double-starred. Twenty quid, he'd put on it. And it had come in fifth!

How much had he left? Not enough to last till the weekend, even.

Things were getting serious.

CHAPTER SEVENTEEN

Ellie woke up feeling depressed. Perhaps she'd caught Thomas' cold.

She tried to focus her mind. If she was feeling depressed after waking up in a warm, comfortable house with a cat for company and the knowledge that she could leave it any time she wanted, then what about poor Neil, banged up in prison for something he didn't do? Well, he had hit a policeman, of course. She wasn't excusing that. He ought not to have done it however much he'd been provoked, and of course he would have to stand trial for it. Hopefully, if she got him a good barrister, he wouldn't get a custodial sentence — or would he? In any case, being in prison now should be punishment enough. Shouldn't it?

She thought about what his daily life must be like. A small cell, shared with someone, probably. Having to come and go as ordered by the warders. Not much exercise. No daily paper delivered for him. No friends popping round to see how you were. He must be worried sick about his gran, too. As for his father . . . least said. Even his last girlfriend had stopped caring for him.

The only person who seemed to care was one silly middle-aged woman with a bad habit of poking her nose in when it wasn't wanted. Well, the silly middle-aged woman might not be brilliant, but she could at least do something to help. What did it matter if people thought her foolish for trying to help? She would give the police the rumour about the man who had disappeared, and get them to search for Jack.

She would speak to Mr Hurry again, see what information he could give about the gardener who must have been working at Mrs Ball's at the same time as him. And stifle any doubts as to whether he'd really existed or not. Possibly she could also speak to the nephew, Mr Ball?

She drew back the curtains in time to see Armand drive off to school. He always went in early. It was still pretty dark and drizzly outside. She pulled on whatever clothing came to hand and went down the stairs, ignoring the winking light on the answerphone. She fed Midge and put some bacon on to fry for herself. She really fancied a bacon sandwich, and — though it was a bit of a fuss for one person — some good ground coffee.

She watered the plants in the conservatory while the bacon fried. Had she overwatered the cyclamen? *Could* you overwater cyclamens?

For some time, she'd been aware of someone or something tapping on the kitchen wall. On Kate's side. She stopped to listen. Was that Kate calling her name?

How odd. Why didn't she use her key and come round, or use the phone?

Was that Catriona wailing?

Had something happened?

Ellie went into panic mode. She turned off everything in the kitchen, picked the bunch of Kate's keys off the hook on the wall and rushed out of her front door, letting it bang to behind her before she remembered that she'd forgotten to pick up her own keys. It was raining, of course. She set the key in Kate's front door. She could definitely hear Catriona crying.

The morning paper hadn't been taken off the floor inside the hall. The layout of Kate's house was slightly different to Ellie's, but the child's cries were coming from beyond the kitchen where an extension to the house matched Ellie's conservatory. Kate's was heated and tiled and used as an all-purpose rumpus room.

Kate was half lying, half sitting on the floor, with her back to the toy cupboard, feebly banging on to the wall beside her with one of Catriona's toys, while the child pulled ineffectively at her mother's hand. Ellie noted the spreading pool under Kate's hips. Her waters had broken, and the baby was coming early.

Kate's eyes were closed. 'Sorry to trouble you, Ellie. Could you take Catriona . . . oh!'

Ellie scooped up the little girl, and gave her a hug. 'It's going to be all right, poppet.' Ellie had learned a lot about keeping young children occupied since she'd had to babysit for Frank so often. 'Shall we go and put a DVD on for you to watch?'

'No!' shouted Catriona, hitting Ellie. 'Want Mummy! Mummy, get up!'

'In . . . a minute,' said Kate, through her teeth. 'Be a good girl, Catriona. Go with Ellie.'

Catriona shook her head violently. Ellie continued to hold the little girl tightly.

'Kate, have you phoned for an ambulance?'

A pause while Kate stiffened, and then relaxed. 'Yes, but I told them there was plenty of time. Just one or two strong contractions about ten minutes' apart. I was going to ring Armand but Catriona fell and it sounded as if she'd hurt herself, so I rushed in here and . . .' She gasped. 'Oh! Oh, Ellie, I think . . . something's happening. It can't be so quick, can it?'

Ellie, survivor of more miscarriages than she cared to think about, knew that it could. She sat Catriona down in her own special baby chair, and gave her a biscuit to keep her quiet.

Kate was wearing a brown jumper over brown trousers. Nice and warm for a winter's day, but not a suitable outfit for childbirth. Ellie dashed to the kitchen for some clean tea towels, looked quickly for some rubber gloves — none in sight — and ran back to Kate, who was very sensibly trying to divest herself of her pants.

Ellie helped her, putting the towels under Kate. Catriona wailed softly to herself, biscuit and fingers thrust into her mouth. Ellie began to pray. If the baby came so early, before the ambulance men arrived . . . oh dear, but Kate was strong and healthy. Perhaps if the baby came now, it would be all right . . . but a lot better if she had it in hospital, in case something did go wrong. Dear Lord, help us!

Someone knocked on the door and rang the bell. Kate's eyes were closed, and she was breathing in gulps. Ellie ran to the front door to let the ambulance men in — actually two women — and directed them to where Kate lay. 'I don't think you'll have time to take her to hospital . . .'

They didn't, but the paramedics knew what they were doing. Ellie cuddled Catriona, carrying her into the hall to phone the school where Armand taught. The school secretary promised to find him and send him home straightaway. Who would look after Catriona while her mother was in hospital? Kate would have made arrangements, of course, but perhaps they didn't cover this week. Ellie tried the babysitter's number, but there was no reply.

She rushed back to Kate's side as the newborn child gave its first cry. He looked full-term. Possibly Kate had got her dates wrong.

'A fine boy, complete with all his bits and pieces.'

Kate was weeping, but her face was smooth and her lips curved in a smile. 'Look, Catriona. Your baby brother.'

Catriona, safe in Ellie's arms, was wide-eyed with astonishment. Ellie discovered she had been crying, too. The baby was the very image of his father, narrow-headed, with a fluff of ginger hair.

'Everything looks just fine,' said one of the paramedics, 'but better get you checked out in hospital'. One went off to get a chair from the ambulance.

Could Ellie look after Catriona while her mother was whipped off to hospital? Mmm. Catriona knew Ellie well, but wasn't used to being looked after by her.

Someone rang the doorbell. It was Felicity, her pretty face sobering when she took in Ellie's serious expression. 'What's wrong? Kate said we'd better work here today because she can't get into her car at the moment.'

Ellie said, 'The baby came early. A boy. Mother and baby doing well. In the rumpus room.'

Felicity rushed through to the back of the house and knelt beside Kate. 'My dear! How wonderful!' Her face was alight with pleasure as she touched the baby's head with her forefinger.

'It's my baby brother,' announced Catriona, standing over her mother in proprietary fashion.

'Indeed it is,' said Felicity, her voice soft. 'Perhaps I'll have a little boy soon, and then they can play together.'

'That would be good,' said Kate, smiling.

For a moment Ellie felt envious of the two younger women's rapport. Of course they would be friends, those two. There was a big age difference between Ellie and Kate, but not so much between Kate and Felicity.

Kate said, 'He was in a hurry. Just like his father.'

The baby snuggled and snuffled on Kate's stomach, wonderfully alive and wonderfully himself.

Catriona transferred herself to Felicity's lap as Kate began to complain about the discomfort of her position, lying on a tiled floor. The paramedic returned with a chair and hot on her heels — having broken all the speed limits on his way over — came Armand.

Ellie felt herself to be redundant. Felicity hovered, with Catriona in her arms. What was it about Felicity that young children would go to her without fear? Armand was ecstatic with joy to see his son, his own mop of ginger hair standing upright on his head from where he'd run his fingers through it.

Mother and baby were put into the chair and removed to the ambulance. Armand said he'd get Kate's overnight bag and follow on with Catriona. Felicity said she'd let them get on with it and would ring later.

Suddenly the room was empty but for discarded clothing, towels and bedding.

Ellie began to clear up, thinking that that's really all she was good for. Clearing up after other people.

She chastised herself. What on earth was she thinking, getting depressed like this? She was as bad as Thomas. Then she realized that this sagging feeling was due to the fact that she hadn't had any breakfast. She must remember to take the keys to her own house with her when she left, or she wouldn't be able to get back in. Kate kept them on a hook just inside the front door. Midge might well have eaten her bacon by now. He wasn't normally a thief, but half-cooked bacon left at the side of the stove might have been too much of a temptation.

She returned to her own house and shut the door on the nasty cold day outside. For a wonder Midge hadn't eaten her bacon, but Ellie no longer fancied it. She'd make herself some good coffee and toast. She'd knelt on the floor beside Kate and her clothes were stained. She'd put them in the wash and have a shower.

Clad in clean clothes, fed, and with her second cup of good coffee at her elbow, Ellie felt able to tackle the messages on her answering machine.

The first was from Diana. 'Mother, please ring me. I think you'll have to have little Frank next weekend. I assume that's all right.'

The second was from Diana. 'Mother, I wish you'd pick up the phone. I've had the most extraordinary phone call from Stewart. He seems to think that I'm not able to look after Frank properly. The very idea! Ring me, soonest.'

The third was from Diana. 'Mother? Where are you? This is urgent.'

Then there was Thomas. 'Ellie, Thomas here. I'm out and about today, looking for another place to stay. Maggie's wonderful, but she's got such a house full already I don't want to put more work on her. One of the churchwardens has heard of a place over the other side of the Avenue, and I'm going to have a look at it later.

'Oh, and by the way, I've just been to see an old friend at the retirement home. He's only recently gone there and is still having a lot of visitors. They tend to fall away after a while, you know. Anyway, he's also heard that story about someone unexpectedly going round the world. He was told that it came from the man's next-door neighbour, but he's a mite confused and couldn't tell me where the neighbour lived, so I'm afraid that doesn't get us any further forward. I'll keep an eye out for this Jack, anyway.'

So maybe there was some substance in Jack's story. Or maybe not. Maybe he was just a will o' the wisp, always leading them on, always just out of reach. Was this second-or third-hand story enough to get the police interested? Ellie couldn't make up her mind.

Ellie didn't feel strong enough to deal with Diana and her problems, but maybe she could do something for Thomas.

She rang her aunt and explained the situation. 'Now, if it's too much trouble or you don't want to be bothered, I'd quite understand. I haven't mentioned it to Thomas yet, but . . .'

'Of course. Send him over. It will provide me with an opportunity to do someone a good turn without lifting a finger to help. Rose said only the other day that she thought he was looking peaky, and she's sure he isn't feeding himself properly. He can have the spare bedroom which is big enough to be a bed-sitting room, and it's en suite. Rose will be delighted to cook for someone who likes a square meal, and I shall sleep better for having a man about the house. Tell him to come any time he likes, though I'd prefer it not to be when I have my rest this afternoon.'

'Thank you, Aunt Drusilla. I'll tell him.'

'Humph. Any news from young Felicity?'

Ellie was guarded. 'I think we can take it that she is pregnant and hopeful. I don't think we ought to make too much of a fuss yet, just in case. Oh, but there is some good news about Kate.' She gave her aunt a blow-by-blow description of the happenings of the morning, which made Miss Quicke chuckle.

'I like that girl Kate. Strong backbone. Remind me to buy a silver christening cup for the boy.'

Ellie blinked. Did people still give silver christening cups nowadays? Miss Quicke hadn't bought one for Catriona. Did Miss Quicke think that only boys merited a cup? Knowing Kate, Ellie didn't think her friend would be best pleased by a gift which took so much looking after. Silver and glass were both labour intensive, weren't they? Should Ellie hint that something in the premium bond line might be a more welcome gift? No. If that was what Miss Quicke wanted, then that's what she should do.

It was important to give Thomas the news quickly. Luckily his mobile was switched on, and she got through straightaway. 'Thomas, do you fancy a large bed-sitting room en suite at my aunt's house, with Rose to cook for you?'

A long silence.

'Thomas, are you there?'

'I can't talk right now. Can I ring you back?'

'I've got to go to the shops and then the police station. Miss Quicke says she'd be delighted to have you stay. Go round there any time except between two and four when she and Rose have their nap. All right?'

'Thank you, Ellie.' He ended the call.

He'd sounded constrained. Ellie hoped he was all right. She'd expected him to be more pleased than he'd sounded. She shrugged. She really must stop this habit of interfering in other people's lives when they were perfectly capable of getting things done by themselves.

She found Mr Hurry the decorator's number, and caught him on the job. He remembered her, all right. 'Hey, I've still got your glove in my van. I'm working the other side of Ealing this week, but I'll try to drop it back to you one evening, right?'

'Thanks. I'd appreciate it. And Mr Hurry, before you ring off—'

'Oh, that ceiling you asked me to finish for your friend. I fitted that in early this morning. The client's happy, I moved her furniture back for her, and I'll drop the bill in to you when I bring your glove over, right?'

'You're wonderful, Mr Hurry. But there is just one other thing—'

'You don't know Mrs Ball's nephew, do you? I could really do with him coughing up for what we've done so far. He says it's nothing to do with him and that I've got to sue his aunt's estate or something. As if I'd know how.'

Ellie crossed her fingers. 'I'll ask my solicitor how to go about it. Look, do you remember the gardener Mrs Ball had in?'

'Not really. I know she said she was going to get someone, but I was working inside and he was outside and that was only for . . . what? A couple of hours, maybe?'

'You did catch sight of him? I mean, there really was such a person in her garden?'

'Sure. But he hasn't anything to do with it, has he?'

'He might have. Did you tell the police about him?'

Silence. 'Mebbe not. Can't remember. I was upset. You know?'

'I know.'

Mr Hurry thought about it a bit more. It probably weighed with him that Ellie was paying the bill for the ceiling he'd just painted. 'You think it's important?'

'I think it was him who dumped the body there.'

'Yuk. I suppose . . . yes . . . thinking about it, that could be right. But the police said they had someone else down for it.'

'I happen to think they're wrong. Could you tell me something, anything, about the gardener? Don't think about it. Just give me what pops into your head. For instance, did he dress like a city gent, or in overalls?'

'Donkey jacket,' he said, immediately. 'You know, one of those big heavy three-quarter length coats with leather elbows and that. Jeans, I think. Big boots. Funny . . . I didn't think I'd noticed. I only caught sight of him through the front door that day when she took him out a cuppa and I was working in the kitchen. Donkey jacket and jeans.'

'Did he look really scruffy? Like a wino?'

'No, not like a wino. Not dirty. More like . . . more like an Irish traveller, if you know what I mean. I wasn't really looking, mind.'

'Was he taller than you, or a squat little man?'

'Hard to tell, in that get-up. About my size, I should think.'

Not that big, then. 'Earrings? Shaved head?'

'Baseball cap. I didn't see his face properly. I think, I can't be sure, the cap was blue, and that his hair was darkish and longish. But that might have been a shadow. That's all I can remember.'

'You've done wonderfully well, Mr Hurry. Lots of people wouldn't have remembered that much.'

'Hang about. I'll ask my mate, see if he remembers anything.' A pause, while he yelled at his mate and his mate answered. 'Sorry, Mrs Quicke. He didn't see nothing, except once he was out at the van, and he come back just as the nephew arrived and he, the nephew, started yelling at Mrs Ball that he didn't want to spend no more money on the garden, and she was yelling back, and he — the gardener — he just stood there grinning at them. Or that's what my mate said. Stood there, grinning. Coupla blackened or maybe missing teeth one side, my mate says. Mr Ball tells the man to go. He pulls down the fence, spiteful like, piles his tools on to his wheelbarrow and off he goes.'

'Wheelbarrow,' said Ellie, thoughtfully. 'You could transport a body in a wheelbarrow, couldn't you?'

'Wouldn't like to try it, myself.'

'Nor I. But maybe that's how it happened. Right under Mrs Ball's nose.'

'You think it was tied in with her death? That he come back and murdered her? Why would he do that?'

'Because she could give a good description of him?'

'So could the nephew. So could my mate, except that he's not one for noticing things much. He only noticed about the man's teeth because he's been in agony himself with a tooth that needs filling only he won't go to the dentist, and that's why he noticed.'

'Point taken,' said Ellie. 'I could certainly ask Mr Ball about him. How long after the gardening non-event did we find the body? You might have noticed the odd smell as soon as it happened.'

'Had a bit of a cold, didn't notice nothing. My mate's the same. There's a lot of it going around. Hold on a sec, I'll ask my mate again.' In a minute he came back. 'We think maybe one or two days. Mr Ball could probbly say.'

'So he could. Thank you very much indeed, Mr Hurry, and if you'll let me have that bill, I'll give you a cheque straightaway.'

'You couldn't make it cash, could you?'

'I'll see what I can do.' Now she definitely had to pay another visit to the Broadway.

First she must make a list of what she needed to do. The library books needed to be taken back for a start. She needed some more washing powder and a congratulations card for Kate and Armand. When she was down at the post office, she must remember to pay the paper bill, too.

Her mobile phone rang, but by the time she'd tracked it down to her handbag in the sitting room, it had stopped. She checked the number on the display. It was Diana, again. Ellie didn't ring back but struggled into her winter boots, found a warm scarf to go with her winter coat, and let herself out into the worst that a November day could do: driving rain.

First she took the bus to the Broadway, to draw out some money. She didn't fancy standing in the rain at the cash point in the alleyway, but went inside to get enough to pay Mr Hurry and tide her over. There was a queue of people waiting to be served inside, and several people sitting on the chairs at the side, waiting for their loved ones to conclude their business.

Ellie spotted a man in a donkey jacket, and giggled to herself that she'd be seeing them everywhere that day. It always happened like that, didn't it? You saw a man walking along with his arm in a sling, and sure enough, you'd see another within ten minutes. This man looked clean and tidy. Not a jobbing gardener.

Stuffing the notes inside her handbag, Ellie took the next bus back to the Avenue. Bother! She'd forgotten to bring her library books. Well, she'd have to return them later. She really must pay her paper bill at the newsagents. She didn't like to leave bills outstanding. Another queue. She couldn't help smiling as she saw a man in a donkey jacket pass by the window. By contrast with the first one, this man was fair and looked like a jobbing builder. There was paint on the overalls under his jacket.

She moved into the cards section of the newsagents, to find something suitable for Kate and Armand. Did she need anything else? Christmas wrapping paper, perhaps? Or how about buying some magazines for Mrs Dawes? How could she have forgotten her old friend! She must make time to visit her in hospital this afternoon. And what about the break-in at Mrs Dawes' house? Had the door been properly secured and what was Angie doing about, well, everything? Ellie thought she'd better try to ring Mrs Kumar, but at that moment she spotted a nice card for Kate, and forgot about it.

She picked up a couple of magazines she thought Mrs Dawes would like, but had some difficulty negotiating around a stolid youngish man who was reaching up to the top shelf for something. She apologized for bumping into him, and he ignored her. The oaf!

She was halfway to the counter to pay for what she'd picked up, when it occurred to her that a lone man who didn't socialize much, might well get his kicks — to put it crudely — from the soft porn magazines on the top shelf of a newsagents. She never looked that far up, herself. Once, many years ago, an old friend had tried to interest her in a campaign to ban such magazines from newsagents' premises. Ellie had spoken to the manager and been told that it was a fact of life that men wanted such magazines, and it was his duty to supply what was needed. Ellie hadn't pursued the matter.

Now she looked along the top shelf with interest. It was much as she remembered it. She supposed even looking at the covers might make some men hot and sticky. She wondered what the magazines were like inside, and decided that she really didn't want to know. The burly youngish man was flicking through the pages of one of the girlie magazines. His face was blank. He put that magazine back, and took down another one.

Ellie found herself moving slowly towards the counter in the queue to pay. After she'd paid for her purchases, she took a deep breath and asked if she might have a word with the manager. A youngish man was produced from the back quarters. Hard eyes, clean shirt and dark trousers. Polite.

Ellie said, 'This may sound strange, but I'm trying to trace someone local for an old friend who's lost his address. He seems to have disappeared off the face of this earth. I know he used to live alone somewhere in this neighbourhood—'

'Lady, do you know how many—'

'Of course. But I wondered if . . . you keep records of people who order magazines every week or month, don't you? I'm not talking about the newspapers you deliver every day, but about the sort of magazines that a single man might buy?'

'Oh. You mean—' he jerked his chin upwards — 'that sort?'

Ellie nodded. 'Have you by any chance been keeping copies of such magazines for a regular customer, someone who's failed to come in to collect them recently?'

'When people go on holiday, sometimes they miss a week. We expect them to pay up on their return, of course.'

'Of course. The man I'm thinking of is not particularly remarkable in any way. Smallish, glasses, doesn't drive a car. Maybe he's been ill and unable to collect his magazines. Perhaps I could settle his bill and deliver them?'

He scratched his chin. Sized her up as a respectable, reasonable customer. Nodded. 'Sounds like someone we know, yes. I'll get them for you. It's quite a pile. I'll put them in a bag for you, shall I?'

She was rather shocked at how many magazines there were, and paid the bill with a credit card, wanting to save her cash for Mr Hurry.

'There you are,' the manager said, handing over a receipt. 'Name and address on the bill, OK? And remind him there's another lot due on Friday. Hope he gets better soon.'

'So do I,' said Ellie, feeling the weight of her package. She wouldn't be able to carry much more. Perhaps she'd better leave the washing powder till tomorrow. Perhaps it would be a good idea to call a cab to drop the magazines round to the customer, just to see if it really was the man they were looking for, and then she could take the cab on to the hospital to see Mrs Dawes. And ring Mrs Kumar. And find out what had happened with Angie. And she supposed she ought to tackle Mr Ball as well, but really, there were limits to what she could do and, come to think of it, she was feeling extremely hungry. Hadn't had much for breakfast, what with Kate's little drama and all.

Should she go home and rustle up something quickly? The magazines weighed a ton. The bag they were in looked rather flimsy. She did hope it wouldn't break open and deposit its contents on the pavement. How humiliating that would be!

'Yoohoo! Ellie!'

She turned round and there was dear Rose getting off a bus, laden with bulky packages.

'So glad I caught you,' said Rose, 'Miss Quicke sent me up to John Lewis to buy some more towels for the guest room. We looked at them this morning when we knew Thomas was coming and decided the old ones were a disgrace. Miss Quicke thinks they may have been bought by her parents before the Second World War, and though of course they're of the very best quality and do an excellent job of mopping up, there's no denying they're getting a bit threadbare. Urgh! This weather! I was going to have a sandwich before I went home as I still have to get some fresh veg. Have you time to join me?'

'With pleasure.' Seeking the shelter of the shops, they scurried along to the Sunflower Café only to find that every table was full, and a couple were already waiting to be seated.

'The new coffee shop?' suggested Ellie. 'We can get a panini there.'

The coffee shop was also full, and there were people standing outside under the awning, waiting to get in.

'Only one thing for it,' said Ellie. 'Let's try the pub at the end.'

'Oh, but, I don't think . . . I've never been in there,' said Rose.

'It's nice,' said Ellie. 'I went there last night, and plenty of women go there alone.'

'Oh, well. If you're sure.'

The pub was crowded, too, but there were people leaving after an early lunch and they soon got a table. Ellie, feeling brave, ordered for both of them at the bar, and was pleased to see that they didn't blanch when she asked for just water to drink.

'Well!' said Rose. 'This is an adventure. I must tell Miss Quicke all about it when I get back. It does perk her up so when things happen.'

'Like Christmas? Do you think everyone will come?'

Rose held up one finger after another. 'Roy and Felicity for certain. Felicity's mother said she couldn't be sure, that she might have another engagement, but we both know she hasn't . . .'

'The very idea!'

Rose grinned. 'Miss Quicke said arrangements were being made to look after both the children who were coming.'

'Both the children?'

'Little Frank and his half-sister Yaz, of course. Stewart and Maria have already accepted. Diana wasn't best pleased about that, but realizes she's got to put a good face on it. Miss Quicke's solicitor, who is a delightful man, and she says he'll pick out some champagne for us. Thomas says he'll have to think about it, but we're sure he'll come, too.'

Ellie wasn't sure how she felt about that. 'Rose, it's going to mean an awful lot of hard work for you, even if my aunt gets some help in, and who is going to look after the children?'

Their food came. Risotto with sea food for Ellie and chicken pie with vegetables for Rose. Rose tasted hers with the air of a chef checking a trainee's first offering. Her face cleared, and she set to with an appetite.

'Well, you know Maria runs a domestic employment agency, though of course she's so busy with the family now that she has to have a manageress, well, she asked the same question and then she remembered that she has a married couple, quite young, Polish, on her books.

'They live locally and would be glad of the extra work over the holidays, and of course the great thing is that they celebrate Christmas on Christmas Eve with a seven course meal but the main dish is carp, would you believe, or was it some other fish like that? Anyway, they have their presents earlier or later in the month, I can't remember which, and Miss Quicke is going to pay them enough so that they can do everything I want done in the house and the kitchen, and all I'll have to do is supervise, and then they'll have enough money to go back home for the New Year to Poland. So what do you think about that?'

'I think my aunt never ceases to surprise me. A couple of years ago she wouldn't have lifted a finger to do anything for anyone else, and now look at her.'

Rose fidgeted with her fork. 'Ellie, you may not quite like this, but Miss Quicke wants to give you a really good present for Christmas, and she's thought of all sorts of things and now she's got it into her head that you'd like a fur coat.'

'What? Me, in a fur coat? I'd look like a barrel! And anyway . . . I don't think I'd feel very comfortable wearing one, Rose.'

Rose looked relieved. 'That's what I said, but I thought I'd better check. I mean, your dear aunt has continued to wear her own fur coat in the winter, and I don't suppose anyone thinks the less of her, but there are people who enjoy shouting at those who wear fur. I told her it wasn't quite the fashion nowadays, and so she's going to think about something else.'

'You're wonderful, Rose.'

Rose gave Ellie one of her brilliant, shy smiles. 'But it's you who are brilliant, Ellie. I mean, it was you who got me out of that horrid council flat with those dreadful neighbours, and gave me the chance to look after Miss Quicke, and have my own rooms in my own part of the house, and people to do all the hard work . . .' She took a sip of water. 'And it's not just me you help, but Thomas and Mrs Dawes and everyone. I always think you're like a knight in shining armour, going round righting wrong.'

Ellie spluttered over her food. 'Rose! Really! Whatever next?'

'Oh, I know the sex is all wrong, and I didn't mean you went around pushing guns into people's faces or beating them up like the private eyes do in those rather peculiar books in the crime sections at the public library, but somehow when things go wrong, you get busy and try to do something about it, whereas we ordinary people wouldn't know where to start and probably wouldn't stir ourselves to take action even if we did think we ought to. If you see what I mean.'

'What I think is, that we need some strong black coffee to bring us back down to earth again.'

Rose got to her feet. 'This is on me. Miss Quicke gives me such a big salary, I never get to spend the half of it, you know.' She hesitated. 'Do I go and order at the bar?'

'Do you want me to come with you?'

Rose stiffened. 'I can manage. I used to go into our local pub with my husband years ago, but he always used to order for me and this is so much bigger, isn't it?'

Ellie pushed her empty plate aside and while waiting for Rose to return, got out her mobile phone and phoned directory enquiries for the telephone number of Mr Ball. She rather thought Mr Hurry had given it to her but she couldn't find it in her bag. The phone rang. It might, of course, be his home number, and not that of his office, in which case, he probably wouldn't be there.

The phone was answered just as Ellie was about to give up. A woman's voice, hard and sharp. 'Yes?'

'Is that Mrs Ball?'

'Yes. Who is it? I never take any notice of sales calls.'

'Neither do I. My name is Ellie Quicke, and it was I who stumbled over the body at your husband's aunt's last week. I wonder if I could speak to Mr Ball, if he's not too busy.'

'He's at work. What do you want?'

'There's some question about the identity of the gardener who Mrs Ball employed to tidy up the front garden at her place.'

'Oh, him. The police have him in custody, already. A Neil something. If you want to know something about him, you'd better ask them.'

'No, not Neil. The other man.'

'If you were wanting him to do some work for you, you'll have to think again. Now if you don't mind I'm rather busy.'

'I wonder if you'd mind giving me your husband's phone number, so that I could—'

No. Mrs Ball had put the phone down.

Rose returned. 'Why the long face?'

'Don Quixote just crashed into a windmill. It's nothing. I was trying to do something to help young Neil, but . . .'

'That's a terrible thing. Poor Neil. We haven't seen him these last few weeks, of course, but he's always good for a laugh when he comes round to cut the grass and he put some new trellis up for us at the back and cleared out the old shed for us the last time he came around, and say what you like, I will never believe he attacked Mrs Dawes.'

'Agreed. She's coming out of her coma, you know. I must try to get round there this afternoon.' Ellie sipped coffee, decided that it wasn't as good a brew as in the coffee shop, but it would do. 'Rose, you've known Mrs Dawes for ages, haven't you? Even longer than I have? What do you make of her and her children?'

'Well, now, we do go back a long way, I suppose. We both went to the primary school on The Green, her with her long pigtails and me with my second-hand uniform. She was really skinny in those days, can you imagine, though I wasn't one of her friends, of course, since she was much older. We always thought she might become a teacher, but she married straight out of school. They had their own little house that he'd inherited from his mother and father when they died, and I was courting myself and ended up in the tower block, which makes it very difficult to be friends with people who own their own homes, if you see what I mean. Angie grew up to be very like her mother, really'

'And the boy?'

'Took after his father, who wasn't much use, as I remember. He worked . . . now where did he work? For the town hall in the street-cleaning department? Never did get ahead, though I can't talk, can I, seeing as my husband didn't do much to set the Thames on fire, either. The girl, Angie; didn't she marry a salesman of some sort? Went north to live and had two or three girls straightaway? The boy married a nice enough girl first time round, though I think it was shotgun, and then they had Neil, and say what you like, Neil's a good boy and he really cared for his gran.'

'I agree.'

'Those two, Angie and the boy,' Rose shook her head. 'Mrs Dawes has never said a word against them that I ever heard, but she doesn't say much *for* them, either, if you see what I mean. But she's always ready to praise Neil and one of his cousins, the one who used to work in the Sunflower Café, the one that went to Australia. The best of the bunch, she'd say. I must go in to visit her soon, only not today, of course.'

Ellie nodded.

Rose sighed, and gathered herself together. 'Well, I must get back, I suppose. Miss Quicke said I should take taxis everywhere to save my feet, and of course I wouldn't normally be so extravagant, but in this weather I think I might, don't you? Especially as Thomas is coming round at four o'clock, and I want to put these new towels in his bathroom before he comes.'

Ellie sat on after Rose had gone, leisurely drinking the rest of her coffee. One of the serving staff came to clear away, and gave her an inquisitive look. 'Was it you here last night? Someone said you was in with Thomas, asking for Jack. You just missed him. He come in after you'd gone. We said Thomas had been asking after him, and he said what for, and we said it was one of his flights of fancy about the man who'd gone to Australia, and he said it wasn't a flight of fancy, but the honest truth, though he didn't know if the man had actually gone to Australia or not.'

Ellie looked around. The pub was still doing good business. 'Is he here now?'

'Nar. Comes in lateish, not every night, but regular.'

'What's Jack's surname? Do you know where he lives?'

'Dunno. Up the hill, somewheres. You keep on coming in, you're bound to catch up with him sometime.'

'I need to speak to him, urgently, about his friend who's gone missing.'

'Not exactly his friend, and not exactly missing. A neighbour, he said, gone travelling.'

'Medium size, specs, not much to write home about?'

A nod. 'Sits in the corner over there, usually. Jake the Peg, I call him.'

Ellie looked a question.

'Jake the Peg, with the extra leg. Remember that song? Rolf Harris? Not that he's got an extra leg, but one of his legs is stiff. Been in a car crash or something. You having some more coffee?'

'No, no thanks. You'll be wanting this table.' Ellie got to her feet, and hauled the carrier bag on to her seat. The bag fell open, and Ellie felt herself begin to blush, as the contents were laid open to view.

A startled glance, and a quickly hidden grin.

'I collected them for a friend,' said Ellie, reddening.

'Takes all sorts, don't it?'

She wondered if women did ever buy such magazines, and if they did, what sort of women? She wondered if there were magazines specially for women who . . . ? She shook herself back to the present task, gathered her things together and departed for the ladies cloakroom.

Whatever next? The ladies was spacious enough. No queues. What she really needed was a large, strong paper bag to hide the magazines in. Perhaps she could buy one at the newsagents? One with Christmas motifs on would be good. Meanwhile, she would ring the police, see if she could get hold of WPC Mills and tell her about Jake the Peg, while remembering that that was not his real name.

She got out her mobile and managed to get hold of WPC Mills. 'Ellie Quicke here. I may have some information for you about the body we found up at Mrs Ball's. I hear there's a local man gone missing, supposed to have taken off round the world at a moment's notice, but everybody agrees it was a most uncharacteristic thing for him to have done.'

'Give us a minute, Mrs Quicke,' said the voice of WPC Mills.

Ellie held on, waiting.

'Go ahead, Mrs Quicke. What's this man's name and where does he live?'

Ellie suppressed the words Jake the Peg. 'He's local, a loner, middle-aged, unassuming, specs. He has the occasional drink at the pub at the end of the Avenue. I've got a lead on him through another local, a neighbour of his called Jack, who's been going round telling everyone about him.'

'The missing man's name, Mrs Quicke?'

Ellie smoothed out the bill she'd got from the newsagents. 'Mr R Standage, Oaktree Crescent, number 14.' It occurred to her that this must be one of the roads not far from Mrs Dawes.

'Mrs Quicke?' Another voice broke in. A man's voice. Not WPC Mills. 'Are you there, Mrs Quicke? Do you know how many calls we receive from the public when we put out a request for information on a missing person? Hundreds.' She knew that voice, which was that of the much-disliked policeman she'd dubbed Ears.

He continued, 'You will be glad to know' — he sounded smug — 'that our missing person has been identified. His widow came forward after we put out a plea to the public yesterday. He disappeared from his last known lodgings about six weeks' ago, at the same time as he threw up his job at the supermarket. Even if I can't spell to your exacting standards, I can't make his name out to be . . . what did you say you thought it was? Bandage?'

Ellie gritted her teeth. How humiliating! 'Standage,' she said, trying to keep her voice steady. 'What about the gardener?'

'Nobody else seems to have seen this mythical gardener of yours. But we have another witness who's placed Neil's van at the scene.'

'Have you asked Mr Ball about the gardener? Or Mr Hurry? They both saw him.'

'Why don't you let us get on with the job, Mrs Quicke, while you get on with yours?'

Ellie was silent.

He said, falsely polite, 'Thank you so much for your phone call, Mrs Quicke. I'm sure you meant well.' He didn't mean it. Triumph oozed from his voice. 'We have, of course, logged your input, along with the hundred other odd calls we've received. Do have a good Christmas, won't you?'

'Thank you, yes,' said Ellie, switching off the phone. She glared at the heavy bag of magazines at her feet. So she'd been chasing will o' the wisps, hadn't she? The police had traced the missing person without any need for her to put herself out, going into pubs — though that hadn't been a bad experience on the whole — and taking responsibility for a stack of magazines which belonged, as far as she was concerned, in the dustbin. She wouldn't put them in the recycling bin, even though Ealing was keen on recycling and had green boxes for collecting household waste of all types.

She wondered about burning them. But they weren't supposed to have bonfires any more, were they? Should she leave them in the waste-paper bin in the pub's loo? Well, no. The bin was more than half full already and she didn't like to think how the staff would react if they found a cache of such dubious material. Besides which, much as she deplored such reading habits, Mr R Standage might appreciate them at some point, even if he had gone off round the world or wherever he'd gone. The best thing would be to drop them off at his place some time later on that afternoon, after she'd been to see Mrs Dawes.

There was just one more thing she had to do before she left the pub. She didn't like carrying such a large sum of money around in her handbag in case it was stolen. There was an inner pocket in her coat, and she transferred the wad to that. Then she phoned for a cab to meet her at the pub, and went outside to wait for it.

* * *

Lee leafed through his haul. Twenty pounds. Not much for a day's work. He'd done better working at the supermarket. Sometimes he thought about going back to work. He had the house now and enough to pay all the utility bills. But going back to work meant he'd have to produce evidence of identity, proof of where he'd last worked and how much money he'd earned that year. He couldn't do that, or his shrew of a wife would be back on his case, wanting back alimony and extra Christmas bonuses and the like.

It was easier this way . . . if only he could work out how to access the bank accounts. The bank statements had come through. He had all that money there for the taking, and he couldn't work out how to get at it, except in fifty-pound lots.

Twenty quid was all he'd made that day. He'd decided to sit inside the bank, since the weather was so bad. Russell's winter coat was too tight across the shoulders, so he'd had to wear his old jacket. Sitting in the bank, he'd watched who drew out wads of money. He'd followed a couple of likely targets out of the bank, but one had got straight on to a bus and it had driven off before he could follow her.

The other he'd followed up to where she'd parked her car on the roof of the multi-storey. Luckily it was fairly deserted. She'd put her handbag on top of the car while she'd fastened her child's seat belt in the back and that's when he'd lifted the handbag and run with it to the lift. He'd heard her scream, but he knew she couldn't leave the child to follow him.

A man and a woman had heard the scream, and seen him run, but he'd done the age-old trick of pointing to the stairs, and yelling, 'There he goes!' That had put them off, nicely. The woman had been reaching for her phone even as Russell got to the lift and pressed the button.

It was touch and go for a moment. The thrill of it. He grinned, revealing teeth which could do with the attentions of a dentist.

Ah, he was the clever one! He got into the lift and pressed the Up button for the roof. He was the only one in the lift, luckily. He opened the handbag, found the wallet and extracted the notes. He didn't bother with the cards because he couldn't use them. Twenty quid. That was all there was in the wallet. He dumped the bag, got out of the lift, and sent it back down again. Someone would find the bag and return it to the woman, who was probably having hysterics by that time.

He'd taken a risk, of course. But got away with it.

What he really wanted was one big haul.

CHAPTER EIGHTEEN

The rain seemed to have set in for the day. When they got to the hospital, Ellie nearly left the magazines in the cab. She would have done, if the cab driver hadn't run after her with them. There was a good newsagents on the ground floor of the hospital, and Ellie went in there to buy a bar of chocolate for herself and to beg for a large stout plastic bag to hold everything in. Sometimes the people behind the till were obliging and sometimes they weren't. This time, to her relief, she got the cheerful young man, and so she went along to the ward feeling slightly more secure.

Mrs Dawes was no longer in the single room. The nursing staff said she'd been moved to another ward, where she didn't need to be so closely monitored. That was an enormous relief because it meant she was making good progress. Ellie was glad now that she'd bought some magazines for her.

The ward contained four beds. Two of the occupants seemed to be asleep, and one was talking on a mobile. Mrs Dawes was awake, half lying, half sitting in bed, a much-reduced bandage around her head. The swelling on her face seemed to be going down, but the discolouration of bruises seemed worse than ever. There was no policeman sitting beside her bed. Was that a good thing or a bad?

To Ellie's enormous relief, Mrs Dawes recognized her. 'Hello, dear.' Her voice was slurred but distinct.

Ellie sank on to the bedside chair, and felt for her handkerchief. 'Lovely to see you getting on so well.'

Mrs Dawes turned her head fractionally to see better. There was still a clip attached to her right forefinger, but otherwise she appeared to be free to move around.

'What a fright you gave us,' said Ellie, trying to hide her emotions, trying to speak softly and not upset her old friend. 'How are you feeling now?'

'Head . . . aches.'

'Not surprising. Shall I ask a nurse to get something for you?'

Mrs Dawes tried to shake her head, but desisted. 'They're very good, really. Tea-time, soon.'

Ellie knew in her head that Mrs Dawes was going to make slow process, but she'd hoped — how silly of her! — that the older lady would snap back to her usual rude health straightaway. Obviously it was not to be. Ellie damped her emotions a little, told herself not to make any sharp movements, and removed the magazines she'd bought for Mrs Dawes from the bag of more suspect items.

'Thank you, dear,' said Mrs Dawes. 'Reading makes my head ache, but I'm sure you meant well.'

Ellie grinned. Perhaps it wouldn't be too long before Mrs Dawes was back, telling everyone what to do and how to do it. 'One bit of good news,' said Ellie. 'Kate's had her baby. A fine boy.'

'Who's Kate?' wondered the invalid.

Ellie hid her alarm, because of course Mrs Dawes knew Kate and her family well. 'My next-door neighbour? Kate and Armand.'

Mrs Dawes closed her eyes. Maybe she did remember and maybe she didn't. 'Nasty old day out,' said Ellie. 'Nice and warm in here.'

'Has there been a frost yet? I told my son to put some fleece on my daphne bush.'

Her son? Had he been down again? What about Angie?

Questions could wait. Ellie said soothingly, 'I'm sure he'll remember.'

'Forget his own head, more like.'

The tea trolley came, and Mrs Dawes was cranked more upright in bed to drink it. Ellie was not offered any, though she'd have loved some as it happened.

Mrs Dawes became almost animated. 'Would you check for me, Ellie? About the daphne bush? In the back garden by the stone rabbit. It's four years old and still needs a spot of attention in the winter.'

'I'll do my best,' said Ellie, wondering if she could get through to Mrs Dawes' back garden through Mrs Kumar's house. Anyway, it would give her an opportunity to check out what was happening there.

'Angie's no good with plants,' observed Mrs Dawes. 'Neil's learning fast, but the finer points of horticulture still elude him.' Her speech was clearing fast.

Ellie nodded, wondering whether to say anything about Neil or not. Probably not. It would only worry the old woman to hear of his arrest and incarceration.

'That policeman,' said Mrs Dawes. 'I told him straight, but he wouldn't listen.'

Ellie nodded, trying to work out what was going on in Mrs Dawes' head at the moment.

'Such stupidity! He thinks that just because I'm older than his mother and have had a bang on the head, I don't know which day of the week it is. He even asked me if I knew who the Prime Minister was!'

Ellie knew this was a test question asked of those suspected of Alzheimer's. She said, 'What did you tell him?'

'I told him to get his ears syringed. How many times do I have to say I can't remember who hit me?'

Ellie tried not to let a sigh escape her. Mrs Dawes handed Ellie her empty cup with a hand that trembled. 'I'm going to have a little nap now, so you might as well go.'

Ellie gathered her things together and went to the nurse's station to see if she could get some information on Mrs Dawes' recovery. 'Doing well,' she was told.

Apparently there didn't seem to be any permanent damage to motor function or speech though, given the age of the patient, recovery would take some time.

Now to see if Kate had been discharged with her newborn son. Down in the lift went Ellie, and on to the Maternity Unit. There she learned that Kate and her son had already been sent home. So there was no need for Ellie to stay at the hospital.

She went into the café, thinking that the last time she'd been there it had been with Neil. Poor Neil. She felt so helpless. So foolish. She couldn't help feeling guilty because her interventions on behalf of Neil had only strengthened the police's belief in his guilt.

She got through a cup of good coffee — it was the best coffee she'd ever tasted out of a machine — and treated herself to a chocolate-covered shortbread. It was no good thinking about diets while she was in such a state.

The rain seemed to be easing slightly. If the clouds cleared, there definitely would be a frost that night. If she couldn't help Neil, she could at least set Mrs Dawes' mind to rest about her daphne bush.

Should she ring Thomas? She hesitated. Would he think she were interfering if she did? Possibly. She didn't know what to make of Thomas in his present state.

She phoned for a cab, and took it to Mrs Dawes' house in Oaktree Road. The wind was drying the pavements and the sky was clearing as dusk began to close in. There was a light on in Mrs Dawes' hall. Possibly a security measure?

There was also — most unwelcome of signs — an estate agent's board nailed to the gatepost. With a sinking feeling, Ellie recognized the entwined signs of the double D, Denis and Diana's agency. For Sale.

Had Mrs Dawes actually agreed to sell her house? It seemed unlikely, given her present slightly confused state. It was not impossible, of course, but . . . no, it was most unlikely. Mrs Dawes valued her independence.

Of course other people — such as Denis and Diana — wouldn't see it that way. Ellie could almost hear their reasoning: Mrs Dawes was elderly; Mrs Dawes had had a horrible experience; she'd probably lost her marbles, and certainly lost her mobility; it would be a kindness to sell her house for her, so that she could go into a retirement home and be properly looked after; it would be best to put the house on the market for her as soon as possible.

Alternatively, either of her offspring might have convinced themselves that they were doing the right thing by putting the house on the market, especially if they thought they could share in the proceeds of the sale. Ellie remembered that Angie's husband was out of work and she had a brood of children to look after, and that her brother had a demanding second wife and new baby.

The only thing that wasn't quite clear was how the two Ds had been able to act so quickly. Perhaps they'd also managed to put a sign up outside Mrs Ball's house already? Well, Mrs Ball's house was too far away for Ellie to go traipsing up there in the dark and it wasn't, she assured herself, any of her business, either.

There were lights on in the Kumar's house next door, so Ellie went up the path, and rang their bell. There was a muted chime indoors, and Ellie remembered that Mr Kumar liked to have his sleep when he came off night shift at the airport. It was Mrs Kumar who opened the door and Ellie hastened to apologize.

'I'm so sorry to trouble you. I hope I haven't woken your husband.'

Mrs Kumar held the door wide open. 'Please to come in. He is doing extra shift today for a friend. I am all alone, and I worry all the time about what is happening next door and I am thinking to ring you, and here you are.'

Ellie followed her hostess into a brightly decorated room crammed with large chairs. There was a huge plasma screen television on the wall and an air of comfort.

'Will you take some tea, Mrs Quicke?'

'No, thank you. I've just had some at the hospital. I was visiting Mrs Dawes, and she seems to be coming round nicely. It may take time, of course. She wanted me to give one of her precious plants some protection against the frosts.'

Mrs Kumar's eyes were bright. She sank on to a big over-stuffed chair, and gestured to Ellie to sit, too. 'I say to my husband, will I go to the hospital to see Mrs Dawes, but he say no, no, she will not wish to see me, so I stay put.'

'I'm sure she will like to see you very soon, but I'm not sure she should be given any unwelcome news yet. That's why I wanted to speak to you. Do you know how the For Sale sign came to be outside her gate?'

'That is it! That is exactly it! I say to my husband, Mrs Dawes loves her house and absolutely she loves her garden, and she is ready to pass on if she gives it up, but he says it is her house to do what she likes. Only, I am not one hundred per cent sure that this is what she likes.'

'Neither am I,' said Ellie. 'Tell me, did her daughter arrange it?'

'Angie!' Mrs Kumar almost spat. 'What a name. She needs a man's name, that one! She knocks on my door and rings the bell loud, loud, to wake my husband, but luckily he has gone to work. She say she stays next door so nothing else is stolen, and her eyes go all round the room and I am thinking that she is looking for all the things that are stolen from Mrs Dawes, and it makes me very much afraid and I wish my husband come home.'

'Oh, dear,' said Ellie.

'But then she say she is to arrange for locksmith to mend the back door, and she is to come back at nights to stay, until Mrs Dawes comes to "rational decision". That's what she say. "Rational decision". Then she is gone, but later there is a terrible shouting next door, and I am going to ring my son to come here to be with me, when it stops.'

'Was it Mrs Dawes' son?'

'Yes, him. The next morning it is him at the door, saying he is going to be coming and going and telling me to get someone to clean up the house for him as he is going to sell it. He intends for me to clean the house for him!'

Mrs Kumar's house was spotless.

Ellie said, 'I was going to do something about it myself. We don't want Mrs Dawes to come out of hospital to see it in such a state. I know a good cleaning agency. Shall I ask them to do it?'

Mrs Kumar flushed with indignation. 'Is he thinking that I have to go out to clean houses, to feed my husband?'

'Probably,' said Ellie. 'I don't think he's a very nice man. You leave it to me, and I'll get it sorted.' Maria's agency would be able to work wonders, even if the carpet would have to be replaced and the walls repainted.

'I am thinking before he says this, that my daughter-in-law and I will go in and see what we can do, but after he say that . . . !'

'Exactly. So did he contact the estate agent, or did they contact him?'

'There are these fliers come through the door. Mrs Dawes has one too, of course. He contacts them, and they come straight over this morning to take photographs and measurements, and then the sign goes up this afternoon. The locksmith is coming, too. He — the son — is still there, and he lets them in. Then maybe an hour ago he comes in to say he is having to go back north, and he talks as if I am his servant, saying to go in twice a day and turn on the lights and turn off the lights and draw the curtains.'

'And you did it. Not for him, but for Mrs Dawes.'

'Yes, I do it.' Mrs Kumar's indignation subsided. 'I turn the heating down low, so there is no pipes bursting, and I am going to clean her fridge, but there is nothing left. Some stale milk and some herbs, and that is all.'

'You are a good neighbour. Mrs Dawes will be grateful.'

'Not if they are selling her house.'

No. Not if her house were sold over her head. Ellie said, 'I don't believe that Mrs Dawes has agreed to sell her house. Not when she asked me to look after one of her plants. I don't think we ought to talk to her about it at the moment, either. She's not fit. I agree with you that in good health, she wouldn't wish to leave the place, but I suppose we must remember that she may not be quite as . . . as strong in future. So we'll get the place cleaned up, and wait to see what happens.'

'But that man is selling the house all the time she is in hospital!'

Ellie reached for her handbag to get out her mobile. 'Trust me to put a stop to that. My daughter is one of the Ds on the sign.' She pressed buttons and got Diana.

'Diana, can we talk? No, not about Frank or the weekend. This is business. I believe you and Denis have been offered the sale of Mrs Dawes' house—'

'Now, mother, don't you start—'

'No, let me finish. I know that it was her son or daughter who authorized you to sell the house, but the fact is I visited her in hospital today and she is recovering fast. In fact, she wanted me to check on something in her garden for her. Does that sound as if she wants to sell?'

'Her son said—'

'The point is, Diana, that it is only five days since she was attacked and no one can tell yet whether she wants to sell or not.'

'At her age, with her injuries . . . her son said the sooner we could get a reasonable deal . . . and you know we need the sale.'

'You were good enough to say you regarded me as your partner,' said Ellie, 'so I'm taking the liberty of giving you some advice. Keep the house on your books for the moment. Keep the For Sale sign up. But if you do get a nibble, don't show anyone round, or accept any offer for it, until we see how Mrs Dawes progresses. All right?'

Diana muttered something, which Ellie asked her to repeat.

'Denis will half kill me, Mother. I can't go back to him now and say that we haven't got the house.'

'I suppose you've got Mrs Ball's house, have you?'

'Yes, of course. But I promised Mr Dawes—'

'Then you'll have to un-promise him, won't you? Meanwhile, I'm asking Maria to clean up the mess at Mrs Dawes' house. The carpet will probably have to go, but we can make the place look reasonable for her return.'

Diana did some heavy breathing, and flicked the phone off.

'So far, so good,' said Ellie to Mrs Kumar. 'If they do start showing people around, will you let me know straightaway?'

'If Mrs Dawes is wishing to sell, my husband is deciding to make an offer for it. Our second son is looking for something in this neighbourhood and we are thinking it is good to have him next door.'

'Yes, of course,' said Ellie, wondering whether this was good or bad news. 'Now, would you like to come next door with me so that we can assess what cleaning needs to be done? Then I'd better see about putting some protection round this famous daphne plant in Mrs Dawes' garden. Have you a torch I can borrow, to see what I'm doing?'

* * *

As Ellie left Mrs Kumar's house, she noticed that the wind and rain both seemed to have dropped, but the air was biting cold on her face. It would do her good to have a brisk walk back down the hill to her house.

The door opened again behind her. 'Mrs Quicke, are you not forgetting something?'

Mrs Kumar held out the bag of girlie magazines. Ellie flinched. 'Oh dear. I collected them for someone. Thank you. I suppose I'd better deliver them while I'm in the neighbourhood. Do you happen to know exactly where Oaktree Crescent is?'

Mrs Kumar gestured to the right. 'Is right behind. This road — Oaktree Road — is going round in a circle, and turning into Oaktree Crescent at the top.'

Ellie thought, She's going to say, you can't miss it. But Mrs Kumar didn't.

Ellie waved goodbye and set off up the road. She'd always been thrown by the way some of the roads on this part of the estate went round in circles or off at angles. She wished she'd brought her A to Z with her. It was all up hill, too.

She reached a junction and paused to take breath. Yes, the road bent round to the right and turned into Oaktree Crescent, just as Mrs Kumar had said. A nice, quiet road with small trees planted at intervals along the pavements. The front gardens were well tended. It looked as if the back gardens in Oaktree Road — where Mrs Dawes lived — backed on to the gardens of the houses in Oaktree Crescent. Pleasant three-bedroomed houses, some with loft conversions.

She consulted the receipt from the newsagents. Mr R Standage, 14 Oaktree Crescent. She was standing by — she sought for the number on the gatepost — number two. She walked along the road till she came to number 14. She wondered if he could see the back of Mrs Dawes' house from his back garden. Probably.

The garden at number 14 looked as if someone had recently been trying to tidy it up after a period of neglect. Someone had cut back a straggly privet hedge. It was the wrong time of the year to do it, of course, but it looked as if it had needed it.

She descended the path and found the doorbell. It didn't seem to be working. She could hear the sound of a television from somewhere inside. She lifted the doorknocker and let it fall. She wondered if she had any beef strips still in her freezer. They took no time at all to thaw, and she could flash fry them with an onion for supper. Should she have rice with them, or a potato or two? It was cold enough to consider carbohydrates.

She wondered how Thomas was getting on.

The door opened, but there was only a dim light on inside, so she couldn't see the man clearly. She held up the bag of magazines.

'Mr Standage?' She had to raise her voice to make herself heard over the television.

A nod. A tallish man. Taller than her, anyway. 'Hold on a mo.' He vanished, and the sound of the television was muted. He returned, turning on the hall light.

Now Ellie was blinded by too much light. 'I was at the newsagents and they were wondering if you were ill or something, because you hadn't collected your magazines. So I said I'd drop them in on my way home.'

He was staring at her, eyes narrowed. A sallow skin, dark hair, good clothes that looked a trifle tight on him. She didn't like the way he was looking at her. She took a step back, puzzled. 'Have we met somewhere?'

He cleared his throat. Shook his head. But there was a sharp, knowing look in his eyes which meant that he knew her, all right.

She'd always considered you shouldn't make instant judgements about people, even though she often found herself doing so. She realized in a flash that she found this man threatening, and that the sooner she was out of there, the better.

She held out the bag but he didn't take it. She made herself step right up to the door — though really she wanted to run screaming from the place — and put the magazines inside the hall. 'The receipt's in there.'

'I'm out of cash. Will you take a cheque, or, I'll drop the money round to you, shall I?'

A rough voice, and — she saw as he bent to pick up the bag — rough hands.

Rough hands meant . . . no! She was jumping to conclusions. Her eyes flickered from his hands inside the house to where a thick, dark jacket was hanging over the post at the bottom of the stairs.

He was smiling, too. 'Come in for a bit?'

His smile revealed a gap in his teeth on the left-hand side.

'No, no,' she said, backing away. 'I have to get back, I'm expecting someone, don't bother about the money, my pleasure, really.'

She could feel him watching her stumble back up the path to the road. For a moment she was disoriented, not knowing whether to turn right or left. Either way should take her back to Oaktree Road. She risked a peep over her shoulder. He was still standing in the doorway, looking after her.

She almost ran along the road, and then her foot slipped as she met a puddle. A crackling sound told her that frost had taken a grip on the pavement. She forced herself to slow down. No point in getting a broken leg and ending up in hospital. Perhaps they'd put her in the next bed to Mrs Dawes.

She'd found the gardener, she was sure of it. The man who'd dumped the body at Mrs Ball's. Had he also attacked Mrs Ball? Ellie's imagination made the connections even while her more logical side refuted them.

Hold on a moment. She stopped at the junction, to reorientate herself, and to try to put her thoughts in order. She pulled her coat collar up. The man she'd seen, who'd claimed to be Mr R Standage, didn't answer to the description she'd been given earlier. The man she'd just met, with the rough gardener's hands and the heavy dark jacket, was nothing like the timid, bespectacled, reclusive Jake the Peg whom the bar staff had described.

Were there two Mr Standages? And if so, which had she just met? Was there any connection with the missing person the police were looking for? The man whose wife was searching for him, the supermarket worker who'd left his job and his digs without giving any notice?

Which was the victim and which the murderer?

And why, for heavens' sake, had the man attacked Mrs Dawes? That is, if he had. There really was no reason to suppose he had, was there? Except that their gardens might, or might not, touch.

Ellie desperately needed to talk to someone about this. Not the police. Not yet, anyway. Thomas would be the ideal person, but Thomas wasn't himself at the moment. So . . . who?

She turned the last corner and saw a well-known car sitting outside her house. Diana. Oh, no! This she could do without. She was too taken up with her thoughts to notice that she was being followed.

* * *

Well, what a stroke of luck. One of the women he'd seen with-drawing a large sum of money that morning in the bank had turned up on his door-step. He could tell she didn't remember where she'd seen him before, but she'd seemed puzzled, had refused his invitation to come in. Had gone off without being paid for the magazines, even. She might well remember soon.

Not that it would do her any good.

He slipped into his coat and followed her down the hill. Even if she looked back, she'd hardly be likely to see him on such a dark night. He kept well back as they came to the little green around the church. The lighting was brighter on the far side, where the road turned into the Avenue, and he wasn't going to follow her down there because some of the shops might still be open, and people returning from work; people who might notice him and remember.

But no. She turned off into a side road and stood by a nice-looking car for a moment, talking to someone inside. She'd got a visitor, then? Well, he could wait till the visitor went. He was in no hurry. He watched the visitor get out of the car. There was something the matter with the newcomer. She favoured one leg and held on to her head. Perhaps she'd been in a car accident?

The man watched as his target helped the other woman down the slope and into a house. One old crock, and one old biddy. A pushover. And plenty of cash to play for. Lights went on inside. The curtains in the front bay were drawn.

Another car drew up in a flurry and parked behind the first one. A fair-haired man got out with some bags of takeaway food, and ran down the path to the house next door. He opened the front door and for a moment was silhouetted against the light within. A child's voice cried out in welcome. A snapshot of the sort of happy family life which he'd never had. Then the door shut.

He was left on the outside, as usual. He'd had a lifetime of being left on the outside. Well, he knew how to even things up, didn't he! He'd make his way round to the back of the house and work out how best to get in.

CHAPTER NINETEEN

Diana had been beaten up and had come to Ellie for help. Ellie forgot about the gardener and steered her daughter through into the kitchen, shucking off her winter coat, and picking an envelope up off the hall floor on the way. The envelope had been left open, and she could see it contained an invoice. Mr Hurry was in a hurry for his money. A shame she'd missed him.

The left side of Diana's face was masked by dried blood from a cut on her cheekbone, her left eye was half closed, and her usually smooth hair looked as if it had been run over by a lawnmower.

'Ouch!' Diana let herself down on to a chair, holding on to her knee. 'I need a drink!'

'You should go to hospital to get stitched up.'

'No hospital.' Yet she drew in her breath against the pain. 'Haven't you got anything to drink?'

'I might have some sherry left. I'll see.'

Ellie rushed into the sitting room, drew the curtains, checked the level in the sherry bottle and clucked with dismay. There wasn't enough left to anaesthetize a child, never mind an adult in shock. Ellie had a flashback to the last time she'd poured out some sherry, which was when Diana and

Denis had dropped round for a celebratory drink. Mrs Dawes often called in after church on Sundays for 'half a glass'. Not this last Sunday of course. And probably not the next one, either.

Ellie took the almost empty bottle back to the kitchen, put the kettle on, and poured some cold water into a basin. Looked round for something soft to use. Ah, paper tissues would do.

'Let's get you cleaned up, then.'

'I need you to take some photos first.'

'What?'

'For proof. In case you need to sue.'

'Why should I want to sue anyone? Oh. Was it Denis who did this to you?'

'Not exactly, no.' She tried to fend Ellie off but Ellie persisted, dabbing gently at the cut and bruised face.

'What do you mean, "not exactly"?'

Diana drew in her breath sharply. 'Am I going to need stitches?'

'I don't think so, but I'm not a doctor. You certainly shouldn't drive in this state. I'm amazed you got here in one piece. I'll call a cab and take you to the hospital, shall I?'

Diana grasped her mother's wrist. 'Let me think.'

'What about your leg?'

'She kicked me on the kneecap.'

'She?'

'Denis' wife. We were . . . you know! Up against my desk. I was trying to make up to him for losing the house. She caught us at it. Hauled him off, kicked my knee and punched my face. It was her ring that did the damage.'

Ellie was torn between saying that it served Diana right, and horror.

Diana felt down her leg. 'Torn my tights, too. I'll have her for this, see if I don't.'

'But Diana . . . what did Denis say?'

'Laughed. Thought it a real hoot. That's why I came here. To show you what they're like so that you can get me out of the agency.'

Ellie took the bowl of reddened water to the sink, and poured it away and tossed the stained tissues into the bin. She then poured boiling water over teabags in two mugs. 'No, Diana. I can't do that.'

Diana hauled her compact out of her handbag to assess the damage to her face. 'Of course you can. You got me into it. You can get me out.'

Ellie fished a bag of frozen peas out of the freezer, wrapped it in a clean tea towel, and laid it against Diana's face. 'Hold it there. It will reduce the swelling. No, Diana. You borrowed money from the trust to start the agency. Contracts were drawn up and signed by both parties. You and Denis guaranteed that the money would be repaid at set intervals. It was not a personal loan from me to you. It was money granted by a trust of which I am only one of three directors. You can't wriggle out of repaying the loan, and I can't get you out of it.'

'Of course you can. You can see for yourself what's happened. I can't be bound to a man who's responsible for this attack on me.'

'It wasn't he who hit you but his wife, and it was your behaviour that provoked the attack. I don't think I'd try suing her, either. I can't think a judge would grant you damages. Now, do you want me to take you down to the hospital to get checked out, or not?'

Diana gasped. 'You surely don't expect me to continue working with a man who laughed when his wife attacked me?'

'You chose him as your business partner. You knew what he was like. You led him on, I suppose.'

'He didn't need much leading.'

'Fair enough. But in future you'd be better off finding another man to go to bed with, and confine your relations with Denis to business matters.'

'I couldn't!'

'Oh, yes you could. Take a good hard look at yourself, Diana. What have you got to show for thirty odd years of life?

A failed marriage, innumerable "encounters" with the opposite sex, a hefty mortgage on a large house and not a single trustworthy friend. You've alienated your relatives by greed and sharp practice, you are on the point of losing your son—'

'Never! How dare you even think that! Did you put Stewart up to it? Is he going to go to the courts to ask for care and control? I can't believe that you'd do that to me, Mother.'

'Believe it,' said Ellie, with a sigh. She took a seat at Diana's side and bent down to look at the rest of the damage. 'Keep that pad on your eye while I have a look at your knee.'

Out of the corner of her eye, Ellie saw something looming up against the conservatory door. She was already bending low to inspect Diana's leg. As she jerked her head upwards, she came into contact with the underside of the table and knocked herself silly.

The glass in the door exploded inwards.

Diana was sitting with her back to the door. She turned to see what was happening as a large, dark-gloved hand felt for the key in the lock of the door — how often had Ellie been told not to leave the key in the lock — and somebody large and dark threw the door open and charged in.

Ellie tried to stagger up, hands to her head, not seeing straight.

Diana's voice went high and thin. 'What . . . ?'

Ellie felt a jolt run through her, and was slammed back against the oven, out of breath . . . out of time.

Diana screamed, but the sound was cut off.

Choked off.

Ellie sagged, putting both hands to her aching head.

She couldn't see straight. Think straight. Tried to get air into her lungs . . .

She had a flashing image of Diana being thrown across the kitchen. Tossed across like a rag doll, flying through the air. It was unreal. Ellie couldn't make sense of what was happening.

Then, incredibly, Ellie felt herself being whirled around and thrown after Diana.

She landed on her side, gasping.

Pain in her side. Down her leg.

Diana wasn't moving. Ellie opened her eyes wide and met Diana's good eye as it slowly, slowly, closed. Diana breathed out, softly.

Unconscious.

The intruder was a man. No woman had monstrously large trousered legs like that. He strode across Ellie's body, his rough boot catching her thigh in passing. He stank of something . . .

Ellie tried to make sense out of what was happening.

The attack on Mrs Dawes. The way he'd tossed Diana aside.

It had to be the same man. Mrs Ball as well?

The gardener.

What to do? The landline phone was in the hall and that's where he'd gone. Her mobile was in her handbag, and she'd dropped that in the hall, too.

He was there now, moving clumsily, shifting the chair that sat by the phone. Opening her handbag. The catch had a distinctive sound. Bumping into the grandmother clock. Cursing.

What to do? She checked her arms and legs, which all appeared to be in working order though it was painful to move her right leg.

Icy air streamed into the kitchen through the broken door in the conservatory. Her poor plants . . .

He was coming back. He lifted her by one arm, twisting it, hauling her upright.

'Where's the money?'

She wasn't acting. She was dazed. But one part of her mind worked it out that he was the man who'd been sitting in the bank that morning when she'd drawn out enough money to pay Mr Hurry. Then she'd turned up on his doorstep, hadn't she, with those stupid magazines.

She said, 'Whaa . . . ?' Pretending to be even more dazed than she really was. Trying to think.

He shook her, hard. Her head snapped back.

'Where is it?'

'What . . . ?'

He picked her up, holding her close in front of him. Marching her out of the kitchen, legs dangling. The phone rang and he froze, holding her still in front of him. Feet off the floor.

She tried to free herself, and failed. He was strong.

The phone rang and rang. The answerphone clicked in. A man's voice. Thomas. Leaving a message for her. He'd call back later.

'Move!' The man propelled her forward to where her bag lay, its contents spilled over the floor. 'Show me!'

She gasped out the words, 'Spent it.'

'No, you didn't, you bitch! I saw you. You put it in your bag, a wad of it. And then you got on the bus straight after. So, where did you put it?'

Where had she put it? She couldn't think. She gasped, 'Kitchen!' At least in the kitchen she might be able to grab a knife, a pan, anything to hit him with.

He reversed direction, still holding her firmly in front of him. Somehow she had to gain herself a little freedom of movement. Diana lay like one dead. Surely she wasn't dead? But he'd killed Mrs Ball, hadn't he? And, presumably, the inoffensive Mr Standage, Jake the Peg?

She stammered, 'I c-can walk.'

He let her down so that her feet touched the ground and, as he released his grip she reached down and took hold of the flesh of his inner leg and twisted. Hard. She'd seen someone do this as a self-defence ploy many years before, and had been interested to see the effect it had had on the attacker.

This time, too. He yelled and released her, doubling over. She kicked at his leg and he staggered. At the same time, an avenging fury rose from the floor and with a banshee wail, swept up a kitchen chair and brought it down on the man's shoulders.

He stumbled and half fell. Diana, still shrieking, brought the chair down on his head.

The man screamed with pain. Diana hit him again.

Ellie could hear the phone ringing. And the doorbell.

And someone thumping on the wall next door. All the noise they were making must be bringing Armand round to investigate.

The man was sobbing for mercy, bloodied hands over his head, bowed to the ground. The chair shattered. Diana stopped shrieking and started gulping. Ellie limped as fast as she could to the front door.

Mr Hurry, looking embarrassed. 'Sorry to come round so late, but I was out with the missus and I just thought that if you'd got the money . . . are you all right? You look . . .'

'Come on in.' Ellie drew him in out of the cold night. 'Can you tie someone up for me? We've just been attacked.'

'Grief!' said Mr Hurry, staring wide-eyed at the man writhing on the floor. 'If that's who I think it is . . . is that the gardener?'

Ellie was delving into a drawer. 'I've got some string here somewhere. I've heard that if you tie a man's thumbs together, he can't move. I don't know where I heard it, but let's try it, shall we?'

He took the string. 'Are you sure he doesn't need the hospital, instead?'

'I wouldn't risk it, seeing what he's done to us.'

Diana was lowering herself on to an intact chair. Her cheek was bleeding again. Her face had ballooned up and one eye was closed tight. Her tights were in shreds, her leg bleeding.

Mr Hurry took note of Diana's injuries and though the gardener was groaning, decided to believe Ellie. 'Are you sure this'll hold?'

'Haven't a clue,' said Ellie, inching her way along the wall to the phone. At that moment, Armand came bursting through the front door asking what was up. Ellie tried to tell him. Gulped tears. Couldn't get the words out. 'Shock!' she said. 'Police!'

Armand took in the scene in the kitchen, with Mr Hurry standing over the injured man on the floor. 'What the . . . ?'

Ellie managed to press the right buttons on the phone at the third attempt. 'Police, please. And hurry!'

* * *

'I saved my mother's life!' Diana was the heroine of the hour. In her attack on the gardener, she'd sprained her left wrist. What with having to keep her arm in a sling, the butterfly stitches on her cheek, her black eye and bandaged leg, she presented the perfect picture of plucky victim to the world.

She blossomed under all the praise she received. Her normally abrasive manner softened since she had to smile a lot when having her picture taken. Her story appeared in a couple of the tabloids and in the local paper, which was all free advertising for the 2Ds agency. Oh, and there was talk of recommending her for a medal for bravery.

She negotiated a deal with Denis that she would run the office during the week, and have most weekends free to be with little Frank. Nobody was convinced that this arrangement would solve all their problems, but it did mean that the agency would continue to function and Frank still see his mother at weekends.

Once the confusion over identity had been resolved, Lee was charged with the murders of his landlord, Russell Standage, and of Mrs Ball. He was also charged with grievous bodily harm to Mrs Dawes, and of assault on Diana and Ellie. Under questioning by the police — not by Ears, but a more senior officer brought in to disentangle the case — Lee admitted everything. He told the police that in his view, prison, without any worries as to where his next meal was coming from, was preferable to having to work in the supermarket to provide for his wife.

Ellie got away with a number of bruises in places she was not keen to have displayed, and put on a pound in weight, due to comfort eating in the days that followed.

She cherished a hope for some days that she might receive a letter of apology from Ears for his conduct of the case. She was saddened but not surprised, that this was not forthcoming.

The police released young Neil with a caution. After all, he had swung a punch at Ears, and in the eyes of the police, that couldn't be forgiven and forgotten.

Ellie helped Mr Hurry to get his money from Mr Ball, and Neil got to redecorate Mrs Dawes' house. Ellie paid for both. Neil got a new girlfriend and began to grow his hair.

Mrs Dawes made a slow recovery. She was transferred to another hospital for physiotherapy but her batteries seemed to have run down. Ellie worried that her old friend might give in to her children's wishes and go into a home. Then, on a routine visit to Mrs Dawes' house, Ellie had occasion to check the meter reading for the gasman, and discovered some wizened hyacinth bulbs in a cupboard under the stairs. Mrs Dawes had put them there to force for Christmas but they'd been sadly neglected and were now only fit for the rubbish bin.

When Mrs Dawes heard this, she was so incensed that she discharged herself from hospital, visited the hairdresser to have her hair dyed jet-black, and appeared in church to tell the flower arranging team that their efforts were a disgrace and that they'd better buck up their ideas now she was back in charge. She had perhaps lost a little of her old edge, for a couple of weeks more she walked with the aid of a stick, but she'd also lost a lot of weight which could only be a good thing.

Felicity continued to keep well, while complaining — with a smile — that Roy wouldn't let her do anything in their house or garden.

In some ways Ellie took longer to recover than Diana or Mrs Dawes. If she could have gone straight to bed and stayed there for a week, being waited on hand and foot, she'd probably have picked up more quickly. But there was Mrs Dawes to visit, and all the Christmas preparations. So she struggled along, telling herself that it was ridiculous to feel so tired all the time.

Perhaps it would have helped if Thomas had come round to see her, but she only heard news of him from others. She knew he'd settled in happily at Miss Quicke's, and that Rose had been spoiling him to her heart's content, but not once did he ring her, or suggest they have a meal together. She wished their friendship hadn't ended like that, but didn't know what to do about it.

The parish held a monster party at the new vicarage on the day after Thomas moved in. Catering was arranged by Rose, courtesy of Waitrose. A team of waiters was provided by Maria at Miss Quicke's request, and altogether it was a joyful occasion to lighten a dark day in early December.

Ellie escorted Mrs Dawes there and helped her up and down the stairs, for the older lady wished to inspect each room, and every modern labour-saving appliance. And to comment on them. Mostly her view was that the parish hadn't needed to spend quite so much money on the latest gadgets, such as broadband for Thomas's new computer, and a coffee machine in the kitchen. On the whole, though, she approved the décor, devised by Roy and Felicity.

Even Diana, who for once had taken time off her office duties to whiz in and out — complete with a slightly unnecessary sling — commented that the underfloor heating and stripped floorboards made a positive impression. A lot of the furniture from the old vicarage had been judged too large and decrepit to keep, but Thomas had rescued his own furniture from storage and after a good polish up from Maria's cleaners, it looked good in its new surroundings. Mrs Dawes approved of the brand-new kitchen and bathroom, but opined that it had been unnecessary to spring to an extra shower room and loo.

When Mrs Dawes grew tired of inspecting everything, she told Ellie to find her a suitable armchair at the side of one of her old friends, and leave her be.

Ellie looked around for someone else to talk to, and found her aunt installed in a high-back chair by the window, overlooking the as yet barren garden. Miss Quicke said, 'I understand Rose and Felicity are planning to create some kind of miniature Hampton Court out there come the spring. I've told Felicity to take care, but she doesn't listen to me.'

Ellie found the right words to soothe. 'I'm sure Rose will see that Felicity doesn't overdo it.'

Kate from next door was there, with Catriona and the new baby in a double pushchair. Kate looked rosy and well. She said they'd arranged a date for the christening, and asked Felicity to be godmother.

Then suddenly the crowd thinned out and Ellie was standing next to Thomas, with nothing to say for herself.

'We're in the way here,' said Thomas, as the waitresses started to clear away. 'Come and see my study.'

He led the way to a quiet room at the back of the house, where his new computer equipment was in the process of being set up. The window overlooked the garden, which still contained some mature trees. Ellie could see that this was where he intended to spend most of his time, for there were boxes of books on the floor waiting to be put into the new built-in shelving, a small television set and some hi-fi equipment had been set up in a corner, and a new Lazy Boy chair was in the process of being unpacked nearby.

'It's very nice, Thomas.'

'It's going to be all right in time. When I've got some pictures up and that.' He unlocked a drawer and took out a small jewellery box.

At once Ellie's heartbeat went into double time. If that was an engagement ring in that box . . . ! No, she didn't want that. Most definitely. Let me out of here!

Thomas looked down at the box, rather than at her. 'I've been wanting to thank you for what you did for me, but I didn't know how. I don't suppose you realized how far down I'd gone when—'

'It was nothing,' she said, hurriedly. 'Honestly, Thomas. Anyone would have—'

'No, they wouldn't. Nobody else saw what you saw, or acted so promptly and so practically. After my old friend died, well, you saw how I was. I was afraid I'd have to go back on medication and be of no use to man or beast for a while. I was fighting it and getting nowhere. And then you rescued me. You're a most unusual woman, Ellie Quicke, and I want to give you this.'

He handed the box to her, but she didn't want to take it, thrusting it back at him. 'Please, no. I don't want anything.'

'I daresay you don't. But I took a long time choosing it, and I showed it to your aunt and she said it was just like you, so you must at least look at it. Keep it in a drawer or something, if you don't want to wear it.'

That didn't altogether sound like an engagement ring, did it? And his manner was not lover-like, either.

She took the box, and opened it. Inside was a heavy Victorian gold locket on a chain. Not a ring. What a relief! She snapped the locket open, to reveal two oval spaces into which you could insert small photographs, or miniature paintings of your loved ones.

'It's beautiful.'

He cleared his throat. 'I thought you might like to put a photo of your late husband in there, or your mother, or someone else dear to you.'

She felt as if he'd punched her in the stomach. She'd heard that widows passed through different stages in their grieving process: numbness, disbelief, anger, denial, loss, the misplaced belief that they were coping and the downward swoop into grief, all over again.

Looking back, she could see that she'd taken a slightly different course. She'd grieved for him and for herself. She'd built herself a new life, convincing herself she could manage very well without his care of her. She'd thought she'd got over her loss and that she might even consider a second marriage.

She'd been wrong. Just at that very moment she felt more vulnerable than ever. What wouldn't she give to have Frank back at her side, willing and able to take over all responsibility for her life!

Of course, one part of her mind she knew that she'd outgrown her dependence on Frank. She'd moved on. She supposed she'd grown up, in a way. She didn't really want to go back to being a cosseted little wifey with no opinions of her own. Not really.

But oh, she missed him. Dear Frank. He'd been the centre of her world, the touchstone by which she had formed all her opinions. Still was, in a way. She remembered, as if it were yesterday, his coming towards her the day they'd first met at the tennis club, holding out his hand to her, smiling.

She turned away to hide her tears. She wondered, a little crazily, if she'd ever get over his loss. She kept her eyes on the locket. 'A photograph of Frank. I like that idea. Yes.'

'I know how you feel. When my wife died, I . . . for a long time. Confused. Of course, one day you might want to put someone else's photo in there. Some time in the future, I mean.'

'Yes,' she said. 'I might.' She found her handkerchief and blew her nose.

'Meanwhile, I'd welcome your advice. Your aunt has very kindly asked me to join you all for Christmas lunch, but I was going to invite Mrs Dawes and one or two others to come here for lunch, thinking they wouldn't be cooking for themselves. Your aunt has been most kind to me and I don't wish to offend her. So, what do I do? Advise me, Ellie.'

THE END

THE JOFFE BOOKS STORY

We began in 2014 when Jasper agreed to publish his mum's much-rejected romance novel and it became a bestseller.

Since then we've grown into the largest independent publisher in the UK. We're extremely proud to publish some of the very best writers in the world, including Joy Ellis, Faith Martin, Caro Ramsay, Helen Forrester, Simon Brett and Robert Goddard. Everyone at Joffe Books loves reading and we never forget that it all begins with the magic of an author telling a story.

We are proud to publish talented first-time authors, as well as established writers whose books we love introducing to a new generation of readers.

We won Trade Publisher of the Year at the Independent Publishing Awards in 2023. We have been shortlisted for Independent Publisher of the Year at the British Book Awards for the last four years, and were shortlisted for the Diversity and Inclusivity Award at the 2022 Independent Publishing Awards. In 2023 we were shortlisted for Publisher of the Year at the RNA Industry Awards.

We built this company with your help, and we love to hear from you, so please email us about absolutely anything bookish at feedback@joffebooks.com

If you want to receive free books every Friday and hear about all our new releases, join our mailing list: www.joffebooks.com/contact

And when you tell your friends about us, just remember: it's pronounced Joffe as in coffee or toffee!

ALSO BY VERONICA HELEY

THE ELLIE QUICKE MYSTERIES

Book 1: MURDER AT THE ALTAR
Book 2: MURDER BY POISON PEN
Book 3: MURDER OF INNOCENCE
Book 4: MURDER BY ACCIDENT
Book 5: MURDER IN THE GARDEN
Book 6: MURDER BY COMMITTEE
Book 7: MURDER BY BICYCLE
Book 8: MURDER OF IDENTITY

THE BEA ABBOT AGENCY MYSTERIES

Book 1: A FALSE CHARITY
Book 2: A FALSE PICTURE
Book 3: A FALSE STEP
Book 4: A FALSE PRETENCE
Book 5: FALSE MONEY
Book 6: A FALSE REPORT
Book 7: A FALSE ALARM
Book 8: A FALSE DIAMOND
Book 9: A FALSE IMPRESSION
Book 10: A FALSE WALL
Book 11: A FALSE FIRE
Book 12: A FALSE PRIDE
Book 13: A FALSE ACCOUNT
Book 14: A FALSE CONCLUSION
Book 15: A FALSE FACE

Printed in Great Britain
by Amazon

39476804R00158